The Fall of Hidden Meadows

Jenna Veirs

To Richard.

PROLOGUE

Seven degrees.

Record low temperatures in the Midwest caused the skin to burn and instant regret about leaving the warmth of the indoors. The wool coat and boots did nothing. I stomped my way through the fresh snow to the spot near the blue spruce. My eyes shut for a moment, dark brown eyes blazing back at me through memory, sunken and melancholy, not as lively and cheerful as they had been eight months prior. He told me never to visit him. How could I not? I wasn't sure when I'd return to Oakville. A plane to my new home waited at the airport, but I needed to see him, feel his presence—something, anything.

"Why does it have to be this way?" The words left my mouth in a puff of cold breath, but no one heard my plea for closure. Was I expecting a response? My gloved hands cupped the curve of my tingling cheeks, every facet of myself questioning, eyes finally opening to reveal the reality in front of me. Even after thirty-five days, I couldn't say goodbye.

Wasn't the fall of Hidden Meadows enough? I sucked in a sharp breath, an attempt to keep my emotions inside, almost enjoying the frosty air singeing my lungs. It didn't matter at this point what I wanted. The only option left was to endure the pain and loss.

My knees cracked when I bent to the grave, cold fingers releasing the single white rose into the fresh powdery snow. My thumb traced the letters on the newly placed headstone. I could no longer pretend he was at work or the store—he was gone. Tears welled in my eyes and rolled down my cheeks. I stood up, frozen with fear, the trip to the cemetery not providing relief.

When I rise, you will stand beside me.

When I falter, you will guide me.

When I fall, you will catch me.

Those words hung in our home for seventeen years in a cheap wooden frame near the fireplace. It never had much meaning to me until today. The thought of living without him never crossed my mind. I was blind-sided, misled by how life should have been, and frankly—destroyed.

The car idled near the iron-gated entrance, waves of exhaust fumes billowing from the cold. I wanted to speak words possessing significance, remind him of how much he meant to me, but I was lost.

This time, I was on my own.

CHAPTER ONE

"All the cool kids are wearing over-sized shirts and printed stretch pants." -Grandma Margo

Why did I get a perm at the end of fifth grade?

My hair had grown out and morphed into a dark mess a few inches below my shoulders. I tugged on the hair pick lodged in my wavy locks. The tangle broke free. I admired my over-sized shirt with a grandfather clock graphic and matching pocket watch printed stretch pants. I had the coolest outfit for the first day of sixth grade.

Throwing my hot pink and green backpack over my shoulder, I skipped out the front door and ran across the street to my neighbor's house. Brenda made the best pancakes, which I opted for over my mom's toaster tarts. As soon as I stepped into her living room, I smelled frying bacon.

Great outfit. New school shoes. Brenda's pancakes.

"Sarah, is that the same backpack you had last year?" Karen stuffed a piece of fatty bacon in her mouth. She was two years younger than me, but mature sporting her mom's red plastic hoop earrings and a loose sweatshirt.

"I've had it since fourth grade." I ignored Karen and focused on the pancakes and bacon. She pulled her black Jansport from the kitchen table bench.

Nothing would ruin today, not even the brat. Of Brenda's three kids, I was closest to Samantha, who was a year younger, and I often played video games with her son, Jack. We were in the same grade.

"Finish up. The bus arrives in ten minutes." Brenda tossed another spatula of greasy bacon onto a plate. My eyes followed the mountain of meat she moved to the table.

We waited in Brenda's driveway for the bus to turn the corner into our sea-of-houses, new development neighborhood —Hidden Meadows. I never understood the name. There were no hidden meadows. I would know. I had been through every blade of grass, and the only thing hidden was our neighbor, Jerry. He liked to sunbathe nude behind his privacy fence. After witnessing middle-aged, hairy Jerry, I vowed that if my soccer ball went over his fence again, he could keep it.

"The bus! The bus!" Samantha jumped up and down excited to ride the junior high bus this year, which transported grades five through eight.

"Calm down," Karen scolded her big sister, making a pouting face while hugging Brenda.

The elementary bus came an hour after ours. Karen had to wait with her mom, and it didn't bother me the little pest was left behind.

My baseball cap was stuffed in my backpack between college-ruled paper and a purple Trapper Keeper. My dad purchased the hat at a Cubs game, and I'd worn it every day since the Fourth of July.

"You are on bus six this year." Brenda helped Samantha get the straps of her backpack on her shoulders.

"Bus six?" I was outraged. "What happened to bus three? Carol drives bus three."

"Does it matter? The bus is there to take you to school. Just remember to get on bus six to get home. You don't want a repeat of second grade." Brenda looked at me as if I had lost my mind.

"Second grade? I didn't get on the wrong bus in second

grade," I said. What was she talking about?

I placed my hat on my head.

"No, but you fell asleep and ended up at the bus garage. Everyone looked for you for two hours," Brenda said. Her eyes focused on the yellow rectangle on wheels turning the corner.

The bus screeched to a stop in front of the cracked concrete driveway. Debbie motioned us to board. I scaled the three black steps to the familiar green seats full of students. At the head of the aisle, I stopped.

"Aren't we the second stop?" I questioned the male bus driver while my eyes searched for an empty seat. Brenda's voice near the door told me not to worry about the bus route.

No seats. There were a few with one kid, but they were eighth graders. You can't sit with eighth graders.

"Sit down!" The bus driver threw bus six into gear.

I tumbled into a seat with a guy dressed in a flannel shirt and Dr. Martens. I glanced up at him. He had facial hair, like an actual mustache. Did he fail five times? He looked old enough to be my dad's friend.

"Little boy, you can't sit here," he said.

My eyes met his from under my baseball cap. I wanted to tell him I wasn't a little boy, but when I opened my mouth, nothing came out. As soon as the bus stopped, I jumped into the seat behind me with three fifth grade girls.

The rest of the fifteen-minute ride I rode with one butt cheek dangling into the aisle. When the driver failed to get the bus into gear, my hands gripped the side of the duct-taped seat to keep from falling into the floor.

My school consisted of a dilapidated structure from 1937 which housed fifth and sixth grade. My grandma attended high school in this building in the fifties and my mom in the seventies. Fast forward to the early nineties where the old Oakville High became Green Street Intermediate.

Nothing had changed since fifth grade. The dingy block walls still looked…well, dingy. The sinus-clearing sewage hung in the air as it did last year. I complained to my parents often my school smelled like crap in the hope they would transfer me to the private Catholic school on the east side of Oakville. Instead, my mom told me to stop exaggerating. I doubted I would pass out from poop inhalation, but I learned my overacting behavior from her.

In third grade, the local news did a story about elementary students using drugs. My mom did what the newscaster suggested. She searched my backpack and found an empty Tic Tac container full of glue.

"Why am I getting in trouble over glue in a Tic Tac container?" I asked in between the tears.

"Were you huffing this?" She lifted the Tic Tac container which not only had glue but crayon shavings and glitter. I admired my work. Whatever I was trying to make looked cool.

"I don't know what huffing means." I raised my eyebrows. My famous are-you-serious face didn't make much of an impression.

"Don't get smart with me! I don't like your mouth. You get this attitude from Karen." She was mad, still holding the awesome concoction of glue, crayon shavings, and glitter.

The woman had zero appreciation for fine art.

"I don't even like Karen," I said.

She told me to go to my room, pointed her finger towards the hall, and had been very skeptical of me, searching my bedroom and backpack daily.

In fourth grade, I brought home an honor student t-shirt. Rather than being proud, Lori Margo started a theft investigation.

In fifth grade, my honor student status changed. I discovered the joy of having an adult hate me for no reason.

Mrs. Crow, my fifth-grade teacher, sent flowers to the

hospital when my grandma had surgery. When I returned to school, every day for three weeks, she passed around a collection bowl to the students. Each day she would call me up to her desk and explain the financial hardship the bouquet cost her. My classmates cast evil glares as they forked over their nickels and dimes, totaling four dollars during her collection period. I told my mom Mrs. Crow hated me, but it all got chalked up to overacting.

"Why would she send your grandmother flowers if she didn't like you?" My mother's tone suggested victory.

"It's part of the sick and twisted mind games she plays," I replied.

My mom contemplated my response. Typically, she would dismiss any notion I provided.

"She spent twenty dollars to mess with you?" Cocking her head to the side, she studied my facial features, which resembled her husband.

"Yes! She would have spent thousands to mess with me, but teachers don't make a lot of money." As I celebrated my checkmate, my mom sighed in frustration.

The sound of Mrs. Crow's annoying voice echoed through the hallway. My feet hurried to the flight of stairs, not wanting her to see me. Mrs. William, my sixth-grade teacher, occupied the first room on the second floor.

I stopped at the threshold. My eyes scanned the classroom half-full of students talking and laughing. I retrieved my crumbled schedule from the side pocket of my backpack.

This couldn't be the room.

Rm. 201, Mrs. Tammy Williams, 6th Grade

A bumble bee made of construction paper hung on the door with *Mrs. Williams 201* written on the wings in black marker. The location wasn't the issue. I didn't know the students occupying the desks. Since Kindergarten, I had class with the same thirty kids who happened to be my best friends. Where was Brittany, Amber, Daniel, Aaron, and Bethany? I heard Daniel's voice. When I looked across the hall, my best friends laughed at the artwork Aaron had created on the board. Why wasn't I in their class?

My stomach churned, not because of the excessive amount of greasy bacon, because I realized what had happened. I didn't make the best grades in fifth grade, which resulted in class demotion.

As paper airplanes soared across the room and rap music blasted from a small radio, I slid into one of the first desks by the door. These kids made me as nervous as the eighth graders on the bus.

I questioned myself once more if I had ended up in the wrong place. I could take partial blame, but the person responsible for placing me with hooligans was meddling, hateful Mrs. Crow.

"Nice pants!" a tall boy in a Michael Jordan jersey yelled. He nudged his friend, and they laughed.

I bent to my backpack to pretend I didn't notice his insult. A few others pointed at my pocket watch printed stretch pants.

"Thanks," I mumbled.

A redheaded girl grabbed a boy's Dallas Cowboys jacket and told him she wanted to wear it. The boys soon forgot about me when Adrianna and Mindy introduced themselves.

Next to my desk, a cork board covered with paper bumblebees showed my classmates' birthdays. I discovered Mindy was forty-six days younger than me. She looked like my twenty-year-old cousin with her perfect blond hair and tight jeans. Mindy possessed confidence when she powdered her nose with a Covergirl compact. I wasn't allowed to wear nail polish.

The rest of the morning was a blur with a cheesy icebreaker

about our summer vacation. I told the class I went to Florida with my grandparents. No one seemed impressed. No one cared.

Mindy pierced her belly button at the tattoo shop on Regency Road. The class wanted to see the sun charm dangling from her navel. When Mrs. Williams told her to pull down her shirt, the guys booed.

Today wasn't going as planned. I needed to regroup. What better way to discuss the enormous mistake of being placed in the wrong class than lunch? The students lined up and followed Mrs. Williams towards the cafeteria.

"Ser-ah!"

I quickened my pace to avoid Mrs. Crow and her fake French accent. Not that I knew anyone from France to be the judge, but the way she talked made little sense. She had lived in our Midwestern town from birth. Her family owned Crow Cement.

No lucky man had snatched up crazy Donna Crow, but she insisted we call her Mrs. rather than Miss. She explained to my fifth-grade class how she earned a master's degree, which deserved distinction from the other teachers. A long story always followed about her first bachelor's degree in psychology, and she would have been faculty at a prestigious university if her mother hadn't fallen ill in 1986.

I yelped when she tugged my arm. Her giant grip wouldn't let go, and I couldn't help thinking banana hands.

"My colleague informed me your mother never used the referral I provided her last year," Mrs. Crow said.

She released her man grip, pulled her green cable knit sweater closed, and cocked her head to the side. Strands of auburn, curly hair stuck out from her messy bun like a matted poodle. She stood a foot taller than my modest five feet, eyes beaming down, and arms crossed.

Add intimidation to the list of her evil villain superpowers.

"I'll talk to her. I need to go." The other students watched our interaction, but I joined the lunch line behind my classmates with my best oblivious face.

Talk to my mom about the referral? No way.

Mrs. Crow called my mother for a parent-teacher conference. The night before my parents drilled me why they needed to attend the meeting. I told them I didn't know, which sent me into a panic to recall every moment in fifth grade. My parents knew I wasn't a complete angel, listening and following every rule. Daniel and I threw pencils until they stuck in the ceiling tiles. I used the bathroom pass to walk the halls. Any chance I could draw, color, or talk—I took it.

Mrs. Crow viewed herself as a clinical psychologist, always analyzing every word and event. During a journal assignment, I wrote about wanting my name to be Kelly. There wasn't much brain power put into the text.

Mrs. Crow stood in front of our class in the same chunky cable sweater and told us once we finished we could go outside early—her mistake. You don't tell kids they can go to recess early if they complete an assignment. If she'd said I could get a month off school by writing a novel in a day, I would have recreated *The Grapes of Wrath*.

The prior weekend my cousin, Kelly, spent the night while her parents attended a business function. My memories of our fun sleepover and the promise of an extra recess made me scribble my desire for a name change. Mrs. Crow turned it into an identity crisis which resulted in getting my parents involved.

"Ser-ah, why on earth would you want to be Kelly?" she asked. A pair of tortoiseshell reading glasses hung from a beaded necklace around her neck, but I couldn't recall her using them to read. She scanned my face in search of some sign of mental illness. I told her I wasn't sure.

Following the parent-teacher conference, I overheard my mom telling my dad Mrs. Crow was a crazy bitch. I laid low and hoped my parents would forget the ordeal.

"Are you going to eat or not?" a raspy voice asked.

Dazed from my Mrs. Crow encounter, I didn't realize I stood in front of the glass lunch counter, which prohibited students from touching the canned, now re-heated food. I pointed to the tray with a chicken sandwich. After I paid, I re-entered the seating area to find fifth graders.

"Excuse me." The mousy librarian assigned to watch the lunch period turned towards me. "Where are the other six graders?"

"Are you in Mrs. Williams' class?" she asked. I nodded. "The six grade lunch period is full. Your class is eating with the fifth graders."

I walked away more defeated.

"Clock pants girl, sit with us!" My classmates roared with laughter, including Adrianna who sat against the owner of the Dallas jacket.

I exited the cafeteria into the hall, a loud thump when I tossed my lunch in a nearby trash can. I ran to the bathroom, a whoosh of heavy sewage smell exited the door. The handicap stall was open. I waited inside, stomach growling with hunger. My optimistic outlook vanished like the setting sun. I wanted to cry but didn't see the point.

When the bell rang, I returned to Mrs. Williams' class as if nothing had happened.

My backpack landed on the living room couch. I released a pent-up breath of air when I entered my bedroom, relieved to be back in my space, where I could shut the door on life. The weight of my body sunk into the floral comforter, my eyes closed, and I fell asleep.

"Did you get home?" I opened one eye like a cat does when enjoying peaceful rest in a sunny spot on the carpet. My mom stood at the door with her hand resting on the doorknob.

I made it home. Look at me. I'm lying on the bed.

"Yeah," I replied.

"Why are you so quiet? Are you up to something?" she asked. Her expression told me she was embarking on a major interrogation.

"Nope. I'm tired."

The cordless phone rang in the living. My mom forgot her parental mission and gravitated down the hall towards whoever dialed our number. Her voice echoed through the house, excited to speak with the person on the other end of the line.

Sitting up, I realized what I needed to do. Talk to Bethany or Daniel. Maybe their first day started rocky too. As I pretended to straighten magazines, my mom returned the phone to its cradle. She left the room, and I headed to my bedroom to make my calls.

I pulled out the long, silver antenna and dialed Bethany's number—her mom answered.

"Can I speak with Bethany, please?"

A rerun of *The Brady Bunch* played in the background. The episode where Marsha took a football to the nose.

"Bethany is at Aurora's house. Can I tell her you called?"

The television made it impossible to understand her mom, but I heard Aurora's house. She moved to Oakville over the summer from California into the nicest house in Hidden Meadows. They had a second story and a pool. Why was my best friend hanging out with the new girl?

"Hello?"

"Um, no. Thanks," I replied.

Without hesitation, I dialed Daniel's number. Three rings. Four rings. Five rings. I was about to hang up when Daniel's little brother answered.

"Hi, Kevin. Is Daniel there?"

"I'm not supposed to be answering the phone," he whispered.

"Is Daniel there?"

The eight-year-old boy needed to stop playing games and hand my friend the phone.

"No." This time his voice was normal. "He is at his girlfriend's house."

"Girlfriend? What do you mean?"

"Bye." He hung up on me.

Girlfriend? Daniel didn't like girls. He told me over the summer when we were playing home run derby with Jack, Damon, and Steve.

My chest felt tight, lungs restricted. I leaned in my desk chair near the window, fingers tapping my lips in rapid thought. This had to be a dream. What if I wasn't dreaming? My thumb and index finger grasped the skin on my forearm.

Ouch!

CHAPTER TWO

"Frank Margo was an engineering major with a shag haircut. I asked him to hang out. He said redheads weren't his type." -Donna Crow

A month later, I fell into a deep depression. Aurora and Bethany were now best friends. How was I going to compete with Miss California? Daniel had a girlfriend, a seventh-grader named Tiffany. Aaron joined mock trial, and Amber became a cheerleader. I rarely heard from my friends. The *My Little Ponies* I packed every day to play with during fifth-grade recess sat on my shelf collecting dust.

Stupid ponies.

I skipped Brenda's delicious pancakes for my mom's toaster tarts. I took a second bite and decided the mass-produced pastries were not as bad as I had remembered. The lack of Karen's mouth during early morning made breakfast much sweeter.

For the first time in years, I stood at the end of my driveway to catch the bus, careful to avoid eye contact with Samantha and Jack catty-corner across the street. The bus driver stopped at Brenda's house, then pulled up fifteen feet for me to cross and board the bus.

"Is this going to be a permanent thing?" Mike asked.

I wanted to ask him if he was referring to my depression or my change of bus stop location, but I wasn't in the mood to be snarky.

"I don't know."

As I moved down the aisle, his rant about the school district only allowing a certain number of stops per bus route faded. I missed Carol. She cared about her students, often baking us cookies and playing games. Mike was a former tow truck driver that couldn't find a job. He didn't care about driving our bus, which was evident by the wadded up school district shirt on the floor.

My left butt check sat on the edge of the seat with the fifth-grade girls, relieved they had not told me to move. The smell of diesel gave me an instant headache. The bus shifted into gear and out of Hidden Meadows.

Mrs. Williams waited for the bell to ring before she got up from her desk to start the day. She was a plain woman in her early thirties, but today she had on lipstick and a pink sweater.

"Today, we will move into our assigned seats," she said. The class groaned. "We will have visitors coming soon for state testing preparation who will want to know your name off the seating chart."

Mrs. Williams ignored April who asked about the visitors. Her attention focused on finding the seating chart buried in papers on the wooden podium

"Amanda." Mrs. Williams pointed to the first seat by the door. The boy sitting in the seat stood up and walked to the front of the room near the blackboard. "Crystal, you are behind Amanda." Mrs. Williams shuffled down the aisle in a good mood. "Sarah, you are behind Crystal, and Jennifer G. is behind Sarah."

I moved to my new desk. Mrs. Williams started on the next row.

"Sam, you are in the first seat. Eric W. is behind Sam. Jett is behind Eric W. Tyler is behind Jett." The students in the seats moved and allowed the boys to take their new assigned seats.

Digging through my bag, I looked up to see someone I had never noticed. He wore a black Fender guitar t-shirt and jeans. His backpack said Jett, with rock band patches and a keychain from Niagara Falls. The boy in front of him, Eric, lived in Hidden Meadows, but I had never talked to him. My eyes met his, and he smiled. I fumbled for my pencil. His light blue eyes danced in my mind.

Mrs. Williams began the geometry lesson, writing the names of five triangles—right, obtuse, equilateral, acute, and isosceles. I looked up to find Mrs. Williams hovering over me.

"Sarah, are you paying attention?" she asked. I batted my eyes twice. Two students were at the board drawing triangles. "I didn't think so. Please draw the class an equilateral triangle."

She handed me a piece of yellow chalk. I hoped no one could read my thoughts. Imagine the teasing if the class knew my feelings about Jett and Eric.

"Well done, Tyler." Mrs. Williams examined a right and acute triangle. "Excellent, Samantha." She stood next to me, looked at my equilateral triangle and then at my face. She was the opposite of intimidating. "Sarah, what is it called when sides or angles are the same?"

"Congruent."

I returned the chalk to her hand, and I sat at my desk before she could say anything further. Mrs. Williams looked surprised. She underestimated me, which wasn't hard to do with my terrible perm and clothes picked out by my grandma.

I wasn't sure if noticing Jett and Eric or my constant misery made me want to change, but I decided my brain would figure out how to adapt to my new environment.

I needed new clothes. Grandma's advice on sixth-grade fashion turned out to be wrong. I had a stack of printed pants, turtlenecks, and kid shirts—let's not mention the matching headbands. But how would I convince my parents after they spent four hundred dollars on new clothes less than two months ago to redo my wardrobe? Fire? Theft? I would have to think of another way because my mom would never buy those excuses.

"Hi, Aunt Gina! It's Sarah. Can I come over this weekend?"

Gina wasn't my aunt, but my Uncle Dan's live-in girlfriend. His relationships never lasted long, but this one had lasted a few years.

"Sure doll. Is it okay with your Mama?" she asked. I walked into the living room with my hand on the receiver and asked my mom if I could spend the weekend at Dan and Gina's house.

"Is Gina on the phone?" she asked.

My mom motioned for the cordless with an expression making it clear she didn't want to mess around.

"Hey, Gina. I didn't hear the phone ring." She looked at me. "Oh, you didn't call." I tried to keep my cool. Sweat beaded where it shouldn't. "I see." Busted. "That's fine she comes over. Are you sure it is okay since Dan is home this weekend?"

My mom walked into the kitchen laughing at their conversation. She wasn't mad when she returned to the living room. I remained calm on the outside, nervous on the inside, watching television.

"Gina's mom is visiting from Georgia. Are you sure you want to go? You hate shopping." My mom sat on the blue couch with peach throw pillows assessing me. You could always count on former swimsuit model Gina to be shopping.

I nodded.

The twenty-minute drive to Dan and Gina's house went by fast. I ignored the country tape my mom insisted on listening to rather than the radio. The way she lip-synced the lyrics made me want to burst out laughing, but I didn't want to ruin her good mood. I needed Gina for shopping.

Our 1989 Buick Regal pulled up to the metal gate, a loud

squeal when the car stopped. My mom rolled down her window, leaned out with a groan, and pressed the keypad.

"Gina? We are here," my mom said.

Broken static, a few beeps, and the gate opened. The Regal drove into the gated community—Pine Ridge. I didn't understand the name. Five pine trees with no ridge.

The neighborhood had pages of rules and regulations. There were times you could water your grass, walk your dog, hang decorations, and Uncle Dan had to get permission if he allowed anyone to stay at his house for over seven days. Too many rules. But my uncle loved the prestigious area. I couldn't picture him living in Hidden Meadows. He couldn't imagine it either as he never visited our house.

His beautiful two-story home, covered in wood siding and stone boasted seven bedrooms, a basement, five bathrooms, a four-car garage, and a resort style swimming pool. Gina skipped out the front door in a terry cloth body wrap, either from being in the tanning bed or the pool. Her blond hair sat in a curly updo with designer sunglasses placed in the middle.

"It's cold today. You aren't swimming, are you?" My mom eyed Gina's attire.

"I've been laying out. Dan installed one of those propane heaters by the pool. It feels like South Georgia. Mom and Tisha aren't here yet. You girls want to get lunch?"

She would not take no for an answer, so we followed her inside while she changed. My mom admired a recent upgrade in the kitchen. I sat on the tan sofa in the main living area. The wicker furniture and beach theme seemed odd for the Midwest, but what did I know?

Gina returned ten minutes later wearing a white jean jacket over a black dress. Even with her model good looks, Uncle Dan had sworn he would never get married. Being a trophy girlfriend didn't bother Gina as long as she had access to his credit card. It seemed like a good gig, but when I ran my hand through my thick, messy hair and remembered my little pot belly, I figured my options of being a trophy anything was slim.

"Let's go girls!"

We followed her to the garage, home of Uncle Dan's toys. Every year he bought a new speedboat with a truck painted to match. I preferred last year's metallic blue to the latest hunter green.

Gina unlocked the red Chrysler LeBaron convertible Uncle Dan purchased for her twenty-fifth birthday. A sudden pang of sadness came over me when I saw the envious look on my mom's face. My dad didn't have money like Dan, and she didn't have a problem reminding him.

Pine Ridge housed the elite. Pine Plaza is where the privileged shopped and dined. I wasn't surprised when Gina pulled into the plaza and parked her convertible in front of a busy café. The expensive awnings over ornate metal chairs and pots of flowers told me this wasn't Burger King.

Attractive people dressed in fitness apparel loitered on the pavement. Gina explained the Pine Ridge Health Club was next door which became apparent when I opened the menu to find no bacon cheeseburgers. I flipped the menu to see the name of the restaurant.

"Muse by Carlos?"

My mom gave me a warning look as if I had planned on embarrassing her with my skepticism. Gina corrected my pronunciation, but I failed to understand. *Moose? Morse? Most? What did she say?* Another warning glance from my mom although I doubt she knew Gina's fancy pronunciation.

"What does fusion concept tapas mean?" I looked up at my mom and Gina after reading Carlos' life story.

My question produced my mom's evil eye and a nudge of the foot. Gina peered over her menu to answer my question, but a thin brunette with a water bottle caught her attention.

"Julie!"

The brunette waved and hurried to hug Gina. I ignored their high school cheerleader conversation and attempted to decipher the menu. Before I figured out my meal choice, Gina ordered.

"We will have the Christie with diets." Gina smiled at the waiter. When he collected our menus, I noticed his name tag—Rian. Did he change the spelling of his name to be trendier? I wanted to ask him. Curiosity bubbled inside of me, but I already had three dirty looks and a nudge.

"Did you know Theresa got a boob job?" Gina asked. She leaned towards the table to keep their gossip private.

"Theresa? She needs more than a boob job." My mom and Gina burst out laughing. They discussed the details of Uncle Ted using money from my grandparents to buy his wife big breasts.

Where is the food?

I scanned the restaurant for Rian. The restaurant staff looked the same in black pants, button-up shirt, and tie. I sipped my diet wishing it was a Mountain Dew, but I kept my commentary to myself.

Focus on the mission.

Gina placed a napkin on her lap. "She had the nerve to come to Carla's birthday party. I said nothing. I'm not married into the family."

Rian weaved through the tables with a large tray, eyes on Gina. My mom put her napkin on her lap eager to eat. My hunger was at a critical level.

"Three Christies," Rian said. He offered us fresh pepper. Everyone said no thanks.

I looked at my plate. I looked at Gina. I looked at Rian and back to my plate. I looked at my mom and back to Gina.

Where the hell was the food?

In the middle of the over-sized plate sat a mini biscuit with a raw piece of fish. On top of the seafood, perched a green

18

wedge of something, topped with a green olive and a fancy toothpick.

"Oh, this looks amazing!" Gina smiled at Rian.

Is she crazy?

My mom plucked the decorative toothpick and ate the green olive. I tried hard to hide my disgusted face. I said a silent prayer of thanks for the bag of popcorn in my backpack at Dan and Gina's house.

"This is my favorite place to have lunch," Gina said.

My mom agreed. She mimicked Gina with a knife and fork to dissect Carlos' so-called masterpiece. I flashed my best fake smile which looked more rabid dog than happy pre-teen.

The olive was edible, although disgusting, but I choked it down with diet soda. I examined the green wedge. It appeared to be a vegetable, but I wasn't confident.

Crunch. Crunch. Crunch.

The diet soda had a strange aftertaste, but it worked as a perfect chaser. I inhaled. My stomach protested when I raised the ultimate question. Could I eat the fish without gagging? Gina and my mom were deep in conversation about Karla's birthday party.

As I poked the fleshy, raw mass, I realized I was not a bad ass. I couldn't eat it. What would I do with the rubbery mess? Muse by Carlos looked expensive, and my mom would lecture me if I wasted food. Saying I was full wasn't an option. I had only had an olive, a crunchy green thing, and three drinks of diet soda.

My fork stabbed the fish. What if it fell to the floor, and I kicked it under the table? That seemed like a logical plan. Accidents happen, right?

Gina's attention turned to me. My fish dangled from the fork, ready to be dropped. The pink chunk wobbled, but I regained my composure.

"You enjoying it, babe?" Gina asked.

"Yes." I envisioned the cheddar popcorn in my bag. My response satisfied Gina enough to return to her lunch and gossip.

My covert fish dropping operation continued. I surveyed the restaurant to be sure no one had eyes on our table. With a slight wrist turn, I was in full cargo drop position. The fork turned left. WHAM! Rian bumped into my chair. The fish launched across the room to an unknown destination. I started fake chewing.

"Sorry," he mumbled. Rian walked to another table to fill a water glass.

Gina and my mom continued talking, not about Carla, but what Dan had planned for the department stores he owned. I cut the little biscuit with my fork and knife.

"Get this off of me! What is this doing in my hair? Is this a joke?" A woman dressed in a blue sari stood up. Her gold bangles clanked every time she raised her hands. She danced like ants were in her pants.

The customers stopped eating, and the employees stopped working. All eyes were on the crazy lady. I chomped my fishy biscuit.

"I want to know who is responsible!" The man at her table roared like a lion in search of prey. "Who put this in my wife's hair? When I find out, I will sue you and this restaurant!" He waved the fish back and forth.

"What is that David?" The woman took shallow breaths, hand clutching her heart. "Is it a body part?"

David sniffed the fleshy mass, and the restaurant patrons made sounds of disgust.

"It's ahi tuna!" David snapped his fingers at a waitress. She ran to him, ponytail swinging, and carried a conversation too low to hear at our table. I was nervous since David didn't want to let this go. Would he question everyone who ordered tuna?

"I liked the food, Gina," I said.

"That's good. I figured you'd ask for Burger King afterward. You are growing up," she said. Gina flashed a quick smile before she paid Rian.

A surge of disappointment came over me. I wanted a cheeseburger, but I had to keep focused on my purpose.

David had the owners, Carlos and Christie, at his table with the tuna resting in his palm. I recognized their faces from the menu. When Gina told Rian to keep the change, I was glad to be leaving.

Gina talked to my mom through the window of the Buick. I watched from inside Uncle Dan's sitting room. Sadness engulfed me, a feeling I tried so hard to avoid with my mother. Nothing I did was good enough. Whenever it was me or something else, she chose something else. Most moms would want to hug their child goodbye or tell them to have a fun weekend—not mine. I wanted a mom from the cooking shows. Over the years, I had become accustomed. What could I do about it? She wasn't like a puppy or a used car. I couldn't put an ad in the paper for someone to take her.

Free Mom. Doesn't cook or clean. Mildly disgruntled. Does a great job talking on the phone. No need to call ahead.

I laughed at my ridiculousness.

Uncle Dan's head peeked out of his office door followed by a wave that indicated he wanted me to join him. As I approached the doorway, he talked on the phone.

"Pine Ridge. Yes." The phone cord was wrapped around his hand. He leaned against his desk. "No, it's not a retirement home. It is the city's most elite planned neighborhood. The damn governor has a home here."

Uncle Dan placed the receiver on the desk and left the women on the line to continue the conversation alone. He stepped into the hall to make sure we were alone. I gave him a confused look.

"Where is everyone?" Dan asked.

"Outside," I replied.

My uncle fidgeted with a frame on his desk. He wanted to discuss the nineteen-year-old bikini model, Tiffani. I knew the next time I saw him, we'd have this conversation.

He peered around the door frame to find the house still empty.

"It wasn't what…" He attempted to justify his actions to a pre-teen. I quirked a brow. He ran his hand through his hair. "I have no explanation because I'm a pig. I'm into pretty girls. Gina is great to have around, but she isn't young anymore."

"She is twenty-five." My forty-something-year-old uncle stared at me as if I were his mother scolding him. If my conservative grandmother found out his behavior, scolding would be the least of his worries. "I told you last month when I saw you making out with Tiffani on your boat—"

"Shh! Don't say her name!"

I started a mental tally of the times he checked the hall for Gina. We were up to four times. As much as I would have loved to talk about his women problems, I had more important issues such as the sixth grade.

"I'm here to shop with Gina. I want to pretend I never saw you making out on your boat."

He relaxed on the edge of his oak desk. The phone beeped since the woman on the line had disconnected. Dan reached for the receiver and returned it to the cradle.

"I didn't know Frank intended to bring you. The last thing I wanted was to get you involved. Your father is used to my crap," he said.

I rolled my eyes.

"It's okay. I will eat popcorn now." I left his office. Uncle Dan popped his head out the door for the fifth time.

"Did she take you to Shit Plate by Carlos?" His eyes lit up, and a large grin spread across his face. I nodded. "There is leftover pizza in the fridge from Lonnie's."

He exited his office and met me in the hallway. Reaching into his pocket, he pulled a wad of hundred dollar bills from his wallet. I watched him count out three hundred dollars like a drug deal in an alley. He placed the currency in my hand.

"You can't go shopping without money." He disappeared into his office and within seconds was back on the phone.

My uncle bought me off.

I felt disloyal to Gina, standing in her home with my blood money, but I had bigger problems. Gina was a grown woman. I needed to survive sixth grade. Stuffing the money into my pocket, I headed to the kitchen hoping for pepperoni and pineapple.

CHAPTER THREE

"Sometimes a man will start to wiggle around, you know, act uncomfortable when attracted to a female. Do you understand?" -Gina Cobb

The bus turned the corner of Hidden Meadows and ran over the begonias near the entrance. Adam lived in the second house on the street. He was the stop before one of Jack's friends and us. I skipped across the street to Brenda's driveway. Samantha eyed me with suspicion.

Seconds later, Mike opened the door, and we boarded. The bus was in motion before I could get to my seat. I sat with a seventh-grade boy. He stared out the window, and I wondered why I had been afraid to sit with anyone besides the fifth-grade girls.

Before leaving my house, I applied bright orange lipstick and used a red banana clip to disguise my perm. My new Guess jean overalls were the latest. I left one strap unfastened like I had seen on a music video on MTV. It hung like a rope of coolness when I walked. There was no doubt in my mind the level of awesome I looked.

"Hi, Jett." I sat at my desk. His eyes grew large, and his jaw dropped open. Eric possessed the same expression when he turned around. "Hello, Eric."

"Oh, hey." Eric licked his lips, eyes locked on the board.

Jett and Eric looked uneasy. This was a good sign. Gina told me men often got uncomfortable when attracted to a female.

"Please take your seats!" Mrs. Williams yelled over the early morning noise.

Something had changed for Mrs. Williams. Today, she wore a different pink sweater and lipstick. The ends of her hair were curled and pinned on the side with a barrette.

Our morning lesson started—Native Americans. All we did was talk about Indians. It's like I had a Ph.D. in Native American Studies. I rolled my eyes and laughed.

"Would you mind sharing with the class what is entertaining?" Mrs. Williams' long, pleated skirt swooshed back and forth.

"Why are we always talking about Indians? There are other people on this earth." After I spoke, I realized I let my new Guess overalls and orange lipstick get to my head.

"You don't think Native Americans are important? You can write one hundred sentences. Native Americans are an important part of our glorious country's robust heritage along with being crucial to many of the battles that took place on our native soil."

Her big sentence was impressive. Mrs. Williams continued writing on the board, and I sat in silence.

The rest of the morning, I put stickers on my purple Trapper Keeper. An Ice cream cone, fluffy cat, neon pencil, zebra with pink stripes, and a rainbow now decked out the front cover. Students lined up at the door. I had forgotten what I dreaded most—Monday gym class. Time to put on shorts and get ready to dodge balls thrown by the gym class heroes. Their only success in life would be hitting a twelve-year-old girl with a kickball.

I tried every trick in the book to get out of gym—asthma, weak ankles, and I even tried to pull the discrimination card. When my dad asked me how I was being discriminated against, I didn't have an intelligent answer.

Today we were climbing a rope to the tall ceiling. It looked dangerous, but Coach Rice said not to worry, he had put a mat below the rope. I doubted the two inches of foam would keep me from breaking a bone.

Mrs. Williams stayed by the door, her attention on Coach Rice. Mrs. Crow never stayed with us for gym. He blew his whistle for the next person to risk their life. Mrs. Williams lifted her chin and shifted her skirt. It made sense now. Every time we had gym, she wore a nice sweater and lipstick.

"Kasey! You're up!" Kasey was not athletic. She struggled to hold the rope and fell to the floor. Coach Rice blew his whistle. "Come on! Get up!"

Kasey's skinny legs tried hard to grab the rope, but she fell again with a loud thud on the blue mat. Kyle Smith ran up to the rope, scaling it with ease. The class cheered when he hung from the top blowing kisses at the girls. He let go with a Spider-man like landing on the mat. Coach Rice patted the baseball star on the back and glanced over his shoulder at Mrs. Williams. She blushed. I felt the toaster tart rising in my throat.

"Looks like we got everyone. Let's use the remaining ten minutes for girls' open gym. The boys can follow me to the baseball field with rakes. The superintendent visits Wednesday. Let's show him we have Cougar pride in the off-season." He clapped his hands, and the boys followed the thirty-something balding man in tight gray athletic shorts.

Mrs. Williams' eyes followed him to the exit. The sun beamed across the wooden gym floors after the doors opened. I wondered how much she knew about Coach Ryan Rice. Maybe Mr. Williams wasn't as athletic, but he had to have more going for him than Ryan Rice.

Last Christmas, I stayed with my great-aunt while my parents went to a holiday party. Aunt Judith wanted me to go to the neighbor's house with her for dinner.

"Honey, you can go downstairs and play in my son's room," my great-aunt's neighbor gestured towards the basement door. The older woman continued her hushed tone conversation with Aunt Judith. "Dinner won't be ready for a half-hour."

I scaled the paneled stairwell to what appeared to be a teenager's room. Baseball bats hung on the wall. Hats from every team were in a case. The most amazing part was the hand-painted mural of a baseball stadium.

"Wow," I mumbled.

The stairs creaked. When I turned around, Coach Rice stood at the bottom of the steps puzzled why I was in his bedroom.

"Sorry, your mom…"

Taking two steps toward me, he held up his hand. He wanted to plead with me not to mention his room, but I didn't give him the chance. My feet sped up the stairs through Mrs. Rice's living room and out the door.

After gym, I changed and went to the water fountain for a drink. Coach Rice over-looked me on his rope climbing list either by accident or as a continuation of our *don't ask, don't tell, live with your mom* agreement.

My overalls were breezy and cool. I loved my new clothes. Green Street Intermediate had the worst ventilation like a sweatshop most days. I continued to drink from the buzzing fountain.

"It's Monday, Sarah!" Kenny Riddle squealed with laughter. I turned my head to see my hooligan classmates laughing.

"Can you not keep track of the days?" Michael Roundhouse roared. He gasped for air in between laughs.

Why were they laughing? I looked down, and realization hit me like a dump truck. I forgot to fasten my Guess overalls when I dressed after gym. While at the water fountain, my days of the week underwear decided to reveal themselves. I pulled up my pants with any shred of dignity I could muster.

"Why do you have on Thursday underwear when it is Monday? Better question. Why are you wearing days of the week underwear?"

Everyone laughed.

The real answer was my mom made sure I changed my underwear daily in elementary school. She wasn't doing her checks anymore. I routinely wore whatever day was clean.

"I don't know," I said.

Mrs. Williams appeared to walk us back to class. I lined up with my peers, careful to avoid eye contact.

I had a feeling I wouldn't survive sixth grade.

After lunch, my classmates went outside for our poor excuse for recess. Last year, we played. This year, we gossiped about the opposite sex, wrote notes, and sometimes threw rocks at oncoming cars.

I was a prisoner at my desk while Mrs. Williams graded papers across the room. One hundred sentences, a complete waste of time, all because I had an opinion about spending too much time on Native Americans. Mrs. Williams rattled off a long sentence as my punishment. I couldn't remember much, something about glory and history. Showing thirty people your underwear makes one forgetful. I scribbled the last few words. My classmates trickled inside with the smell of fresh air.

I walked towards Mrs. Williams' desk with regret. I should have asked her to repeat the sentence. The office was my next stop for being a smartass and not completing my punishment.

I sat the paper on her desk. She studied my writing and pursed her lips

"You have potential, Sarah. Don't waste it," my teacher said. She ripped up my work. Tiny pieces of college-ruled fell into the garbage. "Thank you."

I returned to my desk feeling strange.

Mrs. Williams stared into the trash, eyes watering. Why? I would never know.

In the trashcan were the fragments of one hundred sentences: Coach Rice lives with his mom.

Today was the last day Mrs. Williams wore pink lipstick.

CHAPTER FOUR

"Find me someone who hasn't told a lie, and I will give you the keys to any car on the lot." -Ted Margo

The wooden tree house fell out of the large maple tree during a storm three summers ago. Our family dog witnessed the falling house and refused to go anywhere near that section of our half-acre yard.

Daniel opened the gate, petted Kirby, and scanned the yard for me. I stuck my hand out the tree house door. He made his way across the grass to the tree house which looked like a small replica of our house.

"Can I come in?" He waited in the dirt next to the tree house porch. Although he smiled, something troubled him. Maybe others wouldn't have guessed, but I had known Daniel my entire life.

"Yes," I replied. I scooted closer to the wall to allow room for him to sit down on the wood floor. My parents had donated the table and chairs that once sat in my tree house. I had outgrown the set they said.

"I have never been inside your tree house." He eyed my collection of stickers on the walls.

"You haven't?"

"No," Daniel said with a laugh. "You said only husbands live in a house with a woman. You made Jack and I live on the porch." I flushed with embarrassment, unsure what to say. Everything felt different and confusing. It felt strange to talk about us playing house last summer.

"I doubt you came over to play house with me," I said. Daniel eyed me in a weird way. I changed my mind about Jett being the cutest boy I'd ever seen.

"Will you go to the dance with me?" he asked. The words spewed out to break the odd silence. I looked at him puzzled. Did he say what I think he said? We didn't go to dances.

Play it cool.

"Won't that make Tiffany mad? The dance is weeks away, like Christmas break. Besides, you don't want to be associated with me right now." Please God, let there have been another scandal at school to downplay my days of the week underwear.

"Because you wear Thursday on a Monday? Only a bad ass would wear the same underwear for five days without changing them," he said.

"What?"

He laughed until he snorted. Did Daniel like me? Did I like Daniel? Did friends go to dances together? Would Tiffany be jealous? Should I say no? There should be a book on this stuff.

"Tiffany dumped me. I was hoping we could go together. We can't stay at home while everyone is at the dance." Looking down at his shoes, he sighed, bringing his knees closer to his chest. "Everyone is going with someone. It will look bad if we don't have dates."

I knew about the dance. It's all Adrianna and Mindy talked about during lunch, but going?

"That sucks. Is she going too?"

"Trent Roundhouse," he replied.

"The eighth-grader from our bus? Doc Martens, flannel shirts, and mustache? Him?" I wanted to punch Tiffany.

I wouldn't tell him for a moment I believed he liked me more than friends. In reality, he hoped we could mend our recent humiliations. I would take his embarrassment. Daniel getting dumped seemed better than showing thirty kids your underwear.

"Do you want to stay for dinner?"

"Are your parents home?" He relaxed a little now the conversation shifted from Tiffany.

"My grandma is staying the weekend. They are going somewhere but wouldn't say much about it."

Daniel grimaced as if he had swallowed something bad.

"Your grandma scares me," he said.

I shifted my body towards him, waiting to hear his explanation.

"Daniel, she is one hundred pounds. How does she scare you?"

"She yelled piss off at a group of kids. Crazy if you ask me." He fidgeted like a nervous person.

"Pass Auf?" I asked.

He nodded. "You sound like her."

"No, it's German. It means watch out. Grandma lived in Germany until she met my Grandpa." Even with my explanation, Daniel still thought my grandma was a crazy, old woman that yells piss off to children.

"I'll pass on dinner. My mom is making hamburgers." As he left the tree house, he stopped for a moment, turning to face me. "Sarah, go back to the old you. You will never be happy being anyone but you."

Daniel was right. I never wore orange lipstick and overalls again.

A boring weekend with Grandma was what I needed after my eventful week. She kept to the living room switching the television between sewing and *Jerry Springer*. I spent my time playing *Legend of Zelda* in my bedroom. As I picked up the

Triforce, about to rescue the princess, a soft knock caused me to pause my Nintendo. My grandmother opened the door.

"I'm leaving, dear. It's eight," she said with coat already buttoned and keys in hand.

"Okay. Bye," I said.

My parents hadn't returned, but this didn't deter my bored grandmother. She had enough of making sure I didn't run away or join a cult. After the front door closed, I looked out my window and watched her taillights disappear towards the entrance of Hidden Meadows.

"Piss off to you too," I mumbled.

I changed into my panda pajamas to watch television.

The sound of the garage door opener vibrated the house, a sign my parents were home. I opened the door that led to the garage.

"Where's Dad?" I eyed the empty Buick Regal.

"San Francisco. He is not coming back." She said it as if he had gone to the store to get milk.

"What do you mean?"

"We are getting a divorce, and he is moving to San Francisco." She pulled her bag out of the Buick, eyes looking up at me. Was she going to explain? "Do you know if we have any leftover chicken salad? Grandma said she would make a batch this weekend."

"Dad left, and you're asking about chicken salad?" She walked past me and into the house.

"Mom…Mom…Mom." I followed her to the master bedroom. Tears streamed down my cheeks.

"You weren't upset when Jerry and Leslie got a divorce. People get divorced. They move on. It happens all the time," she said.

"Jerry isn't my dad!" My mom remained calm, which wasn't her usual state if I raised my voice.

"Jerry kicked Leslie out over a fight they had about the neighbor hearing them have sex with their window open. They shouldn't build these houses so close together," she said. She hung her clothes in my dad's empty side of the closet. "My next house will be bigger."

"You shouldn't be telling me this stuff. I'm a kid."

She ignored me.

My mom walked into her bathroom and closed the door. Like most of our conversations, I knew there was no reasoning.

I returned to my room. My body shook from the news. Shock and denial consumed me. I stared at the wall until my alarm went off the next morning.

CHAPTER FIVE

"You cannot control the actions of others, but you can control how you respond." -Dr. Lee Abrams

The gloomy morning sky spat tiny ice pellets, which melted on the warmer ground but coated my clothes and hair. I walked towards the door of the Oakville State University Psychiatric Center, which used to be apartments before the hospital bought the building. My cheeks burned at the thought of anyone finding out about my appointments.

Huffing up the three flights of stairs, I entered the old door into the small reception space. The window gave a clear view of our Buick Regal at the traffic light. My mom waited to turn. Over the last four weeks of my meetings with Dr. Abrams, she would drop me off and return an hour later. The psychiatrist was a waste of time and money in my mom's opinion, but the judge ordered I see someone as part of the divorce proceedings.

"Hello Sarah," the receptionist said. She handed paperwork to a couple. They looked like nice, normal people. I felt sad they were here too. "You can go back. The doctor is ready."

The hallway to the doctor's office had dark blue carpet with snags. Paint peeled around the door frames, some likely no longer opened. I wondered who had lived or worked here before the remodel.

Dr. Abrams left his door open. A boy with glasses had the appointment before me, but not today. Maybe therapy cured him. Perhaps the nightmare divorce inflicted upon him was over. Whatever the reason, he wasn't in the office, and neither was the annoying doctor.

I sat on the faux leather couch with cushions so worn my weight sunk to the hard frame. Throughout the room were pictures of the doctor's family—everyone had dark hair and eyes. His father was a doctor too. At least I assumed since they both wore lab coats in a picture next to his framed diploma. The photographs were second to all the cool items he collected. He must have traveled a lot because none of this stuff came from Oakville. I liked the blue pot with the succulent the best. He preferred avoiding eye contact during our session, which allowed me to look around.

Dr. Abrams appeared in the doorway, took a seat in his leather office chair, nodded, and rotated towards his desk. He wore a wool scarf and matching sweater vest, which was about as cool as my days of the week underwear. I had no idea of his age. No gray hair, but he acted old.

"When we left off," he said. A brief pause to look at his yellow notebook, three pencil taps against the spiral binding, same as last week. "You were discussing Tiffany and her impact on your present situation. Is she your uncle's girlfriend or your best friend's girlfriend?"

"Tiffani is the girl that was making out with my uncle on his boat. Gina is his girlfriend. Tiffany dumped Daniel." He scribbled in his notebook. I would never be a psychiatrist. His notes were probably a grocery list, rather than patient notes or whatever he called them.

"Did Tiffani dump Daniel because she was also with your uncle?" He chewed on the eraser. I wanted to laugh but didn't. Why was this so hard?

"No. They are two different people," I said. Dr. Abrams made a groaning noise as if he had started a deep train of thought.

"In the future, it would be helpful if you would clarify. For example, refer to each Tiffany by their first and last name." He reminded me of Doctor Claw from *Inspector Gadget* with his face turned away, only his fidgeting hand in view. If only he had a cat to sit on his lap.

"I don't know their last names."

On top of his bookshelf sat a silver Star of David. I couldn't believe I hadn't noticed it after looking around the room for weeks.

"Are you a Jew?" I couldn't help but ask. We needed to discuss something besides the divorce.

"Yes, but I don't..." His chair turned. If Inspector Gadget wanted to see Doctor Claw, he only needed to ask about his faith.

"My grandmother is Jewish," I said. I hoped this would propel him into some lively conversation about what he did last Hanukkah.

"You said your family is Catholic." He flipped through the pages on his lap for a note about religion. His notebook wasn't a grocery list.

"For a psychiatrist, you don't listen." I crossed my arms to ward off the chilly air from the single pane, frosted windows. The small space heater did a poor job heating the large office.

"For a thirteen-year-old girl, you have a big mouth." The doctor turned the chair to face me and tossed his notebook on the desk. "You are also avoiding your problems. You are deflecting, placing blame, acting out— "

"Maybe I am sick of everyone acting like selfish brats. Maybe my life was perfect before sixth grade."

It bothered him not to have his notebook, but he didn't move.

"What do you mean by selfish brats?" His words were cautious.

I wanted to scream.

"My parents are getting a divorce because my mom wants

one for no reason. For my dad to afford our house and an apartment, he had to move to San Francisco for a job. Jerry and Leslie are getting a divorce because Leslie doesn't like that Tom and Sue heard them having sex. Uncle Dan cheats on Gina because twenty-five is too old."

The gates opened, and all the bottled up words came rushing out.

CHAPTER SIX

**"Married women rarely ask for commitments." -
Ryan Rice**

"Brenda?"

I stared at Daniel in disbelief.

"It's true," he said.

"Brenda and Coach Rice?"

He nodded and stuffed his baseball uniform into a blue Cougar duffel bag. Daniel's house had the same floor plan as mine. Our rooms were identical except for the décor. I would much rather have his tan walls than my gaudy rose wallpaper.

"Jack said his dad has been sleeping on the couch for a while. Maybe it was because of Coach Rice? Jack must hate his parents are divorcing."

My eyes widened at my friend, but he was oblivious.

My head rested on Daniel's pillow, which smelled like a sweaty boy. Daniel eyed me lying on his bed. Something had changed between us, but it was hard to explain. We no longer played outside, sometimes video games, watched television, or walked around the mall.

"Do you want to do something this weekend?" Daniel asked. "Steve wants to see a movie at the dollar place."

Margie's dog barked next door. The dumb creature howled and whined at everything.

I sighed. "We are meeting Donny's kids at Funland." Saying the words made me cringe. Donny made a terrible situation much worse.

"I thought you liked Funland? Who is Donny?" I forgot I had not debriefed Daniel on my mom's new boyfriend. She wasted no time getting back into the dating pool.

"Donny is my mom's boyfriend. He is a total loser. I met him for the first time last weekend, and the guy lives above his mom's garage." I closed my eyes to vent life's angst.

Daniel joined me on the bed. I rolled from my back to my side, our faces inches apart. Did he know he filled me with butterflies? I needed him more than ever. He remained the last piece of normal in my life.

"Donny has a skull on the coffee table in his living room. He is weird." My heart pounded to the point I couldn't breathe.

"A skull is weird," he whispered. The tip of his index finger traced the outline of my palm. I inhaled through my nose, a feeling of dizzy mixed with anticipation when he explored my wrist.

The sound of Daniel's name echoed down the hall. We scrambled off the bed in a way one does when guilty. Mrs. Klein burst through the door. Daniel sat in a desk chair, and I leaned against the window frame like a mannequin.

"Hi, Sarah. I didn't know you were here. Usually I have to yell at the two of you to keep it down. No video games today?"

Each of us looked at the black television screen.

"I was only stopping by for a minute." I smiled at her.

She reminded Daniel to do his homework when she left the room.

"The dance is next Friday. I hope you didn't forget." Daniel played with a paperweight from his desk.

"No, I didn't forget. Are you sure you still want me to go? Tiffany broke up with Mr. Mustache."

I wanted to be certain Daniel wanted to go with me.

The corners of his lips turned up.

"I'm over Tiffany. You're my best friend." He walked me to the door. I bit the inside of my cheeks to keep from smiling. My heart warmed with his words. I wanted to hug him but didn't.

After I left Daniel's yard, I ran home. I needed help. After two rings, I heard Gina's Southern accent on the other line.

CHAPTER SEVEN

"Lori hung with the cool crowd in high school. She smoked and drank, skipped school, drove around Oakville like she owned the town. I don't know what she ever saw in Frank Margo." -Donny Nelson

It made zero sense how my mother could divorce my father and end up dating a man who lived with his mom. I wanted to say something to her, let her know the entire situation bothered me, but she was incapable of reasoning. She told me I would understand when I became an adult.

Our car pulled out of the driveway and headed towards the end of the neighborhood. The tacky Christmas decorations stood out in the gloomy frost. Country music played in the background, but I was too busy thinking about Gina to care. She agreed to help me find a dress before the dance.

"You are quiet today," she said.

She watched me stare out the window after our Buick pulled into the parking spot at the chain restaurant. I didn't know the name of the place as they all looked the same.

"Sorry."

If I said anything about Donny, my mom would take it as an insult. She knew I didn't like him. Grown-up wisdom wasn't required to know my mom's boyfriend was a loser. My mom knew Donny from high school. She said he wasn't one of the cool kids when they were younger. Did she not realize his coolness hadn't changed?

An overwhelming feeling of dread came over me when I saw Donny at the entrance of the restaurant. The knockoff football jersey paired with the acid washed jeans did little to impress me. At least my dad dressed like an adult with a job. My mom waved with a level of enthusiasm I didn't know existed. Our car doors opened, and we began the walk to the lunch from hell.

"Hey, kiddo!" Donny smiled at us. He introduced his children although I didn't need introductions. My mom shared their life stories the night before.

Tara was three years older. She played the flute at Eastside High. In person, she had over-processed blond hair and a retainer.

Michael was in the seventh grade at Eastside Middle. The hair on his head was a messy jet black coated with dandruff and oil. He only needed a beard and acid washed jeans to be his father's twin.

Stacy was the youngest, two years younger than me with light blond hair and an attractive smile she inherited from her mother.

They lived in an apartment with Donny's ex-wife on Martin Luther King near the old skating rink. Did my mom think I cared to know these people?

As we followed the hostess to the table, my mom leaned closer to my ear. "Can you please try to say something?" I looked at her confused. Donny and his spawns picked up plates at the salad bar.

"I thought you wanted me to be on my best behavior?" Another Lori Margo no-win situation. I gave her my best smile. She returned it with a glare.

I sat in my chair, fidgeting my napkin on my lap. After two nudges of the foot, I got the hint that my mom wanted me to leave the table. The thought of eating food from a buffet setting always grossed me out.

Someone slopped food into the other containers. Was I the

only one who cared the ranch dressing had stray pieces of cheese and chunks of ham floating on top?

"Have you been here before?" I asked Tara because I knew my mom was watching.

Grasping her plate with two hands, she walked around the bar until she stood next to me. I looked up at her dark roots. Gina wasn't kidding when she said you shouldn't dye your own hair.

"Listen, I don't like you. I don't want to be around you. Our parents are moving in together, and there is nothing I can do about it. My mom is so pissed. We live in a shitty apartment on the river while my dad lives in a house. He doesn't give us any money. My grandma is kicking him out of her garage for not paying rent."

I stood dumbfounded, listening to my heart thump in my eardrum. The words made me feel so powerless. My hope for the best year of my life shriveled up like the day old spinach on my plate.

"Umm. What?"

"You heard me. I. Don't. Like. You," she said. The black eyebrows under her blond bangs raised.

"I don't care if you like me. What do you mean they are moving in together?"

Donny needed a place to live. Lori Margo had a home. I wanted to scream, throw things, and climb into a dark hole.

I ignored Tara, kept my cool, and returned to my seat to eat my salad. My life would turn to hell if I made Lori Margo mad. The sweat on my palms made it difficult to hold a fork. I needed my dad. Talking on the phone wasn't enough. I bit my lip hard to distract myself from the oncoming tears.

"Your mom tells me you like Poison and Twisted Sister?" Donny stuffed a fry into his mouth. "I don't date women with kids. When I found out you and I have so much in common, I couldn't say no." He moved his hand over to my mom's arm.

"What is Twisted Sister?" I knew I should've kept my mouth closed and agreed.

"Metal!" Donny played a fake air guitar. Michael played invisible drums. Tara and Stacy laughed while I sat in my horrible nightmare I didn't ask to join. "I've got all the albums. We can listen to them while we watch stock car racing. Most girls don't like the noise. Your mom said you talk about cars and bands all the time."

Death metal? Stock car racing? All because he didn't want to date someone with kids. I was almost a teenager. My diapers no longer needed changed.

Even though my mom wasn't the greatest mother, she did nothing illegal. I couldn't say she beat me or neglected me. Telling Donny that I liked death metal or not hugging me when she left my uncle's house weren't reasons a court would deem her unfit to be a parent. I was a paycheck. As long as I lived with her, my father would give her money. No one at this table wanted me. There was no way to sugarcoat the fact.

"I don't like death metal or stock car racing. I have nothing in common with you other than we both live with our mom," I said. This should have been the moment I smacked my hand against the table and yell roasted. Instead, my mom squeezed my arm until I winced in pain. Donny laughed, the only reason I wasn't killed at the restaurant. The other kids sipped their drinks and searched their plates for food they could pretend to be eating. No one wanted to join me on my downward spiral.

After my loose tongue at the restaurant, we skipped Funland, and she grounded me for a month. My dad was the buffer, often getting me out of trouble, but with him gone, I stayed on lockdown.

While everyone dined on turkey at my grandparents' house, I enjoyed a peanut butter and jelly sandwich. The solitary confinement suited me. Besides, I didn't like turkey, and I couldn't stand the Fischers.

I never noticed the surrounding drama until sixth grade. The status of relationships or wrongdoings never crossed my mind. If a person was sick, I found out if they died. Situations had to be extreme before I had any clue.

I spent many nights wondering why the world had changed. Was I more mature? I dismissed maturity. A part of me still wanted to play with pony toys, no matter how uncool. Was it my parents' separation? The divorce seemed to be the least dramatic event going on around me.

"Are you ready? You have an appointment with Dr. Abrams." One hand rested on her hip.

I put on my coat, not saying a word to my mother.

CHAPTER EIGHT

"Life goes on no matter if you like it or not." -Dr. Lee Abrams

The tips of the receptionist's nails tapped the counter. Her hair stood three inches taller, clothes twice as tight, and eyeliner heavier than usual. She gazed out the frosty window into the night sky. The lights of Oakville twinkled for New Year's Eve to begin. Dr. Abrams stepped into the hall and motioned for me to join him.

Our session started the same way. He did a brief recap of what we discussed the previous week; then we moved to new stuff.

"My mom grounded me."

He turned his chair towards me.

"I told her new boyfriend he is a loser that lives with his mom. He is moving in with us next week, his kids too."

"How does this make you feel?" My eyebrows shot up at his remark. "Okay, dumb question. Terrible, I suppose." His frankness took me off-guard. "It is unprofessional for me to discuss my personal life, but my parents also divorced. My father married another woman within a year. I was fifteen."

"But that was a long time ago."

He laughed.

"I'm not old." He paused. I waited for him to give me a number. "Twenty-eight."

A person near thirty was old.

"What should I do?" He remained quiet, only the sound of the space heater and his pencil tapping the spiral notebook filled the room. "I am stuck. It's hard pretending I am okay with the divorce." I swallowed hard. "And Donny."

"As children, our parents structure a routine. Once you become an adult, life changes. You must have goals too."

"I'm nowhere close to being an adult." I shivered. My weight shifted to align myself with the old space heater.

"You are a teenager—"

"Not yet." Goals wouldn't fix a stupid divorce.

"Close enough. You won't always live at home, Sarah. My point is you must consider what's next. For example, the classes you take in high school may affect what major you pursue in college. Perhaps you will choose a trained skill over attending a university."

He brushed lint off his dress pants. "You need goals. A way to focus on the future, because like it or not, you cannot change others. You cannot make your mom get back with your dad. Your neighbor will start an affair with the gym teacher whether you think she should or not. That's life."

The blue hatchback rental car pulled into the driveway on New Year's Day. My dad arrived in Oakville the night before, a relief since Donny was moving in on Thursday. Ignoring my mom, I ran outside and hugged him around the waist. I hadn't seen him in weeks. We didn't talk much because of the long distance charges. His arms wrapped around me, squeezing me breathless, only letting go when my mom cleared her throat. I never realize how much I loved him.

"She is grounded. I mean it. No friends and no activities." Her evil scowl made my dad agree. "Please make sure she gets to school on time. Where are you staying?"

"Does it matter? I don't ask you about your boyfriend. Why

should you care about my business?" My father never spoke a harsh word to anyone. Her mouth dropped open. "Traveler's Motel. I'll have her back soon. She will call you." He turned to face me. "Get your suitcase."

I buckled my seat belt. In less than a minute, my dad had the car moving through the neighborhood. The wooden sign went out of sight in the side mirror. Sadness loomed, and I knew Hidden Meadows would never be home again.

We were staying at Traveler's Motel. The thought of the homeless bums hanging outside the dilapidated one-story motel still seemed a better alternative than spending two weeks with Donny and his kids.

My dad remained quiet, not saying a word since leaving. My view of the man in the seat next to me changed. I no longer saw him as an adult with life figured out. Maybe it was my fault I thought adults were invincible. The tired lines running through my dad's face made it clear I was not the only one dealing with personal struggles.

"Something wrong?" He shifted his weight towards me while the rental car idled at the red light.

I shook my head no. In fact, everything was wrong. Neither my dad nor I could change my mom's decisions. We were forced to deal with the crumbled pieces of our former lives as she picked out new sofas with Donny. I sighed. The rental car pulled into a gas station near the highway.

"I am not grounding you. She told me what you did or at least her version. We aren't staying at Traveler's Motel with the hookers either," he said.

I laughed. It wasn't supposed to be a joke, but he never used vulgarities. An uneasy smile spread across his face. I leaned across the console to hug him.

"Where are we staying? I'm not grounded? But she—"

"We are staying at Dan's. Your mother prohibited me from staying with my brother."

I did not understand why we weren't allowed to stay with my uncle.

"Keep it between us. I am trying to avoid conflict. What did you do to Gina?"

"Nothing. I need Gina's help to find a dress. There is a dance Friday." I didn't care about the dance, but I cared about Daniel.

"Do you still want to go?" I nodded. "Then go, but don't tell your mother," he said.

We shared a smirk of victory.

"Trust me. I won't."

CHAPTER NINE

"She had the purest heart, a wicked smile, and a hilarious sense of humor." -Roddy King

The last day of school break started out perfect. The smell of meat frying in the kitchen filled my nostrils. Rolling over, I tossed the pink and purple quilt on the floor. Shelves of beauty pageant trophies and tiaras lined the wall. Gina called it the hobby room although I wasn't sure why her childhood daybed and porcelain dolls constituted as a hobby. Who was I to question the room's name? Besides, my alternatives were Traveler's Motel or my home, which would soon occupy my mom's boyfriend and his three kids. The door creaked when someone knocked.

"Hey babe, breakfast is ready. I made cheesy grits," Gina said. Her footsteps disappeared down the hall.

A second knock on the door. My dad entered in sweatpants and a university t-shirt. His casual consisted of dress clothes with no tie. All of his engineer friends wore the same. Sweats?

"Gina is taking you shopping today. I have errands to run this morning—adult stuff. Is that okay?"

I ran my hand through my wild bed head. Did it matter what I thought? My thoughts consisted of two things—the divorce and Daniel. I couldn't wait to go dress shopping for the dance. The adult stuff needed shoved aside today.

I strode down the hall in pajamas to the kitchen. A steaming plate of food waited on my placemat. Leave it to the

Southerners to mix hot cheese into grits for breakfast. I crumbled my sausage into the bowl, relishing in the cheesy, meaty taste. Gina had a glass of water to wash down her homemade granola bar.

"Do you want me to do the dishes?" I gestured to the sink, an attempt to be as good-natured as Gina. She shook her head no. My meal moved in my stomach, enough grease and cheese to kill a person.

No more cheesy grits.

"Martina will clean this afternoon," she replied. Uncle Dan's last housekeeper wore short skirts and a halter top. Gina selected Martina—sixty years old, overweight, and wore a giant wooden cross around her neck.

"When will you be ready to go?" She had on a denim jumper with metallic buttons. The curled ends of her hair bounced when she moved. Gina gave one last tug on her boot laces, eyes looking up at me.

"Five minutes. I need to put on jeans. What if we see my mom?"

The last thing I wanted to do was cross the dragon lady by going out while grounded. It didn't matter what Frank Margo said I could do. If Lori Margo found out, I would be the one taking the blame.

"We are going to the bridal shop in Pine Plaza. She won't be there." Gina dug through her purse for car keys.

"Rule nothing out," I mumbled.

Even with the convertible top up, the heater couldn't keep the car warm. Gina didn't seem to mind. With my new dress hanging in the back and shoes in the trunk, we pulled into the driveway. My stomach growled for lunch. Three hours of shopping burned off the morning grits.

"Who is that?" I pointed to the kid sitting on Dan and Gina's porch. He looked about my age with black hair, tan skin, and stylish glasses.

"David King's son." I gave her a blank stare. "He was at the restaurant when we ate lunch with your mom." She rolled her eyes. "As always, he made a big scene and claimed someone threw fish in his wife's hair."

I let out an uncomfortable chuckle. In my defense, the tuna wasn't supposed to land on her head.

"Why is his son at your house?"

Gina parked the car in the garage, and the boy greeted us as we stepped out of the LeBaron. She eyed the neighbor's kid with curiosity, not answering my question.

"Hey, Roddy!" Her smile caused the boy to light up. He had a crush on Gina.

Pretty girls had life so easy.

"Hi. I'm locked out again. Can I use your phone?" he asked.

Gina gestured for him to follow us through the garage and into the kitchen. Tossing her purse and keys on the counter, she reached for the cordless mounted on the wall.

Roddy dialed a phone number as he walked into the living room. I was unsure why he felt he needed privacy.

"Is his name Rodney?" I whispered to Gina.

Roddy paced near the wicker coffee table, disappointed in his conversation.

"I think so. Do you know him?" she asked in a loud whisper.

He lived in the elite neighborhood while I came from the middle-class neighborhood. People on my street drove used cars and attended public schools. Gina looked very skeptical that Roddy King and I ever crossed paths.

"No," I replied.

"It's Radhey," he said. I flushed with embarrassment. "My mother's family is Indian. No one can pronounce my name. I've been Roddy since first grade." He returned the cordless phone to its cradle. "Thanks, Gina. My dad won't be home until midnight. I left a message with his service, but they said he is in an eight-hour surgery." He sighed.

I couldn't imagine David King having the focus and patience to perform a fifteen-minute surgery. *Who put this scalpel upside down? When I find out, I will sue you and this hospital!*

"Do y'all want to grab something to eat?" Gina already had her keys in hand. We had planned on leftover Chinese, but there wasn't enough for three. This kid was stuck with us, like it or not. It was too cold to make him wait outside for eight hours.

"What's with the dress?" He turned around in his seat and gestured towards the garment bag hanging on a hook. I scrunched in the back since Roddy's six feet was too tall for the tiny bench seat.

"A dance this Friday." I smiled at him.

"It is very nice." He flashed his perfect teeth.

"Thanks. Gina helped." She vetoed the teal gown with fluffy sleeves and white bow.

Not Muse by Carlos again.

The thought of another fishy biscuit gave me the most terrible stomach pains when we pulled into Pine Plaza. To my surprise, we passed the entrance and drove around the back of the building to a place called Pete's Meats.

"Pete's is my favorite," Roddy said.

"Dan loves Pete's–too much." She glanced over her shoulder and tapped her stomach with a slight grin.

Roddy and I talked while we had burgers and curly fries. I found out he was thirteen, played tennis, loved video games, and went to Oakville Country Day School. He received the Disney version of my life. I left out the part of staying with Uncle Dan. Roddy didn't need to know my dad moved to San Francisco because of the messy divorce brought on by my crazy mother.

"I can't believe you play *Super Craft*! Too bad your Uncle doesn't have *Super Craft Four*."

"He has four and five," I said, bragging.

"What? No way! *Super Craft Five* released in Europe last Tuesday. It doesn't come here until next month."

"Uncle Dan's college roommate is on the board of Super Craft Games Worldwide." Roddy looked impressed. "Do you want to play tonight?"

"That's like asking me if I want to breathe," he replied.

My eyes grew tired after playing five straight hours of video games in Uncle Dan's basement. I beat Roddy six times. My victories didn't seem to phase him. He lounged with a leg over the leather chair, game controller in his hand. Neither of us took our eyes off the television when my dad came down the stairs. He watched us for a few moments before speaking.

"Sarah, you need to take a shower and get ready for bed. School starts early."

I tossed the controller towards the television.

"Next time I won't take it easy on you," I said.

"Easy on me? You beat me every time!" We laughed.

My dad picked at his fingernails, not paying attention to our conversation. He seemed worried, and I felt uneasy.

"Do you go back to school tomorrow too?" I asked.

"Yes." He stuck his tongue out in disgust.

I scaled the steps to return to the hobby room. I enjoyed hanging out with Roddy King. He wasn't cool like Jett, athletic like Daniel, or cute like Eric, but he was smart and kind.

Once he found out more about me, I knew I would never hear from him again. The private school kids didn't hang out with the public school kids. It didn't matter. I liked Daniel. I sank into the daybed with thoughts of him. My eyes closed, and I fell asleep without showering.

CHAPTER TEN

"I need a warning label. Explosive. Dangerous. Toxic." -Brent Hayes

A voice yelled my name from down the hall. Daniel weaved in and out of students loitering by their lockers. I shoved my math book into my backpack.

"Where were you this morning? You weren't on the bus," he said while trying to catch his breath.

I slung my heavy bag of books over my shoulder. Daniel and I walked towards the six grade classrooms on the second floor.

"My dad dropped me off. I am staying with my uncle for two weeks." We stopped at the top of the stairs. "Crazy divorce stuff." I hated talking about my situation.

"Oh. Are we going to the dance on Friday?"

"Yeah," I replied in a calm voice, although I had a billion butterflies in my stomach. *I am going to a dance with Daniel Klein.*

"Good," he said. The teachers shut their doors. "See you later."

"Bye." Watching him walk away, I bit my cheeks to hide my smile. I wanted no one to see how happy Daniel made me.

"Ser-ah, let's go." Mrs. Crow towered over me with her hands on her hips. I walked past her into Mrs. Williams' classroom. She followed and closed the door. Why was Mrs. Crow here? Her delusion brought her to the wrong floor. "Quiet everyone! Find your seats!"

The woman's voice was a megaphone—a sound I could live without. Two minutes of her was enough to make me hurl myself out the window. She was a fifth-grade teacher and would never be my teacher again.

"Hey Chunk, sit down," Mindy said. She eyed my few extra pounds. I wasn't over-weight, but I wasn't thin like her. Mindy and Adrianna decided my new nickname the first week of school. I hated the name, but in the big picture, it was low on the list of what sucked most.

"Chunk has a name, Mindy," Jett said.

"Listen up, everyone!" Mrs. Crow shouted. The classroom grew silent as everyone wondered why Banana Hands stood near the blackboard. "Mrs. Williams will be out for a month. She had to have an unexpected surgery."

"Is she going to be all right?" Amanda asked without raising her hand. Mrs. Crow frowned at Amanda but didn't reprimand.

"Like you care." Amanda stuck her tongue out at Brad. I didn't like him either. He called me Bucky when he wasn't referring to me as Clock Pants Girl.

"That's enough—"

"Why are you here? Where's the sub? I put my vote in for Miss Rupert." Brent's friends cheered.

Miss Rupert subbed for our school district. The boys loved flirting with the large-chested blond who giggled at their immature remarks. Tommy put his hands in front of his shirt to show Jeff the size of Miss Rupert's anatomy.

"Boys!" Mrs. Crow put her hand on her heart. "State testing is in two weeks. I will take over until Mrs. Williams returns. Principal Marsh doesn't want a substitute teacher in sixth-grade classes until after the testing."

Brent booed.

"Perhaps you should see Principal Marsh." Mrs. Crow made her way down the aisle where Brent sat with his feet propped up on the cluttered craft table. Last Thursday we glued popcorn kernels to construction paper.

"No thanks." Brent's hand ran through his long hair. He puckered his lips at Mrs. Crow.

Brent Hayes was a notorious troublemaker that lived in a run-down trailer park on the edge of town. When his mind decided to make trouble, it was best to stay clear of him.

"Let's not play games today, Brent." The teacher walked away, not wanting to deal with the troublemaker, but his expression said *let's play games*.

He leaned towards Eric to whisper. Brent raised his eyebrows and Eric nodded. Anticipation sparked excitement in the classroom, which Mrs. Crow did not pick up on. She continued talking about state testing as she wrote the criteria and pass rates on the board.

"Brent went out the fire exit," Eric spoke in a tattle-tail way.

Mrs. Crow whirled around, stomped down the aisle to Eric's desk where she cocked her head to the side. Eric pointed to the metal and glass emergency exit.

The stairs to the ground were missing; only the platform remained intact. Not to mention, the door locked when shut. We weren't allowed to use the fire escape. The class knew this information. Mrs. Crow did not.

A whoosh of cold air filled the room when the door opened. Mrs. Crow flung herself onto the metal landing and looked down towards the damaged stairs for Brent. She yelled his name twice with her hands on the railing. Distracted by the prospect of dragging Brent to the office by his hair, Mrs. Crow let the door shut behind her. Some of the class found this funny. Others were worried.

Once the door clicked shut, Brent jumped out of the supply cabinet. Mrs. Crow discovered Brent on the inside. Banana Hands tugged at the locked door, screamed Brent's name, banged on the glass, and demanded he open the door.

"Save me, Brent," he said in a Southern belle voice, fanning his face and clutching his chest.

"I mean it! Open the door!"

Our side of the building faced the woods. No one would hear her cry for help. Her only chance was returning through the fire escape door.

"Nah," Brent said. His eyes scanned the room. "Eric, fetch me the roll of paper. I don't want to see this bitch."

Brent didn't think his plan through.

What would happen? We couldn't leave her on the fire escape forever.

"Now what?" Eric asked.

"We use the paper to cover the glass," Brent replied.

Several of my classmates joined the troublemakers. They cut and taped paper to the door. I pretended to sort assignments in my Trapper Keeper. Mrs. Crow pleaded with others in the class to open the door.

It was not a mystery I didn't like Mrs. Crow, but I didn't feel the need to lock her out on a cold fire escape. What if something bad happened? I could have opened the door, but I needed to survive sixth grade. Being called Bucky or Chunk would seem like nothing if I dared to rescue Mrs. Crow.

I did nothing.

In a matter of minutes, the glass disappeared with brown paper and tape. I was glad they covered the door. I didn't want to see her pleading face, covered in tears. The class cheered. Brent ran to the podium, arms flailing to quiet the room. He had commandeered sixth grade.

"Someone will bust us if we make too much noise," Brent said. His weight rested on the tall, wooden stool near the blackboard.

"What do we do now?" Ray, a football player, asked.

Brent tapped his hand against his holey jeans.

"What do you want to do?" He eyed the class like a magic genie with a wish to grant to his followers.

"Go to the mall!" Kelsey shouted.

"I think someone will notice if we go to the mall." Jett looked up from his doodle of a zombie playing guitar.

"What do you think, Chunk? Should we go to the mall?" Mindy asked. "Maybe get you another makeover."

A few kids laughed. My cheeks warmed with embarrassment. The bully walked towards my desk, a giant smirk on her face. She slapped my Trapper Keeper before her hand squished my chin. Mindy forced me to make eye contact.

"You won't need one. Daniel will go to the dance with Tiffany De Luca." My heart pounded, one of its new habits, either from fear or truth. "Oh, that's right. You don't know she wants him back." She made a pathetic face. "A guy like Daniel Klein shouldn't be with someone like you. He will say yes when she wants him back. Tiffany goes to second base."

Brent removed Mindy's hand from my face. "Tiffany goes to third. Been there. Done that." He grinned at the other boys who idolized him. "Take a seat and leave Margo alone."

I couldn't breathe.

Was Daniel going to throw me over for Tiffany? I knew the answer. The worst part was knowing before it happened. How was I going to compete with base rounding Tiffany?

I couldn't.

CHAPTER ELEVEN

"Any guy would be stupid not to choose Tiffany De Luca." -Daniel Klein

Daniel caught up before I climbed into the rental car to leave school. He explained Tiffany wanted him back, and I should be happy for him. I stared at him, eyes watering, as the ship blew up and sank to the bottom of a deep, dark sea. When I slammed the car door, my father said nothing. Neither of us had a desire to talk about life. I wanted to return to my temporary home in Pine Ridge and sleep.

At seven, I woke up from my nap. No one bothered to call me for dinner, but I wasn't hungry. As I looked into the mirror at my sleepy reflection, a soft knock sounded at the door.

"No, I don't want cheesy grits," I said. The door creaked when it opened. "Go away."

"That makes two of us." Roddy King stood in the doorway. "Whoa. What happened to you?" He took a step back with his palms in the air

"Bad day. What are you doing here?" I tried to sound pleasant. He leaned against the door frame of the hobby room in his private school uniform. The pocket of his jacket had a crest with a lion's head.

"I wanted to hear about your first day after break. Maybe you want to play *Super Craft*?" I didn't respond. Life had sucked every last bit of energy out of me. He continued rambling. "My day was uneventful. We had lacrosse camp sign-ups even

62

though it isn't until summer. You know how it works. They always want the check and permission slip months in advance."

He couldn't be further from reality. I didn't know. Public school kids didn't play lacrosse. Expensive camps weren't our thing either.

"I had a terrible day," I said. My eyes returned to the mirror again. I looked like I felt—a girl on a sinking ship to a black abyss.

"It couldn't be that bad. You have only been back to school for one day." He invited himself in and sat on the daybed while I remained at the vanity. Roddy surveyed the hobby room with interest. Before he had time to ask meaningless questions about Gina's trophies and dolls, I told him the events of my dramatic afternoon. What did I have to lose? I wanted to tell someone, not my family or Dr. Abrams.

"Whoa!" Roddy took his glasses off to clean them on his shirt. "It's rude not to follow through with plans." He returned his glasses to his face. "What happened to the teacher?"

"Who?" I zoned out for a moment. "Oh, Mrs. Crow. I let her out."

"You did?" The disbelief on his face was almost comical. "What did the other students do?" He literally hung on the edge of his seat.

"Everyone agreed to go to lunch to not raise any suspicion. I pretended to go to the bathroom while the class waited in the food line." His mouth hung open. He wanted to ask another question but was too afraid to interrupt the most exciting story ever told. "I opened the door."

"What did the teacher do?" he asked after a moment. The palms of his hands pressed against his dress pants.

"She looked scared. I think she expected the teacher's pet, Amanda, or the janitor to rescue her. Not me." I moved a strand of hair from my face. "I saved her life. She didn't say thank you."

After I released Mrs. Crow from her fire escape prison, she went to the office to find Principal Marsh. I slipped back into the lunchroom. The rest of the day, we dealt with Principal Marsh's interrogation. Locking a teacher out on the fire escape seemed to have bigger repercussions than sixth graders could have anticipated.

"What if she tells everyone you were the one who opened the door?" Roddy's eyes grew to the size of cantaloupes.

"I told her I would tell the principal she touched my private parts." With a look of shock on his face, he laughed at my threat. "I'm kidding. She said nothing."

"Can I go to your dance with you on Friday?" he asked. I looked at myself in the mirror and then to him. "Public school sounds awesome."

"What's the deal?" I whispered to Amanda the next morning. "Where is Mrs. Crow?"

"She is suing the school for emotional damages. My mom said Mrs. Crow told the school board she almost died in the cold," Amanda replied. The acid in my stomach burned my insides. "Mrs. Crow is pressing charges against Brent and Eric. Some of the others, too."

"We are getting in trouble?" Jett asked. Amanda looked disappointed. "That is bullshit. We didn't lock her out on the fire escape."

"We didn't come to her rescue," Amanda said. Jett tucked his pencil into the metal spirals of his notebook.

"Does Principal Marsh not remember sixth grade? I couldn't open the door. Brent would have kicked my butt." Amanda agreed with Jett along with a few eavesdroppers.

The conversation made me nervous. My classmates didn't ask who released the teacher. Did Mrs. Crow tell the police? Would it come out in court? My life would be over. Why did I set her free? I couldn't stand the woman, but I didn't want to be a bully. No one deserved the humiliation, not even Mrs. Crow.

With all the controversy, test preparation wasn't a priority. School administration and police questioned my classmates alone and in small groups. Green Street Intermediate turned into a crime scene with police radios and flashing lights.

I didn't say much when questioned, only giving Officer Franken my name and agreeing when Amanda said we were too afraid to act. He dismissed us. I joined the sixth grade lunch period for the first time all year.

"Sarah!" Daniel skipped across the room to greet me. When he reached for my arm, I jerked away, joined the line, and ignored him. "Are you mad at me?"

"You don't get it, do you?" Tears welled in my eyes. Gina said men were idiots. She wasn't exaggerating.

"Get what?"

His face was blank, but he knew. We both knew. He thought I'd always be his back-up when he needed me. The tears left their reservoir, streamed down my face, a salty taste cascaded across my lips. Grabbing my arm, he pulled me through double doors and into the hall. We weren't supposed to leave the lunch room. When footsteps echoed through the hallway, Daniel shoved me into a janitor's closet.

"I didn't think you'd be mad. You should be happy for me," he said.

"Happy for you?" My eyes burned like a roaring fire in the darkness. "I like you, Daniel, as more than friends. It's…" I couldn't stop crying. He tried to touch my shoulder, and I slapped his hand away. The mop handle fell into a shelf of cleaning supplies. "I can't do this anymore."

I stormed out of the closet, down the hall, and out the emergency exit. The loud buzzing of the door stopped once it closed behind me.

By the time I realized I had left school, I was a mile down

Green Street almost to the intersection of Regency Road. I let out a deep sigh, relieved to be away from the dilapidated hell hole full of police and stupid boys. What was I going to do? I was in over my head. A voice inside said I needed help.

Five rings. No answer. I tapped the pay phone receiver against the glass, cars speeding along Green Street. The tears returned.

"Hello? Hello?" A faint voice came from the phone. I put the receiver to my ear.

"Dad? Is that you?"

"Yeah. Sarah, is something wrong?" He sounded sleepy.

"Yes. Everything. I need you to pick me up."

CHAPTER TWELVE

"When I saw the little bastard standing near the office, I wanted to knock him senseless." -Frank Margo

The blue rental car pulled up to the curb with my worried father behind the wheel. Once inside and seat belted, he moved to a parking spot near the end of the shopping center lot. The warmth of the heater did little to thaw my frozen arms. What was I thinking leaving school without a coat in January? Shifting his weight to face me, he didn't say a word, only remained in his seat with a blank, defeated face.

"I can't do this anymore!" I screamed while sobbing without tears. "I don't fit in at my school. I have told you, but no one listens. My friends have changed. Daniel broke my heart. If I can't trust him, who can I trust? I lost my best friend!" My dad flinched. "Then there is you and my mom. She says awful things sometimes."

"You should ignore her and keep to yourself," he said.

If he believed his remark helpful, he was wrong.

"Keep to myself? Not say anything? That's terrible advice. You should know." My knuckles turned white from squeezing the seatbelt.

"Are you referring to me?" His eyes narrowed.

"Maybe I am."

This wasn't the direction I intended to go. I didn't want to pick a fight with my dad, but he let my mom walk all over him.

The divorce moved along because he didn't contest. He didn't fight for custody or the house. At the end of his two-week vacation, before returning to San Francisco, he was to meet with the lawyers to complete this mess on paper. Lori Margo was victorious while we were left to rot and suffer.

"I am doing this for you, to keep your life as normal as possible," he said. The back of his head rested against the stained headrest. "I took a job thousands of miles away so I could keep you in your home."

"It's not my home anymore. When I go back, another man and his kids will live in our bedrooms. She bought bunk beds! I have to share my room with two girls. Did you know she told me I could call Donny my dad?" I turned the knob to shut off the heat. The car felt July rather than January.

He clinched the wheel, inhaled, his face crimson with frustration. A couple fighting near the shopping cart corral took our attention away from our conversation. They climbed into their beat-up van and sped off, a trail of white smoke fumed from their exhaust.

"Sarah, I want you to live with me. I want your mom out on her ass, but if I say those words to my attorney, there will be big consequences. Do you understand?"

I shook my head no. Didn't anyone understand the real world was a new concept? Six months ago, I played with *My Little Ponies* and thought fish stick day at school was life's biggest tragedy.

"You might have to change schools. We will sell the house in Hidden Meadows." He paused for a moment. "I wouldn't want to upset you or have you be conversation because of your parents. Not to mention, the legal costs."

"Oh." I had considered none of the consequences.

"Do you understand, Sarah? I've been weighing my options the past few days with Dan and the lawyer. I don't like giving in to your mom, but I will do anything for you." My father closed his eyes in prayer. "Can I be honest?" He opened his eyes. "I'm

68

an educated adult with no answers."

"Okay," I said.

Adults without answers was scary territory.

"What do you want? Do you want me to continue or pull the trigger on this nightmare?" he asked with a large serving of desperation on his plate.

Trigger?

Divorce wasn't a world war, but I had the ability to drop the bomb. The question remained—could I live with the aftermath? Did I have a choice? I wasn't sure. Life had no certainties.

I followed my gut.

"No, I can't continue living this way. Please fight for me."

In only a few words, I had given my orders for the fall of Hidden Meadows.

I remained in the car while my dad went into Green Street Intermediate. Swollen and red from crying, my face looked as if I had fallen down a flight of stairs. We agreed I'd go home.

"I saw Daniel in the office," he said. I didn't realize my dad had returned to the car. He shivered from the cold, pressing his hands to the car vents. "He will call you at Uncle Dan's tonight. I gave him the number."

"Dad!" Crossing my arms like a pouting child, I glared at him. "I don't want to talk to him!"

"Sarah, listen to the boy. He is concerned about you." He collected his thoughts. "You said he broke your heart?"

I forgot I mentioned Daniel during my crazy rant.

"He asked me to a dance and then wanted someone else." The short version of a more complicated ordeal. I would not tell him about lying on Daniel's bed as he ran his fingers over mine. "Daniel thought I'd be happy for him."

My dad laughed. I let out a frustrated sigh. Putting the gearshift in reverse, he backed the car out onto Green Street.

"Sorry. Men don't think. I'm not making excuses for him, but we aren't like women," he said.

"What do you mean?" It seemed guys lived on their own planet. Girls didn't plot to lock teachers out on a fire escape or doodle guitar playing zombies. Girls didn't throw kick balls at other girls for fun or wonder who could run up a flight of stairs the fastest.

"Guys aren't wired the same." He motioned for another driver to go and stopped his explanation. "Hear what he has to say. If it sounds like a load of crap, move on, but listen."

CHAPTER THIRTEEN

"Maybe when I'm thirty I will have enough courage to tell Sarah how much I like her." -Aaron Wells

Daniel never called.

We made eye contact, by accident, for a moment. He looked away, attention on Tiffany. She begged him to dance with a tug on his arm and pouty lip. He smiled. She twirled in her tight dress, which left my heart defeated. The colorful lights swirled around the darkness of the school gymnasium. I couldn't believe my best friend was no longer talking to me.

"Let's dance," Roddy whispered, his warm breath near my ear. I closed my eyes for a moment, inhaling the scent of his father's cologne. A tear escaped my eye, rolled down my cheek, and splashed on the waxed floor.

"Hi," Amanda said. She wore a magenta dress; one Gina would have said no way to buying. "Who's your friend?"

I wiped my face before anyone noticed.

"Roddy King," he replied. My date released me to extend his hand. Amanda shot me a curious look. I shrugged.

What sixth-grader shakes hands?

"Amanda MacDermot with only one T," she said. Roddy raised a brow. I shrugged again. "Are you new here?"

The gym lights brightened for a fast song. Aaron's arms flailed in unusual circles as he lip-synced Salt-N-Pepa. *Ooh, baby, baby. Baby, baby.* Aaron moved like a funky chicken and smiled.

"No, I go to Oakville Country Day." Roddy tilted his head to face mine, a warm expression on his face.

"Oh, okay," Amanda said. A few kids standing nearby eyed me with the prep school kid from the other side of town. I wanted to be with Daniel, but I liked the way my classmates looked at me with Roddy King.

Roddy threaded his fingers through mine. He led me through the gym, into the entry hall lined with cases of trophies. The sound of muffled music carried through the double doors. I joined Roddy on the wooden bench.

"Something wrong?" he asked.

"I am thinking about my family." I lied. Daniel possessed all my thoughts whether I wanted him to or not.

"Tell me," he said with a maturity far beyond thirteen. Roddy pushed his glasses up his nose, prepared to listen.

I told him about my parents and their messy divorce. I knew once the words left my mouth, he wouldn't want anything to do with me. When I told him about Donny living with his mom, he laughed.

"I had fun hanging out with the public school kids tonight," he said.

The chilly January air disappeared when his soft lips touched mine. I thought kissing a boy would be gross, but it wasn't. Sixth grade continued spinning at a speed faster than I could handle.

The Hidden Meadows sign caused an uneasy grumble in my stomach. Until a few months ago, the entry, surrounded by boxwoods and begonias, was a symbol of home. That comforting feeling vanished.

"Remember what we discussed," my father said. He sat close to the steering wheel, hands clenched at ten and two. I nodded, not sure if I could pretend to have zero knowledge of the fall of Hidden Meadows.

"Okay."

My response did not sound convincing, but my dad said nothing, only risked a slight glance. He knew he was feeding me to the wolves. I had never been a deceptive person, a trait my father and I shared.

"We will get through this."

The car idled in the driveway of our home. Donny's dented car with no hubcaps loitered in my dad's former spot. My heart beat at hummingbird speed to the point of dizziness. I sucked in a deep breath.

My mom stood at the door, hand on her hip, waiting. She would lose her mind on Monday when the lawyers notified her about Frank's change of plans.

Two days.

My dad stayed in the car, a smart decision on his part. I pulled my suitcase and backpack from the backseat. With a slight wave, he watched me disappear into the house. I took one last glance through the picture window. The car vanished at the end of the street, on its way to the airport. He would return to Oakville in two weeks.

Fourteen days.

Divorce was war. It sucked choosing sides. My mom gave me no choice. For years people had told me you have to deal with the repercussions of your actions. I didn't understand what those words meant until today.

CHAPTER FOURTEEN

"Someone needs to move the dented piece of shit out of the Margos' driveway. I can feel my property value dropping by the minute." -Jerry Bunn

Donny lounged in my father's chair; his attention focused on auto racing. Was he smoking a cigarette? I inhaled the hazy air, then coughed. My mom shot me a hateful glare. What was she thinking? The cordless rang from the kitchen like a summon to its master. She disappeared without a hello or glad you're home.

"Can you move?" Donny motioned with his hand. I hadn't realized I stopped in front of the television.

"Sorry."

The wheels of my suitcase rolled over the carpet towards the sanctuary of my room where I could avoid lung cancer. Music played from the other side of my bedroom door, and when I entered, I didn't recognize my space.

Teal paint covered the gaudy rose wallpaper. Above my bed hung a flag with a marijuana leaf. Brent often wore a t-shirt with the same image. The two girls said nothing as I examined the masking tape marking our spaces. Anger bubbled up inside of me with nowhere to escape. I wanted to kick the crap out of everyone and everything in the house. Instead, I climbed onto my bed and pulled out my favorite book series, *The Babysitter's Club*, from my backpack.

"Are you going to read all day?" Tara hovered over me, arms

crossed.

I glanced up from my page, irritated she interrupted me during Claudia's sleepover. Tara smacked the book out of my hand and yanked my hair.

"Stop it," I said.

Tara lunged on my bed and dragged me to the floor. We kicked, elbowed, and pulled hair until I shoved Tara into the dresser. We stood, both panting from our squabble.

"You think you're so smart," Tara said.

We moved like boxers expecting a punch. Tara stopped, smiled, and raked her fingers down her face, drawing blood.

"Can we please—"

"Lori!" Stacy put her hands over her ears after Tara's bloodcurdling scream. My mom stood in the doorway in seconds. "Your daughter pushed me and scratched my face. I only asked what she was reading." My mom stomped past Tara, smacking me hard across the mouth.

I gasped from the shock. The tips of my fingers went to my stinging face. My mouth opened to speak but as I looked around the room, I realized no one cared what I had to say.

"Take your pillow and blanket." My mom pointed towards the door. "You are sleeping in the laundry room. This week has been perfect without you."

"You can't be serious."

The girls snickered. My mother kept pointing.

I looked at smirking Tara, then to fuming Lori. I picked up my belongings, traveled down the hall to the small laundry room. Over the years, I had put up with Lori Margo's craziness, but today she reached an ultimate low. Was she making me sleep in the laundry room? I wouldn't cry, because even though I was in hell, my dad's life was worse. He dealt with the adult side of the mess my mom insisted on creating.

Somewhere in the middle of my thoughts, I fell asleep and didn't wake until the next morning. The only sound in the smoke-filled house came from the heat pump. I tip-toed to the kitchen, taking a few snack cakes to hide in the laundry room. The front door slammed. I peeked into the living room to see my mom.

"Where is Donny?" My feet shuffled from the pent-up anxiety.

"He took the kids to his ex's apartment. I can't stand that bitch."

I swallowed hard, uncertain if I should ask additional questions.

She walked towards her room, leaving me on my own. I couldn't bring myself to go back to my bedroom. It was no longer mine. I never expected my parents to get divorced. Only people on television moved their boyfriends into their husband's house. My back sank into the pile of dirty laundry, and I said a silent prayer for survival.

Hours later, while eating a stashed cupcake, Donny returned. I continued to read, not moving from my spot near the dryer.

"Where the hell have you been?" Lori screamed in the living room.

"Where I have been is not your business," Donny said. I heard his footsteps on the linoleum followed by the refrigerator door opening in the kitchen.

"It is my business. Were you with her?"

"Shut your mouth, woman," Donny said. A kitchen cabinet slammed and glass shattered on the floor. "Is your daughter here?"

"Yeah. She is sleeping in the laundry room," Lori replied.

"Why?"

"Because she is weird like her father. I don't question the stupid shit she does."

Their conversation faded like the worn pair of jeans on the laundry room floor. Warm tears streamed down my face, but I wasn't crying. Her words stung, but they always had. I took a deep breath to prepare for the wrath about to come.

One more day.

CHAPTER FIFTEEN

"Poor Sarah Margo. I doubt she will ever recover."
-Jared Wells

Amanda changed the past tense form of the words on the board to present. Mrs. Williams studied the board with careful eyes, followed by a brief discussion about present simple versus perfect. I could die of boredom, but I put on my fake paying attention face and zoned out.

"Mrs. Williams." The intercom hissed and popped. "Can you send Sarah Margo to the office to leave for the day?"

Excitement surged through me as I shoved my Trapper Keeper in my backpack. *My dad returned to Oakville early!* Before the intercom could change its mind, I skipped to the office, bag over my shoulder.

My joy came to a halt when pissed off Lori Margo and deadbeat Donny came into view. I hesitated, a confirmation to my mother I knew today's news. Her eyes narrowed to cat-like slits. My gut said Donny intended to dump me into the Oakville River. Fear flowed through my veins, but I remembered to take my dad's advice and pretend I knew nothing.

Bonnie and Clyde led me to the Regal parked in the handicap spot. The duo didn't say a word. Their silence caused my lunch to return to my throat.

Donny sped to the end of Green Street and turned left onto King Street towards downtown. I would have stayed up all night reading had I known today was my last day on earth. Before I could do anything rash like jump out of a moving vehicle, we pulled into a law office.

"Come on," Donny said. He reached for my backpack and placed it in my arms. On the bright side, the river was at least five miles away.

The brick office had a waiting room with four chairs. My mom and I sat near the window while Donny picked his teeth with a free toothpick from the counter. I watched the four lanes of traffic stopped at the light near the gas station. Footsteps echoed on the tile. A man in a light gray suit appeared in the reception area. His bald head shone like a clean mirror. I wondered if he used a product to make it shiny on purpose.

"Let's go to my office," the gray suit man said. We followed him to a nautical themed room. The pier posts with ropes were over-the-top, but who was I to judge? I had a marijuana leaf over my bed. "You must be Sarah." He smiled, but it wasn't real. The insincerity in his eyes told me he had a habit of faking. "I am Peter Cranfeld." Pete turned to my mother. "Are you sure you want Sarah present?"

"She is the cause of this mess." My mother glared at me like a petty teenager.

"How am I the cause of your divorce?" I told myself to lay-low, but how was I to blame?

"Please have a seat. Let's review the paperwork," Pete said. A burgundy folder on his desk had our name typed on the tab.

"No," Lori said. She turned to face me with fury in her eyes. My friends would point out she lived up to her dragon lady nickname. "We were days away from settling, and he changed his mind. What did you tell your father?" Lori narrowed her eyes. "Who changed his mind?"

Donny blew out an irritated breath.

"Nothing. Nobody," I said.

Lori smacked me hard across the face. Pete shifted in his executive chair. The impact did nothing to my overall numbness.

"Explain to my daughter what is happening," Lori said to Pete. He hesitated for a moment.

"The court has declared the house as separate property since Frank acquired the parcel prior to marriage. Frank listed the property with a local Realtor three days ago. He has a cash offer and a closing date in two weeks." Pete continued at Lori's urging expression. "Your father is pursuing full custody with no child support or alimony payment."

"What does that mean?" I asked. My voice and body shook with each word I didn't understand.

"It means I am out on my ass without a dime because of you!" Pete held up his hand, but Lori ignored him. "You did this. You've been plotting to get back at me."

I bit my shaking lip, metallic blood trickled in my mouth, a sense of disillusionment surrounded me.

"Is there anything we can do?" Lori asked. Her watering angry eyes never shed a tear. Satan didn't cry.

Pete shuffled the paperwork, wishing he wasn't involved in this circus either. I marked lawyer off my career options.

"The judge declared the property as your husband's asset—"

"Ex-husband," Donny said.

"They're still married." Pete turned back to Lori.

"The judge lives across the street from my brother-in-law," Lori said.

"Are you implying Judge Dannon is favoring your husband because he is your brother-in-law's neighbor?" Pete asked. He folded his hands on the desk. "Good luck proving it."

"How can he have a buyer? No one has toured the house." Lori asked.

"I don't know. Perhaps you should ask him, but selling his

80

property for market value is not illegal. Although the property is his by the court decision, he has agreed to split the profit. Your husband is also willing to take care of your legal fees and outstanding debt. It's a very generous offer as you won't be starting your new life with yesterday's burdens." Pete handed Lori a folder. "Frank does not legally have to give a dime from the sale and could fight to have you responsible for half of the debt. A spouse never volunteers to pay for the other's legal fees."

Pete eyed Donny touching a golf trophy on the shelf near the door.

"I am getting screwed over!" Lori screamed. Pete seemed unaffected by his client's outburst. He wanted Donny to stop fingering his mementos. "You think this is because of Donny? I pissed Frank off by moving my boyfriend into my house."

"My job is to advise you on legal matters," Pete replied. Lori stared at Pete as if demanding an answer. "I think your husband wants your daughter."

"Are you saying I should agree?" Lori sobbed like a bad school play.

"What do you want?" Pete asked.

"The house, alimony, and child support," she replied. Lori wasn't upset anymore.

"The house isn't an option. Your husband is refusing support and wants full custody," Pete said.

"Can't I fight for alimony and child support?" she asked.

"But at what cost? Your husband may decide not to split the proceeds of the property, pay your legal fees, and cover the marital debt." Pete put on his fake sympathy face. "You work ten hours a week. It will be difficult to prove you are better off financially to care for your daughter."

"Are you on Frank's side too? I bet the Margos are paying you off. They flash their money around to get whatever they want," Lori said in a continued rage.

"I am not working for your husband's family," Pete said. Donny dropped a golf ball on the floor. The lawyer pursed his lips together. "Frank has agreed to enroll your daughter in private school. He has provided documentation to the court for his intention to purchase a home after the divorce is final." Lori frowned. Donny flipped through a brochure from a small table near the door.

"He doesn't have a job in Oakville. He can't move my child out-of-state!"

"Frank accepted a position at Oakville State University on Friday," Pete said. His gold watch beeped, a button on the side stopped the noise. "His lawyer informed me early this morning."

"I am out on my ass in two weeks?" Lori asked.

Pete remained quiet.

"I didn't think the jerk had it in him to be so nasty," Lori said. Her face changed. "What if Sarah tells the judge she wants to live with me? Will I get the house?"

Pete loosened his tie.

"Mrs. Margo, I have told you several times. Judge Dannon has ruled the property as Frank's asset." Pete muted the ringing phone. "The judge decides custody, not the child. If you want to fight for your daughter, I suggest you do the same as your husband. Put together proof she belongs with you— employment and living circumstance. I will assist you however I can."

"Forget it," my mother said as she stood. I remained in my chair, without feeling or words. She stared at me, for at least a minute, contemplating. The lawyer stayed behind the desk. "If I can't have my home, I don't want stuck with a child." She snatched her handbag from the floor.

"Call Frank. Let him know he can pick up his kid." Lori walked through the threshold of the lawyer's office. Pete stood up, disbelief on his face.

"Lori, please think about your actions," Pete said. He touched his bald head as if he once had a habit of running his fingers through his hair. "If you walk out the door, Frank will get custody. The judge will not overlook your conduct."

"I'll show up to the court date to sign the papers and pick up my check." She paused by the door. "He isn't expecting child support, right?"

"No," Pete replied.

Without a second glance, Lori Margo left the law office.

The receptionist brought me a cup of water, placed a folder in her employer's hand, and closed the door. A clock on the wall ticked in the silence.

"Sarah, I need your father's number," Pete said. He kneeled in front of me with a yellow legal pad resting on his thigh. The tip of his pen ready to scribble the information.

"I…I don't remember his number," I replied with chattering teeth. A tornado of thoughts and words spun in my brain. I didn't know what would happen next. Did I go to foster care? That's what happened to Johnny Butler after his mom went to jail for drugs.

"Your family owns the department stores, right?" Pete asked. I nodded. "Can they reach your father?" Pete dug through a magazine rack near his desk.

"Yes, Uncle Dan knows his number." Pete flipped through the phone book to find the listing for the department store's main office. He picked up the receiver, fingers touching the advertisement to hold his place on the page while dialing.

"Hello, Darlene. I am calling from Duncan and Cranfeld. Can I speak with Dan Margo?" A few moments passed. Pete fidgeted with a crystal award shaped like a diamond. "Hello, Mr. Margo, this is Peter Cranfeld. I represent Lori Margo. Sarah is in my office. I need to get in touch with your brother." Pete nodded. The lawyer glanced at me. "I'd prefer not to discuss matters over the phone…King Street near the Value Gas Station." He hung up the phone.

The ceiling in the hobby room was smooth, not bumpy like my bedroom ceiling. Former bedroom, I corrected myself. My bags sat near the closet, a reminder of my temporary situation. My uncle convinced Judge Dannon to grant custody to him until my father returned to Oakville. My mom was right about Uncle Dan knowing the judge. Ken Dannon had a drink with Uncle Dan while they discussed me and a charity golf event.

It didn't matter if the judge favored my uncle—my mom left me. If she couldn't have the house, she didn't want me. Preteens weren't known for reflection, but when I thought about our lives, my dad held the illusion of our family together.

My dad and I didn't want the divorce. We were content with pretending Lori was a decent wife and mother. For whatever reason, Lori couldn't continue playing along. I wanted to believe she and Donny had an undeniable love, but she displayed the same contempt for Donny as she did to my father.

Gina peeked her head around the door frame. I looked like a poster for depression symptoms. Dr. Abrams had one in his office with a lady tugging at her hair. The caption above her head said, "I can't take life anymore!" On the bottom, a medication promised happiness again.

"Roddy is here. He's downstairs." I shook my head no. "It might keep your mind busy." I turned my head to the side. Gina clutched the door, blond hair and puppy dog face.

"Did my mom drop off my clothes?" I asked.

"No." Gina opened the door. "Your uncle had Shantel drop off clothes for you from the store. You should have enough for the school week unless you don't want to go."

"Did my dad say I could stay home?" I sat up.

"No, but I will deal with your father and uncle." She sat on her childhood bed and wrapped her arms around me. Gina smelled like tanning lotion and expensive perfume. "Feeling sorry for yourself doesn't help." Gina's lip quivered. "I've had a bad day or two myself." A tear rolled down her cheek, but she smiled before hugging me. "Go downstairs and play video games with Roddy. I will order pizza."

I didn't argue.

CHAPTER SIXTEEN

"I see human capacity tested daily, but the expression on Lori Margo's face when she walked out on her daughter made my stomach churn." -Peter Cranfeld

My feet swung back and forth on a wooden bench, in a long hallway, outside the courtroom door. People walked by with folders of paperwork for whatever business brought them downtown. A woman in holy sweatpants and flip-flops asked the security guard what office accepted payments for property taxes. Why did my dad make me wear a dress? I felt ridiculous wearing navy blue polka dots. Dr. Abrams exited the double doors, which made a loud sound when they closed.

"Everything okay, Sarah?" he asked. I shrugged. "If you need to talk, I am always available."

No one told me Dr. Abrams would be at the courthouse. Maybe he wasn't here for me. Perhaps he was paying taxes. His figure disappeared through the security area. I wouldn't see him again. What was the point? Talking wouldn't change my situation.

The wooden doors opened, followed by my parents, their lawyers, and two strangers in suits. My mom looked pleased. I hadn't seen her since the day she left me at Pete Cranfeld's office. A part of me wanted her to acknowledge me, explain or apologize, but the reasonable part knew she wouldn't. My dad motioned for me to follow.

In a small conference room, I sat next to my dad and Jared

Wells, his lawyer. My mom and Pete Cranfeld were facing us across the table. I had no clue what was going on, but I figured a woman involved in a divorce would display upset and heartbroken emotions. Mine looked like a lottery winner.

Mr. Wells, who happened to be Aaron's dad, slid the paperwork across the metal table to my mom. I felt embarrassed he might tell my friend about my parents.

"Five thousand dollars!" my mom yelled. Her finger traced along the fine print. "I thought I was getting half the house. You are a lying asshole. This check should be seventy thousand. The only reason I agreed to give you Sarah…"

My dad's wicked laugh sent tension through the room. She stopped ranting. The lawyers exchanged looks as if they had seen this a thousand times.

"How do you figure?" my father asked his ex-wife, a look of amusement on his face. "The house sold for $95,000. After the commissions, taxes, debt, and legal fees, we have $10,000. Divide the total in half, and you have $5,000 each."

"The debt wasn't that much," she said in a nasty tone.

"Hotel rooms must be expensive," he said. She opened her mouth. "You did such a splendid job hiding your debt; even you couldn't find the amount."

"How am I supposed to live? I need at least fifty thousand."

Frank shook his head, putting the paperwork and check in a green folder.

"You did this for money," I said. A moment passed before I heard my own words. I wasn't asking. I was telling her. My mother looked at me, eyes narrowed as if I had done something wrong.

"Your father screwed me over!"

"Bullshit!"

"Sarah, watch your language." My father reached for my hand, but I stood up. The folding chair crashed to the floor.

"All of this mess for five thousand dollars," I said. Anger pooled in my blood and circulated. "I hope it was worth it."

Tears streamed down my face creating tiny puddles on the waxed floors. I ran as fast as I could in dress shoes towards the exit. The sound of my name echoed down the hall. I turned to see my parents and their lawyers with their folders and briefcases.

"I am never getting married!" The hustle and bustle of the courthouse hall came to a standstill. "Do you know who got screwed over today?" I looked at Lori Margo. "Me!"

I was a raging bull, slumped on the pavement against the car tire, dark hair warm from the winter sun. My white tights had a snag, but what did it matter? Today not only changed my life but would haunt me forever. I would never get over the divorce. My father appeared in the sunlight with his hand shielding the brightness from his eyes.

"I've been looking for you." He tossed paperwork on the hood and dropped to his knees beside me. "I don't know what to say."

"I am not mad at you," I said.

"That's good."

"What are we doing to do? We are homeless with no money." My dad put his arm around me, enveloping my head against his chest.

"I have a job, honey. We aren't homeless. I hoped to show you a house today." I pulled away from his chest. "If you like the place, we will put in an offer. We can use the money we received from the settlement to purchase new furniture." He reached for my hand, knees cracking as he stood. "Gina can help you decorate."

"What about Mom?"

Frank pressed his lips together. "I offered to take her back for your sake."

"What did she say?"

"She told me to rot in hell." The clouds moved in the sky, casting a gray hue on the sunny day.

"She wanted the money, didn't she?" I wanted confirmation Lori Margo was a shitty mother who only cared about herself.

He nodded.

"It's over. We have no choice but to move forward. Let's get lunch. The real estate agent is meeting us at the house in an hour." The keys jingled when he attempted to find the ignition.

"Does she want to see me?" I buckled my seat belt. My dad looked at me, not sure what he should say. "You can tell me."

"You can see her whenever you want, and I told her the same." He started the car. "She is living with your grandparents. The lawyer will provide her with our new address and phone number once we move."

"Where is Donny?" I asked. I wondered why they weren't living together.

"According to Teddy, Donny moved in with his ex-wife. Your mother told Theresa." Frank adjusted the air conditioning vents. "I don't want to talk about Donny anymore."

"I hate her." My fingers pinched my nose to avoid the burn of oncoming tears.

"Hate is a strong word. I'd prefer if you used dislike."

"When I say dislike, I still mean hate," I said. A soft smile formed on my father's lips. The car reversed from its spot towards our new beginning.

"You and I are so much alike," he said.

"I hope so," I whispered.

CHAPTER SEVENTEEN

"Everyone has an experience which changes the course of their life. It isn't until time passes you realize how much." -Gina Cobb

I tried to talk myself out of going to the gym. Work was more hectic than usual. Not to mention, I was exhausted from trying to finish my degree a semester early. Whenever I started this conversation with myself, I touched my stomach to remember my little potbelly in sixth grade. Today, weight didn't matter, and I promised myself an iced mocha from the coffee shop next door to Oakville Health and Fitness.

I frequented the location near work because I found being within a mile from my apartment talked me out of running. The university location was much nicer, built for busy professionals around Oakville State.

After changing into shorts and a t-shirt, I stepped onto the elliptical, put in my earbuds, and pushed the timer. One hour of running in exchange for a delicious, chocolate coffee drink. I moved to my playlist, not caring if the guy using the stationary bike across the room noticed me dancing.

The television on the wall showed footage of a high-speed car chase on the highway. I stopped my music to find out what happened. A guy on probation stole his grandma's pills and her van. I pressed play to resume my dance track.

Two minutes left on the timer.

The machine beeped for the cooldown. My pace slowed to a

walk. I sipped my water as the final minute counted down in large, red numbers. The man on the elliptical beside me stopped his workout to check his buzzing phone in his bag. Was he new here? No bags on the floor. He released a frustrated sigh, bent over to catch his breath, and tousled his wavy hair. A white t-shirt clung to his body, revealing he didn't reward himself with high-calorie drinks.

"Bad day?" I watched the weather on television. The final seconds elapsed on the monitor, followed by three beeps.

"Blind date set up by my meddlesome mother." The man returned the phone to his bag with his back towards me.

"Ouch. Good luck." When I stepped off the elliptical, and he stood to face me—we knew each other.

"Oh. Hey," he said.

"Um. Yeah. Hi."

Two minutes before seeing his face, I admired his athletic legs and sculpted back. We hadn't seen each other in eleven years. I thought I'd never lay eyes on him again. Time had passed. We were different people in a different stage of life. The look on his face told me he didn't see me as the awkward preteen.

"You going tonight?" The voice of a stocky, middle-aged man chimed in next to us. The creep stopped to scan my body with his beady eyes. "If I am interrupting something, I can wait."

"No." I flashed a polite smile. Without giving the men a chance to say anything further, I picked up my water bottle and bolted towards the door.

"Why weren't you at the club last Thursday?" The stocky man's voice echoed through the gym. He had zero volume control.

"Not my scene. Excuse me," he said.

I was close to my car when he called my name. Part of me wanted to talk to him, but it was weird. The last time I saw him, I was a kid in the middle of my parents' mess. Not to mention, his patient.

"Dr. Abrams, sorry, I didn't want to interrupt you and your friend." I fidgeted for my keys, stopping next to the door. He jogged towards me with a smile. Although it had been eleven years, he looked better than I remembered. The casual workout clothes suited him.

"Coworker from the hospital." He shifted his messenger bag to his other shoulder. "Do you live around here?"

"No. I work at the plant. It is much easier to hit the gym after work. I have a bad habit of skipping out if I go within a mile of my apartment."

He chuckled. Had he ever laughed?

"You look great. If you skipped the gym, no one would notice." His face flushed. "You work at the plant?"

The word weird flashed over and over in my head. Was this not strange to him? Maybe he saw former patients outside of work.

Make small talk. Go home. Never return to this gym location.

"Yes." The smile on his face turned downward. "As a mechanical engineer. I am finishing my master's degree this semester."

"Impressive," he said.

"Do you work around here?" Playing catch-up with people was an interaction I avoided. I hated the awkwardness of reminiscing about the uncomfortable past. Dr. Abrams and I shared no memories I wanted to relive. I would need something stronger than coffee if we started on the divorce.

"At the Oakville Medical Center." He gestured towards the large, glass buildings a few blocks away on the edge of Oakville State's campus. "I left private practice eight years ago. The hospital is hectic, but it suits me." The way he stared at my face through his brown eyes unnerved me.

A phone buzzed again.

He reached into his bag, rolled his eyes, sighed, and returned the bothersome device. I opened my car door to put my bag and water bottle in the back seat.

"Don't mind me. I was heading to the coffee shop to get an iced mocha."

The line between his brow creased, and the corner of his lip raised.

"Do you care if I join you? My mother can wait," he said.

I nodded.

My small talk and dash plan failed. We walked across the parking lot towards the coffee shop. People were everywhere—at tables, in line, waiting near the door. My former psychiatrist placed his hand on the small of my back to guide me through the patrons in need of a caffeine fix.

As we waited, I could have kicked myself for agreeing to have coffee with Dr. Abrams. What could I have done? My excuses were terrible and lame. Besides, he seemed genuine in wanting to catch-up.

My iced mocha gushed whipped cream over the sides of the plastic cup. I licked my straw, basking in my reward like a beach vacation. Dr. Abrams smiled and took a careful sip of his black coffee.

"Iced mocha was my reward for working out for an hour after work." I blotted my mouth with a napkin. "So good."

"I should have ordered the same." He gazed at his black coffee with disappointment. When he looked up, we laughed.

"There is always tomorrow." I raised my disposable cup as if toasting champagne. He clicked his coffee against mine.

"Touché," he said.

Employees yelled the names of drink owners.

"Your phone is ringing again." I wasn't sure if he was ignoring the call or couldn't hear it.

His lips twisted. He looked at the screen.

"My mother is relentless," he said.

"She set you up on a date?"

When he made eye contact, the smile was no longer on his face.

"In her words, I am too old to be single. She arranged the meeting for next Friday. The woman is thirty-three, teaches second grade, and a good Jewish girl." He held the phone near my face, and the description read what he said aloud. I smiled. "You think this is funny?"

"I think everything is funny, Dr. Abrams. You told me so once." My comment took him off-guard, and he laughed. I wondered if he felt strange laughing with me over coffee when our past consisted of therapy sessions.

"Please, call me Lee." It was odd for a moment as we crossed the barrier of Dr. Abrams to Lee.

"Well, Lee. I must be going. I have an important meeting tomorrow."

He helped me out of my chair and ushered me through the mob of people. A barista couldn't find Kyle, who ordered the chai tea latte. Dr. Abrams held the door for two women to exit the coffee shop. I waited on the sidewalk.

"Are you working out tomorrow?" Dr. Abrams asked. The full moon illuminated the parking lot better than the lampposts. I had no intentions of working out two days in a row. I needed an excuse.

Dead grandma. Dog ate my homework. Knitting sweaters for the homeless. My goat broke a horn.

I had nothing.

"Yes."

"I hope to see you tomorrow." He shifted his bag.

We weren't sure if we should shake hands, hug, or do nothing. I opened my car door going with do nothing.

"Bye."

CHAPTER EIGHTEEN

"It's important to follow your heart, but take your common sense with you." -Waitress

Five minutes remained on my elliptical timer. The machine next to mine stayed empty. When he asked if I was working out, was he making conversation? It bothered me he didn't show, even though I didn't want to see him. I shouldn't have had coffee with him. Maybe he came to his senses and joined a different gym.

The elliptical beeped as the final minute counted down. On the bright side, I worked out two days in a row and no iced mocha afterward. My body needed real food after skipping lunch to prepare for the department spending reduction meetings.

I threw my gym bag into my trunk after changing into my black suit. If I stopped to eat, I didn't want to be in sweaty gym clothes. A black car parked. As I opened my side door, Dr. Abrams rolled down his BMW's window.

"Hello," he said from his driver's side door. "I had difficulty discharging a patient. I would have been here earlier." He wore a pale yellow dress shirt, silver tie, and gray dress pants. The ripped corduroy pants were a thing of the past. I felt weird admitting to myself he looked good. He checked the time. Even the watch on his wrist matched his polished look.

"I already put in my hour." I thought he'd go inside for his workout. Instead, he joined me near my car.

"Do you want to have dinner? I am on call tonight, but I should be okay as long as we stay close to the hospital."

I was starving. He'd make a better meal companion than the cat. I hadn't been out to eat with a man since Roddy. My dad and uncle didn't count. I knew I should say no.

Remember, Sarah. He knows all the bad stuff about you.

"You will miss your workout," I said. I needed to remind him why he was at the gym.

"You're not the only one who bails on the gym." His easy smile caused me to return a grin his way.

Was this a date? Roddy and I broke up two years ago. I gave him the it's not you, it's me spiel after we left a Christmas party. I didn't want to tell him I couldn't stand his parents, or the fact we didn't have sexual chemistry, not that I had much expertise in the matter. But I couldn't spend a lifetime bumping heads and faking orgasms. By not telling him the truth, he refused to move on. He hoped I would change my mind. Instead, I avoided him.

"Okay. If you get flabby, it's not my fault," I said.

As he shook his head with a smile, he helped me into his car. I recalled his 80s Corolla parked in front of the therapy place. Dr. Abrams had moved up in the world since I last knew him.

We drove in silence a mile down the road to a twenty-four-hour diner. I told myself this wasn't a date. Older men were not an option. I didn't want to date a younger man either.

"Is this okay? It is the diner, the hospital cafeteria, or the burger place."

"The diner is fine."

He opened my door. The tips of his fingers touched my back on our way to the door. Only two cars remained in the lot.

"I am starving. I didn't eat lunch," he said. Dr. Abrams closed his menu, eyes studying me as I searched for my meal choice.

"I skipped lunch today. We had a meeting with company leadership about cutting costs. Our plant is in danger of a shutdown."

Before he could respond, the server stood at our table with her notepad. She had more tattoos than I could count.

"I want soup and salad. The dressing on the side. No bacon." It seemed he regretted jumping in and ordering first. I told the waitress to bring me the same.

"Why haven't you eaten since this morning? Are you nervous about your big date?"

He didn't find my teasing funny.

"No. I'm the Chief of the Psychiatry Department. I am busy, but I wanted to see you." He studied my face for a reaction. I remained neutral.

Part of me wanted to see him. Perhaps my former psychiatrist felt forbidden. My life had grown serious and boring with a full-time job and school. Dr. Abrams was a grown man, not a twenty-something frat boy playing beer bong.

What was I doing?

The waitress returned with our salads, and I coated my lettuce in dressing. I didn't want to respond to the fact he wanted to see me.

"You brought up my date. What about you? Are you dating? Do you have a boyfriend?" He put another fork full of salad into his mouth.

I swallowed hard. "No dating. No boyfriend."

"Attractive, intelligent girl without a boyfriend?" His eyebrows lifted to his hairline. He waited for an explanation, deep brown eyes searching me with intensity. I sucked in a breath after I took a drink to wash down my dinner.

"Relationships are hard. I don't need complicated right now. I am building my career and finishing my education. Why do you need a relationship to be happy?"

"Do you want to call my mother and have this conversation with her? I am successful, but my mother believes my brother's career at the dry cleaner is more worthwhile. He has a wife and four children."

"You aren't ready for a family?" Dr. Abrams told me he was twenty-eight, eleven years ago. No way would I ask him his age now.

"It is the expectation I marry a Jewish woman and return to the neighborhood. I'm not there yet."

Our soup had arrived, but he hadn't touched his bowl. I took a few bites. It tasted no different than canned soup from Walmart. I moved my spoon around the chunks of potatoes.

"Do you date outside your community?" It was an honest question, but I regretted asking. Did he think I was interested?

"No." He shook his head. "A few women I never brought around my family. My mother would go ballistic if I dated outside the faith." He paused, considering his words. "I mean no offense. She is a kind woman, she only wants—"

"No offense taken. I get it."

People of the same religion, race, and socioeconomic standing minimized the complications in families. I had known it all too well with Roddy's family.

The night air sent chills down my spine when we left the warm diner. Dr. Abrams clicked the car remote; taillights flashed a yellow hue across the pavement. He opened the door and guided me into the passenger side. When he sat in his seat, a green glow illuminated the dark car. Reaching down to retrieve his pager, Dr. Abrams' hand brushed my leg by accident. I felt something unexplainable. We made eye contact. I needed to break the tension, but I couldn't string together a train of thought.

"Dr. Abrams—"

"You need to call me Lee." His cell phone rang. The tension put on hold.

"This is Dr. Abrams…That's strange…This is the first page I have received. I'll be there soon."

He put the car in drive and within moments, we were next to my car in the empty gym lot.

"Thanks for dinner. Good luck on your date." He grimaced. Once I closed the door to his car, I unlocked my own.

"Would you meet me for lunch tomorrow?" Lee asked from the open car window. I clutched my door, either from fear or excitement. "You work close."

"Yeah, sure." I pulled a business card with my cell phone number from my handbag. "Let me know when and where. I have more flexibility than you. Engineering isn't life or death."

Lee didn't laugh at my joke.

"Goodnight," he said.

The taillights of his car disappeared towards the medical center. I questioned my actions. It was obvious he was interested in me. Was I interested in him? I didn't want a relationship, but neither did he. It would never work. Neither of us cared.

CHAPTER NINETEEN

"Lust makes sex dangerous." -Marta Malone

Oakville had the worst traffic in the morning because everyone worked in the same five-mile radius. I was too tired to care about music. Most of the talk radio shows were geared towards mindless idiots. Today, the hosts called to prank a local business. If the caller convinced the old man at the floral shop to say *ass*, she would win concert tickets

Once at work, I had to deal with the usual complaints. Most engineers were not great with people. I became the representative for the engineering department, due to the fact I didn't hide from people. This honor came without a title or a pay increase.

"The project can't be completed in the time frame you suggested," I told the balding, middle-aged man with Plant Section Five, Supervisor on his badge.

"I want to speak to an engineer," he said. It went from department helping department to nasty in a hurry.

"You are speaking to one. I have already voiced your concerns with my team. We don't have the resources."

The supervisor left to find another answer.

I leaned back in my chair and flipped through the folders on my desk. Marta, the department secretary, walked into my office. She dropped into the seat in front of my desk, legs crossed, and a magazine rolled in her left hand.

"He was a real a-hole," Marta said. I looked up at her and nodded. Marta meant well, but her busybody ways irritated me. "You dressed pretty today, Sarah. Are you hoping to impress Todd in sales?"

Her manicured eyebrows moved up and down, which made my stomach sick thinking about Todd Hanover. There wasn't anything wrong with him, other than he was annoying, sweated too much, and wasn't someone I'd want to be around.

"No, Marta." I continued rummaging through my paperwork stack for a project proposal. Marta blew out a breath and chuckled.

I paid extra attention to my appearance today, but lunch with Lee was not her business. Besides, she wasn't my mom. Marta took the hint and left.

The remainder of the morning I crunched numbers. When I looked up, Marta stood at her desk with Todd. They gazed into my open window like I was an animal at the zoo. Todd took my glance as an invitation. He had received five date rejections from me since July.

Why didn't I shut the blinds?

"How's the life of an engineer?" Todd asked.

Salespeople and engineers were opposites. Did he have no idea he got under my skin?

"Number crunching and living the dream. Did you need something?"

He sat in the chair Marta vacated, head tilted to the side. I retracted my original assessment of Todd. My opinion changed to complete creep.

"Why won't you go out with me?" I gave him the annoyed face I reserved for my mother. "You are single. I am single. We are young."

"Todd, this is not appropriate. I told you no. Nothing personal." I flipped the power strip. Todd looked me up and down with a brief lick of his lips. I wanted to vomit on him.

"Marta said you dressed up for me today." I looked up at him from my crouched position as if he had lost his mind.

"Marta needs to mind her own business. I don't mean to be rude, but I have a ton of work to do."

He left my office, a quick exchange with Marta as he exited. I dialed Marta's extension. When she answered, I asked her to come into my office.

She stood in the doorway, nervous to enter. "I was only trying to help. You are so focused on your school work," she said.

Before I spoke, my cell vibrated in my desk drawer. My facial expression gave her the hint to leave. She held her hands up in surrender. When I looked at my phone, it was a text message.

Lee: Can't meet you for lunch. Sorry.

I hated disappointment. This stemmed from the divorce and being traumatized by my mother. I kept telling myself nothing was going on with Lee. The guy had a date with another woman next week, a marriage prospect.

My phone buzzed again.

Lee: Very busy. Dinner instead at the diner at seven o'clock?

I replied yes.

The BMW idled in the parking lot when I arrived at the diner. Lee opened my car door, dressed in a black suit with a white dress shirt. I wore a form-fitting gray sheath dress with beaded jewelry and flats—the reason Marta thought I wanted Todd.

"You are beautiful," he said.

A few awkward moments passed between us as we contemplated if we should hug, shake hands, or do nothing. Do nothing seemed to be the trend.

"Thank you. Do you wear suits to work?" Dress clothes didn't seem practical at a hospital. We walked towards the entrance.

"No. I lectured at the medical school and had an administrative meeting."

We ordered the same meal and discussed our day. I could never talk about work with my friends. Lee took an interest, not finding it boring. Leaning back into the booth, he watched me pour sugar into my iced tea.

"Thanks for meeting me. I needed time away from family and work," he said. A child cried in a high chair at the next table.

"I can relate. Thank you for inviting me," I said.

Lee handed the waitress our bill as we left the diner. I shivered in the night air, wishing I would have brought the matching jacket to my dress. Once at the car, he opened my door, his hand guided me into the driver's seat. I let out a breath, amazed by the same intense feeling from the night before. He gripped the open car door. Rather than asking me to meet him to work out, lunch, or dinner—he appeared nervous.

"It was fun, Sarah. Drive safely."

Lee climbed into his BMW.

CHAPTER TWENTY

"I feel terrible keeping a big secret from Sarah. Once I tell her, we can no longer be friends." -Bethany Adams

Thanks to the plant supervisor's big mouth, I had to work a half-day every Saturday for a month. He convinced the plant manager his team could complete the project quicker if an engineer were available on Saturdays. Having an engineer available meant paying someone to sit and wait for the possibility of a question. Did anyone see the irony of the recent cost savings meeting?

I promised Bethany I would meet her at the mall at one to browse bridesmaid dresses. She was getting married in six months. I couldn't tell her no when she asked me to fill the role of maid of honor. We had rekindled our friendship in seventh grade. Bethany and I transferred to St. Elizabeth the same year. That's where she met Craig. I had never been a fan of her fiancé, but I was doing my best to keep my mouth shut.

A few minutes before one, I noticed her at a table in the food court, engrossed in a bridal magazine. My mind had zero interest in marriage or wedding paraphernalia. I relied on my acting skills whenever Bethany expected excitement.

My friend waved both hands while I put on my best smile. Bethany stuffed the magazine into her quilted bride embroidered tote, almost knocking over a little boy to greet me. She wrapped her arms around my neck, a squeal of euphoria escaped her mouth.

She released our hug. "Is something wrong?"

"No. I have been at work all morning."

The smell of food court Chinese made my stomach growl. I didn't have time for lunch.

"That's not it. What's going on?" Bethany always insisted.

"Let's look at wedding stuff!" I mustered fake enthusiasm, hands waving like a stripper jumping out of a cake.

I couldn't discuss Dr. Lee Abrams with my best friend. The synonym for Bethany was Catholic good girl. She ignored me for weeks after I told her I slept with Roddy our freshman year of college. How would she react to me considering an older man, who used to be my childhood psychiatrist, and would marry another woman determined by his family?

We crossed the threshold of the bridal boutique a minute later. Bethany's mind had moved on to wedded bliss.

"Craig and I have our wedding blog live. It's basic—how we met, high school and engagement photos, guest book, and a poll for cake flavors." Her eyes twinkled. "Do you know red velvet is winning?"

I smiled at her happiness, although I wanted to say don't marry him. She placed a tiara on top of her head.

"It's perfect," I said. Bethany squeezed me. I shrugged at the cashier when Bethany skipped down the dress aisle humming a processional tune.

After working fifty hours, I spent the weekend at my apartment doing nothing. On Monday, I worked until nine. I returned home to find my cat had spent his day dragging my dirty clothes into the kitchen. Tuesday and Wednesday, I spent at a workplace diversity conference downtown. Thursday returned to my typical routine. First, the gym to work out. Second, a delicious iced mocha with whipped cream.

Most members of Oakville Health and Fitness didn't use the machines in the back because the cardio theater was near the front. Today's movie was *Legally Blonde*. I didn't care to run in the dark.

As I maintained a decent pace, I heard the machine next to mine start. My attention stayed on the lawn care infomercial. Even though I didn't have a yard to water, the British man convinced me I needed a hose small enough for my pocket.

"I'm sorry I haven't called," he said.

I whirled around. My neck popped. I grimaced. "No need to apologize." I continued to watch television as if I hadn't noticed we hadn't talked in days. According to the elliptical timer, another six minutes passed.

"You okay?" I asked.

"No. Did you have plans last weekend?" He took a long drink from his water bottle. I stepped off my machine when the timer beeped. Lee pressed stop on his elliptical.

"I worked Saturday morning then spent the afternoon with my best friend. Sunday, I hung out with my cat and watched movies." I wasn't about to tell him my furry friend and I had a *Dawson's Creek* marathon.

We moved towards the exit with our water bottles in hand, an awkwardness between us as we stepped into the chilly evening in our athletic apparel. Dim parking lot lights highlighted his five o'clock shadow when we stopped near our parked cars. I wrapped my arms around his neck. By instinct, his arms went around my waist into a warm embrace.

"You looked like you needed a hug." I crinkled my nose when I uttered the words.

What was I doing? My cheeks heated with embarrassment. I didn't hug men. I wasn't a hugger period.

"Yes." He rested his head on mine for a moment. "All better now."

I removed myself from the intimacy I initiated. "I have an early day. Are you working out tomorrow?"

"No. I have a date with Miriam," he replied with a tone more like a dental appointment than a dinner with a woman.

"That's right. I forgot." I grinned, which he didn't find amusing.

"What? Do you want me to call you to discuss the details?" he asked.

"Would you? I would love to hear about your magical evening." I sucked in my lip to keep from bursting into laughter.

"You are a troublemaker," he said. The lights of his car flashed yellow when he clicked his remote. I opened the rear door of my car to toss my empty water bottle on the floor.

"I have been called a troublemaker by you before," I said. He shook his head with a slight grin.

"If you want to hear the details, I will call you." He put his bag into his trunk.

"Great. Can't wait. It will be like we're girlfriends."

"Oh." The lines on his face hardened.

"I am kidding. It will be fine, Lee."

Would he call me about his date? I wasn't sure, but I would have been lying to say I wasn't curious.

CHAPTER TWENTY-ONE

"Soft lips turn into passionate tongues. Slight brushes become impatient hands. I find myself intoxicated with the build-up." -Lee Abrams

The dryer in my unit wouldn't turn on. Angela, the property manager, said a broken dryer didn't constitute an emergency. I disagreed. The washer and dryer was the main reason I lived in Riverhaven—another ridiculously named community. The complex sat next to the interstate, nowhere near the river, and not a haven. I should have stayed at my dad's house, but I felt he used me as an excuse not to have a relationship. We never talked about what happened in sixth grade or mentioned Lori Margo. I hoped my absence would somehow permit him to move on. He dated no one after my mother.

Angela repeated several times the availability of the laundry facilities at the clubhouse. Who wants to wait for clothes to dry in a small room full of noisy machines? College had traumatized me with stories of stolen clothes. On a Friday night, while my friends were out, I dropped seventy-five cents into the community washer to wait. I felt a sense of peace knowing my Walmart socks were not in danger.

The laundry room had three sets of washers and dryers across from a vending machine. The fluorescent lights overhead burned my eyes after a long day. I flipped the switch off. The glow of the vending machine illuminated the room. At work, the engineering team toured the plant with a potential client. My feet ached from walking in heels. I sat on the dryer, kicked off my shoes, closed my eyes, and waited for the load to finish.

My phone rang.

I squinted to see the caller on the screen and looked at my watch—10:10 pm. Shouldn't he be on a date?

"You aren't calling from the restaurant restroom, are you?" I giggled.

"Are you home by chance?" Lee didn't laugh.

"I am doing laundry at my apartment complex clubhouse. My dryer broke." My bare feet moved back and forth like a child.

"I'll be there in ten minutes."

Without another word, he hung up. I tossed my phone into my bag. Why was Lee coming to my apartment?

The main door opened in the clubhouse. A tall figure appeared in the laundry room doorway, lit only by the red glow of the Coke machine. I remained on the dryer, feet dangling, my palms resting against the warm metal surface.

He stood in front of me, casual pants and shirt with a hint of cologne as if he had been on a date. A minute passed with nothing but the rumble of spinning darks.

"Shouldn't you be on your date? I could have waited to hear the details of your magical evening."

His conflicted eyes burned with an intensity I couldn't match.

"Sarah."

I shrugged my shoulders. He didn't live or work near Riverhaven. The rundown mall closed last summer. All the good restaurants were at least four exits away. Why was he here?

The soft buzzing of the Coke machine acted as an

accompaniment to the rhythm of my racing heart. Lee took his hands out of his pockets and moved until the front of his thighs touched my dangling legs. His hands rested on the dryer, on both sides of me, in an authoritative way. Air moved into my lungs as if I had stopped breathing for a moment.

Please tell me why you are at my apartment and not on your date.

"She didn't have a chance," he whispered. His warm breath trailed across my cheek and neck, towards my ear. My usual joking, sarcastic-self took a back seat. What was Lee doing? The dinners and flirting seemed harmless. This moment was dangerous.

"Why is that?"

He moved away from my ear. The tip of his index finger traced across my lower lip with smoldering eyes gaging my reaction. I licked my lips, pressing them together after his finger left my mouth.

"Don't pretend to be clueless."

I sat up straight, to show confidence, but why? I didn't want Dr. Abrams. He leaned forward to brush his lips against mine.

"I couldn't stop thinking about you," he said.

I kissed him back, then hesitated. Lee tugged up my skirt in a way Roddy would have never dared. I sucked in another gulp of air when his hand went under my panties. The base of his thumb pressed against me and moved in a skilled, circular motion.

Oh, my.

Just say no.

I parted my legs further and allowed him to work. My hands moved to his chest, unsure if to stop him or explore his body. Lee kissed me hard, mouth minty and warm, his free hand touching my breast. The kissing stopped. This was my chance to tell him no. The way he looked into my eyes with a potency of desire lured me in. I counted my three shallow breaths, mind and reasoning gone before I kissed him.

The laundry room became a whirl of lust and curiosity, which traveled at a speed too fast for me to process. His belt jingled. A wrapper tore. I gasped when he entered me. My nails dug into his back to steady myself. The unlevel dryer crashing back and forth overpowered our moans.

A shadow holding a laundry basket appeared in the doorway but left when they realized the noise wasn't coming from the laundry machines. I wanted to tell the visitor I'd never done this before or don't stare at the mailbox tomorrow.

It could have been minutes or hours; I wasn't sure. Lee released hard, hitting his knees against the dryer. I spent more time thinking than being in the moment, a habit I had during intimacy.

The room lit up green along with the familiar buzzing noise. Lee reached for his pager in a mess of crumpled pants on the floor. He pressed the arrow button, a quick sigh while reading the message.

"Shit." He tugged his pants up and planted a hard kiss on my mouth. "I need to go."

My fingers grasped the metal appliance to steady myself. What was I thinking?

CHAPTER TWENTY-TWO

"When my mother set me up with Lee Abrams, I cringed. Everyone knows his reputation." -Miriam Eppel

Marta and Tim were also victims of half-day Saturdays. I stared at my computer screen when Marta walked by the door. She wasn't my boss, but I didn't want to have the why-do-you-look-so-tired conversation.

I couldn't sleep. I returned to my apartment after Lee left with a million thoughts racing through my mind. What happened? Why did he leave? He didn't call or text. What was I thinking?

Marta argued with a man. I stood up and walked to my doorway to find Lee in hospital scrubs, messy hair, and a need for a shave. The dark circles under his eyes matched mine. He hadn't slept either.

"I told him you were busy," Marta said. The nosy secretary stood with her weight shifted to one side, hand on hip.

"It's okay," I said. Marta's curious face disappeared when I closed the door. "How did you know I was here?"

"Your car is in the parking lot. I was on my way home from the hospital." He closed his eyes in exhaustion.

"Do you want something to drink?" He shook his head no. I sat on my desk, which resembled the night before. My cheeks warmed to the memory.

"I can't have a relationship with you." He opened his eyes.

"I know." His words stung. I didn't want a relationship with him, nor did I want rejection. Lee stood, flashed a fake smile and patted my shoulder like he had handled the situation.

"Let's have dinner tonight."

I gave him my sham smile and nodded. Thirty seconds after Lee left, Marta rushed into my office.

"I didn't want to get you in trouble with your dad. I've partied all night before." She made an excited motion with her hands. I flinched. "You said your dad is single, right?"

My foggy brain couldn't follow why she had taken interest in my father. No one ever asked if my fifty-something, engineer dad was available. He once bragged to a woman about his graphing calculator. The man had no game. Forty-something Marta dressed in bright dresses and loved karaoke.

"He is single, why?"

"You never mentioned he's a doctor." Marta laughed. "Give me his number. I'll call him. I'm what they call a modern woman." She batted her eyelashes, coated in enough mascara to repair the crack in the parking lot.

She continued talking, but I stood in shock. Marta mistook the man I slept with to be my father.

"He likes women under twenty-five."

Marta's mouth formed a speechless circle. She contemplated for a moment, pursed her lips, batted her spider lashes in irritation, and whirled herself out of my space.

The rest of the afternoon I slept without setting an alarm. My fingers raked my messy bed hair as I considered what to wear. Was this a date? More than likely, he would say we made a mistake, be friends or whatever guys say after a hook-up. But why did I feel the need to wear my sexiest panties?

A knock sounded at my door at exactly six. I looked myself over in the mirror, pleased with my denim skirt and black top. When I opened the door, the smell of his expensive cologne confirmed the granny panties belonged in the drawer. He kissed my cheek and placed a box in my hands.

"Cookies from the Pine Bakery," he said. Lee's eyes roved my body. When did a guy last notice me? Besides Todd. It only counted when you wanted the attention.

Did I want Dr. Abrams? Lee. The answer was no. My actions said yes. Why?

"I love this place." He grinned. I told him one night how much I loved cookies. "Do you live in Pine Ridge?"

"I live in Pine Villas. I own a condo by the square," he replied. Lee looked around my two-bedroom townhouse.

"My uncle lives in Pine Ridge."

"Dan?"

"Yes. Do you know him?" I placed the cookies on my bar. Lee touched a picture of Gina and Aunt Penny in a frame.

"He is the HOA president of Pine Ridge. I met him at a meeting once," Lee said in a strange tone.

"He had a party when he won the homeowners' election. He gave a speech and everything. You would have thought he won a Senate seat. Don't be surprised when Uncle Dan erects a bronze figure of himself by the gates."

Lee flashed me a preoccupied smile. "Shall we go?"

Once he loaded me into his car, we drove towards downtown. He didn't say where we were having dinner. I gazed out the window at the familiar exits passing on the highway. My mind wandered when the Green Street sign appeared. The same memory always played. Daniel and I fighting. Alarms sounding as I stormed out the emergency exit. Frank Margo's sleepy voice when I called for help. The fall of Hidden Meadows.

I never drove past Green Street.

"I am sorry I left last night." He glanced at me in the passenger seat, memories fading when he spoke. "Emergency pages are part of the job."

"What happened last night?" I wasted no time getting to the point. His expression turned comical. "Not with me. Miriam."

"I am not ready to settle down. My mother claims mutual respect grows into a loving relationship." Lee took his attention off the road, gauging my reaction. "Pleasing my family is important, but I decide." He sighed. "There is no attraction with Miriam. A healthy sex life is vital to a relationship. I don't want a housewife."

"Did you tell Miriam she didn't meet your non-housewife standards?"

"I told her I didn't see a future." He took a deep breath. Lee wasn't telling me something about last night. "My mother put me in a terrible situation. This is how mothers get their way."

"I wouldn't know. I don't speak to mine." The look on his face was sympathetic. To my relief, Lee's cell phone interrupted our conversation.

"This is Dr. Abrams." A woman spoke with urgency, but I couldn't understand the context. "Have you tried paging Dr. Michaels? I am not on call tonight and rather busy at the moment." More frantic speaking while Lee nodded his head. "I'll be there in fifteen. Has she had anything for this episode?" Lee scratched his head, rattled off pharmaceuticals, and ended the call.

A large frown creased wrinkles on his brow. He did a u-turn towards the medical center. "We need to make a quick stop at the hospital."

The elevator stopped on the fifth floor. Lee punched a code on a keypad, and the sliding glass doors opened. A woman in scrubs greeted us. She rattled off details with flustered hand gestures.

"You can wait here," Lee said, voice calm, unlike the nurse. They disappeared.

A woman worked on a computer behind a glass window. She answered a black, corded phone, which contrasted the abundance of the color white. I looked for something to occupy my time, but the reception area was bare.

"I need your identification," a voice said out of nowhere. A short, pudgy woman with a pasta stain on her white sweatshirt barricaded the door. She held a clipboard. "You're new here. It's hospital policy."

"Okay." I fumbled in my purse to locate my driver's license. She snatched the plastic card from my hand. The middle-aged woman scanned my license as if reading a two-hundred-page book.

"Twenty-three. Maybe twenty-four. I am bad at math," she said. The woman clicked her tongue in a sequence. "Young." She looked up for a moment, only to return her attention to my identification. "One hundred and twenty pounds? A lie if I've ever heard one."

I flushed with embarrassment. Who calls someone out on their weight? I've had a few iced mochas and a plate of cheese fries for dinner here and there.

"One twenty-five," I said. The woman laughed, coughed, and bent over to catch her breath. I watched her with a blank face.

"No, honey. You are dreaming." She returned my license. "I will give you yellow clearance since you are with Dr. Abrams. He brings all of his girlfriends here." She scribbled a note on the clipboard.

"Is that so?" I asked, half-disbelieving and half-curious. Was this woman trying to check my sanity?

"Hundreds of them." She winked three times.

"Hundreds is a large number."

"You know how these doctors are, one minute they are into you, the next you are back to being the hired help." She paused. "I am his boss, Barbara Sue, but you can call me

Barbie." She stuck out her hand, and I shook it.

Lee reappeared through the door. He signed a chart for the nurse, who seemed relieved by whatever happened behind closed doors. Lee joined his so-called boss and me in the reception area.

"I was keeping your latest girlfriend company. I made sure she stole nothing this time," Barbie said to Lee.

"That's good. Thanks, Barbie. Have a good night," he said. Lee touched my back and urged me towards the elevator.

"You aren't leaving, are you? The other doctors are lazy. They sit around and play computer games and order pizza."

"I'll be back on Monday. Keep the staff in line."

"Yes, sir." Barbie saluted Lee. She marched down the hall with her clipboard.

Once the elevator doors closed, Lee wrapped his arms around my body, head resting against mine. The warmth and smell of him sucked me into a trance of intoxication. I needed to keep my head in the moment.

"What was up with your boss, Barbie? She wanted to see my ID. Not to mention, she told me you have hundreds of girlfriends."

Lee laughed. The metal door opened on the ground level, not far from the physician parking lot. Lee said hello to a group in scrubs who took our place in the elevator.

"Barbie is a patient. She says many colorful sentiments to put it politely."

"She seemed weird but together."

Lee studied my face with a slight smirk.

"Last week, Barbie had her privileges taken away because of a physical altercation with another patient over who's turn it was to sleep with a baby doll." He opened the car door. I slid into the seat, but he remained standing near the passenger side in thought. Lee bent to see my face, hand clutching the door frame. "Let's skip dinner."

Somewhere between pleasure and regret, I inhaled a deep breath into the satin pillowcase. He rolled to his side, a quick swipe of his forehead to remove the sweat. My eyes focused on the small beam of light coming from the bathroom.

"Why don't you date?" Lee asked.

"I suck at relationships." I rolled to face him. My stomach made an embarrassing grumble. When he said skip dinner, I thought he'd at least feed me at his place. "What? Do you have a psychoanalysis about me and relationships?"

"Never crossed my mind," he said in a dry tone reminiscent of my therapy sessions. He was prompting this conversation. The arrogant look on his face said he would tell me anyway. "You will always prefer unattached relationships to avoid being hurt. You don't trust men since your mother cheated on your father for two years."

"What?" I narrowed my eyes. "My mom started dating a month after my parents separated. She wasn't..."

Lee inhaled air through his teeth. I sat up.

"Shit," Lee said. He propped his weight up on his elbows. "You didn't know?"

"No." My nervous hand raked my wild, bed hair until it looked like the before shot in a shampoo commercial. "I can't believe this."

"I'm sorry," Lee said. He sat up, blankets covering his nude waist. "I thought you knew—"

"My dad knew?"

"Sarah, I don't feel comfortable—"

"Fuck feeling comfortable! My mother cheated on my father for two years?"

"Yes. I shouldn't have said anything. The affair came out in court."

The scene of sitting on the wooden bench in the courthouse was a memory I never allowed to surface. Out of nowhere, I felt sick when I thought about my father. I wanted to drive to his house, hear the truth from him. What was the point?

"Can I have water?" I asked Lee.

"Sure."

I watched his nude shadow leave the bedroom. My body sank into the mattress, in a tangle of sheets and pillows, equally as lost and upset as I had been a decade prior.

CHAPTER TWENTY-THREE

"If two systems are both in thermal equilibrium
with a third system they must be in thermal equilibrium
with one another. Simple, right?" -Dr. Ina Rosenberger

My family and friends mingled around the private party
room of Benny's BBQ. Even though my dad had arranged my
graduation celebration, he had help. The red tablecloths and
centerpieces were not his work. Gina and I made eye contact
from across the room, which held dozens of hungry people
waiting to eat. She gave an excited wave. Party planning was her
element.

Her attention returned to Uncle Dan. She instructed him to
move the tin of macaroni closer to the green beans. I chuckled
to myself at his face when Gina told him no to putting the
desserts on the same table with the food.

"Marta, have you met Dr. Margo, Sarah's father?" I
overheard Tim say to Marta. My dad said his pleasantries to the
nosy secretary. Tim was my father's former student, ten years
before I attended Oakville State. I grinned. I doubted she
would ask for his phone number now.

A warm hand grasped my shoulder. I whirled around to find
a tall build, chestnut hair, and perfect lips I never considered.

"Aaron," I said. He wrapped me in a warm hug.
"Congratulations on getting into law school."

"Congrats to you, Margo," he said with a shy smile. Bethany
came up behind us and poked Aaron in the back like we were

in fourth grade.

"Look who showed her face," Aaron said to Beth, who leaned against our childhood friend. "It has been a few years. Are you still with Craig?"

"He couldn't make it," she said with hesitation in her voice.

Was there trouble in paradise? I was afraid to ask.

"Too bad. I once played video games with Craig for two days straight during our sophomore year." Aaron laughed. I forced a smile at his accurate summarization of Craig. "We didn't play again. My parents would have been pissed if I flunked college because of video games." Aaron's enthusiasm always made me smile. "This is like a Hidden Meadows reunion. All we need is Mrs. Shiltz-Potts."

"I don't need her burning down Benny's BBQ during my party."

The three of us laughed at the memory of our former, haphazard neighbor. She caught her couch on fire at least once a year from falling asleep with a cigarette. Not to mention, dumping hot fireplace ashes into a pile of leaves or leaving a candle near a stack of old newspapers.

"I haven't been to Hidden Meadows since my parents moved. Do your parents still live in the same house?" Aaron asked me.

"No. My parents divorced. We moved the summer after sixth grade to a house off Regency Road. My dad still lives there," I said without emotion. "I went to St. E." I looked at Bethany. "Your parents still live in Hidden Meadows, right?"

"Yes." Bethany fidgeted with her engagement ring.

It was not until college our group of friends from the neighborhood had reconnected, except for Daniel. He didn't go to Oakville State. I never asked what happened to him. If he married Tiffany, lived in a giant house, and had two beautiful children—I didn't want to know.

"Man, Sarah." Aaron scratched his neck. "I forgot…"

"No worries. It's ancient history," I said.

My joy disappeared when my mother and a man entered the banquet room. Ancient history had come to bite me in the ass. My eyes met my dad's from across the room. We didn't need to exchange words. He didn't invite his ex-wife. Why would he? He could not stand her. I spent most of my teens begging not to see my mother. I left Aaron and Bethany at the buffet. My stomach grumbled leaving the pulled pork behind. Although my mom saw me, she headed towards my dad in the corner where he talked to Dr. Rosenberger, one of the engineering professors.

"Lori, you can stay but no trouble," Frank said to his ex-wife in hushed tones.

She was not here to celebrate.

"Is this your girlfriend?" Lori pointed her index finger at my professor. Dr. Rosenberger wore a designer suit. A few strands of gray lined her tight shoulder-length curls.

"Ina is a colleague and one of Sarah's professors." He forced a smile. "Sarah was Ina's graduate assistant last year."

"The department will be lost without her," Ina said. My mother was not here to play meet the faculty. "I'm sorry. I don't believe we've met."

"This is Sarah's mother, Lori," Frank replied, deadpan.

I joined their huddle because I wanted to be wrong about my mom. The delusional part of me hoped she'd hand me a card.

"Hello, Sarah." Dr. Rosenberger squeezed my hand. "Congratulations. I was telling your mother how sad the department will be to see you go."

"Thanks so much. I'll be sad to go, but the Ph.D. program is not off the table."

Ina touched my shoulder. The corners of my dad's lips moved upward with pride. My mother narrowed her eyes.

"Shouldn't you be thankful you got through college?" Lori

122

asked.

Ina picked imaginary lint from her suit. I wanted to hide under a rock, a very large one where no one could see the depths of my humiliation. My father's face flushed, his postured stiffened, he cleared his throat. He wanted to drag my mother out of Benny's BBQ and toss her into traffic. I knew the scowl.

"The food line has died down," Ina said to my mom's guest. "Come, let us eat and leave these three to talk." The man in dirty jeans and work boots followed.

"Our daughter graduated college at the top of her class two years ago. You weren't there. Today, we are celebrating her master's degree."

My mother shrugged because she didn't care about education. I died a little inside. How could she not give a damn?

"Did she tell you she is screwing around with her psychiatrist?" Lori asked.

Everyone stopped eating. The chatter gone. Say the word screwing and people will stop and listen. I flashed a fake smile at my cousin, Shelly.

"Watch your language, Lori," Frank hissed. "Why did you come here? You want nothing but trouble."

"I am family!"

Frank shook his head no.

"You quit the family when you took up with Donny." He aligned his head to nod towards his ex's date in line with Ina. "Or Johnson's Asphalt and Tree Service." Frank read the back of the man's t-shirt.

"So you don't care your daughter is a slut? I should have never given you custody. You did this." The words exited her mouth with brutal force, piercing, like a stab with a sharp blade.

I opened my mouth to justify my actions, plead with her to

be nice, but only air left my lips. Out of nowhere, Gina joined our feuding group.

"You have the facts wrong, like always," Gina said into my mother's face. "If you ever speak this way to Sarah again, I will rip every goddamn hair out of your trouble-making head." Gina had a grip on my mother's arm "It's time you left."

"Just because you can't have children doesn't mean you can have mine," my mother said. The two women struggled towards the door.

"What were you thinking, Dad?" Each follicle on my scalp tingled with anxiety. "Marrying her." I nodded towards the exit. A calm breath escaped his lips, eyes averted from mine, watching the doorway as if Lori's ghost wouldn't leave.

"That's the problem—I wasn't."

CHAPTER TWENTY-FOUR

"She was no longer the chubby kid from Hidden Meadows, but it didn't change my parents' opinion. They destroyed our relationship. No matter what I said or did, Sarah wouldn't take me back." -Roddy King

The colorful evening with my mother would not leave my thoughts. Most of the time I could sleep it off, but her malicious actions crossed the line. Not to mention, the scolding I received from Gina in the kitchen at Benny's BBQ.

People had seen us together, so she said. Lee had a reputation as a man whore—Gina's words, not mine. No decent man wants someone promiscuous, as if she can talk.

"Baby girl, we are having this conversation because I love you," she said. The kitchen staff had cleared out the moment the blond in heels stormed in with me in tow. I cried on the shoulder of her white blazer.

"What should I do?" I asked in between sobs. Her palm held my head against her.

"First, you will dry your eyes and go back to your party. Second, you tell that man you can't see him anymore."

"Why are you upset today?" he asked. Lee glanced towards the passenger side as he merged onto the highway. No matter how he phrased his questions, he sounded like a psychiatrist.

"My mother made a scene at my graduation party. I'll save you on hearing the transcript version of the confrontation."

I could never gage his thoughts or feelings. Maybe he

should marry whoever his family chooses because I could never imagine Lee caring much about anyone.

"Ignore them." He switched lanes to get off at the medical center exit.

Did I want to know his thoughts? When he discovered me looking in his direction, he moved his hand to my thigh. "I need to stop at my office for fifteen minutes. We won't miss the exhibit."

I didn't care about famous paintings, but he insisted. If I were honest, I had nothing in common with Lee Abrams. We had a messed up history together. I needed to take Gina's advice and be done with Lee. I would tell him after the exhibit.

"You are only working fifteen minutes on a Saturday?"

"I am a medical student advisor. One of my students failed their boards. This student passed the second time, but cannot understand failing once is a black mark on a residency application."

"This student cannot get a residency?" I didn't have a clue about the process of becoming a doctor. First aid training at work didn't count as medical experience.

"The student will get a residency, but not a competitive one. This person's parents are very successful, which makes the predicament more difficult." Lee pulled into the parking garage. "A quick meeting. I promise."

I sat on a metal bench in a long corridor between the hospital and medical school. Large windows overlooked a field with a red sculpture, which resembled a giant gumball machine. My stomach growled. I clicked my phone to see the time. Ten minutes had gone by, boredom had set in, and people watching wasn't an option.

"What are you doing here?" I looked up from my daze to see the last person I would have expected. He wore a tie and held a green folder. I blinked twice whether to moisten my eyes or make sure I wasn't imagining him.

"Hey."

"I'll repeat myself, Sarah. What are you doing here?" The light from the large window became shadowed as he stood over me, arms crossed. "I moved on after two years. Do you want me back or are you here to see the prep school kid who failed his boards?"

Had Roddy King lost his mind? What was he doing here? Then I remembered the day he showed me his acceptance letter to the Oakville State University School of Medicine. His parents blamed me for their son not going to a more competitive school. Dr. King and his wife went to Johns Hopkins.

"I'm sorry. I'm not here to see you."

Roddy narrowed his eyes. The night we broke up drifted into my memory. For the second time in our lives, he was angry with me. How could I explain I wasn't here to see him?

Lee appeared out of his office. The set of keys jingled at the door lock. I stood up, a foot shorter than Roddy, mouth open with no words.

"You ready to go?" Lee asked. He placed his hand on my back to guide me, oblivious to the situation. How would I know the Kings?

I risked a glance over my shoulder at Roddy, uncertain how I felt about the encounter. My ex-boyfriend put his hands up as if wanting an explanation. I stepped into the elevator while the doors closed on my past.

CHAPTER TWENTY-FIVE

"You're one decision away from a different life." -
Tim Sanders

The back of my head rested against my car seat. A song I
loved, but didn't know the title, played on the radio. Work was
exhausting, more than usual. After a moment of relaxation in
my apartment complex parking lot, I turned the car off and
reached for my bag on the passenger side. Lee would be here in
thirty minutes. He suggested dinner. I said yes, even though I
wanted nothing more than pajamas, soup, and the couch—the
benefits of living alone.

I needed to tell Lee tonight. No more one last time. The
gym near the closed mall would have to do because I couldn't
run into him. I couldn't be seen with him again. The
disappointed look on Gina's face at Benny's BBQ wouldn't
leave my head, neither would my dad's words about my mother.

That's the problem. I wasn't thinking.

When I opened the front door, I stopped in the foyer. A
blond rummaged through my refrigerator for a diet. She
popped the tab and took a sip.

"Your landlady let me in," Bethany said when she turned
around.

I couldn't believe Angela let someone into my apartment
without my consent. I didn't give out keys for a reason. My
apartment was my haven from the world. Bethany knew
nothing about Lee. I wanted to keep it that way.

Bethany moved to the living room with her drink, used tissues littered my coffee table. *Yuck.* I made a mental note to bleach everything after she left. Bethany had been crying—puffy cheeks, red eyes, and an empty Kleenex box she took from my upstairs bathroom.

I moved to the chair next to the sofa, heart racing in fear. Something was wrong. Bethany came here for help. The situation reminded me of my desperate pay phone call in sixth grade. Following my father's example, I waited for Bethany to tell me the reason for her tears.

"I'm pregnant," she whispered. The words hung in the air. Her hands rested in her lap, reminiscent of the nuns at St. Elizabeth. High school flashed through my mind, a brief image of Bethany on the first day of ninth grade. She transferred schools too. Our friendship renewed. "Say something!"

My daydream dissipated into the pile of snot rags on the table. I didn't know what to say. Bethany was the definition of pious—going to church, praying for everyone, and often lecturing my foul language, including the word crap. How many times did she ignore me in college when Roddy would joke to Craig about getting laid? Premarital sex is a sin she would say in her mother's voice.

"What do you want me to say?" I asked.

No one cries into an entire box of tissues when happy. Her eyes narrowed when she looked up. My mind needed to process her words. Holier-than-thou Bethany had gotten herself knocked up.

"You are the last person who should judge me!" Bethany stood and toppled over the coffee table, hands scattering tissues on the floor.

"I swear I am not judging. You took me by surprise. I didn't know you and Craig were having sex." Bethany returned to the couch, tears moistening her cheeks. "You are getting married soon. This could be a happy surprise, right?"

"No! My parents think I'm a virgin. You know what my

mother is like."

"You have dated Craig for years. It wouldn't be a shock—"

"Sarah!" More sobs with upset hand gestures. "I don't have sex with whoever I want like you."

An overwhelming need to put her in her place came over me, but I ignored the urge. I only had one real boyfriend plus Lee. Who was she to judge me? I wasn't sitting in her living room crying over an unwanted pregnancy.

"What did Craig say?"

"Craig says we have drifted apart. He doesn't want to get married. He doesn't want the baby." Bethany swiped her face with the bottom of her shirt.

"What an asshole!"

"You never liked Craig!"

"Maybe this is a good example why. Are you sure you're pregnant?" I tried to keep the conversation moving. She nodded.

"If I tell my parents, they will kick me out. I have no husband and no parents." Bethany cried until her body shook in waves of tremors. She picked up a used tissue from the table and blew her nose as loud as a horn.

"Beth, you can stay with me. I have an extra bedroom." Empathy wasn't my strongest attribute. I didn't want Bethany dealing with her predicament alone.

"What? You want to save me since you make more money?"

"No, Beth. I am trying. You know I'm not good with emotions."

"I can't believe I will join your rank of slut."

My sympathy was running out of gas.

"Wait! You break into my apartment. I offer you help, and you insist on insulting me. What have I ever done to you?"

Bethany gave me a cold look, one too close to my mother's.

"You have no idea what people are saying about you," she said.

Bethany knew about Lee.

"I don't care. This isn't about me." That was a lie. I hated people being judgmental. They needed to mind their own business.

"He used to be your psychiatrist." The smug tone of her voice irritated me.

"It accelerated the get to know you part of the relationship," I said.

"Why do you think everything is a joke?" Bethany grabbed her purse from the table. She marched towards the foyer in a rage. The door flung open to reveal Lee on the small stoop, hand in the air to knock. "Get out of my way!"

Bethany bumped into Lee. I followed my raging friend to her four-door Chevy. Bethany fumbled for her keys, items spilling from her handbag to the pavement.

"Beth, come on. Let's talk. I want to help." I tapped the glass of her window, but she refused to roll it down.

"Don't you get it? Every time we hang out, you will see a hypocrite," she said. Bethany started the car. "Don't ever talk to me."

"No one is perfect. People make mistakes," I said. We stared at each other through the dirty glass. I wasn't sure if I was giving Bethany or myself words of comfort.

"Everything seems to go your way, and you don't deserve it!"

Throwing the car into reverse, she slammed on the gas, without a care of what she might hit. The tan car speed out of my complex.

Bethany had loving parents, a free college education, and a body she didn't have to do an exercise to achieve. I couldn't believe she would claim I somehow had a better life than her. Nothing came to me from pure luck, only hard work.

The door to my apartment remained opened, small beams of light filtered onto the linoleum floor. I stepped inside, eyes adjusting to the dark living room. Lee's hands covered his face on the couch where Bethany sat minutes earlier. The cat hid under the kitchen table, a place he went when stressed.

Now what?

"I am sorry," he said.

"No reason to be sorry. This drama is not your fault."

I leaned into the back of the chair, ready to be alone with my cat, in pajamas. My favorite purple ones were clean. I needed the purple ones.

He sobbed. I hoped I would wake up from this outrageous nightmare. All this dream needed was a floating blue panda or a flying pig.

"I don't know how this happened. I do, but—"

"No big deal, Lee. I am already over it." Closing my eyes, I massaged my temples while taking shallow breaths. Since when did Lee have emotions?

"How can you be calm?" Lee asked. I opened my eyes to find him on the floor next to my chair.

"Because bad stuff happens to people sometimes." I cared about Bethany, but everyone pays for the consequences of their actions.

"What are you going to do?" His eyes watered as he reached for my hand, gripping it with fear.

"Nothing. Wait it out. See what happens."

The edge of his lips formed an outraged circle. Why did he care about my friend? He told me days ago to forget about my mom.

"I think people will notice if you do nothing, Sarah. How can you be so naïve?"

"Naïve? People get knocked up when they don't take birth control or use condoms," I said.

"No birth control?" His cheeks turned a dark crimson. "You said—"

"I said what?" I shook my head in confusion. "Like I said, not my problem."

"It's my problem?" Lee stood. He eyed the discarded tissues on the floor. *Gross, I know.*

"No, it's Craig's problem."

"Craig?"

"He is the father of Beth's baby." Lee let out a breath of frustration, eyes burning a hole into me for an explanation. "Bethany is pregnant. I found her here when I got home. We argued. She left."

"You are not having a baby?"

"No. Why would you think such a thing?" He pulled the positive pregnancy test out of his pocket. The little stick, with two lines, made a soft tap when placed on the table. "Oh. She must have taken the test here. I didn't realize you thought Bethany's issue was mine."

"I came close to a heart attack," he said.

"Lee." I looked into his dark eyes. "I need to get out of Oakville. Everything is a reminder of the past. I go twenty miles out of my way to avoid Green Street. Every time I feel I have moved past my mother, she appears and starts trouble. I don't want to leave my family and job, but I need a new start." My mind drifted to Tim's email flagged at the top of my inbox. "I am tired of the drama. Bethany confirmed my decision."

Lee squeezed my hand. Now that he wasn't in trouble, he returned to his baseline lack of emotion. The room grew darker whether from the lack of sunlight or our conversation.

"It's a relief. I planned on ending our relationship today," he said. Lee stood, dinner forgotten. "We caused immense gossip. In hindsight, we should have been discreet. Lesson learned in the future."

"In the future? You plan on dating another young, former

patient?" I asked.

Lee walked towards the door and grinned.

"Good luck, Sarah Margo."

The office phone rang ten times before Tim's voice mail picked up. I thought about hanging up, staying in Oakville, being with my family, but I couldn't. The time to start a new life was now—no turning back.

"You have reached Tim Sanders, Manager of the Research and Development Division. I am away from my desk, but if you leave a detailed message, I will return your call."

Beep.

"Hey Tim, it's Sarah Margo. You mentioned an opening in New York City in your weekly update email. If the position is still available, I would like to be considered."

I let out a deep breath. The anxiety of the past left me alone with the unknown of the future.

I called my dad.

I texted Gina.

I bought boxes.

CHAPTER TWENTY-SIX

"I have set Sarah up with every hot male in New York City. She's not interested. Alex swears she's not gay."
-Deana Dash

My apartment building didn't have an elevator, but the old, brick tower had cheap rent for Manhattan. I tugged my suitcase up six flights of stairs, both hands and every ounce of strength to make it to the landing. Snow continued to fall outside. The holiday vibe would end on Monday morning when I returned to work. I took a moment to admire the flakes swirling in the wind outside the stairwell window. Returning to New York after visiting Oakville always felt strange as if the two places were battling to be home.

"Hey girl," Deana said. She stood in the doorway of her unit next to mine. "Five years ago today, we met in this hall."

I attempted to catch my breath.

"Really? It's been that long?" Deana nodded. My twenty-ninth birthday was less than a month away. It had been five years. "How was your Christmas?"

"Another year without my parents killing each other. My youngest brother was home from Penn State. We watched Christmas movies. Dad made a Tofurky. Nothing exciting. I've been waiting for you to return for two days." She smiled. "You spend time with your dad?" Deana shoveled a fork full of pasta into her mouth.

"Yes." I smiled at the memory of being curled up next to the fire, warm afghan around me, in my childhood home. "We made fettuccine, drank too much beer, and I had a great time at Uncle Dan and Gina's Christmas party." My suitcase thumped against the trim of my apartment door. "Gina is visiting in a few weeks. You are welcome to shop with us."

"Sounds fun. I'm glad you are taking time off work." Deana stepped back inside her threshold, not wanting to have the Sarah works too much argument. "I will see you at the bar Wednesday for wing night. The perfect guy will be there." An evil grin spread from cheek to cheek of her flawless face.

"Oh, no." My head peeked around the corner of my door at my smirking friend. "I am done with men."

"You haven't even started with men." Deana leaned her tall, blond, fitness trainer body against her door frame.

"I've had enough setups. Remember Matt?"

"What was wrong with him? If I remember correctly— good-looking, software engineer, and a beautiful apartment in Lenox Hill." Deana pursed her lips together as if there was no way I could argue.

"Yes. You are correct about his job and housing, but he also ran a porn site in his free time." Deana failed when she tried not to laugh. "Sorry, I couldn't overlook the pornography hobby."

"What about Tom?"

"Mister dressed head-to-toe in company apparel? Even his watch and shoes had his corporate logo." I wasn't sure if I should laugh or cry over my dating history. "You told me not to be a snob, so I gave him another chance. When he showed up for a second date in a company logo tracksuit, I couldn't see him again. It's like he was trying to sell me insurance."

"Fair enough. Erick?"

"The guy with the dangling earring and lisp?"

"I prefer the name Tharah over Sarah." Deana bit her lip to keep from smiling. "Okay. The guy from Alabama who interned at your company."

"We are not talking about him."

"Why not?" She giggled like an elementary school girl. "I heard a lot of noise coming from your apartment. You refused to give me the details. I asked Alex and Cassie if they knew—"

"You asked our friends? Fine, there was noise. I screamed when I found him naked on the couch. When a girl says she has to use the restroom, it doesn't mean strip down and be waiting."

The amused look on Deana's face made me flush a thousand shades of red. He had a nice body and tattoos in the sexiest places. Why didn't I go for him? Then I recalled him singing *Thunderstruck* at the top of his lungs while dancing, still nude.

"Your friend from Oakville. The one you have dinner with sometimes," Deana said. She looked towards the ceiling as if trying to recall his name. "Anthony?"

"Aaron," I said. We met up a few months ago when he was in town on business. Just dinner between childhood friends. "He isn't interested in me."

"Are you sure because—"

"I am a lost cause Deana Dash. Please give up on me." I pushed my suitcase further into my studio apartment, almost squashing the cat against the wall.

"No, you're not, Sarah Margo. There is a man smart and weird enough for you somewhere." She tapped her fork against the bowl.

"That's reassuring. I have work to do. I will see you on Wednesday." I shut my apartment door.

New York welcomed me, but it wasn't where my heart rested. I loved my job and friends, but I missed my family. Moving to the big city provided me with a life I couldn't have in Oakville, and my dad reminded me every time I told him I missed home.

On my contacts screen, I pressed my dad's number. After

137

four rings, the 80s tape answering machine he refused to get rid of played the same message.

"Hello, Hello," he said over the recording. He cursed under his breath followed by a few beeps to stop the tape. "Is that you, Sarah?"

"Dad, it's me. My flight had a two-hour layover in Charlotte. I am at my apartment."

The cat jumped on my fold-out couch, which stayed a bed unless I had company. My attention went to the window where street lights shone into the cold, evening sky.

"Thanks for calling me. My first class is tomorrow at eight. You know how I obsess over my syllabus the night before," he said. I could hear his smile, and in return, my lips curled upward. My heart grew heavy.

"I didn't think the department chair taught classes. Dr. Dune didn't when I was a student. What are you teaching?" During our time off, we didn't talk about work.

"Two Mechatronics courses, a morning and an afternoon slot three days a week." My dad yawned. The clock in the kitchen displayed quarter after nine. "Honey, is it okay if we talk at our usual time?"

"Yes. Eight o'clock on Saturday morning because people love waking up early on the weekend."

My father had the goofiest laugh.

It's not funny, Frank Margo.

"I love you," he said.

"I love you too."

Single digit temperatures made morning even worse. I pulled my heaviest wool coat out of my closet, an effort to keep from freezing to death during the twelve-block walk to the office. The cat remained nestled in the comforter, one green eye half open.

"I'm leaving. Don't worry. I wouldn't want to disturb you." The black ball of fur closed his eye, satisfied with his impending day of rest.

My key stuck in the lock. I tugged, paint chips fell to the floor, but my keys remained dangling above the doorknob. I couldn't be late on my first day back from vacation. Debbie went crazy when staff showed up two minutes past eight. My gloved hands tugged harder until my keys jingled free.

The heels of my boots clacked against the stairs, down the six flights to the ground level where the superintendent snoozed in a folding chair. My building didn't have a doorman or a fancy name, but it met my budget. That's what I told myself every time I wanted to move.

I hustled in the cold, scarf covering most of my face until I stood in front of my high-rise office building. Construction crews were busy working on the exterior, adding a Mackgale-Berrell sign, the first sign of change since my employer sold to the foreign conglomerate in November.

"Watch it!" A construction worker scolded a woman texting in the taped-off area near the new electronic sliding doors.

I shuffled inside with a group of people trying to reach their floor by eight o'clock. No one knew Mackgale-Berrell's intentions, but at least they were making improvements. The worn out lobby now boasted new furnishings and artwork in neutrals and blues.

"Move!" A woman shoved me aside to get on the elevator. I mumbled sorry and packed into the small space with fifteen people. All of us were five minutes late. Angry woman's vein throbbed on her forehead.

When I got off the elevator, a security guard scanned my badge, which hung under my coat, with a digital scanner. I beeped like a can of peas at a grocery store checkout. We didn't have security guards on my floor before. I gave the new addition a curious look, but he motioned for me to continue through the main doors.

There were many offices on my floor, engineers and displaced management roles from other departments. Now that Mackgale-Berrell had bought the building space shouldn't be an issue.

"Was your Christmas good?" Ethan asked. When I turned around, he had on a brown sweater over his dress shirt. Even with the chunky knit, he looked like a lanky boy.

"Yes."

My eyes searched for our boss. I could do without a lecture on punctuality from the devil in a tight pantsuit.

"Debbie is off today," Ethan said. "Maybe she's at home reading up on engineering since she is the manager of our department."

"I have more faith in the existence of Santa Claus," I said.

"What is funny?" Raj asked. He was the opposite of Ethan —short, brown-skinned, and a well-fed gut covered by one of his many plaid dress shirts.

"Nothing. Sarah and I were discussing Christmas. Did you enjoy your week off?" Ethan asked Raj.

"I don't celebrate Christmas. It was a mandatory paid week off," Raj replied.

When he walked away, Ethan held up his hands in mock surrender.

"Did you go anywhere for the holidays?" I asked Ethan.

"My parents live in Poughkeepsie. I cleaned out a storage shed with my dad." He paused and then opened his mouth.

I waited.

"We are behind on the Massey-Carter project. I'll see you later," I said. Ethan remained near the copy machine, mind somewhere else.

I closed my office door, ready to dive back into reality.

CHAPTER TWENTY-SEVEN

"She named the cat after her dad. Enough said." -
Alex Winchester

Three voicemails, sixteen texts, and a picture of Alex
wearing a lavender scarf. I sat at my desk staring at the selfie of
tall, tan, and handsome on my phone. My first week in New
York, we sat at the same table in our building's cafeteria. Alex
worked at the accounting firm on the first floor. We hit it off,
and I liked him the way I did Daniel in sixth grade.

Two days later, I spotted my new crush outside with a petite,
artsy type. My heart dropped to my gut, a feeling that often
kept me away from the opposite sex. Alex introduced me to
Cassie. I hated her for snatching up the gorgeous, smart
Alexander. When I asked how long they had been dating, they
roared with laughter at the naïve girl from the Midwest. I
invited Alex and Cassie to join me at a local bar with my
neighbor, and the four of us became best friends.

Me: Cute scarf. No wing night. We are behind at work.

Alex: I do not accept your answer, Margo. You have skipped
out on the bar for two weeks. No one has seen you.

Me: Not true. My cat, boss, and three coworkers have seen
me.

Alex: I'll see you at seven. My search party is coming to find
your workaholic-self if you no show. I own this city. You
cannot hide.

"There you are," Debbie said. I dropped my phone into the

trashcan like a guilty middle school kid. "I need to see you, Raj, Ethan, and Samantha in my office." Before I could ask questions, she was out the door and on to her next victim.

"What's going on?" I whispered to Raj when I joined him outside Debbie's office door. He shrugged.

"No gossiping, Sarah," Debbie said from behind me with Samantha and Ethan in tow. "Close the door, Raj." Our boss sat in an executive chair, tapping her fake nails against a three-ring binder. "It appears our new CEO, Warren Wallace, wants the four of you for a conference next week in Berrell." Debbie flashed a picture on a document of a man in his fifties.

"I thought the CEO's last name was Mackgale?" I questioned.

"What gave you that assumption?" Debbie asked. My eyes went to the folder with the Mackgale-Berrell logo, but I decided not to point out the obvious.

"I can't go to Berrell next week," Raj said. "I told the company no travel when I accepted the position."

"What you told the previous company is irrelevant now," Debbie said with an annoyed look. "The four of you are going. I'm not sure why." Raj spoke, but Debbie motioned for him to remain silent. "I will send you the details via email. You leave tomorrow morning. Off you go."

I returned to my office to retrieve my phone from the trash. My friends would kidnap me for wing night. Their persistence added to the stress of leaving tomorrow morning for Berrell. The thought of going somewhere I knew nothing about and working at the corporate office made my stomach ache.

Me: Alex has texted me sixteen times. I can't come tonight. The CEO requested four engineers to attend a conference in Berrell. I leave in the morning.

Deana: That's tomorrow. My friend Jeremy from work will be there, and it's almost your birthday. The last one before

142

thirty.

They weren't letting me skip.

Me: I'll come as long as Jeremy is not a setup.

No response.

CHAPTER TWENTY-EIGHT

"Experience Berrell's rich history, tucked away in its forts and castles, ancient ruins and stone streets. From fine dining to beautiful beaches, and the set of *Cross Hill Manor*—make the island country of Berrell part of your memories." -Travel Berrell

We arrived at The Hotel Rowan after midnight with a bad case of jet lag. A plaque outside the four-story, old building dated 1791. A porter ushered us inside while another unloaded our bags. Floral runner rugs lined the stone floor to the wooden desk near the wall. An abundance of live and artificial flowers stood on metal plant stands. Each window had heavy, floral draperies, and the furniture reminded me of my grandma's couch we donated after she passed away. Each of us took our keys—actual metal keys—and went to our rooms.

Ethan smiled at me as he unlocked the door next to mine. *He better stay next door.* I disappeared into my room, not wasting a second to lock the door. Berrell was strange. The surroundings were nothing like home, and the people we met spoke with an odd version of a British accent.

The shuttle driver told us he learned about America from *The Andy Griffith Show*. I smiled inside. Wasn't he in for a shock? I doubted he would ever travel overseas to learn the truth about Mayberry. Then again, I never thought I'd be walking into a hotel room thousands of miles from home.

The furnishings were modest, a twin bed and armchair. When I read about the island country of Berrell, I pictured

Barbados, a luxury hotel with a lazy river, not a frigid, old mass of land in the English Channel. I had never traveled overseas.

I turned the metal handle on the clawfoot bathtub. Water trickled out of the spout into the metal base. I waited, cold and naked, for the tub to fill. After five minutes, I stepped into two inches of cool water. Goosebumps covered my skin from my scalp to my toes. I shivered each time the washcloth touched my body.

After my polar bear challenge, I climbed under the itchy covers with a *Berrell Guidebook*. The mattress was worse than my college dorm. Gina bought a mattress topper to stop my complaining. I needed one now. The guidebook fell to the floor when I tried to reposition myself. Perhaps the world had weird toilets, no showers, and slept in small beds.

Debbie's email said Mackgale-Berrell was across the street from the hotel. I glanced at my appearance in the small mirror, pleased with how well I looked considering the jet lag. When I noticed the time on my watch, I groaned. Two in the morning in New York.

I left my room, said goodbye to the cheery porter, and walked across the stone street. All the buildings were old. Streets and streets of gray earth, built hundreds of years ago, were a perfect companion to the gloomy sky. Why didn't I ever go anywhere sunny?

The corporate office mirrored our new updates in New York, shades of blue, modern, yet comfortable. I followed the conference signs, no one in the building but me, to a conference room where four people sat engrossed in their devices. Paper name cards lined the tables. I found mine, *Sarah Nicole Margo, United States of America, Mechanical Engineer*. Was my middle name necessary? I felt like an ambassador to a foreign country.

More people arrived, and I settled into my chair. On the left, *Joan Goode, Berrell, Technical Writer* and to the right, *Richard T. Newport, England, Materials Buyer*. Richard, dressed in a bow-tie and knitted vest, shook hands with a pale man with freckles in a green dress shirt. I couldn't follow their conversation, a bunch of acronyms and the mention of a plant in Nord-Pas-de-Calais.

I didn't know what Mackgale-Berrell did outside of our office. For months, as our company struggled, there was a lot of tension between the staff. The Oakville plant where I started was down to a skeleton crew as the company owners looked for a buyer. When Mackgale-Berrell purchased us, we were happy to keep our jobs.

By the time lunch came around, I couldn't stay awake. Samantha and Raj sat across the room, not paying attention to the human resources man giving a presentation to seven Americans—two I didn't know—six employees from France, four men from London, and twelve people who worked at the home office. Part of me hoped I would be the cool kid from New York with everyone asking what it's like to be from an amazing city—like Aurora from California in sixth grade. No one cared, which wasn't a big shocker.

"You have an hour for luncheon," Davey, the HR coordinator, said.

The employees stuck with their cliques and left the room. The New Yorkers remained in their seats. Raj typed on his laptop. Samantha flipped through a magazine she purchased at the airport. Ethan used a pencil and drafting triangle on a piece of paper.

"Are you guys eating?" I asked. Raj ignored me. Had I ever seen him eat non-Indian food? Samantha shook her head, returning to her gossip article. Ethan said no thanks without moving from his calculated position.

I left my chair to wander through the halls in search of a vending machine. The internal clock in my head had no idea what meal I should eat. I felt terrible. A map in the *Berrell Guidebook* showed an American restaurant a few blocks from Mackgale-Berrell called The Bistro.

Did I have the energy to walk a few blocks? My level of

tiredness increased. I paced the floors in search of non-existent vending machines. I swiped my phone's screen to see what Google had to say about my food situation.

I blinked twice.

A man hovered over me, hands cradling my head, fingers twisted into my hair, and a knee between my thighs. The collision happened so fast, neither of us had a chance of staying upright. I inhaled a deep breath, eyes the color of deep water studied mine as if he recognized me. I crinkled my nose. What was that awful odor? The man's eyes widened at my look of disgust. It wasn't him. He smelled clean, like scented soap or a mound of fresh laundry next to an open window. To my left, scattered on the floor, I found the stinky source in the form of a fish sandwich. I questioned the judgment of people who could stomach food which once lived in water.

"I am sorry," I said. He offered his hand to pull me to my feet. I stumbled and fell into the tall man's chest. He seemed reluctant to release my hand as if there was a familiarity between us. We didn't know each other. He wasn't from New York, and he sure as hell wasn't from Oakville. When he let go, he straightened his sweater and ran his hand through his reddish, brown hair. My attention returned to his spoiled lunch. "I'm eating at The Bistro. I can replace your—"

"Sir, line three. Nigel says the call is urgent," a woman said. She tapped her shoe in a manic rhythm. The fax machine buzzed. A phone rang while the other line beeped. I was interrupting their workday.

"It's all right. I won't have time for lunch today," he said in the same accent as the others in Berrell. The blue eyes behind his dark-framed glasses remained serious, not a hint of joy on his face. Why was he staring at me? The woman cleared her throat, and the man followed her like a lost puppy.

The cloudy sky misted icy rain pellets into the dreary atmosphere. Why would anyone build a company here? When I passed The Hotel Rowan, the porter nodded, returning to his conversation with the manager. A mix of salt water and local cuisine filled the air with a fishy aroma. My cheeks flushed at the thought of spoiling someone's lunch while typing on my phone. The humiliation heightened by the fact he was gorgeous. Why did he have to be tall and athletic? I preferred to collide with the janitor, old enough to be my father, and a pot belly big enough for triplets.

A comforting scent of American junk food floated through The Bistro. I was thankful to whoever put an American-themed restaurant in Berrell. I didn't need to be tired and sick from local food.

Fellow Americans waited in a long line to order from a giant menu board at the end of the black ropes. I had no idea tourists visited Berrell. Sure, they had a tourist guidebook, but so did Oakville. It didn't mean anyone visited the place. Berrell had beaches, but no one would swim in winter coats. Perhaps, the tourists received a group rate for an off-season discount to the island of gray and gloom. My exhaustion beat out my curiosity.

The tables were full. A heavyset man in a Kansas City Chiefs jersey lounged against the wall with his wife, who wore a period piece costume. They took a bite of their loaded hot dogs in-sync. The woman wiped the pickle relish from her lip, and the husband laughed.

"What do you recommend? I do not eat American food."

When I turned around, Fish Sandwich Guy stood behind me in line. He no longer wore a sweater, but a wool coat over a button up. The tie under his coat was so beautiful—pink tartan. He flushed when he caught me staring at the top of his shirt.

"I am having pizza." Clanging dishes and conversation created a noisy background. "I hope I didn't take you away from something important." My nostrils sucked in air to avoid dying from embarrassment.

"It can wait. I missed breakfast this morning. Do you know it's unhealthy to miss breakfast?" He undid the toggles on his coat, deep blue eyes on the large menu, lips twisted in contemplation.

"I never miss a meal."

Don't yawn. I didn't want to ruin his lunch and then act like a bored teenager.

"Good for you. It keeps you healthy," he said. A relaxed smile spread across his face. I grinned back like a crushing school girl.

"May I take your order, please?" The cashier saved me from the humiliation.

I never checked out guys. Why was I smiling? Twinkling around men only encouraged their pursuit, but he wasn't flirting. The man was hungry. I ruined his lunch.

"Give me two slices of pepperoni and a diet."

Fish Sandwich Guy seemed out of his element when he surveyed the menu.

"Please give me the same order." He pulled a credit card from his wallet. The cashier swiped the plastic while she placed two cups on a tray.

"I would have paid. I am the one who ruined your lunch."

"Nonsense. My eyes were on documents rather than watching my steps. Besides, what man allows a woman to pay for a meal?"

"Many do." I had known my fair share of men who would let a woman pay. Tracksuit guy made me split the check plus tip down to the last cent. The jerk ordered lobster when I had a burger.

"You are not from New York."

He watched me fill my cup with ice and did the same. Fish Sandwich Guy flinched when ice sputtered out, pieces landing on the black commercial rug below our feet.

"Is it so obvious?" Did I say y'all? If so, Gina was to blame. "How do you know I live in New York?"

We sat near the trash cans at the only open table.

"I have experience in the U.S. You don't sound New Yorker," he said with a look of hesitation. "The only American division Mackgale-Berrell owns is in New York City."

"I grew up in the Midwest. I moved to New York City five years ago for a job opportunity," I said because a fling-gone-bad-with-your-childhood-psychiatrist didn't sound as nice.

The food runner yelled our number. Her eyes scanned the packed restaurant. I waved my hand. She delivered our pizza, tossed a handful of napkins on the table, and told us to enjoy.

"Odd way to serve food," he said. With skill, he placed a paper napkin on his lap. The way he looked at me unnerved my man-hating ways.

"You have your fair share of weird customs."

At the next table, two women pointed and giggled at my lunch buddy. Were we back in elementary school? He seemed oblivious to the attention.

"Provide examples, please." He shifted his weight towards me, elbows on the table in a mocking way.

"Um. I'm not sure," I said. He laughed. "I've been here less than twenty-four hours. Give me time to compile my list."

"Fair enough. I look forward to hearing your cultural discoveries."

Both of us picked at our pizza, neither admitting how terrible the food tasted. It had to be better than seafood.

I groaned at my watch still in Eastern Time.

"The time zones are killing me. I couldn't stay awake this morning." We tossed our trash into the can. Fish Sandwich Guy fastened his coat and adjusted his glasses. "Are you participating in the projects this week?"

"No." He took a final sip of his drink, tossed it in the trash, and held the door for me. "I'll be at the presentation at four."

"It's the CEO talk, right?"

The dampness in the air made me wish for my comforter at home. There would be no snuggling with the scratchy floral blanket on my little bed at the hotel.

"I believe so," he said. He pulled his phone from his coat pocket to check the time. "I hear the CEO talks are boring. Are you sure you can handle it with your jet lag?"

I sighed.

"I'll survive the old guy somehow."

"We never introduced ourselves," he said with a shy smile.

"I'm Sarah."

We stopped on the pavement, eyes connecting for a moment before he spoke.

"I'm Iain. It was a pleasure meeting you, Sarah from New York."

"You too, Iain from…here." I looked around and made a model-like gesture with my hand. He laughed before disappearing into a door in the lobby.

My voice, the one that didn't use words, deep inside me said there was something about Fish Sandwich Guy. I ignored her.

CHAPTER TWENTY-NINE

"You only benefit from the magic of new beginnings if you are brave enough to start over." -Joan Goode

The large auditorium reminded me of Ross Hall at Oakville State where I had Dr. Morton for Biology. Employees filed in, extra cheerful to be socializing rather than sitting at a desk. The New Yorkers were missing. I could imagine Samantha skipping a meeting, but not Ethan and Raj.

"Hi," Joan said. I flashed a fake smile. "Can I sit with you?" Before I could respond, the awkward girl in over-sized glasses, white leotards, and a burnt orange tunic plopped into the chair next to mine. "I am nervous."

"Why?"

She sat near me during the HR orientation, not giving me a moment of peace with her questions about what it's like to fly over the ocean. Joan had never left Berrell.

"The auditorium is large. We never have conferences," Joan replied.

"Why start now?"

Joan shrugged. She organized her foldout desk with a notebook, pencil, and highlighter. I hoped note-taking wasn't required. It would feel like Biology 101 again. Joan gestured towards a gray-haired man in a tweed suit. Her mouth moved close to my ear.

"Mr. Wallace doesn't like Americans," she whispered. Did she forget who she was sitting with? I must have given her a dirty look because a look of panic crossed her face. "I meant no offense, Sarah. You're a lovely person. A smart person but —"

"Good afternoon," Mr. Wallace said into a microphone over the chatter. "Good afternoon." He repeated his welcome to the final employees entering the room.

My coworkers were still missing. I didn't care. Raj complained, Ethan flirted in a weird way, and Samantha chomped her gum like a horse eating peanut butter.

"Please take your seats, and we shall begin. A quick reminder to turn off your devices to avoid interruption."

"Did you have a question, Darcy?" Mr. Wallace asked. I failed to understand the woman's question, but I heard Mr. Wallace rambling just fine. Iain was correct. The CEO was a snooze fest. I opened my training materials to fake interest.

"He started our company at twenty," Joan said. "My father worked for his family." Joan grew quiet. She had her own memory lane, one I hoped she wouldn't drag me down.

I reached into my bag for *The Oprah Magazine*. After digging through my folders, I realized I left it in my suitcase. *Damn. No finding my life's purpose today.*

"Hello," the loudspeaker said.

My head shot up so fast, my neck popped. Why was fish sandwich guy on stage in a suit jacket? I looked around the room in a panic. No one seemed surprised to see my lunch buddy with the microphone.

"I hope our visitors have settled in well," he said. A few mumbles from the crowd. He took a step to the side of the podium, searching the crowd with his eyes until he found me. "I'm Iain Mackgale, your CEO and host for the next two hours. Why am I giving an introduction? You should know who writes your paycheck."

The crowd laughed. I sank into my seat like sand in a sinkhole.

Iain Mackgale is the CEO? I had lunch with the CEO? Wait. I ran into the CEO and ruined his fish sandwich. My level of freak out caused my exhaustion to disappear. I couldn't believe I told him how weird I found Berrell or how boring I found the conference. I didn't make it sound that bad, did I?

Yes, I did.

Iain's eyes burned into mine from the stage at an intensity someone had to notice but didn't. He was mocking me in front of everyone. Had I ever been more embarrassed? Not even days of the week underwear could top this one.

"This week I want you to dig deep and come up with the solutions for some of our greatest challenges." Iain flipped through pages on the podium. "We have an Inbox for suggestive improvements. Senior leadership and I select what we believe to be the most business-critical regarding operation and cost. It appears Gregory has the teams arranged."

Iain moved with confidence on stage, microphone in hand. Fish sandwich guy was supposed to be a normal employee, like Richard, the buyer, or Enzo, the personal assistant.

"When you receive your team assignment, don't think there has been a mistake if you're outside your field. We need fresh perspectives on daily operations."

Iain spent several minutes explaining how to calculate cost savings. He had an example in his presentation, which displayed the breakdown of a task divided by the wage the employee earned. The equations had the room lost.

"We need a numbers person—an engineer." He scanned the crowd. "Sarah Margo from New York City." I never told him my last name. He ascended the stage stairs into the aisle with his microphone like a game show host. He stood at the end of my row, three seats from me. "Can you calculate the cost savings for example two?"

I studied the PowerPoint slide on the wall, nerves in

154

complete freak out mode. *Please God, let the math find its way into my brain.*

"The new procedure takes two hours less a day. The division operates every day. Two times seven days is fourteen. There are three employees in the department doing less work. Fourteen times three is forty-two. The average wage per hour in U.S. dollars is $27.75. Total hours times average wage would be your cost savings for the week."

The crowd grew quiet, all eyes on the CEO and the dumbass who had no clue about her lunch buddy.

"Which would be?" Iain waited, microphone up to his mouth, the crowd curious if I knew the answer to the million dollar question.

"Um…$1,165.50."

The crowd took a deep breath when I rattled off the number. Iain smiled. He knew the answer too.

"Well done! Sarah Margo, from New York City, is the new point of contact for cost savings."

Iain returned to the stage.

I returned to my panic attack.

CHAPTER THIRTY

"The Americans were disinterested creatures, always yawning and using their phones. Why did we bother bringing them to Berrell?" -Davey Finch

During the summer of 1996, I went camping with Uncle Teddy, my cousin Diane, and her two best friends. I couldn't recall their names, but they were twins with rhyming names like Stacy and Tracy. After a terrible weekend of bug bites on top of poison ivy, I vowed I would never camp again. The Hotel Rowan wasn't too far from the great outdoors.

My room didn't have a climate control panel to adjust the temperature. A large vent blasted at random very warm or frigid air towards the bed. I tossed and turned until I realized sleep would not happen. When I tried to turn on the bedside lamp to read, the bulb blew. Kicking the scratchy comforter onto the floor, I went to the bathroom to flip on a light.

I studied my reflection in the mirror for a moment, pale from no sleep, before deciding to put on yoga pants. I needed to run.

"Where is your fitness facility?" I asked the hotel employee watering plants in the lobby. He held the watering can close to his chest in thought. "A place to run. It's raining outside." I nodded towards the dark window, splattered with water droplets.

"We don't offer a fitness facility, miss." He placed his watering can on an end table. "We do, however, offer a lovely breakfast of tea, toast, and jam."

"Thanks." I should have known a hotel with no television wouldn't have an elliptical. Tea and toast for breakfast again? The Hotel Rowan needed to take a lesson from Holiday Inn Express. People wanted cinnamon rolls and sausage links.

"Miss." I turned around. "You work for Mackgale-Berrell, right?" I nodded. "There's a fitness room on the first floor for employees. We park our vehicles near the entrance door in the alley."

I smiled.

"Enjoy your day, Miss."

The hotel shuttle wasn't hard to find, parked in an alley next to Mackgale-Berrell. I hoped the badge reader would give me access to the building. A loud click unlocked the door when I swiped. The lights were off. A sign with a running man and arrow illuminated the ceiling green. Why not have the word exit? It took me forever to understand what the signs meant at the airport.

I flipped the light switch to find Mackgale-Berrell had a nice fitness facility at the corporate office. My tired legs climbed onto the elliptical, unwilling to run before the sun was up. A loud grumble came from my stomach. Once again, I had no idea what meal to eat.

I had no desire to return to Berrell after this week. The hotel sucked. The weather was worse than New York. I couldn't adjust to the time zone. No one talked to me, except for Joan, and she used me to ask questions about flying. Not to mention, I made a complete ass out of myself to the CEO, which was the main reason I couldn't sleep. I closed my eyes, a soothing breath into my nose, before picking up the pace.

Lay low. Finish out the week. Go home.

"Good morning, Sarah. You are starting your day early." Iain Mackgale closed the door behind him.

What the hell was he doing here?

I was on a carnival ride spinning to the point of sickness. I peeked over my shoulder, sweat beading on my forehead, and gave him a polite smile. Wisps of his reddish brown hair were damp from a recent shower. I continued to run like my work out was important. I risked another glance. He stepped onto a treadmill, index finger hovering over the settings. The man was even better in athletic clothes.

Nope, not phased by his hotness.

"Good morning, Iain." I returned my attention to the television playing on the wall. "I couldn't sleep."

He laughed. Why was he laughing? Did he know I found him attractive?

"What's so funny?" Please don't say you saw me checking out your nice chest. *What is wrong with me?*

"No one calls me Iain." The bottom of his shoes pounded against the machine, a reminder he was behind me. I felt self-conscious I wore my gray yoga pants—the ones which made my butt look extra chubby.

"That is your name, right?"

"According to this badge, yes." He paused. "It also says CEO." Our paces quickened as if trying to keep up with one another.

"Do you work out here every morning?" I asked. I couldn't see his face but heard him chuckle. He knew I wanted to change the subject. I made a mental note to join an all women's gym when I returned home.

"No. I prefer to run outdoors near my home, but it's raining," he said.

Iain slowed his pace to remove his ringing phone from his pocket. I risked a quick glance, our eyes met for a moment, and I felt annoyed. Did he always shower before he worked out?

"Mackgale." He answered his phone, listened for a moment, followed by an exaggerated sigh. "I am downstairs on the treadmill. Let's move the meeting earlier, around seven. We can remote from my conference room."

I couldn't handle anymore conversation with Iain Mackgale. Part of me feared I would get fired for my stupidity. The other part found the CEO captivating. Either way, the situation was dangerous.

While he continued to talk, I picked up my bag and left before his call ended.

CHAPTER THIRTY-ONE

"Who deals with more assholes? Me or toilet paper." -Jessa Turner

Each team had a project manager, ours was Alan Simpkins, who worked as an operations manager in Berrell. The short time I spent with him, he obsessed over how to impress Iain Mackgale, rather than discuss our project. We had three days. On Friday, we would present our data and proposal in front of everyone at corporate.

"It's almost lunch, Alan. Shouldn't we decide what everyone should do?" Jessa asked. Alan's jabbering mouth stopped. He narrowed his eyes at the beautiful secretary. "I emailed you the outline from Gregory."

Alan clicked on his laptop. "Jessa can be the historian. Richard and Seth can data mine. You and you can be available for when the others need help." Alan pointed at Christian and then to me. I shrugged when Christian shot me a weird look. What was I suppose to do? Alan didn't want the New Yorker or Londoner on his team.

"Do you understand what scalability means?" Alan asked me. I couldn't hide my bitch face.

"I do have an engineering degree." My tone was drier than the desert.

"From an American university." Alan looked at Richard and Seth who continued to work on their laptops. Christian coughed. Jessa giggled. "There is a difference."

For once, I kept my mouth shut. I didn't need to get fired for fighting with an operations manager at corporate. I was already on the CEO's radar. Iain knew my name. He saw my chubby butt in yoga pants.

I finished my real work while a manager, buyer, file clerk, language specialist, and a secretary tried to put together a project on scalability in manufacturing equipment. Who needs an engineer?

Besides, Iain Mackgale wasn't here to care if I didn't contribute to the group. As I was leaving the fitness facility, I overheard him say he was departing for France after his morning meeting. By the time he returned, I would be home.

"It has to be perfect," Alan said to the group. Alan dabbed at his moist dress shirt with a handkerchief. "Mr. Mackgale has high expectations."

It wasn't hot. Why was he so sweaty?

"How would you know?" Jessa asked. I took Richard and Seth's method and pretended to work. Christian propped his feet on the table. "You have never worked with him."

"I have watched his television appearances and have read every article written," Alan said on the defense.

I wanted to laugh at his response. During my childhood, I had watched *Aladdin* a dozen times. It didn't mean I knew him.

"He is a fusspot if you ask me. I filled in for his secretary last year," Jessa said. Richard and Seth stopped working to join the gossip.

"You did?"

"The worst week of my life. He had me ordering his dry cleaning and lunch. A smart, rich man like Mr. Mackgale with no woman?" Jessa looked in my direction.

Why did I feel guilty?

"Did you…" Alan panicked when Iain appeared in the doorway.

Our CEO overheard the entire conversation, but he stood unaffected with a hand in the pocket of his gray dress pants. He wore a blue sweater over his white dress shirt. I loved the way he looked in glasses—so smart and sophisticated. What was I thinking? What happened to France?

"I've received worse than fusspot." Iain bent to scroll through the work on Alan's laptop. "No, not feasible," he said to the operations manager. "Did you run the numbers by Sarah?"

"Who?" Alan scratched his head. Sweat poured down his face, and I hoped he had an extra shirt.

Iain turned towards me. "After lunch, educate Alan."

I nodded. Iain strolled out of our room like he owned the place.

When lunch came around, the group separated. Most went to Chipper's, a local seafood place, but no one invited me to tag along. I walked to The Bistro for two slices of mediocre pizza. Bad American food beat the unknown.

My feet hurried across the gray, stone street, arms wrapped across my chest to ward off the cold wind coming from the ocean a few blocks away.

Happy American tourists stepped out of The Bistro. Had they heard of the Bahamas? I stepped aside to allow an elderly woman with a walker and her husband to exit the restaurant. A man held the door. The couple disappeared into the street.

A shy smile crossed his face, mixed with conflict and relief. Why? I didn't know him to have an answer, but I couldn't take my eyes from his face. We stood on the threshold, world blurring into the dreary streets.

"What are we having today?" Iain asked in a soft voice.

I exhaled a deep breath.

"I'm boring. Pizza again."

"You are far from boring." We joined the long line. "I will try the corn…dog. Promise me you will run the company if I get sick?"

I laughed. Why was he here? He admitted to disliking American food yesterday.

"I promise as long as I get your pay." We shared a grin. Sticking out his hand, I shook it as if brokering a deal.

"Are you okay with me eating here?" Iain smirked. He was testing me. I left the gym without saying goodbye.

"It's a free country. I think."

Iain laughed. We stood in line with people chatting, kids screaming, fryers bubbling, and cash registers beeping. I looked at the menu again.

"Have you compiled your list?" Iain asked.

"My list?"

A woman pointed at Iain. Her friend whispered. He noticed the exchange but brushed it off. I was glad to be no one of importance.

"You promised me odd cultural differences."

We were next in line. Iain removed his glasses. The depth of his blue eyes could swallow me like the ocean surrounding us.

"You can't handle my level of brutal honesty." I scanned his satisfied face, unsure if he was joking.

"Try me."

CHAPTER THIRTY-TWO

"Do you want to know the worst part of the workday? It's the people. They are bloody awful." - Richard Newport

On Friday, hours before our presentation to corporate, Alan still would not allow the group to view the project files. It was clear the way he interrupted me he believed either women or Americans were idiots—maybe both. Whenever the group spoke, Alan started a rant about knowing senior leadership better than us.

"We will work through lunch today," Alan said.

His words ruined my day. What if Iain was at The Bistro? Then reality came around. I didn't want a relationship. Iain was out of my league. Why was I thinking about him?

Since Alan wouldn't allow me to have any part, I came up with my own figures based on my experience working at the Oakville Plant. I needed to contribute somehow.

"You're unrealistic with your calculations," he said after opening my email.

My eyes moved from my laptop to Alan. I left an email to Deana about new cat treats in the pantry on my screen.

"Everything has a life-cycle. Nothing goes on forever, and we must compensate for those variables. Equipment needs replaced," I said. People needed upgraded too, and Alan would've been my first choice.

"The two of you best agree. We present in an hour." Jessa gave us a warning look.

"Let's present Alan's proposal," Seth said. The guy spoke three words all week, too busy playing games on his phone.

We were getting roasted this afternoon. I couldn't wait to get home. After hitting send on my email, I shut my laptop and waited.

The thought of presenting a project created by Alan made my stomach sick. I glanced at our project manager. He loaded his files to the shared folder with victory on his face.

The first group to present did a project on transportation. Iain sat in the front row asking questions, verifying data, and assigning tasks to others for follow-up. The first group was near flawless, wearing matching t-shirts with a fictitious group name.

"Next group," the CFO said. The gray-haired man flipped through the notebook. Warren Wallace dressed as if it were 1965. "Alan Simpkins, I believe. Please introduce your group and what you are presenting."

"Hello," Alan said in his salesperson's voice. "We are presenting scalability of equipment in a manufacturing setting."

Our group stood on stage, also hearing the project results for the first time. As soon as Alan's figures illuminated the projector, I cringed. Alan had the face of someone getting promoted this afternoon.

Warren stood to get a better view of the figures.

"Alan, I worked in manufacturing prior to Mackgale-Berrell," Warren said. He adjusted his reading glasses. "What about the life-cycle of equipment? There are no figures for depreciation. You must account for failures, which lead to repair costs and replacements." Warren scanned our group. "Did anyone research?"

Iain tapped his pen against his portfolio. I made the mistake of making eye contact. The CEO stood up. I hoped my panicked face was enough to make him not single me out. With his arms crossed, Iain whispered to Warren.

"Your topic was scalability as in the capacity to change in size or scale. Let's put your project on hold. I would like to see this group in my office at six," Iain said.

A few people whispered in the audience.

Iain returned to his chair, attention focused on his notebook. Warren called the next group. Our team did the walk of shame back to our seats. Although I sat several rows away, I had the perfect view of Iain texting on his phone. He was pissed.

Iain Mackgale had an office fit for a CEO, furnished with a hand-carved wood desk next to a ten-person conference table. Framed awards lined the wall over a black, leather couch, which offered a perfect view of The Hotel Rowan. Behind the door hung a dry cleaning bag and dress shoes.

"If we get sacked, I will claw your beady-eyes out," Jessa told our project leader.

Alan looked terrified, his skin clammy and greenish. He kept quiet. I knew his plan—throw us under the bus and save himself.

At exactly six, Iain came into his office and closed the door. He walked to his desk without a glance at the people occupying the chairs. Alan cleared his throat. I had heard our CEO arrived to work before sunrise and stayed until sunset. Today was no exception. He looked tired.

"Your group had one week." He stood at the front of the conference table observing us. "We spent an afternoon going over data documentation and the expectation. Did any of you pay attention?" Jessa spoke, but Iain held up his hand. "I will not ask for an explanation. I don't have time for scapegoating." He cleaned his glasses on his sweater. "The senior team hand-selected this group based on your skill sets. I am disappointed. To spend valuable time in front of senior leadership is an opportunity many do not earn. You will go back to your regular roles and complete this project." Alan moved his hand as if to ask a question, but decided against it. "I want it emailed by Friday next. Your managers will follow-up."

Iain went to his desk to retrieve a folder. Looking up at us with an irritated look, he added, "Your continued employment with Mackgale-Berrell depends upon what I receive." Iain took his dry cleaning off the back of the door and left.

"Bloody fusspot," Jessa said. The group remained at the table, stunned. "I hope you're happy, Alan. We are all getting sacked."

"Excuse me," I said to the group. "I have a flight to catch."

I needed New York City. My desire to impress the CEO diminished—saving my job was my only concern.

CHAPTER THIRTY-THREE

"We were sacked. The entire bloody team." -Alan Simpkins

I had the best chance out of my group to come up with a project good enough to save my job. I couldn't recall a time where I was this stressed. The tip of my finger traced the numbers in the Excel spreadsheet, ones I had checked ten times. A knock on my door startled me from my work daze. I closed my laptop and wrapped my robe tighter.

On the other side of the door, Deana clutched a large, brown bag of Chinese food. She hurried past me to the kitchen cabinet where she helped herself to a bowl.

"What? I don't eat rice from containers." She continued to scoop fried rice. "You haven't returned my calls or texts. You landed on Saturday. It's Wednesday."

"Sorry. Last week was terrible. I am so behind." I pointed to my laptop on the kitchen table.

"That sucks," Deana said. She offered me a bite of her second egg roll. I shook my head no. "Come out with us. You need a break." A chunk of egg roll fell out of her mouth. I grimaced.

"I can't tonight. There is a large possibility I will lose my job. It's a long story."

I changed my mind about the Chinese. Deana handed me a bowl and a fork. I was much too Midwestern to master chopsticks.

"When is your work due?" Deana rummaged through the brown takeout bag for more duck sauce.

"Friday. The project needs to be completed by tomorrow. Berrell is several hours ahead of us." I stuffed my mouth with sweet and sour chicken. Deana smiled. "I missed New York City food. I might go out this weekend if I'm employed."

"What will you do if you get fired?" Deana packed up her Chinese to take next door. Her check-to-make-sure-Sarah-is-alive duty fulfilled.

"Move back home and become a spinster." The thought of being almost thirty in my childhood bedroom made me cringe.

Deana laughed. "The spinster part is your choice. Men are always interested." She clutched her food bag like a new baby.

"You sound like my Aunt Gina." I opened my laptop to hear its familiar chime on the log-in screen.

"You give no one a chance. What about Derrick or Jeremy?" Deana waved at me like I wasn't paying attention.

"Derek wanted a fling. Been there, done that. No thanks." I typed my password. "Jeremy…what can I say about him?"

"There's nothing wrong with Jeremy," she said. I shrugged. Maybe not, but I wasn't interested. Jeremy excited me as much as sugar-free jello. One of her hands went to her hip. "You haven't had a boyfriend since I have known you. Should I remind you of your age?"

"Nope, my aunt did at Christmas. Apparently, I am almost thirty."

Deana sighed. She realized I wouldn't like any of her man choices.

Please give up on me.

On Thursday, I submitted my project via email to Iain Mackgale's secretary. When Friday afternoon arrived, I still had no response. I checked the spelling of the email address fifteen times to be sure. Did I expect an immediate response? Logically no, but the thought of getting fired had me crazy. I couldn't sleep, even after taking enough Benadryl to sedate a rhino.

At four o'clock, Debbie stopped in my office to say she wanted to see me before I left. The cheesesteak from lunch balled up into a knot inside my stomach. A mental image of me unloading a moving truck at my dad's appeared in my head.

Debbie motioned for me to sit in a chair. She argued with her teenager on the phone over video games. It seemed the kid won the argument. Tossing her cell phone into her purse, she studied me for a moment.

"What happened in Berrell?" Debbie leaned forward, hands folded on her giant calendar. From her freckled, middle-aged face to her cigarette smelling office, there was nothing I liked about my boss. I didn't even like her name. She had single-handedly ruined the name Debbie for me.

"I had a very arrogant project manager. He wouldn't take anyone's feedback. When it came time to present—"

"Did you say something to him?" Debbie unfolded her hands and tapped her red, fake nails on the desk.

"Yes—"

"Did you ask probing questions to understand his position?"

I sunk deeper into the office chair.

"He wanted to impress senior leadership." None of us could persuade the self-interested jerk. "Alan was—"

"This is a big opportunity for you. Engineers are not great communicators, but you need to try if you're representing our department at home office." Debbie licked her lips, followed by an audible smack. "You will not be going next time. We can discuss your actions during your review." I stood up to leave, relieved I wasn't terminated. Debbie snapped her fingers to get my attention. "Mr. Mackgale's secretary emailed me about your presentation. It appears it was acceptable."

CHAPTER THIRTY-FOUR

"I asked Deana out a dozen times. She tells me to meet her at the bar. It's a set-up with her friend, although the girl has a gay boyfriend." -Stan Stinger

The bar, walking distance from my apartment, had an Irish name no one could remember. I wore my favorite jeans, boots, and a plum sweater. The bar didn't have a sign or tourists, only a wooden door, locals, and a blacked out window.

I pulled the handle to reveal the same scene on Wednesday nights. Random locals filled the fifteen scattered tables. A group of guys and a skinny redhead played at one of the two pool tables, next to the single restroom and broken dart board. Mark, Deana's boyfriend, tended bar with the owner, Roxanne, who Deana didn't like.

Deana hugged my neck while holding a bottle of light beer. Cassie waved and returned her attention to Steve, who always had the funniest stories.

"Still employed?" Deana gazed at me with her arms around my neck, her cold beer resting against my back.

A guy in a jean jacket played a Nirvana song on the digital jukebox. The song took me back to junior high, to Jett. He loved grunge music. In high school, he formed a band. Bethany and I went to see them play at the theater downtown. Jett pretended not to know us. Even though I had a boyfriend, I was crushed. I looked much better in eleventh grade than I did in sixth.

"For now."

Deana lead me towards a table, arm around my neck.

This wasn't her first beer.

"You have to meet Stan," Deana whispered into my ear, lips bumping into my lobe. I gave her an irritated glance. She giggled.

His anticipating eyes said set-up, and I groaned.

Dark brown hair, decent build, and nice teeth—he was most men in New York City. Deana introduced us. I pulled out a chair, and she abandoned me with a stranger. My meddling friend waved from the bar where she socialized with her boyfriend.

Stan worked on Wall Street. Deana must have thought two intelligent people with nerdy jobs would hit it off.

Wrong.

I developed a bad habit in elementary school of making mental tallies when I suffered from boredom. Today's mental tally involved the phrase, *Awesome Sauce*. Stan said it seven times.

I told him my profession. *Awesome Sauce*. He asked if I lived in Manhattan. *Awesome Sauce*. Stan grew up in the Northeast. I grew up in the Midwest. *Awesome Sauce*. When I was ready to explode from *Awesome Sauce*, Alex came through the door like a guardian angel. I waved like an excited diva. He returned the wave, confused by my enthusiasm.

"Hey babe," I said. The wooden chair fell over when I stood. I hugged my friend. He glanced at Stan. Alex kissed my lips hard, hands grasping the side of my head. When he released me, he grinned.

"Sorry. Work kept me. I am yours now," Alex said.

Stan narrowed his eyes at my gorgeous boyfriend. What was I supposed to do? I left my phone at my apartment, which eliminated faking an emergency.

Alex unbuttoned his jacket to reveal his tight button-up and skinny jeans. The tips of his perfect hair stood up with gel.

"You promised me a game of pool last night." I motioned to the empty pool table like a model at a car and camper show.

"Did I?" Alex enjoyed the game too much.

"Yep. Over at my apartment where you stayed— remember?" I picked my wristlet up from the table.

"Right. How could I forget? Shall we?" Alex threaded my hand into the crook of his arm, then flashed me an awkward grin. We turned towards the pool table.

"It was nice chatting with you, Stan." I smiled over my shoulder.

"Real smooth," Alex whispered at the pool table.

"Maybe he thinks we are together," I whispered back. Alex released my arm and stepped back in shock. He over-dramatized the situation.

I racked the balls. Stan wouldn't stop watching us.

"Honey, no one thinks we are together." Alex stood still. "Is now a bad time to tell you I've never played pool?" He leaned on his pool stick with a contagious smile.

"Is that the look you give your male conquests?" We stood face-to-face, pool sticks in hand. What a shame Alex didn't like women.

"Is it working?" Alex brushed a strand of hair from my cheek. "Let's get out of here." I swallowed hard. "Deana honey," he yelled at our friend by the bar. "Sarah and I are leaving."

She looked confused but waved while continuing her conversation with Mark and his friends. Their names were Heath and Ramon. Deana had tried setting me up with them too.

I didn't say goodbye to Stan.

Once outside, Alex and I walked towards my apartment. We were quiet for a few minutes, only the sound of random cars and scurrying rodents surrounded us.

"Thanks for rescuing me. I hope I didn't ruin your night."

Alex put his arm around me. "What are friends for? Besides, did you see his shoes?"

I laughed. I hadn't seen his shoes. No part of me was interested in Stan Stinger, the Wall Street guy, from New Jersey. In all honesty, Stan was a decent guy. Part of me wanted a relationship. Who wouldn't want someone special? But every time my inner voice said no. Shoes didn't matter. Career irrelevant. I never arrived at the part of caring about the little details. The answer was already no. I wondered for a moment if I needed therapy and laughed at the irony.

"If you're not ready for a relationship, you're not ready. Okay?" I nodded, grateful someone understood. "Sometimes people prefer dating more casual—I do." Alex stopped in the street to look at my face. "You are..." He stopped talking when I winced. "How long has it been, Sarah?"

"Five years." I winced once more. Alex screeched so loud I put my hands over my ears.

"I apologize for screaming. I'm shocked." Alex checked the time on his phone, putting it back in his pocket. I made the no worries hand gesture. We stood in front of my building like a scene from a romantic comedy, except I wouldn't be inviting the guy in for coffee.

"Goodnight, Alex. Thanks for walking me home." My keys were crammed into my wristlet. "Are you heading home?"

His grin illuminated the darkness in the street. "Honey, my night hasn't even begun."

On Sunday evening, I did laundry, changed my sheets, and brushed the cat—against his will. The rest of the day's sunlight shone through the large window onto the hardwood floor. The cat sunbathed until the microwave beeped. My furry friend wanted his share of my dinner. After the ambush setup, I didn't want to leave. Microwaveable macaroni was fine. Running into Stan would be embarrassing since I ditched him for a gay guy.

My cell phone rang.

"You home?" Deana had a mouthful of food.

"Yeah. Why?"

The call disconnected. Three seconds later, she knocked. When I opened the door, Deana was in pajamas shoveling popcorn into her mouth from a metal mixing bowl.

"Turn it to channel thirteen," Deana demanded. She plopped onto my clean linens.

"Don't you have a television?" I knew the answer—a 1980s cabinetry model her parents gave her two years ago. Deana carried on about how vintage it looked.

"Stopped working last month." I offered her the remote, which she snatched and pointed at the television. "I watch my show at Mark's place, but he is working tonight."

"Don't you have a key?"

A catchy dog food advertisement with a Pomeranian playing a baby grand piano played when Deana stopped at her channel.

"No. We don't do keys." She fished in her bowl for chocolate chips mixed into the popcorn. The no key policy seemed like Mark's idea. I had never had a relationship serious enough to discuss keys.

"This is the show?" I raised an eyebrow when the recap displayed a European country manor with a guy wearing a crown. "This is a period drama. You are more of a reality television with drag queens kind of girl."

"You haven't seen *Cross Hill Manor*?" I shook my head no. "Oh my God, Sarah Margo. It is the hottest show right now." Her eyes fixated on the television. "Prince Dirkin is hot. He's played by Drew McGrew—the guy from the zombie show. You do know Drew McGrew?"

"No. I watch little television." She ignored my lack of coolness.

"Prince Dirkin never used to spend time at his country estate until he fell in love with his kitchen maid, Charlotte. They cannot be together because Prince Dirkin's father will disinherit him. Charlotte just found out she is pregnant, and her father ends up murdered." Deana spoke as if this was historical fact rather than a fictional show.

"This sounds so dumb."

She threw my pillow and missed me. There were several requests in my email I had not completed. *Cross Hill Manor* started, Deana stopped talking, and I worked.

An instant message dialog box appeared on my screen. I sighed, readying myself for Debbie's lecture on being more productive during the week. When I clicked the blinking message, it was not my boss. Instant messages through our system displayed the employee's name, a photo (badge or personal), and the employee's title.

Iain Mackgale, Chief Executive Officer

The picture was neither a badge photo nor a personal photo, but a nice professional headshot in a black designer suit.

Iain: Working on a Sunday?

My heartbeat pounded to a speed faster than a hummingbird. Deana munched on her snack, too enthralled in *Cross Hill Manor* to care. What should I do? I couldn't ignore him. What should I say? Maybe answer his question.

Me: Playing catch-up.

Iain: I hope you're not cross with me over the project.

Me: No, not your fault.

Iain: I found your proposal impressive. Your manager should have informed you we are using it for the leadership round table.

Debbie gave me the impression I was lucky to have a job still. This wasn't the first time she lied or mislead someone.

Me: Thanks.

Deana offered me her mixing bowl when she caught me staring at her over my laptop. I shook my head no. Deana returned to the television.

Iain: I have a high-level project in Berrell. Interested?

I wasn't interested. The petty side of me wanted to stick it to Debbie for lying. She said I would never return to Berrell.

Me: Yes.

Iain: I will see you soon.

He went offline.

Deana's cell phone played an upbeat ringtone. She answered the call, eyes on the television. A man shouted in the hall. Deana blinked a tear down her cheek, said okay, tossed the phone on my bed, and left my apartment. I had never seen Deana upset in the five years we had been friends. I did not want to eavesdrop, so I continued to stay at my kitchen table. When I heard Deana scream, I ran to the door.

"Is everything okay?" Mark's rage frightened me.

"Your friend is a phony. She uses men for money." Mark raised his voice. I stepped closer to my door. "Did you know her name isn't Deana Dash? It is Heather Ann Murphy. She's had plastic surgery. Did she tell you about her work?"

I didn't know what to say. So what if Deana changed her name? If she had work done, whatever. This couldn't be the reason he was mad.

"He's with someone else." Deana sobbed. "He doesn't want me."

"You're pissed I'm onto your games. I'm out of here."

Deana went into her apartment and slammed the door. Mark stomped down the stairs. Mrs. Martinez opened her door to see the commotion but closed it when the hall emptied. I entered Deana's apartment without knocking to find her sobbing into a pillow on the bed. My throat tightened as I recalled Bethany five years ago.

I couldn't lose Deana.

"I am sorry," I whispered.

When she rolled over, her face was swollen from crying. Her mascara stained everything it touched.

"If you don't want to be friends anymore, I understand." Deana wiped her snotty nose on her sleeve.

"Because your birth name is Heather? That's ridiculous!" I touched her hand, and she held mine. "We are best friends."

"Can we be spinsters together?"

I laughed. "Absolutely."

CHAPTER THIRTY-FIVE

"I grew up on a farm. City life was never for me,
but I needed the money and Oakville didn't have jobs." -
Tim Sanders

Debbie insisted on seven o'clock morning meetings. I took a
sip of coffee, sank into my typical seat next to Ethan, relieved
I wasn't the one presenting. An unexpected, familiar face
entered the conference room. He shook hands with Arjun.
Debbie introduced Tim Sanders. What was he doing in New
York City?

"Hello, Sarah," he said. I stood to greet Tim, who bear
hugged me. "It's been a long time."

Someone needed to tell the man people don't hug in the big city.

"Five years." The room watched us, not realizing Tim used
to be my boss.

When Iain Mackgale bought my former company, he sold
the Oakville plant. I understood why. Even when I worked
there, the plant hemorrhaged money.

"Your dad was great at the Oakville Engineering Convention
downtown."

Tim had gained a few gray hairs and pounds but hadn't
changed. He reminded me of home, and the feeling warmed
me inside.

"I went too. He was brilliant, but I am biased. Who knew
someone could make heat transfer sound so exciting?" Even

though my dad taught at the university, he was nervous lecturing for a professional conference. Afterward, we stuffed our faces at the all-you-can-eat steak buffet before returning to our little brick house.

Debbie hurried everyone into the room. Once she shut the door, our group faced forward. We were ready to get this meeting over. No one seemed to care about Tim or why he was present.

"What's everyone working on this week?" Debbie asked. She tugged at her olive green skirt to hide her lacy slip, which always showed.

Raj presented an automotive project, involving six types of windshield wiper blades tested on three different windshields. He had the products broken down by how they performed in the rain, snow, and normal conditions.

"Raj," Debbie said in her typical irritating tone. "I asked for this week, not what you have been doing the past three months." Raj looked defeated. He worked hard for the client.

"It's great, Raj," I said. "The models you constructed are top-notch."

Debbie cocked her head to the side and exhaled.

"I agree," Tim said.

Debbie flashed a fake smile at Tim, one of those half-ass trying to be professional ones.

"Does everyone know Tim Sanders from our former Oakville Plant?" Debbie crossed her arms. A few people nodded. "Since Mackgale-Berrell has sold the Oakville plant, Tim has taken the Senior Operations position over this department."

I restrained myself from jumping out of my seat in celebration. Debbie now reported to Tim, who unlike Debbie, was an engineer and a great manager.

"Debbie, I'd be happy to speak about my transfer." Tim walked to the front where Raj disconnected his laptop from the projector. "Since our company has been acquired by Mackgale-Berrell, we are seeing larger and more diverse projects—manufacturing, automotive, corporate, and so on. By the end of next year, our company will be the largest consulting firm in the world. There will be no matter of business we can't handle. Our engineering division will grow. The great news is this means big opportunities for you." The room filled with excited chatter. A few months ago, we thought we'd be out of a job.

"So we aren't closing?" Luke asked.

"No. I will spearhead the growth in our department and assemble the best teams for our major accounts." Tim handed out a packet. "Raj, Ethan, Luke, and Sarah—I will rely on your seniority to help me through this transition. You all will be going to home office with me next month for three weeks."

Debbie interrupted Tim. "Sarah cannot go to home office. There was an incident." She made a face of pretend disappointment.

"It looks like she will be going," Tim said to Debbie. The queen wasn't used to being challenged. I'd pay the price of jet lag to see Debbie knocked off her high horse. "I received an email from Iain Mackgale's assistant this morning."

Three missed calls from my dad. I had missed our usual Saturday morning chat. Scrolling through my contacts, I searched for his cell phone number. The sound of travelers rushing to and fro filled the airport with chaotic noise. The wheeled carry-on I tugged behind me added to the commotion. He answered on the first ring.

"Hey, Dad!"

"Where are you? It's noisy."

"London. Sorry. I forgot to tell you I switched to an earlier flight to adjust to the time zone change." My loud voice earned a dirty look from the older woman next to me.

"I'm glad you called me back." Wind rustled against the phone. "I'm driving to Ted's. Call me soon to tell me about your trip—day or night."

"I'm staying at The Hotel Rowan again. I love you, Dad." Every time we talked, I missed him and Oakville.

"I love you. Please be careful."

After our call ended, I placed my phone in the zipper pocket of my carry-on. My stomach grumbled, but I didn't have time to eat. The flight itself wasn't long. The process of waiting, boarding, and unloading consumed the time.

Once at the terminal, I sat in a blue chair near the window. A man searched for an outlet to charge his phone. He climbed under a bench and let out a helpless cry when his device died.

An airport employee called sections, even though only eight people were waiting for this flight. When it was my turn to board, I followed the attendant and another passenger out a door, to the runway where our small plane sat ready to fly us to the English Channel.

I sat in my seat, near the window, lights sparkling in the distance from whatever was nearby. An overweight woman plopped into the spot next to me with an erotica novel—the kind with a shirtless man on the cover. After a few disturbing moans and hearing *get it girl* three times, I put on my headphones and closed my eyes.

A short time later, the bump of the plane landing woke me up. The night sky twinkled on the tarmac in Berrell as we taxied to the airport terminal not much bigger than a single-family home. I exited the cabin, hair blowing in the salt water tainted breeze.

An airport employee waited near the entrance for the eight passengers to arrive on the last flight of the night. "Do you need transportation to your lodgings?" he asked the exhausted group.

"Yes," I replied.

"I need a lift," a man said.

I climbed into an old van with two strangers en route to The Hotel Rowan. The worn shocks felt every bump and turn. My stomach ached like I'd been at an amusement park. I clutched the arm rest, focusing my attention on the moon illuminating the tall blades of grass near the rocky coast. After a few minutes, the sleepy lights of Berrell City lit up the sky.

The driver stopped outside the hotel and passed my bags to the porter. The others stayed in the van. Where were they staying? I looked down the street, irritated at the possibility a modern hotel with a shower and a bed bigger than a cot existed.

"Welcome back, Miss Margo," the porter said. I followed him into the floral lobby to get my room key.

"I am glad to be back."

The porter turned on the light, placed my bags inside, and asked me if I needed anything. I said no, and he left.

A double bed with a white, fluffy duvet and pillows sat in the middle of the floor. On the wall, a flat-screen television next to a wooden desk and two armchairs. I peeked into the bathroom. No shower.

"You can't have it all," I muttered.

My accommodations had improved. Maybe luck. Perhaps the others complained. Whatever the reason, I wasn't telling anyone I had a big bed and flat-screen. I kicked off my running shoes and plopped onto the bed with my phone.

Three missed calls.

Alex wanted me to go to the gay bar with them. I sighed. The music was too loud for conversation. Not to mention, I had a lady fan I didn't want.

To my surprise, it was an Oakville area code—my mother. Every time she called, I felt nervous. No matter how many times I told myself I am a grown woman, anxiety still surged through my body. How did she have power over me decades later? The last time she called, a year ago, she asked for three thousand dollars. When I told her I didn't have the money because living in New York was expensive, she called me a liar and recited her typical *your father promised to always take care of me.* I'm sure he did in 1979. She ended their marriage. How could she not understand reality? When I reminded her, she called me a colorful name and hung up.

I couldn't shake the restless feeling, but I was done with drama. Over five years ago, I left it behind. Lori Margo would not bring her issues into my life. My finger hovered over my phone until I pressed delete and chose my happiness over her.

CHAPTER THIRTY-SIX

"Long locks of hair rippled in the misty wind. The crashing waves thrashed near her figure. I couldn't determine who held more power—the girl or the sea." - Iain Mackgale

Tim waved his hand in front of my laptop screen with his bag over his shoulder to leave. I pulled out my earbud and smiled. Raj stood behind him, not happy to have two weeks left in Berrell.

"We are doing an early dinner," Tim said as he motioned to Ethan to join us at my workspace in the conference room. "Chipper's."

Raj made a look of disgust.

"Another time, Tim." I shut my laptop and unplugged my power cable. "I am sightseeing. Julia and Claire recommended a place called William's Folly."

According to my coworkers, the breathtaking view of the sea attracted tourists from all over the world.

"I am surprised you're taking their advice," Tim said in hushed tones.

Julia and Claire were the adult Berrell versions of Adrianna and Mindy from sixth grade—complete bitches. They were the assistants assigned to babysit the Americans; neither of them liked us.

"Only on sightseeing," I said. Tim grinned. "You guys have

fun. I will see you tomorrow." I turned to Ethan as I exited our conference room, which we dubbed Team USA's office. "Can you email me the Jasper files?" He nodded. I hurried out the door before Ethan asked to join me.

Years ago, walking a mile along dim streets would have scared me. New York City had made me tougher and more comfortable with pepper spray. After I passed the last building on the street, I came across the worn, bronze sign for William's Folly. Claire said it was best at night. I was having a hard time understanding why. Only one street lamp illuminated a group of benches. The cloud-covered moon gave enough light to see the sidewalk. I couldn't see an amazing ocean view as Julia said.

Water crashed—loud in the distance—somewhere in the darkness. I left the sidewalk, grass squishing beneath my feet. The intensity increased, and I found myself intoxicated with the unusual building rhythm. With each step, the sea called my name.

"Sarah!"

I moved quicker, exhilarated by the heightening of my senses. The wind blew harder, and droplets of water coated my skin. I inhaled a deep breath; salt cleared my sinuses. Breathing became easy. I was weightless. Mist surrounded my body, strands of hair whipped in every direction as I stood like a sea goddess in the middle of a dream.

"Sarah!"

The voice felt familiar, but it wasn't coming from the sea. My magical experience halted when I turned around to see Iain Mackgale running full speed towards me in a dress shirt and pants. The sound of water intensified into a rumble, then to roaring thunder.

Iain Mackgale tackled me at full speed onto the ground, rolling through wet, rocky soil. He rolled his weight on top of me, ripping the back of my dress shirt with his hand. He held me tight.

In a half second, I had no time to question his actions, because the noise grew and exploded into a wall of salt water. Even with Iain's weight, the water carried us several feet through gritty rocks and dirt, leaving us on the cliff.

Silence, except for trickling water, provided a strange contrast from the moment prior. I turned my head to gag the fishy, salt water out of my mouth. No longer a sea goddess but a nasty, wet mess with my disheveled CEO on top.

"My God, are you trying to kill yourself?" His eyes blazed, saltwater dripped from his nose to my cheek. Iain hadn't been in the office this week.

I cried.

"Please, don't cry. I didn't mean to raise my voice. A few more steps and you'd be in the sea, rather than filthy and soaked," he said with his hands holding the sides of my face, every pound of his weight on me.

"They said the view is amazing after dark. I shouldn't have listened to those bitches," I said in between girlish sobs. My stomach ached like a hard punch.

"The view is quite amazing, but from a distance in the daylight." Iain removed himself from me, offering his hand. Once on my shaky feet, I stumbled into Iain as his wet, sandy arm wrapped around my back. "Every seven minutes water builds in the caverns below the cliff. When the pressure becomes too much, seawater rushes over this point. There are many local legends involving this cliff. William Berrell lost his life in 1799 in this spot, hence the name William's Folly." We walked as if coming out of war, arms wrapped around each other's back, towards the benches near the sidewalk. "Tell me who told you."

A darkness came over his face. The tips of his fingers brushed sand from my cheek. I couldn't find the words, which were somewhere in his blue eyes. Maybe it hadn't clicked in my head how close I had been to my own foolish demise. I couldn't believe Claire and Julia hated us enough to harm me. Mean girls never grow up.

"No," I said after a moment. "I am embarrassed." How did I not notice the word folly in William's Folly? I felt dumb being rescued by Iain Mackgale, who no longer looked sophisticated, but homeless. Although, the wet shirt plastered to his chest was a nice sight. "How did you know I was here?"

"I live outside the city and travel this road home," he replied.

"Thank you." I risked a glance at his face. He returned my gratitude with a shy grin.

"My pleasure. Besides, I can't remember the last time I went sea bathing after dark in clothes." Iain grinned with satisfaction.

My cheeks burned with a level of embarrassment only he could accomplish. We stopped on the sidewalk near his car, examining each other in the light from the street lamp. Two buttons from my blouse disappeared in the chaos. My nude bra showed.

"Would you like to come home with me, change and have supper? I'm sure I have something you can wear. Or I could take you to the hotel if you prefer?"

"I can't get in your car." I lifted my dripping arms. A clump of seaweed fell to the pavement.

"We have to drive, regardless. I don't plan to walk." Iain glanced at his Lexus and cringed. "Do you enjoy duck?"

"Yes." I lied.

"Please have supper with me. I want to be certain you're okay."

The way he offered made it impossible to refuse. I nodded. He walked to the driver's side and took me off guard. Did men no longer open doors for a lady?

"Are you driving?" Iain grinned. He raised an eyebrow and waited for my response.

"No." I realized driver and passenger sides were opposite in Berrell. If I didn't feel like an idiot ten minutes ago, I did now.

"Sorry, I'm a fish out of water here."

"Literally," he said.

CHAPTER THIRTY-SEVEN

"Run a full dossier on Sarah Nicole Margo. If you discover anything suspicious, have a detail assigned to her when she returns to New York." -Nolan Martin

The Lexus left the city lights behind. Iain said he lived twelve kilometers from Berrell City. My brain struggled to remember how to convert to miles. I had been on this road a week earlier in a van with strangers. Iain passed the turnoff to the airport. A wooden sign etched *Rowan*, and below, *Dona Nobis Pacem* stood on the side of the road.

"What does the sign mean?"

Iain looked over at me, amused by my curiosity.

"Grant us peace. Rowan and Crossleigh fought most of the eighteenth century. The locals still hold a grudge." Iain downshifted when an animal scurried in front of the car.

"I have never heard of Crossleigh."

"It used to be a village east of Berrell City; now it's only an estate." Iain looked uncomfortable. "Many left the rural areas for opportunities in the city." He paused for a moment. "It's funny how places and people evolve. You like history?"

"I do."

My hometown didn't have a rich history. People showed up, said let's call this place Oakville, and nothing had changed other than a new gas station on King Street and some outlets on Regency Road.

A few minutes later we arrived at a large iron gate surrounded by a stone wall covered in greenery. I never considered Iain's private life, but by the look of the gate, he lived up to his CEO status. Unlike Dan and Gina's gated community, this gate had a small office to the side with two security guards. The guards opened the gate when they recognize the silver Lexus. My heart pounded in my chest although I wasn't sure why. Perhaps I didn't want to get fired.

Each piece of property looked to be a few acres, marked with a small number near each gate's call box. He punched in a code, the gate opened, and the Lexus proceeded down the driveway to a large one-story home, lit up and landscaped.

Iain drove to the back of the house and pulled into a three car garage. The back wall of the garage had racks of bikes, skis, and sporting equipment. When Iain pushed a button on his key ring, the garage door creaked close. I stepped out of the car, feeling more gross as the salt water dried. Iain held his phone to his ear.

"I'll need the Lexus cleaned tomorrow...salt water on leather." Iain smiled. "Don't ask." He motioned for me to follow him into the house. "No, you don't have to drive me. I will take the Merc."

"I am so sorry," I said.

He did a terrible job suppressing his amusement. We went through a small hallway, which led to a large living space.

"Never a dull moment with you." He paused, deep in thought. "Don't fret—my car needed a proper cleaning. Wait here."

He disappeared through double doors. A moment later, he handed me sweats, a long-sleeved t-shirt, and socks.

"Follow me." We walked through the kitchen into a hallway with several doors. "This is the guest room. Towels and toiletries should be in the linen closet. If you finish before I do, please make yourself at home." Flashing a polite smile, he disappeared into the hall.

I shut the door, running my hand along the white bed frame with yellow pintuck duvet. Above the headboard hung a painting of sunflowers, which added a feminine touch. I wondered if he hired a designer or had a girlfriend. My reflection stared back at me from the full-length mirror. The type who landed the Iains of the world weren't covered in dirt and sand. It didn't matter because I wasn't interested.

I wanted to jump up and down when I walked into the bathroom—an actual shower. The claw-footed bathtub at the hotel had lost its charm after the second night.

Hot water poured through my salty hair, leaving evidence of the sea on the shower floor. I hoped Iain had a housekeeper because the thought of him scrubbing my filth added to the humiliation.

The shower was heavenly. I wouldn't have another until I returned to New York in sixteen days. I dressed in over-sized sweats along with the white, long-sleeved t-shirt with the number six on the back. The front said *Bleed Rugby*.

I left the guest room to find Iain in the kitchen dressed in running pants and the same t-shirt, except he was number seven.

The duck and potatoes were served on porcelain plates next to formal silverware. Iain opened a bottle of champagne, retrieved two glasses from a cabinet, and poured. He turned around with a slight smile. We eyed each other for a moment in our casual clothes. Iain looked like a normal person, in his house, showered, and preparing dinner. I never thought about my coworkers outside of work.

"Would you like champagne?" He offered a flute with pink bubbly liquid "I have other options."

"I love champagne. Thank you." I accepted the drink.

He lifted his glass.

"To Sarah Margo not being swallowed by the sea." Iain grinned.

"To your weird Berrell sense of humor." I lifted my drink to toast. Our glasses brushed together with a slight clank as Iain laughed.

"Cheers."

He pulled out the chair at the breakfast bar for me to sit. The kitchen looked similar to an American kitchen with granite countertops, stainless steel, and maple cabinets.

"Do you have a cook?" The duck and potatoes tasted like fine restaurant quality. Iain was too busy to be a secret chef.

"My housekeeper cooks when I am in town."

"Does your housekeeper live here?" I regretted asking. My curiosity got the best of me. Iain didn't seem to mind.

"She leaves before I get home. That is the way I prefer it—my home is my escape from the outside world." Iain studied me with a fork full of potatoes. "Does that make me sound strange?"

"No. I love being home alone. Most days I have to tell my neighbor to leave. She doesn't like living by herself."

Iain refilled my glass. I savored one more small sip. There was a rule somewhere which stated don't get drunk with your CEO, but when would I ever drink champagne this expensive again?

"I try to buy most items from Berrell," Iain said after dinner. My face warmed when he caught me admiring an embroidered throw on his sectional. Iain grinned when a sock fell from the blanket.

"Sorry, I entertain little."

"I love this painting." I pointed to a painting of horses running through a village. Iain held his champagne in one hand, the other in his pocket. "There is something real about the village—it's extraordinary."

"I agree." Iain stood close, our attention on the horses.

"That's Crossleigh a hundred years ago." Our focus left the art when his phone rang on the entryway table.

"Don't mind me. I am the one crashing your free time." Tonight was a pity invite because I listened to the mean girls.

"I wouldn't call it free time." His tone changed when he answered his phone. "Mackgale…Are you serious?…Do you have any idea how this is affecting our reports?…The data will not populate…I have given them three days…This is business-critical…Okay, tomorrow at seven." He tossed the phone on the table. "I'm sorry."

"No need to apologize." He joined me next to his ottoman.

"My life is a chaotic mess. I feel uncomfortable when others take part." I had to stop myself from reaching up and touching his face. He looked so beautiful, so vulnerable.

"Are you having database troubles?" He gave me a look as if he found my question inappropriate. "I do work for Mackgale-Berrell. Anything you tell me stays between us."

"IT cannot seem to bridge the new databases, and they have been working on it for three days." He sighed in frustration. "We need the reports, but the data will not populate."

"SQL?"

"Are you familiar?" Iain asked

Am I familiar? Please, SQL was child's play.

I didn't want to overstep my boundaries. "Yes. I would love to help if I can."

When I volunteered, I assumed I would look at the issue tomorrow, but he led me to his home office next to the guest room where a large wood desk took up most of the room. One side had plants and photographs. On the other wall, built-in bookcases held first editions and trinkets—nothing about the cozy room said CEO.

Iain motioned for me to sit in his leather chair. He leaned

over me, too focused on powering up his laptop to notice his chest touched my shoulder. The smell of him was nice— scented deodorant and washed clothes. He stood up, crossed his arms, checked his watch, and waited for the login box to appear on the computer.

"I need to know the database names. Also, how you need the information to populate," I said, now in work mode. Iain spent the next ten minutes explaining what he needed. I took notes in a company notebook. "I have what I need. As far as the actual data, I won't be paying attention to the numbers, only linking databases."

"I trust you," he said. Iain turned towards me when he reached the door. "Would you like tea?"

"Sure." I was relieved he didn't offer alcohol.

Why did I offer to help? I should have gone back to the hotel, thanked him for dinner and the ride. Being around Iain Mackgale was comparable to playing with fire. I kept walking the line with him. I had dissed Berrell, the conferences, mistook his identity, bombed a project, looked like I wanted to kill myself, and now… I offered to fix the major problem a team of skilled people couldn't fix. What was I thinking? Yes, it was playing with fire, but I found myself to be the moth, attracted to the flame, whether I wanted to admit it or not.

This wasn't stupid boredom like Lee. I liked Iain, although I ignored reality. I had trouble seeing Iain as a successful businessman from a foreign place. I'd seen him eat a corn dog, work out, and microwave potatoes in sweatpants.

The door creaked open. He carried a tray with a full tea service. I watched him serve tea in floral patterned cups and matching saucers. Would it be bad to laugh?

"How do you take your tea?" He looked up from the tray.

"I'll have the same as you." I knew with-ice-and-sweet-enough-to-tranc-a-diabetic was not an option. He poured milk into the steaming cup of tea. The two items didn't go together.

"Do you mind if I work here?" Without waiting for an

answer, he produced another laptop from a bag and set up in the wing-backed chair near the bookcases.

Iain typed with a contemplative expression on his face. He removed his glasses and rubbed his eyes with his hand.

"I am finished," I said. The laptop displayed two o'clock.

"You fixed it?" Disbelief and relief were evident in his question.

"Yes, I did."

Take that IT department.

My legs were numb from sitting so long.

He did nothing to hide his eagerness, and once he saw the numbers, he looked up at me in amazement.

"You fixed our issue in three hours when IT couldn't in three days." He scrolled through the reports. "This is incredible. Thank you, Sarah." I loved the way he looked at me.

"No problem. I am glad it's fixed."

"David Larson is proficient in database management according to Warren," Iain remarked to himself.

"David Larson is an idiot. Sorry, I have no filter when I'm tired."

He stood. We were close, too close.

"Should I terminate him?" Iain's voice changed to cold and distant. "No need to answer. David is unacceptable." He clicked a pen in his hand. It is late." Iain strained to see his watch.

"I should get back to the hotel. We don't need an office scandal when I show up in the boss' clothes." I raised my arms. The sleeves of his rugby shirt hung off me.

We left his office and headed towards the garage.

"Scandal is the last thing I need," he mumbled.

He picked up his keys from the entry table. We returned to

the door we entered hours ago. Iain loaded me into his black Mercedes SUV and yawned when he backed out of the garage. "I am skipping my morning run."

"Me too." I yawned.

"I appreciate your help tonight. If I can ever help you, please ask," Iain said.

"You saved me from being fish food. It's the least I could do."

CHAPTER THIRTY-EIGHT

"The night I finally had the courage to tell Sarah I had feelings for her, she wasn't in her room. I knocked. No one answered." -Ethan Wyatt

Joan's constant rambling made the day drag on. Tim and Ethan helped the caterer set up trays for our lunch. We were in the main auditorium, and Tim invited anyone we worked with during our three weeks to eat with us.

"I love catered lunch. The New York office should visit more often," Joan said.

"It's Tim. He brings the party wherever he goes." Joan had trouble following my American slang. She did the same weird smile when she didn't understand.

"Do you leave tonight?" she asked.

"Tomorrow morning." I took a drink of my bottled water.

"I want to visit the New York office. If I do, will you show me around?"

I didn't answer Joan. Instead, my attention moved to the door where sunglasses and a navy suit entered. I had not laid eyes on him since the evening I visited William's Folly two weeks ago. Iain removed his shades, surveyed the room, and stopped his search. We shared one of those unspoken moments. His eyes said he rushed back to Berrell before I left. Was I crazy for considering such insanity?

"Don't be daft," Joan whispered in my ear. She gave me the

yeah-right-you-don't-know look. "He never dates, isn't friendly, and his parents would have you murdered."

"When you visit New York, we should go out," I said to Joan. Iain walked towards us; my gaze never left him. "My friends would love to meet you." My friends couldn't care less, but I didn't want Joan to continue talking about Iain.

"That would be brilliant." Joan showed more excitement than the rest of her coworkers combined. "Mum would be in shock if I found an American beau."

Iain sat in our row, three seats from us, and worked on his phone. Joan watched our CEO, wheels turning in her head.

"There's an away team opening. I saw a posting in the opportunities portal," I said.

"Oh, so soon. I'm a trifle nervous," Joan said.

Iain shook his head at Joan's remark.

"Lunch is ready," Tim said into a microphone. Someone remarked, and Tim laughed. "Do I look like I miss a meal?" Tim patted his stomach.

My phone buzzed in my bag. I couldn't imagine who would call me now. Deana wasn't up at seven in the morning. Alex didn't start until ten.

Unknown: Dinner tonight minus the sea bathing?

Iain typed on his phone, revealing nothing. He glanced my way, and our eyes connected. Joan was still contemplating her imaginary New York trip.

Me: Stalking HR records for my phone number?

Iain: A perk of the position. So?

Me: Pick me up at William's Folly at 7:30 pm?

Iain: Yes.

The remainder of the afternoon we finalized our projects from the past three weeks. With Tim in charge, our work was flawless. At five o'clock, he told the New York group to return to the hotel to pack. We would meet downstairs at seven in the morning to take the airport shuttle.

Once in my room, I changed into the only pair of jeans I had packed—the tight, dark denim Alex said made him reconsider his sexuality. When I pulled my hair out of a bun, it fell into soft waves. *Yeah, that never happens.* I looked date-worthy. This wasn't a date. What exactly would I call having dinner with my boss's boss's boss's boss? I heard Gina's Southern accent say, "It's called a bad idea."

Gina's fictional voice had a point. Why did Iain Mackgale keep spending time with me? Maybe he was a sleazy person who hooked up with secretaries and female coworkers. Perhaps he wanted me for my SQL powers or my mathematical expertise.

Looking at my watch, I knew I couldn't call Deana since most of her clients were in the afternoon. I didn't have time to think about Iain's intentions. I needed to start walking.

The mile walk felt great, even in boots. When I approached the bronze sign, William's Folly didn't have the majestic appeal it had two weeks prior. I shuttered thinking about what would have happened if Iain had not driven by. Thoughts of my demise disappeared when the Lexus pulled alongside the curb.

He opened the passenger side door with a brief pause to study my face. I gave him an exaggerated smile, and he laughed. His gorgeous face made me nervous. I slid into the car with my eyes on the windshield.

"You are quiet tonight," Iain said after a few minutes of silence. The dash lights illuminated our faces. His dark eyelashes were visible through his glasses.

"Tired. My jerk of a CEO insists we sit in a conference room discussing metrics all day."

He didn't laugh. I forgot my sense of humor didn't always translate.

"Metrics, please." Iain scoffed, amusement not only reached

his lips but his eyes. "You and Joanie were gossiping."

Thank God for the darkness because I flushed to the point my cheeks burned. I knew he heard Joan.

"She said your parents would murder me for talking to you." I hoped he would elaborate why Joanie would make such a comment. He didn't explain, only laughed.

"I wouldn't say they would go so far, but I exclude nothing with my parents." He navigated the dark road with years of experience.

I rubbed my clammy palms on my jeans. "Joan thought I was checking you out, which I wasn't." I needed to make it clear Joan had delusional thoughts.

"Interesting." He smirked, pleased with my girl talk confession.

The iron gate to his property opened. Iain put the Lexus in reverse, parking near the front door. The engine shut off, he looked at my hands folded on my lap and left the car to open my door. My boots stood on paver stones, under the night stars, wind blowing a cool breeze. Iain punched a number into a keypad on his door.

"Do you mind if I change before we eat?" he asked.

Moments later, he returned in denim and a gray sweater. I was happy Joan wasn't here to witness me staring at him. Iain's cheeks flushed. I followed him to the kitchen. He knew I was checking him out. How embarrassing.

"I want to show you something."

Please, don't be a weirdo.

My mind fluttered back to when Mr. Perfect with the Lenox Hill apartment said the same phrase, to reveal his adult website. The date ended and the phrase *I want to show you something* made me apprehensive.

Iain pulled a large dish from the fridge and grabbed two bowls from the cabinet. He nodded towards a set of french doors and carried our meal on a tray. Were we eating potatoes and meat from a bowl outside?

We walked through the grass, quite a distance from the house to a stone patio, visible by decorative lanterns and a fire. I first smelled the salty air, but the view—infinite water glistening under the stars.

"Wow."

"Sea without the bathing," he said.

"Am I ever going to live down William's Folly?"

We sat on a cushioned patio sofa with our warm bowls. My thigh brushed against his when I reached for my wine glass on the small table. He stirred his food and shook his head with a big smile.

"I guess I will wait until you do something embarrassing."

"Looking forward to it." Iain took a sip of wine and watched me examine my bowl. "Cottage pie—beef and potatoes. Nothing outlandish, I assure you." I let the comfort food and beautiful atmosphere relax me to the core.

"Do you eat out here often?" My Berrell coworkers took dinning more serious than work. They rolled their eyes when we scooped food from catered trays. "It seems a little…"

"American?" Amusement crossed his boyish face. "You may be surprised to find I lived in California for five years."

"An American-sympathizer—tell no one. It explains the diluted accent."

Iain choked on his wine followed by a few coughs.

"Diluted?" The intensity returned to his face as he processed my remark. "I prefer well-traveled." The corners of his lips turned up. "Do you want me to tell you why people dislike you?"

"Wow, let's get straight to the point." I sipped my wine. I preferred to sit around and stew about it rather than know the real reason my Berrell coworkers ignored me.

"You brought up American-sympathizer. It's nothing

personal. It's likely my fault." The sofa shifted when he oriented himself towards me.

"It's good you're not talking crap about me."

"No crap talk." Iain licked his lips. "For years, Berrell has relied on agriculture and trade. As time and technology changed, so have the job opportunities. The older generations don't want to leave their homes, and the younger generations don't want to leave their families."

"You provide jobs for people who would be forced to relocate." I shifted my weight towards him, our knees touching.

"I enjoy giving back. Mackgale-Berrell has offices in New York, London, Paris, and Vienna, but I chose to be here." A jagged breath escaped him. "It wasn't until I showed interest in the U.S.—buying your former employer and real estate in America caused uneasiness." A hint of a smile crossed his face. "Take Joanie for example. She will never leave Berrell. I doubt she will muster the courage to apply for an away team. Where would she work if I left?"

"Would you leave?" I bumped his leg when I placed my bowl on the table.

"I would love to say no, but how can anything be absolute?" The lines on his face hardened. "Will you stay in New York forever?" Before I could speak, he continued, "Unlikely. Most are born to live a linear life. You have already moved once, broken your straight line."

"I envy the linear."

"You do?" He tossed a blanket from behind him on my lap as the wind picked up. "That's surprising."

"I'm not sure what's next. I have no absolute plans beyond this moment." Our focus was only on each other.

"I understand." He raised his wine glass. "To those that wander."

I wasn't sure if he said wander or wonder. Clicking our glasses together, we sat in silence digesting more than cottage pie.

CHAPTER THIRTY-NINE

"I never trusted Sarah Margo." -Raj Sood

Monday morning, I leaned in my office chair with a jet lag fighting iced mocha. Debbie barged in, without knocking, wearing her typical two sizes too small pantsuit. She leaned on my desk. Why did she have to touch everything?

"What did the CEO want with you at home office?" She had waited twenty-one days to ask. I forgot she existed. My mind had already replaced her with Tim.

"I don't know." My answer did not satisfy her nosiness. "Do you think he talked to us? If he had a reason for me to be there, I wasn't informed."

This was true—I didn't talk to him at work. Debbie rolled her eyes, huffed as she strutted towards the door.

"I'm glad you're back. We are so behind." Debbie leaned against the frame like a bikini model. I tried to hide my you-annoy-the-piss-out-of-me face. "Promise me you won't go to Berrell again."

"I don't make promises, Debbie."

She left my office. I heard her tell Raj she was going to smoke. Whenever someone asked about Debbie's whereabouts, I told them to check the smoke deck on the roof. It became a not-so-funny joke in our department.

"I didn't see you on the plane," Raj stood in the doorway holding a stack of reports. He insisted on printing everything.

"The airline upgraded me to first class." Paradise in the sky.

"That's strange because a man rescheduled due to an overfull flight. He received a free ticket and two hundred dollars." Raj thought everyone was a conniving liar.

"That's weird. I guess the airline made a mistake."

Raj motioned to someone in the hall. A tall, dark-haired man in his early thirties joined Raj at my door.

"This is Ben Wilcox. Today is his first day. He is the temp employee manager." Raj left after his introduction.

"How long have you worked here?" Ben asked to make polite conversation.

"I have been here for five years. Two years prior at our former Oakville Plant." I flashed a fake smile. Ben had an odd demeanor. The way he looked over my office made me nervous.

"A few of us are grabbing a drink tonight. Would you care to join us?" Ben put his hand in his khaki pant pocket.

"Thanks, but I have plans with friends." He frowned in a way suggesting I made the wrong decision. "I returned from our home office on Saturday. It takes a few days to adjust to the time differences. I am drinking coffee because it's morning, but my stomach is growling for dinner." Ben did not find my rambling cute, so I stopped talking.

"Another time," he mumbled.

The phone on my desk rang while my cell phone buzzed loudly in my purse. Before I could decide which to answer, an instant message popped up on my screen—Iain Mackgale, CEO. I stared at the flashing message as the ringing and buzzing continued. The phone on my desk stopped, but someone insisted on getting a hold of me on my cell. When I retrieved it from my bag, I saw three missed calls from Gina.

"Hello," I said with the phone against my ear.

"Why aren't you answering your phone?" Gina asked.

"I am at the office. Sometimes I work while at work." Iain's message made my heart beat double. I clicked accept.

Iain: Can I call you tonight?

"I'm getting married!" Gina squealed. People in the background cheered. Gina getting married and Iain messaging me at the same time was crazy.

"To who?" I asked.

"To your uncle, silly girl," Gina said. Laughter erupted on the other end of the line when Gina repeated my dumb question.

"Oh my God! Congratulations. This is exciting news. Have you set a date?" Uncle Dan and Gina getting married? I had to pinch myself to make sure I wasn't dreaming.

"Six weeks from Saturday."

"You wanted a big wedding. Is that enough time?"

I replied yes to Iain's message.

"Honey, I planned this in the fall. I gave your uncle the ultimatum last month. We went to the Riverfront for dinner over the weekend, and he asked—two carats on a platinum band." Her happiness was contagious. "I wanted to call you, but Frank said you were traveling home."

"I got home late Saturday."

I waited for Iain's reply.

"You will have a special place at the ceremony, next to my mom," Gina said. I didn't care I wasn't in the bridal party.

"I can't wait." Tears welled in my eyes. "Let me know if you need anything."

"Baby, I have to run. I promised your dad I would pick him up at the University. His truck is in the shop, and he has refused a loaner from Teddy." Gina told someone to leave the shipment in housewares. "Any travel expenses you have from the wedding, send to your uncle. Love you."

"Love you too." I laid my cell phone on my desk.

Why did Iain want to call me? He said tonight which meant at home.

"Are you waiting for something, Sarah?"

I looked up to find Ben Wilcox in my office again. The tip of his index finger brushed dust off a shelf.

"Yes. Ethan is sending me files." He looked at me as if I was a liar. "Did he send you here to relay a message?"

"Watch yourself."

He tapped the door frame twice as he left. The excitement of Gina's wedding disappeared like a child letting a balloon go into the sky. Ben Wilcox had a problem with me, and I didn't know why.

CHAPTER FORTY

"Your hotel room has been ransacked. There is a car behind me with two men. I need you to find a place to lay low until James calls. This is Martin."

The workday was a blur. I couldn't recall one significant event except for the emergency meeting. Debbie received an email the CEO would visit in the morning. She called us into her office, discussed every possible scenario to make her appear to be a good manager, and told us not to speak to Mr. Mackgale unless spoken to.

Are we kindergartners?

I wasn't surprised about the corporate visit. After my near-death experience, Iain and I talked on the phone a few nights a week. Nothing major—our favorite books, television shows, music, and the happenings of our lives. During our last conversation, he asked if we could meet for a drink since he'd be in town. Iain said he would call at four when his flight landed in New York City.

It was now seven o'clock.

I found myself deep in regret for talking to him. Once again, someone disappointed me, and my mind went crazy with a million reasons why he didn't want to see me. *You're not good enough. Not pretty. Too weird.* For the first time, I stopped freaking out. Rather than over-analyzing why he hadn't called, I picked up my phone and texted him.

Me: You okay?

Instead of a text reply, he called. My finger hovered over accept in freak out mode. What if he called to tell me not to call him? Maybe I misunderstood, and he didn't want to have a drink?

Stop freaking out.

"I'm in the midst of a disaster." Tires swooshed through puddles. Out the window of my apartment, droplets drizzled in the street light.

"I understand if you can't—"

"I don't have a hotel to meet you for a drink."

"Where are you?"

"In New York somewhere." He paused. "My temporary assistant booked a room in Los Angeles rather than New York."

"Why? We don't have an office there."

He groaned. "That's what I said. She claims she has little knowledge of the United States. I am firing her as soon as I return to Berrell. Hold on a second, Sarah. She is phoning now." Without waiting for my response, Iain put me on hold. Three seconds later, he returned. "No rooms in the city right now—zero. A sporting event, fashion show, and a concert seem to be the reason." He let out a frustrated breath.

"We can figure this out at my apartment. I'll text you my address."

Iain didn't argue. Thirty minutes later, he knocked on my door.

I expected to see the polished CEO. Instead, he wore jeans and a Manchester United t-shirt under his wool coat, fastened with one toggle. I was in yoga pants with a stretchy sweatshirt, the kind which hangs off the shoulder revealing a sports bra. Before I could say hello, he pulled me into his arms, warm from him, wet from the rain. I recalled the night we worked on the databases, his wonderful smell, still present and better when pressed against him.

"Thanks," he whispered. The top of my head became a resting spot for his chin. Meanwhile, his luggage sat outside my open door.

"I thought people from Berrell weren't huggers," I murmured against his chest. Alex's famous hugs weren't this good.

"You're confusing us with the British." He broke our embrace.

I hadn't planned on inviting him over. Iain and I were friends, but he owned the company that provided my paycheck. The phrase *conflict of interest* wouldn't leave my mind.

"You look as if you have had an interesting evening," I said. The bottoms of his jeans were wet, hair a mess, and his luggage was the victim of a muddy puddle.

"You don't receive the best treatment when people don't know you." Iain smirked.

"Welcome to the real world." I smiled and paused. "Unless you're one of those rags to riches stories."

I helped Iain roll his bags into my studio apartment. He looked around for a moment. I lived here to save money to buy a house and go back to school to earn a doctorate. He made me self-conscious.

"No." His face grew serious, eyes surveying my face

"My place isn't much, but it's close to everything." I walked towards my beeping stove. "Are you hungry? I reheated leftover chicken and baked potatoes. There should be enough for both of us."

Tossing his coat on my bed, Iain joined me in the kitchen.

"No pizza?" He faked shock.

"Sorry to disappoint."

"I am the opposite of disappointed. Do you have any wine?"

I shook my head no, not wanting to admit I consumed the last bottle while reading a grocery store romance novel in the bathtub.

He contemplated for a moment before unzipping his suitcase. "This wine was purchased for Marco." He held up a bottle.

Marco was the site leader of the New York office. There were at least five managers in between us. I had never talked to him. He didn't socialize with the minions.

When Iain handed me the bottle, I couldn't help but notice the price tag still attached. The cost was in euros, but I did a rough estimate in my head. "We can't drink this! This is a three hundred dollar bottle of wine!"

"Four hundred. We are drinking the wine." He rummaged through my drawers for a corkscrew. "It has been a long day. I shouldn't have traveled without Martin."

Iain helped me set the table and serve the food. He poured the wine. We clicked our glasses together.

"How's it taste?"

"It's fantastic. Totally beat my ten dollar bottle," I said.

Iain checked his phone with one hand as he used a fork with the other. I realized for the first time how stressful his life must be leading an empire like Mackgale-Berrell. I seemed ridiculous for groaning over a fifty hour week.

Iain's phone played a classical ringtone. He stood up, told me it was Warren, and moved near the window to answer.

"Mackgale." Iain sighed. His free hand touched his forehead. Rain pelted the window where he stood.

I ate my food and pretended I couldn't hear. How could I not listen? I lived in a studio. The cat peeked from under the bed. He couldn't fathom a man in our apartment.

"There was not a miscommunication. I despise the word." He listened for a moment. "I'll reach out to you tomorrow afternoon, evening your time." He tossed his phone on his suitcase.

No one had found him accommodations.

"You are welcome to stay here tonight." He looked around my studio and stopped at the sofa bed. "I have an air mattress I sleep on when my dad visits. It's small. You can have my bed."

"I can't imposition you." Iain bit his bottom lip, followed by scratching his ear.

"It is my bed or the street corner. It's okay. You'll find a hotel tomorrow. No one will know you roughed it for a night."

He laughed.

"Where's the shower?"

Our eyes traveled to the only door.

"Towels are in the cubby." I poured myself another glass of wine. Iain motioned for a refill. I topped off his goblet. "You drink in the shower?"

"Tonight I do."

A tall figure in button-up black pajamas exited the bathroom in a haze of steam. He stayed in the shower until every drop of hot water left the tank. When he came closer, I glimpsed his initials embroidered on his shirt pocket, like the ones in over-priced catalogs.

"Hot pink towels?" Iain scrubbed his hair. "I never imagined you and hot pink."

"The towels were gifts, along with the flamingo shower curtain. I didn't picture you being a two-piece pajama guy." I thanked God he wore old man pajamas. What would I have done if he walked out shirtless with boxer briefs?

"I wasn't planning on a spectator before bed. Mum sends me pajamas for my birthday every year. She has since I lived in California for school." Iain put on his glasses and searched his laptop bag.

I watched him for a minute. He found his phone charger and glanced around the room for an outlet.

I plugged the air mattress into the wall to inflate. The air compressor roared, a cross between a vacuum and a freight train. I prayed Deana had plans because I didn't want her coming over. She would ask too many questions. Maybe flirt with Iain. Even worse, know I liked him. Then she would tell everyone. Iain would be mad. I would get fired over nothing. Debbie would use my empty office to store cartons of cigarettes and tight pantsuits. I inhaled needed air.

After Mark dumped Deana, she wasted no time getting into a new relationship—Sven worked on the Euro-Dumplings food truck. Deana had spent every night with him.

After I made my inflatable bed, I found a key in my drawer reserved for the lucky person in charge of feeding my cat when I traveled. I handed the key to Iain then rattled off how to get to the office from my apartment.

He climbed under the covers. I braced the twin air mattress to keep from flipping over.

"Sleep well, Sarah."

"Goodnight, Iain." I threw my fleece throw blanket over my head.

CHAPTER FORTY-ONE

"The guy makes a billion a year and brings me a fifteen dollar bottle of wine from a gas station." -Marco Romano

Hotels opened on the other side of town, but Iain didn't want to ride the subway. Iain said on a phone call he trusted one driver. He mentioned his father and spoke softer, so my eavesdropping ceased.

I told him he could stay at my apartment. When he offered me money, I refused. His presence wasn't an inconvenience. Maybe weird he was okay with my studio, but I liked talking to him at night.

He came up behind me two blocks from my apartment. Iain finished typing and tucked his phone away.

"You are leaving work early tonight," I said.

"Yes. I've worked enough fifteen hour days this week. Do you have plans tonight?" Iain had a serious face like we were conducting official business.

"Friday night is Chinese food and a movie. If you are interested, you can take the cat's place on the couch." His face lightened a little at my offer.

"I need a night off. Where do you get Chinese?" Iain admired the buildings.

"Uncle Ping's, a block north of my building next to the twenty-four-hour market." I gestured up the street.

"I'll get the food." Iain dodged a lady pushing a stroller with a quick hustle to get across the street before the traffic light changed.

After I scaled the six flights of stairs, I headed to the shower before he returned. Even though I speed washed my hair, I opened the bathroom door to find Iain sorting Chinese containers.

"Perhaps this is a tad excessive," he commented to himself.

I agreed. The five containers of food and egg rolls were enough to feed the entire sixth floor. For being a CEO with a team to cater to his needs, he wasn't afraid to take care of himself. I loved the way he made himself at home.

"Are you ready to eat?" he asked.

"I'm always ready to eat."

Iain hung his suit jacket on a peg, rolled up his shirt sleeves, and uncorked the wine. The Chinese restaurant didn't sell booze. I eyed the bottles with suspicion. He shrugged when he saw my expression. In return, I nodded towards his purchase.

"The market sells spirits. The Indian fellow said this is their finest bottle. A value for twenty dollars."

"Getting all fancy up in here," I said in my best New York accent.

Iain shook his head and suppressed a smile.

"If you speak in a New York accent again, we can't be friends." He poured the wine and took a sip. "My cologne tastes better."

Iain grimaced.

I drank and coughed. "Wow."

"Tell no one what I'm about to ask. Do you have anything we can mix into the wine?"

"Like what?"

"Check the refrigerator."

The bright light in my fridge lit up the dark corner in my kitchen. Iain surveyed my pajama pants and fitted tank top. Was he checking me out? There was no way.

It slipped my mind when I changed—no bra. I didn't have roommates. When I held the bottle of vodka to show Iain, my nipples aimed directly at him.

"Vodka maybe?" I peeked in the fridge again. "Cherry juice or Coke? Ranch dressing? Taco sauce?"

He laughed. Did he know about the nipple situation?

"Surprise me."

As soon as the bathroom door shut, I hurried to my wardrobe to put on a sweatshirt. A minute later, he appeared in gray sweats with a white t-shirt.

"What movie are we watching?" Iain asked.

I scooped a large mound of pork fried rice onto my plate. He watched me with curiosity, either wondering why I hadn't poured the wine or why I put on a sweatshirt. He smirked, then grimaced when he sipped the wine. My cheeks burned for a million embarrassing reasons. Where does one hide in a studio apartment?

Iain added vanilla vodka and a splash of cherry juice to our wine glasses.

"Anything you want to see?" I bit into an egg roll. One down, fifteen more to go.

"I can't tell you the last time I watched a movie," he said.

"Let's rent a comedy." I climbed on the couch part of my bed with my plate.

He scrolled through movies with the remote while balancing Chinese on his legs. Iain took a drink of his wine and rested his head against the back of the couch. He put the remote in my hand.

"Ladies' choice," he said.

"Good. I hate having movie wars. Alex and I always fight. He has the worst taste in movies—tearjerkers and kid flicks."

A shadow crossed Iain's face.

"Is Alex your boyfriend?" He took a bite of an egg roll.

The thought of Alex being my boyfriend made me smile to the point my face hurt.

"No. Alex likes guys. He is much prettier than me."

"That's not possible."

We didn't talk much during the movie. The empty bottle of wine sat in between us like a third party, not tasting any better no matter what we added. When the end credits rolled, Iain cleaned up the plates and put away the Chinese. I brushed my teeth, followed by organizing the blankets on my air mattress.

"You aren't going to bed, are you?" Iain twisted his watch. I shrugged my shoulders indifferent to going to sleep or staying up. "Shall we watch another?"

Iain selected a crime thriller, which guaranteed to give me nightmares. I agreed, not wanting to be the party pooper. I turned off the lights and returned to my spot next to him. He tossed part of the comforter on my legs, and we relaxed into the cushions for movie number two.

I woke up in the middle of the night with the television screen saver illuminating the room. My head rested against his chest. The warmth of his closeness engulfed me. I wanted to snuggle closer, not move, enjoy his beautiful, sleeping face, but I needed to get back to my air mattress.

I moved with caution to free my arm wedged near his side. Instant mortification occurred when I discovered my other hand rested on his athletic thigh under the covers, not too far from a certain place. I hoped this had happened after he fell asleep. This was not a date. The thought of Iain waking up to find me on his chest with my hand near his nether regions was enough for me to creep out of bed like a criminal in the night.

I realized two steps from my mattress that I had to pee. Could I hold it until morning?

I tiptoed to the bathroom, closed the door, and turned on the light to retrieve the box of feminine products I stuffed in a cubby. As I tugged on the bin on the top shelf, three bottles of nail polish fell to the floor. The noise was loud, but the glass didn't break.

When I came out of the bathroom, Iain stood in the middle of the room with his arms crossed. Between his posture and breathing, he seemed upset. Had someone called?

"What are you doing?"

Chills went down my spine at his tone. Iain didn't move from his place between the air mattress and bed.

"Going to the bathroom." I continued to my inflatable destination.

"Were you trying to take a picture of me?" He stepped in front of me with his eyes dark with betrayal. A dozen emotions passed through me from running away to punching him.

"What? Have you lost your mind? Please tell me this is a screwed-up night terror, or your tight t-shirt cut off the circulation to your brain?" He grabbed my wrists and held me hostage. "What the hell, Iain?" I thrashed like a fish out of water.

"Tell me what you're doing." His feet were planted on my wood floor.

"It's not your business but, I started my period today. My apartment isn't large. I crammed the box in the cubby above the towels. Take a look—Kotex with wings. The wrapper is in the trash can."

Iain released my wrists. The lines of his face hardened further, stress turning to regret.

"I can't believe you thought I'd take a picture of you sleeping. It's great you think I am a weird creeper." I tried to calm myself. "You need to get over yourself." If he came near me again, I would knee his balls so hard he would wish he never set foot in New York.

"You could make more money with one photo of me in your bed than you could working as an engineer for ten years." The tone of his voice possessed a defeated edge. Iain sat on my bed with his attention on his shaking hands.

"No one will pay me money for a picture of you. There are corporate executives all over the city—no one cares." My eyes watered from anger and exhaustion. "I fell asleep next to you by accident. When I got up, I needed to use the restroom. I'm clumsy—"

"You don't know who I am?" Iain stood up. "You never looked me up or read a tabloid? You spent weeks in Berrell. No one told you?"

He expected me to stalk him on the Internet.

"I don't have time to stalk people." That was a lie. My weekends were never busy. "I wasn't popular in Berrell. No one confided their deep, dark secrets."

"Look me up." He walked past me, through the door, into the hallway without a coat or shoes.

Instead of beauty sleep, I spent the next twenty minutes discovering the truth about my temporary roommate.

With fuzzy house shoes and robe to battle the overnight air, I walked down the stairs to find Iain, on the third floor, hunched with his face in his hands. He couldn't have gone far with no shoes or money. I sat next to him, not sure how to start.

"So?" Iain mumbled through his hands.

"So what?"

The stairwell didn't have heat; cool air entered the building every time a tenant opened the entrance door.

"I assume you found the information." He removed his hands, eyes moist with tears.

"You are the eldest son of a duke. A period drama is filmed at your family estate, Crossleigh Manor. You have a title you inherited from your second cousin who died two years ago skiing in Europe, but I can't remember the name." He glared. "It's early in the morning. Give me a break." He said nothing. "I don't care about a television show or titles. Why are you upset with me?"

Iain Mackgale graced the cover of most tabloids, due to IPIQ Productions' period drama, *Cross Hill Manor*. A recent article speculated about a connection between the storyline and Iain's life, although he refused to comment when interviewed. I wish I had watched the show. When Deana described the plot, it sounded like a cheesy soap opera. I couldn't imagine Iain being associated with so much drama.

I also wondered why his parents would allow the show if it caused controversy for their son. Cross Hill Manor's popularity explained why tourists flocked to Berrell.

"I can't get close to people," he whispered.

A door opened on the floor below us, but no one came up the stairs.

"I don't know what to say, Iain."

This wasn't a situation I came across—ever. I wasn't comfortable asking him questions.

Two months ago a magazine referred to him as *The Virgin Prince* since he never dates. Two of his former boarding school classmates confirmed to the magazine Iain was not gay, even though he was photographed vacationing with an American man. It made me squirm thinking about what my former classmates would tell a journalist.

Besides being the heir to his father's title, he was the heir to his maternal grandfather's shipping empire in France. I was a loser for stressing over who would take care of my cat when I visited Oakville.

When I glanced over at him, my mind traveled back to the night of William's Folly. He didn't like others seeing his chaos. At this moment, I realized what he meant.

"If everything I read is true, why are you sitting here with me? You're the lord of this and heir of that."

His lip trembled. He studied my face for the damages. This man always had it together, but not tonight, in the stairwell of a rundown apartment building in Manhattan with the girl from the Midwest.

"You are a smart and funny person. I don't get the privilege of having friends. People use me. I was waiting for the moment our friendship ended, and you would sell me out for money or a few minutes of fame." He sucked a jagged breath into his lungs. "I can't take back my behavior, but I can apologize. I have really fucked up." He paused for a moment to wipe his face. "The money is adding up for you."

I couldn't believe he expected I would sell him out although I understood. The Internet had pages of former classmates, coworkers, and relatives who took the cash.

"Iain," I whispered. He expected comforting words. "Shut up."

I stood and offered him my hand. He accepted without question, fingers warm between mine. All I wanted was sleep, to get rid of my headache, to make him go upstairs and sleep too. We returned to my apartment, and I plopped on my air mattress.

Girl, you thought he was trouble yesterday. You best run and fast.

Fictional Gina butted in too much. I closed my eyes, feeling warm tears run down my face. Why? Who knows? I was a mess with men. If they were trouble, I was interested. My mind went to my father, to Lori Margo. Perhaps he had the same pattern. We were attracted to the worst possible matches. Maybe that's why he never dated. I inhaled a deep breath, careful to be quiet as Iain laid on the bed four feet away.

Be nice. Let him go home and never talk to him again.

Thank God Gina would never know.

CHAPTER FORTY-TWO

**"I chickened out. She was too happy. I couldn't." -
Frank Margo**

Like clockwork, my dad called at eight in the morning. I
reached for my phone on the table, the air mattress wobbled,
and I tumbled to the hardwood floor. The sleek case slipped
through my fingers, a faint male voice coming from the device
next to my head. When I said hello a second time, my dad
asked if everything was okay.

"Yeah, why wouldn't I be okay?" I looked around the room
for Iain. Did he go back to Berrell? His luggage sat next to my
closet.

"You sound panicked." Wind blew against the phone, an
indication he was outside. My family joked my dad's yard
looked cleaner than the inside of his house.

"No. I stayed up late last night. Your call scared me."

Frank Margo made a groan implying he didn't buy my
answer but didn't want to know either.

"All right. Go back to sleep and call me later. I love you."

"I love you too."

My back ached on the floor, a thud when I sat the phone
next to my side. Sleep deprivation made analyzing last night
impossible.

The door opened. Iain stopped when he spotted me on the
floor like a turtle on its back. He wore his sweats from last

night with a wool coat, two Styrofoam containers in his hands. The area along his jaw showed a shadow where he hadn't shaved.

"My dad calls every Saturday morning." I picked up my phone and stood.

I recognized the amazing smell from the diner, but my stomach ached. Not to mention, the throbbing headache. I placed the tips of my fingers on my temple, not finding relief.

Iain put the food on the TV stand. "I'm sorry."

"Let's forget it, okay? If you get crazy again, I will kick you in the balls." His lips turned upward. "Totally serious. I spent every recess in second grade against the wall for nut kicking."

"I believe you. I'll be on my best behavior."

Rather than rehash last night, Iain went to the kitchen to retrieve plates for the food. He liked to eat on dishes rather than out of a container. I would have eaten out of the Styrofoam—less clean up.

"When is the last time you took a vacation?" I stuffed a piece of bacon into my mouth.

"Never. My holidays are working outside the office."

"That's your problem. You work too much." Even though my stomach said no, I couldn't resist an omelet with cheese and mushrooms.

"I have seen the hours you log each week. What about your work-life balance?" Iain removed his wool coat and joined me at the table.

"I take vacations. Last fall, I traveled on a ten-day train tour of Canada with my dad. On Thursday, I am flying home to spend the weekend with my family. Rather than argue over our lack of lives, why don't we do something today?"

"Outside of this building?" Iain asked while chewing a sausage link.

"Yes."

Iain winced. "You will end up a tabloid story."

I left the table. Iain watched me walk to my closet. After a moment of digging through my mess, I produced a Yankees hat and my dad's knock-off aviator sunglasses he forgot.

"Put these on." He hesitated but accepted the merchandise. "No one will know you from Ralphie, the hotdog vendor. I am showing you the city."

He chewed his food with contemplation.

"No one has ever been so direct." Iain tapped his finger on my table. I wondered if he would go on a rant about his title or the billion-dollar global corporation he ran.

"In this house, your lordship, the cat ranks higher than you," I said with a smirk. Iain's mouth opened as if to respond. "I need to change."

"Sarah." He turned to make eye contact. "You can be direct with me anytime you wish."

I gave him my be-careful-what-you-wish-for face and closed the bathroom door.

The weather wasn't too bad, somewhere in the mid-fifties, on top of the open-air tour bus with the twenty-four tourists. The tour guide provided clear ponchos in case it rained. Iain insisted on wearing his, so I ended up wearing mine. We sat in the back with our hot chocolates, feet propped up on the empty seats. The older couple two rows in front of us asked if this was our first time in New York City.

"Yes. Is it yours?" Iain asked the man in his surprisingly good American accent. The wife nodded with too much enthusiasm.

"We are having a great time," she told Iain. Her husband pointed towards the water. She took a second glance at Iain.

"Nice accent," I whispered. He put his arm around the back of my chair and leaned closer.

"When I was in boarding school in California, I would pretend to be American," Iain said into my hair. "That's where I met my best friend, Tyler. We are still close. I can be myself around him without worrying if our conversation will be tomorrow's news. This isn't my first time in New York. Tyler is a restaurateur and chef. I decided recently to become a partner in his business here. I'd been here a few times before to look at the real estate I bought."

He turned his face towards me, his breath warm against my face, eyes so deep blue. The sounds of the city faded, distorted with more than the motion of the bus. A large drop of rain smacked my skin. I squealed like a girl. Iain wiped my cheek with his fingers.

"You getting off the bus?" the woman asked. She adjusted her City Bank visor.

"Yes," American Iain said. It took everything I had not to laugh.

"This is Battery Park," I said. We followed the older couple.

When we got off the bus, Iain pulled his phone out of his pocket. I eyed the device with disapproval. His lips spread into a big smile.

"I'm not working. I want a picture of us," he said getting into selfie mode with his camera. After he snapped it, we looked at our cheesy smiles and tour bus ponchos. "Perfect." He put his phone away. "I'm keeping your father's sunglasses."

CHAPTER FORTY-THREE

"She walked through the door with the real life
Drew McGrew, the worst human being on the planet." -
Cassie Long

The second week of living with my temporary roommate
started the same—he left before I was out of bed and returned
after I had dinner. On Wednesday, he returned a few minutes
after six.

"Hello," Iain said in a chipper voice. He closed the door.
Today, he wore black dress pants, a white button-up, and a gray
sweater. I smiled at him, then wheeled my large suitcase near
the kitchen table.

"Are you going somewhere?" Iain asked. His chest touched
my back when he helped me shove the suitcase against the
wall. I gave him another smile. Sometimes I went overboard
when packing, but I needed options. I pushed my carry on
against the larger bag.

"Wing night at the bar."

"I doubt you're taking suitcases to a bar." When we made
eye contact, I felt strange, unsure if the sensation was good or
bad.

"I am flying to Oakville in the morning." I realized he wasn't
leaving until Friday. "Sorry, I forgot to tell you. You are
welcome to stay here." He continued staring at me. We were
standing close, too close.

"You told me. I didn't realize it was this week." Iain looked at his watch. "I am coming with you" He walked away, not waiting for my response.

"What?"

Iain closed the bathroom before I could say anything further. I didn't want to be the weirdo trying to talk to him through the door while he did whatever guys do.

When he emerged a few minutes later, he had changed into jeans, kept the dress shirt and gray sweater, but added the Yankees hat. I couldn't help checking him out. *Bad Sarah.* I hoped I didn't say *bad Sarah* out loud.

"So you are coming with me to the bar?"

Picking up my handbag, I walked towards the door with my keys. Iain followed. That was a relief. I thought he meant home to Oakville for a moment.

"Bar and Oakville." Iain held the door open. His cologne improved the smell of the old building's stairwell.

"No. No. No." I stopped near the stairs, bumping into him when I turned around. His handsome face grinned at my attempt to be authoritative. I even put my hand on my hip.

"You said I needed time off. I am taking a holiday." He leaned against the wall and waited for my response.

"Yes. I suggested you take a vacation to the Cayman Islands, Australia, Nova Scotia, or any other place rich people go."

"Nova Scotia is for rich people?"

"I have never been. You should go. Let me know if I'm right."

"Nah. Besides, you need a wedding date." Iain gave me the grin of someone who had won the argument.

How did he know about Dan and Gina's wedding? I didn't tell him. When he was showering, I was on the phone over the weekend. He must have heard part of the conversation, the pathetic part about me being close to thirty and not having a date. *Thanks for bringing it up, Gina.*

"You can go to the bar, but not Oakville. Maybe I already have a date." I paused. "Are you sure you want to go to the bar?"

"You don't have a date," he said. We walked down the stairs towards the lobby. "You said it's a dive. Locals and artists, right?"

I nodded.

The streets were full of cars, no one walking but us. Misty drizzle coated the windshields.

"Alex and Cassie are meeting us. You will not meet Deana. She refuses to go after her breakup with Mark." Our eyes met for a moment. "Mark is the bartender." He made a noise of understanding but didn't inquire further.

Once we arrived, Iain held open the door. A gush of warmth escaped into the night. The fried food and spilled tap beer lingered in the air and on the floor.

"Sarah!" Alex yelled in an over-the-top dramatic voice. Pushing past Iain, he hugged me in an exaggerated rocking back-and-forth manner. "You look tired, gorgeous." The t-shirt he wore matched his golden eyes.

"Busy week at work." I gestured towards Iain with my hand. "This is my coworker." Alex looked at me as if I had said I brought an elephant to the bar. "He is in town from Berrell." I tried to break the awkwardness that Alex was a professional at creating. "Iain, this is Alex."

They shook hands.

"Can I get you a drink?" Iain asked.

"I'll drink whatever you are drinking." As he turned to go towards the bar, I added, "No tequila. Nothing tomato. No orange juice either." The thought of orange juice and alcohol made my stomach churn. A faint smile flickered across his face at my random requests.

"Seriously." Alex pulled me towards him, fingers digging into the flesh of my upper arm. "Did you bring him for me? Please, tell me you brought him for me." The fake begging with his hands together freaked me out. "Sarah, he is so damn hot, and the sexy accent is even hotter."

"Stop," I hissed. We both glanced at Iain paying for drinks at the bar. "He isn't into guys."

"Are you sure?" Alex possessed zero ability to tell gay from straight. If they were attractive, they were an option. "Observe his clothes." Alex motioned his hand up and down. I thanked God Iain faced the bar rather than us.

"I am very sure."

Alex squealed with excitement. "Is the decade drought over?"

"What?" Iain walked towards us with drinks. "It hasn't been a decade!"

"What hasn't been a decade?" Iain asked. He carried two glasses of whiskey.

I accepted my drink, glared at Alex, and watched Iain close his eyes for a moment after he took a sip.

"Sarah hasn't waxed a car in almost a decade." Alex laughed like a crazy hyena. Iain shrugged.

"Ignore him."

My cheeks flushed with embarrassment. I hoped our cultural differences would keep Iain clueless about Alex's jesting. Whatever the case, Iain took my advice.

Cassie and Steve whispered at a table near the broken dartboard with a basket of wings between them. When we walked over, they looked up in a way one does when they've been caught gossiping. After I introduced my friends, the five of us chatted about the weather.

"Are you going out later?" Alex was his usual antsy.

"No. I have to catch an early flight." This was true, but I didn't want to go to the gay bar Alex frequented.

"Not buying the early flight. You don't want to go to *my*

bar," Alex said. He did an exaggerated head motion. If I moved like him, I'd need a chiropractor.

"That drag queen always hits on me. Last time he sat on my lap!"

Alex loved my conservative Midwestern culture shock.

"Roxanna is not a queen!"

"You mean that's a woman?" There was no way a six-foot-tall person in combat boots could be a female. Iain laughed at our argument.

After two glasses of whiskey, I felt as warm as a slow-burning fireplace. Iain looked relaxed with the sleeves of his sweater pushed up chatting with Alex about soccer. Alex knew nothing about sports.

"Be careful going home," Alex said. We hugged. "I'm leaving too. It's time to get my night started."

His smile made me grab his chin like I was his mother. I wobbled from the alcohol. Iain held my elbow for stability.

"Behave Alexander. I will see you when I return to civilization."

CHAPTER FORTY-FOUR

"Home is not a physical place on a map or a structure made of tangible goods. It's a person. In each other's arms, a couple is at home." -Rev. Douglas Smith

A flight attendant made announcements in the aisle while holding a fake seatbelt. I closed my eyes to relax and think about Gina's wedding. Today, it hit me. Gina, the mother or sister I never had, was becoming a Margo.

Bliss stopped when the tapping noise wouldn't go away. I opened one eye to discover the woman next to me texting on her phone. The tips of her fake nails made the sound of an antique typewriter. She could text fast. I couldn't help but watch her tell whoever Lydia was about the rip-off Prada bags she purchased out of a car trunk. The speed-texter glared at me like a dirty, little eavesdropper.

A layover in Chicago meant a flight on a large plane, the ones with three seats in a row. I always found myself in the middle seat which stunk, sometimes literally if you sat next to the wrong person. I didn't know the knock-off Prada lady in the aisle seat, but I knew the man sitting by the window—my CEO who would not take no for an answer.

I said yes when he loaded his suitcase into the cab with mine. I didn't want another conversation at a family function about how I am a weird asexual who doesn't have a boyfriend. Not to mention the awkward suggestions of men I should date, followed by *you're too pretty to be single* or *there has to be someone*. Part of me didn't want to get their hopes up by bringing a date. The other part felt weird bringing someone like Iain Mackgale to Oakville.

The longer I knew him, the more the disparity in our lives widened. At first, he was a foreign guy at a bistro, then my CEO, and last week I discovered he has a title and another after his father dies. Wasn't there rules about fraternizing with common folk?

When I called my dad at the airport to tell him Iain was coming, he knew the name. According to my father, Iain frequented the financial channel with his grandfather, Aldric Aleron, the billionaire shipping tycoon who had deemed Iain his successor. At one point, he owned the Oakville Plant where I used to work. He had to know something about my behind the times Midwestern town. Why did he tag along to my family wedding?

I couldn't ask him.

Iain Mackgale complicated everything. I liked him, more than I wanted to admit, but he made me nervous. I allowed myself to get close to him with late night phone calls and daily texts. The last twelve days he had slept in my room. Wanting Iain would lead to heartbreak—there was no question. After this weekend, I needed to keep my distance.

"Tell me about your family. Who will I meet?" Iain asked.

"You will meet my dad, Frank, and his two brothers—Dan and Teddy. Dan owns a chain of department stores. Gina is the bride. Dan and Gina began dating when I was in elementary school." I paused for a moment to calculate how many years they dated. "Teddy married my mom's cousin. It's his second wife. He owns a car dealership." Before I could get to Aunt Penny, he asked the forbidden question.

"Will I meet your mother?"

"No. She divorced my father when I was in sixth grade. The house we are staying at is where we moved after the mess." My hands turned clammy. Deana and Cassie were my best friends, and they knew nothing about Lori Margo. I wanted to leave the past where it belonged.

"Do you have a relationship? Sorry, I can't read your life story on the Internet."

"She contacts me when she needs money. I don't give it to her, which results in name calling." Iain placed his hand on mine and squeezed. "I have three aunts, many cousins, and dozens of family friends. Gina has a large family. They are coming from Georgia." Iain's thumb caressed my wrist.

"I know you didn't want me to come—"

"I don't bring guys around my family." My cheeks burned to a deep crimson. The most embarrassing weekend of my life was coming. "Please don't take offense if they think we're dating."

A big grin spread across his face. "No offense taken. Real relationships aren't my strength. I will settle for a fake one with a beautiful American."

I couldn't hide my grin.

Iain watched the luggage turn at baggage claim. Retrieving his bags wasn't something he did, but he didn't complain. Iain stood next to me like all the other real mortals from our flight. He gave me a slight smile when he caught me staring.

My attention moved to the conveyor belt where Iain reached for his suitcase. No one else had leather with embroidered initials on the pocket. Mine passed by a moment later, a hand-me-down Samsonite from Gina with a blue ribbon tied to the handle. Iain lifted my bag over the metal railing, strapped the expensive leather to the worn Samsonite, and placed my carry-on against the handle.

"I have traveled a time or two," he said. I flushed. Was he a mind reader? Iain smirked with satisfaction. "Where do we go next?"

"Rental car pickup." I nodded towards the sign.

We followed the ropes which seemed ridiculous because a

line of fifty people never formed at the Oakville airport. We waited at the *wait until called* sign.

Chad, according to his name tag, waved us to come to his cash register. I declined his ten attempts to add insurance and upgrades. The rental car expense was crazy enough without extras. Chad handed me the key along with the paperwork. Iain stuck his hand out, wanting to drive.

"Follow me out the door, folks," Chad said.

I realized I went to middle school with Chad Montgomery. He looked different—bulging belly, gray hair around his ears, gold-framed glasses. I doubted he recognized me. Chad never shut up in school. He would have said something. I guess my name didn't sound familiar. Margo wasn't cool like Esposito or Bourgeois.

"No." Iain returned the keys to my former classmate. "This can't be my first time. I always imaged it...special." Iain shook his head. Chad fidgeted with a pen. "There is no room in the back. I am certain the audio system is unacceptable. This vehicle mirrors a girl's roller skate." Iain circled the car, looked at me and then Chad. "Did you see her boot? It doesn't make me eager to put anything inside."

"Um. Sir, I...don't..." Chad put his pen in his pocket and rubbed his palms against his khaki pants.

When Iain said boot with his accent, it sounded like butt. Unlike Chad, I had been to Berrell. The boot was the trunk, not my ass.

"He is referring to his first time driving in the United States," I said. Iain looked at me as if I told Chad the sky was blue.

"I drive a top-of-the-range," Iain said as he surveyed the parking lot full of rentals. "We need a model with class and power."

"I think I have what you're looking for, Mr. Margo," Chad said.

"Lead the way." Iain's grin was triumphant.

Twenty minutes later, we were cruising down the highway in the luxury model of the roller skate. Not only did it feature power locks but a sunroof and mini spoiler. I flew forward again. My seatbelt locked me in place.

"Sorry," Iain mumbled. He switched lanes. "I'm not used to driving an automatic on the wrong side of the road."

"Car manufacturers make automatics to make driving easier."

"Damn." Iain mistook the brake for the clutch. His hand rested on the automatic shifter between us.

"I can't believe you have never driven in the U.S." I held on to the cheap door handle anticipating more abrupt braking. "Take the next exit."

"I was young and couldn't drive when I lived here. Between larger cities and having a driver, I have had no need to drive." He smiled. "This is not what I pictured. I wanted my experience to be like an American music video."

My chest vibrated with laughter.

"I am serious." Iain's face flushed.

At last, he was embarrassed.

"Okay, let's do it."

I rolled down the window, fluffed my hair, and cranked up classic rock. We sang at the top of our lungs until the luxury roller skate reached my dad's street.

Frank Margo refused to live beyond ten minutes from the interstate. He commuted twenty minutes to Oakville State. Uncle Ted had suggested my dad sell his house and move to a nicer suburb, Lake Washington, which would add thirty minutes to his drive. My dad would tell his brother he was happy where he lived. Then Ted's wife, Theresa, would suggest someone he should date. My annoyed father would tell them he was fine with his single life. I believed him. I'd said the same many times, but was I being truthful? Was I thrilled being alone?

I turned down the music and directed Iain to the older 1970s neighborhood with brick ranchers. Ours was at the end of the street on an acre lot with a cracked asphalt driveway from the oak tree roots.

"This is it." I pointed to the brick house with a blue 1994 Chevy Silverado parked in front of the garage. Out of the corner of my eye, I risked a glance at Iain to gauge his thoughts. I didn't possess the gift of mind reading, but he seemed happy to be here.

As he parked the car, the living room curtain opened. My father strolled out the door and stopped on the sidewalk to greet us, already in dress pants and a tie. Although he had salt and pepper hair, I still pictured him thirty-five in my mind.

"Hello," Iain said to my dad before I could get out of the car. My dad extended his hand.

"I'm Frank Margo, Sarah's dad."

"Iain Mackgale" He took the older man's hand. I stood on the pavement, unsure how I felt about Iain being chummy with my father.

"Please call me Frank."

"Iain."

"How was your flight?" My dad followed Iain to the trunk of the roller skate.

"Not bad. Short. Good company," Iain replied. He handed me my purse from the trunk. Iain lifted our suitcases onto the driveway, a clicking sound as he pulled out the handle.

"I love your property," Iain said. His eyes surveyed the mature trees and green grass. My father beamed with pride because he loved the place too.

Once we had our bags inside, I felt relieved to be at home— real home, not my New York City apartment. Nothing had changed. I couldn't think of any changes in the past ten years.

"Iain, you can put the bags in Sarah's room at the end of the hall." My dad motioned towards my bedroom door.

"No. Iain is staying in your den."

"No." My father turned to Iain. "Sarah's cousins from Kentucky are staying with us. They didn't have money for a hotel but wanted to attend the wedding."

Iain had on his corporate face.

"We can't sleep in the same bed," I said in my teenage girl dramatic voice with my hands on my hips. This amused the men.

"Oh, Sarah." My father put his arm around me. With my boots on, we were almost the same height. "I'm not a prude."

"We are not together. What if Iain is embarrassed?" The problem wasn't the room.

Take that Frank Margo.

"Iain, are you embarrassed?"

"No," he replied with a smug grin.

Maybe Iain wasn't embarrassed, but I was. My father had the nerve to laugh.

"Fine."

I huffed the Samsonite down the hall. Iain followed, chuckling to himself.

Iain surveyed my childhood bedroom. My horse figurines on the dresser sent me to a new level of shame. He touched the miniature grooming supplies. I hoped he realized I hadn't groomed fake ponies in two decades.

A picture of Bethany and I at our senior prom sat on the shelf in a red frame. I called her many times over the years. When Aaron and I met for dinner last year in New York, he tried to contact her, but she didn't return his call. Bethany never returned mine.

"What is this contraption?" Iain pointed at my daybed,

covered in the purple comforter I begged my dad for in high school.

"I am guessing you have never seen a daybed?" He shook his head no, still looking at the not so modern marvel. He grabbed the faux iron rod of the bed and shook it. "Easy with the merchandise, buddy."

"Sleeping will be interesting," he mumbled.

Glaring at him, I unzipped my suitcase to find the dress I packed for the rehearsal dinner. Iain took the cue and left me to change.

The house wasn't large. Their conversation about Iain's interview with *Forbes* echoed to my room. My dad told Iain he found the piece inspirational. Iain thanked him and told my father a behind the scenes story about the interviewer. They laughed. My cheeks burned as I slipped into my pumps. Why did Iain being in Oakville embarrass me? I survived clock pants, days of the week underwear, and an awful perm.

When I joined the men, my father held the paper picture frame with cartoon mountains from our Canadian train tour. I remembered the photographer taking the picture in Jasper, real mountains in the background, like it happened yesterday.

"Is the portrait from your holiday?" Iain asked while holding our trip memento. "What?" Iain studied my humiliated face. My crazy father laughed. He sat in the squeaky recliner with his hands clasped together.

"Tell him about our trip," my dad said.

Iain sat on the couch eager to receive the details. I was positive he wasn't expecting what I was about to tell him.

"My wonderful father booked us a train tour for ten days." A quick glimpse of my dad made me smile.

"I got such a good deal, Iain!" Frank Margo's eyes were alive with amusement. I couldn't help laughing too.

"We boarded the train. Everything seemed great. Once we got into our room, we noticed a tiny double bed coated in rose petals with a bottle of champagne on ice." Iain wasn't following, so I got to the point. "My father booked us a couples retreat."

Frank slapped his knee and roared with laughter. Iain laughed at my dad's over-enthusiasm. I shot them both a not funny face because a couple's retreat with your dad was an ultimate low.

"Admit our trip was a great time," my father said.

"We had the best time." I leaned down to hug my dad. In return, he patted my back, planting a kiss on my cheek.

"The women were so envious. They thought I had money to get a hot babe like Sarah." The clock on the mantel chimed. "We need to leave in fifteen. Are you guys going to be ready?"

Iain and I waited for my father on the small, concrete porch, the home of an old bench and a dead plant. The weather felt perfect for a wedding weekend—not too hot or cold. Iain slipped his phone into his pocket when my father appeared at the door.

"Are we taking your rental car? There are file boxes in the truck." My dad locked the front door with his massive key ring. Why did he have so many keys?

"Let's ride together in the rental," Iain said.

My dad eyed the lime green roller skate with a small spoiler. I would rather walk than own this weird automobile.

"Sweet car," my dad said. Iain and I shared a smirk. Frank noticed our exchange and motioned for the keys. "I'm driving. It's not every day I get to drive a sports car."

Iain tossed Frank the keyring. The men occupied the front. I sat in the back like a kid in elementary school.

"Where is the dinner?" Iain asked.

The car reversed out of the broken asphalt driveway onto the street.

"My brother's house across town." Frank glanced at Iain. "Dan does well for himself. He owns several stores. My father started the business. He hoped I'd work with Dan, but I didn't have a knack for managing people. I was always a mathematics guy."

"Like your daughter." Iain turned to face me. My dad's proud grin beamed in the rear-view mirror.

CHAPTER FORTY-FIVE

"She looked at him with stars in her eyes. All I could see was trouble in a five thousand dollar suit." - Gina Cobb

Cars cluttered the yard and the street—ours was the crappiest. I stepped outside the roller skate into the Kings' grass. Lights and decorations hung in pure Gina style. Soft party music played in the distance. The sun had set, only a hue of orange on the horizon.

"Hey," Dan said. His cheeks were rosy. Two guys slapped my uncle's back on their way inside. "The party people are here!"

"Not quite," I mumbled. Uncle Dan sat his drink on a table. He hugged me and swayed with my face smashed against his chest. "Hello, Uncle Dan."

Dan broke our embrace, hands gripping my arm. We stood on the porch with the lights from inside illuminating us.

"When did I see you last?" He couldn't remember, not too far-fetched considering the smell of alcohol coming from his breath.

"Mrs. Shiltz-Pott's funeral," I replied. Dan let out a thunderous laugh.

Iain studied us. What normal people laugh about a funeral? My father shook his head.

"Mr. Pott worked for my uncle. I never knew him. His wife, Mrs. Shiltz-Pott, lived in the neighborhood where I grew up.

The minister performing the memorial referred to her as Emma Shit-Pot." I tried to hide my smile.

"This girl has a dark sense of humor like her uncle. Don't let her tell you otherwise. We laughed our asses off in the car," Uncle Dan said. He downed the rest of his drink.

"Dan," my dad said with a nod towards my date. "This is Iain, Sarah's friend."

Dan and Iain shook hands.

"Nice to meet you. Sorry, I forgot my manners. I was happy my beautiful niece came." Uncle Dan noticed his brother's displeased face. "I've had too much to drink tonight, Mom. Any sane man can't get married sober."

"You couldn't survive without her." My dad ushered his brother inside, tired of standing on the dark porch.

Gina stood in the center of the living room surrounded by people. As always, she looked amazing in a white dress with extensive crystal beading, which sparkled in the light when she moved. My purple sheath dress paled in comparison, but she was the bride, and few women could compare next to Gina in stilettos.

"Hey, baby girl." Gina placed her wine glass on the waiter's tray. She dodged a waitress carrying a platter of hors-d'oeuvres then wrapped me in a warm embrace. I missed her. She said hello to Iain.

Iain's phone buzzed in his pocket. When he looked at the screen, he groaned and twisted his lips. Uncle Dan knew Iain's discontentment. He was no stranger to working all hours.

"My office is the second door. Use whatever you need," Dan said to Iain. He squeezed Iain's shoulder and headed to the bar for another drink.

"I'll be here when you're finished," I said.

Iain nodded and disappeared down the hall.

"Can we talk?" Gina asked with a hint of irritation in her voice. Before I could say yes, no, or maybe, she had me by the arm leading me into the downstairs bathroom. I thought she wanted me to undo her dress to use the restroom or see if she had a run in her pantyhose. "I thought you were bringing a *friend* from work?" The Southern accent was in full throttle.

"I brought a *friend* from work," I said in my teenager-in-trouble voice. What was up with sixteen-year-old Sarah making a comeback?

"Iain Mackgale is not a *friend* from work. He is the CEO of a billion-dollar corporation," Gina said.

"Did you ask for his resume?" I continued my bratty responses. Gina sighed.

"Your father called me today," Gina said in a low voice, still holding onto my arm. We stood against the dark wood vanity. I noticed the new hand towels and made a mental note to tell her I liked them later. "I doubt you'll ever learn Sarah Nicole."

"Learn what?" She let go of my arm. I rested against the wall next to the trickling toilet. I never liked this bathroom.

"Date people in your own league. A school teacher, bank manager—"

"My league?" I was unwilling to allow her to suggest I wasn't good enough. I reached for the door, but she barricaded my exit. "Seriously, Aunt Gina?"

"Seriously, Sarah?" Gina bobbed her head like a diva.

"First. I am not dating Iain. I didn't want his company, but he is here. Second. I have no desire to date a school teacher or a bank manager." I raised three fingers. "Third—"

"You have a problem with school teachers? My brother is a school teacher." Gina held the door handle behind her back.

"Is he single?"

"Yes, but he's fifty."

"Damn. You have already prohibited me from older men." I fake sighed.

"I will tell him you're interested." Gina smirked. She grabbed my shoulders. "I care about you and don't want you to get hurt, okay? Iain can have any woman he wants. You are someone new and different, but your novelty will wear off. Then what? The best scenario is you have a broken heart. Do you want to lose your job?" Gina's worrisome face upset me.

We hugged.

"I get your point, and I'm sorry. Can we not talk about this now?"

"Okay." Gina looked in the mirror at her blond hair in a partial up-do. "Let's put on our party faces." Gina gave me a cheesy, beauty pageant smile.

My fake smile looked like I had eaten rotten eggs. Without another word, Gina opened the door, and we were back to playing happy family.

Iain sipped a cocktail near the dining room with Uncle Teddy, whose dress shirt hung untucked. Their conversation appeared serious. Were they talking about cars? A waiter offered me a glass of wine on my way to join my uncle and work friend. I took a drink; fruity liquid slid down my throat with a velvet finish.

"I thought your boyfriend was a doctor?"

Teddy was never my favorite uncle.

"I told you twice I'm not a physician," Iain replied for me. He pointed towards Teddy's untucked shirt. "You are the one who insisted on showing me your…hip."

My uncle shrugged. He thought Iain was unhelpful.

I grabbed Iain's arm, pulled him towards the basement door, in the direction of Uncle Dan's game room. My whole world was crashing down around me. This feeling happened in Oakville often. I sank into the brown leather chair.

"Are you okay?" Iain asked. "If you are worried about your uncle—"

"Showing you his hip?"

"His ass. I was trying to be decent." Iain's lips curved upward into a soft smile. He sat on the chair's arm. "Do you think you're the only one with crazy relations? If you met mine, you would see you don't hold the monopoly."

"There is trouble at *Cross Hill Manor*?"

Iain grimaced at the mention of the show. "Those are fighting words."

"Okay, I will never mention *Cross Hill Manor* again after I ask you one question." Another one of my bad habits was pressing my luck.

Iain groaned.

"I don't watch the program, but I will grant you one question on this subject." He did a genie granting a wish wave.

"Why did your parents allow the show at their home?" Home was a poor word choice—estate, mansion, or castle would have worked better. I didn't know what to call where they lived, nor did I know whether I should address Iain by a title.

He hesitated. "My parents needed the money. My father loves to tell a barrage of other reasons. I hope you keep what I said to yourself."

"You can trust me." He studied my face. Others had told him the same. "Aren't your parents wealthy?"

"My father's belief is gentlemen shouldn't work. He spends and gambles more than the estate profits. I have helped to no avail." Iain exhaled a breath. His family situation seemed to weigh on his mind. "It's terrible to be at the estate when IPIQ is filming. Most of the living spaces are full of people and camera equipment."

I stood up. He remained sitting on the chair's arm. We were at eye level. The way he studied me caused my breath to stop. I wished I could read him the way he could me.

"Like everything else, generations change. He refuses to

understand someone has to pay the bills. Perhaps he doesn't want to grow up. Only he knows." The space between us was warm. I wanted to step into his arms, but I had pressed my luck enough tonight. "No one has a perfect family. Let's go upstairs."

When we returned upstairs, the party had moved to the backyard to start dinner. Gina made her own rules. This rehearsal dinner had more guests than most weddings. She wanted to include employees who worked for Uncle Dan but weren't invited to the ceremony. I stared at the metallic centerpieces, complete with silk magnolias and doves. Love and happiness sounded fine, but cakes and invitations did nothing for me.

Iain pulled out my chair. My dad sat next to Iain. Iain laughed while he removed his napkin from his plate.

"What's so funny?" I leaned closer to Iain.

"Nothing," he said. The men shared a smirk. "Frank wants to leave after dinner."

Dan hired a country band, influenced by Gina's relatives, for after dinner. My father hated country music. It was no surprise he didn't want to stay.

"Sarah," my dad said in a hushed tone. He made certain no one was listening. I leaned over Iain, closer to my dad. "There is a Rambo movie marathon starting at ten." At that moment I knew where I acquired my weirdness—Frank Margo.

"What's Rambo?" Iain asked, also keeping his voice low. Gina's mom was on the faux stage talking into the microphone of a karaoke machine.

"You haven't seen Rambo?" Frank asked too loud. His outburst caused a few shushes and dirty looks. Iain shook his head no. "We are leaving after dinner because you need to see Rambo."

"My dad has a weird obsession with Sylvester Stallone." I

didn't hear my dad's reply because a server poured our drinks.

"Can I have water?" Iain asked. He eyed the iced tea like a dead rat. The irritated server left without another word or providing tea for the rest of our table.

"I can play American all day, but I can't drink tea with ice."

"I won't judge because I will not eat fish mousse." My tongue moved around as if getting rid of the flavor. The server returned with a pitcher of water and filled two glasses.

The three of us ate our catered chicken parmesan while others told stories about Dan and Gina. No one cared about our presence.

"It's time to go," Frank whispered. He wiped his mouth with the cloth napkin.

"I didn't get dessert." I wanted a piece of cheesecake. Iain sat in the middle of our hushed conversation.

"Meet me at the car. I will rectify the situation." Frank motioned to the door in covert operation mode.

"If you are stealing desserts, get enough for everyone," Iain whispered. Frank nodded in approval.

"It's Stallone time."

CHAPTER FORTY-SIX

"I didn't sleep that night, only gazed at the two beautiful girls in bed with me, imagining the possibilities." -Iain Mackgale

When I walked into the kitchen in my gray sweats and university t-shirt, Iain and my dad huddled around a bakery box. They looked up at me like kids caught with candy before dinner. It had been awhile since the last time I saw a Pine Bakery box. The memory played in my mind as real as the cookies in front of me. Lee, in my apartment foyer, the evening after we did laundry. It took awhile after moving to New York to see how naïve and stupid I had been. I will be more discreet next time rang through my head for years. Was I being stupid again?

"You took a whole cheesecake, a pie, and a box of cookies?" I asked. The men snickered, still eating. My dad moved to the coffee maker and filled the pot with tap water.

"Gina had Dan's beer fridge in the garage stuffed with desserts." My dad's smirk was visible in the dim kitchen. "Ted will get blamed if anyone notices."

"Frank is the good brother," I said.

Iain handed me a cookie, and I took a bite.

The kitchen table became my waiting area while my dad brewed coffee. He also wore gray sweats and an Oakville State t-shirt. We were odd, matching twins. Iain had on running pants and glasses.

Even though I had seen Iain outside of the suits, it wasn't until tonight I saw him, relaxed on my father's couch. He wasn't the CEO or the foreign guy. I gazed in a dreamy way as he laughed with my father. If it weren't for his accent, one would assume he belonged here.

As he pulled my dad's checkered throw blanket around him, Iain noticed my dreamy gaze. The dark lashes around his eyes widened. I didn't want him to think I was checking him out. So what does a girl do? I gave my father the same look. Frank Margo returned my gaze with perplexity.

"What's going on?" Frank asked.

Iain shrugged his shoulders and returned to Rambo. With as much oblivion as I could muster, I walked to the kitchen for a drink. My father's eyes watched me leave the room.

Yep, I am an idiot.

I returned to the living room with water. Iain turned off the television. My dad did his usual night checks—a habit I inherited. He flipped on the porch light for my cousins.

"Diane and Jim will be here anytime." Frank peeked out the mini blinds into the darkness of the front yard.

Diane was my dad's favorite niece and Uncle Ted's daughter. She was five years older than me with two young children— Haley and Madison. Haley, my little twin, was four, and Madison was two.

"Why is Diane staying here?" I sipped my water. Uncle Ted's living room could swallow our house. He had plenty of space.

"Diane doesn't get along with Theresa." My dad did a poor job of hiding his contempt of his sister-in-law. Theresa, being cousins with Lori Margo, possessed similar qualities to his ex-wife. "Theresa is a troublemaker. I told Diane they could stay here. I know you love her girls." He referred to Haley as Little Sarah.

"Are you leaving the door unlocked?" I motioned towards the deadbolt. My dad had one thought—sleep.

"What's with the twenty questions? It's Oakville. The most exciting event on this street was Don Burton's knee replacement." Frank was halfway down the hall.

"There's crime here. What about those thugs at the bus stop on Regency Road?"

The men laughed.

"Iain will fight off the burglars. He watched Rambo." Frank stood in his bedroom doorway.

"He wouldn't even touch iced tea tonight!"

With arms crossed, I stood in the living room outraged by their lack of safety. I was thinking like a New Yorker!

"My BB gun is in the closet if you want to keep watch, Sarah." Frank Margo spoke his final words for the night and closed his door.

"I once was a hooker." Iain bumped into me. "I can be hard and bolshy."

Was he serious? I couldn't hide my disgusted expression. Maybe he didn't understand the word hooker. It's like when someone tells the foreign exchange student bitch means teacher.

"Wow. I'm concerned you're sleeping in my bed."

I gave up on the unlocked door. We went to my room.

"It's a Rugby position." Iain grinned.

Fluffing the pillows on the daybed, I looked over at him relieved.

"That's good. I wouldn't want you fighting the burglars off with something hard and bolshy." What did bolshy mean? I made a mental note to search the word.

Iain flushed. "It's not ladylike to discuss my hard and bolshy."

We went from serious to cracking up over an odd dick joke.

"A Rambo-loving-engineer that steals cheesecake raised me

—this is as ladylike as it gets."

I should have got a queen like my practical father suggested, but I wanted the same daybed as Gina. Maybe I thought I would turn blond and gorgeous by sleeping in it. Another mistake made by a middle-schooler.

It took ten minutes to get us settled into the faux-iron-rod-work-of-art with Iain squashed against the back and me dangling off the end.

No touching.

It would be so much easier if we could snuggle together in the middle. He was still the CEO, and I sat number one on Gina's crap list. Even though I hated to admit it, she was right about me.

The image of coming home to Diane's husband, Jim, every night wasn't appealing. He was nice, but I couldn't spend every night with a guy watching television and talking about his job at the cable company.

It wasn't just the guys like Jim. I didn't care for the successful ones either. If I were honest, my parents' divorce screwed me up. Opening up to people made me uncomfortable unless I knew there was no chance of a relationship. Here was the dysfunctional part—I preferred relationships that would never work. These relationships would never make it past Sarah Margo's emotional fortress, which had a moat, twenty-foot walls, and complete with flaming arrows and rocket launchers.

"Are you awake?" Iain whispered.

I continued to lie still, afraid to roll into him or off the bed. My breathing remained the same as I pretended to be asleep. He needed to go to sleep, leave me alone with my depressing thoughts.

"I wanted to be certain you were asleep and not trying to touch my thigh." He chuckled to himself.

What? He knew?

Without thinking, I rolled over and pinched his side. He squealed like a girl. The movement on the daybed was too much, and half my body fell towards the floor. Iain caught me by the hips with his hands. My back arched in an erotic pose when the door opened. The blood rushed to my head. My eyes struggled to focus, and I prepared myself for an embarrassing parental lecture.

"Can I sleep with you?" Haley asked.

"Sarah," Diane said. She flipped the lights on to find me hanging off the bed, shirt pulled up due to gravity, with a gorgeous man holding my hips. "Oh my God. I am so sorry!"

"This isn't what it looks like." I sat up and flushed a thousand shades of red in the dark. I climbed out of bed and hugged Diane. "It's good to see you. Yes, Haley can sleep in here. This is Iain." I paused. "He works with me."

Although I worked for him, he didn't correct me. Diane seemed hesitant about Haley sleeping in the room with us, but she said nothing. She looked tired from driving, and Haley had her mind set. My little cousin climbed into the daybed in front of me.

Diane flipped off the light and left the three of us squashed. Haley snored within seconds. I couldn't kick Haley on to the floor, but I couldn't expect Iain to sleep like a stiff board against the iron railing all night.

Before I had a moment to analyze the situation, Iain wrapped his warm arms around me, pulling me against him. I melted into him without hesitation. My small frame fit against his large body. Together we were like a lock and key.

In the past, I would lighten the mood with one of my snarky comments, but my words disappeared somewhere in his arms.

We didn't talk, only slept.

CHAPTER FORTY-SEVEN

"Haley has more game with boys than Sarah." - Diane Collins

The next morning I woke to an empty bed and a quiet house. I opened the living room blinds, only the rental car and the truck in the driveway. Diane must have gone to Ted's house.

The smell of coffee lingered through the kitchen. I poured myself a cup. My great-grandmother's clock on the wall ticked to 9:30.

Why didn't anyone wake me up?

Laughter came from the backyard. Wrapping my robe around me, I walked outside, wood smoke lingering in the air. My dad and Iain lounged in lawn chairs around the homemade fire pit.

"Sarah, can you grab my phone off my desk?"

Without an answer from me, he continued to chat with Iain. My presence had no effect on their conversation. Once I returned, I handed my dad his flip phone. He entered Iain's contact information into his outdated device.

"Good morning," Iain said.

I replied the same back and sat in the empty lawn chair. I realized why no one used this chair; half the straps were loose. My butt sagged below the metal frame.

"I'm leaving next Friday. Where should I stay?" Frank's face was serious; my presence was meaningless to these two.

"You can stay at my townhouse in London. We can dine Saturday evening."

Does anyone see me?

"Are you sure?" My dad stood up and poked the fire pit. Flames shot up when the embers shifted.

"It's empty. I'll be there for the weekend. BBC is doing a feature on Mackgale-Berrell on Monday. Afterward, I am flying to Paris for two weeks." Iain handed Frank the newspaper.

"Are you traveling abroad?" I asked.

My father complained about downtown Oakville and dreaded flying to New York. I scratched my messy bed head. A townhouse in London, a feature on BBC, and flying to Paris for two weeks? Why was he here, in Oakville, sitting in a twenty-year-old lawn chair?

"Yeah," my dad replied with caution. He sipped his coffee. "You can come with me." He offered to be polite, but his tone said he wanted to go alone.

"No thanks. Couples retreat was enough for me. I'm out of vacation time." I smiled at my dad. "Besides, you will never get a lady with me around."

We chuckled.

"How long have the two of you been out here?" Between the newspapers, empty cookie box, and burnt logs—it appeared they had been outside for hours.

"Since five," they replied.

"I wanted to show you an article." My dad picked up the newspaper and flipped through the pages. "The school you attended for fifth and sixth grade is being demolished."

So what?

I gave him a shrug. The last thing I wanted to talk about was Green Street Intermediate.

"The health department received complaints over the years, but it wasn't until last month they discovered the entire underneath of the building is raw sewage." He handed me the paper. "I wonder if it was dilapidated when you were a student."

CHAPTER FORTY-EIGHT

"Sarah's boyfriend was from one of those New York City escort services." -Theresa Margo

The Oakville Riverfront Resort was downtown's finest—nothing compared to New York City, but the residents of Oakville didn't know otherwise. Gina booked the penthouse suite for the night. The hot tub on the balcony bubbled next to the matching bathrobes hanging on a rack. For Oakville, this was fancy stuff.

Gina invited a dozen women, including me, to get pampered. Forty-something-year-old women giggling over hair products and dresses was hilarious.

When I told the bride I didn't need my hair fixed, she ignored me and motioned for the stylist. She didn't trust me to do my own hair. We were getting family pictures. Not only did she pick out my dress, she handed me a pink tie for my dad.

The bride and her bridesmaids, all blond and most with breasts as fake as their spray tans, posed for a photo on the terrace. The stylist tugged at the knots in my hair before putting mine in a updo. Before I could thank her, she was removing Grandma Cobb's curlers.

I closed the bathroom door and stepped into the metallic gray dress. It was tight and short. The left shoulder had a thin strap with chiffon and crystal detailing.

"We are heading upstairs," Gina said. The herd of bridesmaids in hot pink picked up her long, white train.

Most brides in their forties wore a simple dress—not this one. Gina once told me the highlight of a Southern girl's life was her wedding day.

Shoe boxes, cans of hairspray, and tote bags with each bridesmaid's initials littered the penthouse. I closed the door and laughed to myself. Uncle Dan had been with Gina long enough to expect the condition of his hotel room.

My phone buzzed under my clothes in my tote bag. My dad and Iain were meeting me at the hotel. I didn't want to drive separate but neither of them wanted to wait around with females.

Iain: We have arrived. Where are you?

Me: I'm in Gina's room. I'll meet you in the lobby. I need to put my stuff in the car.

Iain: Okay.

The elevator was confusing.

Ground Entrance. Ground Main. Ground Front.

I searched for a sign explaining, which option stopped at the lobby. The no smoking sign didn't help. I pressed Ground Main. The elevator opened on the level above the lobby. The main staircase went up to a series of ballrooms. I spotted the front desk below and decided not to get back on the elevator.

Holding onto the railing, I steadied myself in the stilettos. I never wore heels this high, but they were gorgeous with metallic straps and crystals.

With only a few stairs left to go, I spotted my dad and Iain waiting by the windows. They both had one hand in their pocket, attention towards the parking garage where cars were in line to park. As if they sensed my presence, my father and so-called date turned to see me making my final stair without falling.

"Wow," my dad said. I didn't turn towards Iain's face, afraid to see his reaction. "If you didn't have a date, I would be hesitant to leave you alone." My father pointed at Iain. "I shouldn't worry leaving her alone with you, should I?"

"Perfect gentleman."

Them liking each other was weird. My dad staying with Iain in London was weirder. He wasn't my boyfriend. I would be an ass for saying anything to my dad. He was excited to travel, and I didn't want to disappoint him. I was the one who somehow put everyone in this bizarre situation.

I handed my dad the pink tie. He groaned and loosened his striped hand-me-down. My Aunt Penny waved when she entered the lobby.

"I will wear a pink tie because she does so much for us," he mumbled. Aunt Penny mouthed something to my dad. He shook his head confused. "My big sister is summoning me. I'll meet you inside."

Once my father disappeared with the Margo clan, I turned towards my date, tall and gorgeous, blue eyes close to mine. His tailored black suit and silver embossed tie matched me. Even though I grumbled about Gina picking out my dress and accessories, I was thankful. How could I stand next to a man as put together as Iain Mackgale?

Without taking his eyes from mine, he reached for my hand and planted a kiss on my wrist. My stilettos wobbled.

"You are beautiful," he said.

"Thank you."

Alex was right. Iain's accent was sexy.

"What's in the bag?" Iain asked.

"Monogrammed cloth napkins, a candle, bubbles, candy, and a t-shirt that says, g*ot the man in the right department.*" The t-shirt confused him. "Gina's friends make t-shirts with catchy phrases related to the groom's career. *Just what the doctor ordered* and *laying down the law* were two examples I heard while getting ready." I shrugged, not understanding it either but everyone in the bridal party loved the shirt.

"Do you want a big wedding one day?" Iain asked. I sucked

in a breath, either from the chilly air outside or the question.

"After you go through a messy divorce, you are less likely to sit around romanticizing about weddings," I replied with too much honesty.

"You're divorced?" He stopped to look at me, eyes squinted and posture rigid.

"I meant my parents' divorce."

I pressed the car remote button and tossed my bags into the lime green roller skate. We stood for a moment, illuminated only by a distant light in the parking garage.

"You told me you have trouble getting close to people. I do too," I said. My voice shook when the words left my mouth. Iain bit his lip. "I had the same boyfriend in high school and college. I ended it because his family hated me. They live next door to Uncle Dan, the brown Tudor on the right. After him, I had a fling with my childhood psychiatrist." His mouth dropped open. I shouldn't have told him. "I've been on some bad blind dates courtesy of my friends. You must date all the time."

My heart ached with jealous images of him making out with a blond and redhead on his private jet. The girls took turns trying on expensive bracelets while a brunette filled a bathtub with champagne.

I couldn't read him.

"No." He exhaled. "I told you people only want me because my position or wealth can benefit them." I touched his hand. He threaded his fingers through mine. "I spend my time closing deals, traveling, and fighting off lawsuits."

Iain closed the distance between us. The moisture of his breath moved against my lips. I didn't like being vulnerable, but I loved the way he looked at me.

"Hey! You two stop necking and go inside!" Uncle Ted walked past our car with Theresa. Ted's physique in a suit looked more penguin than man.

"I want to punch him," I muttered. Iain escorted me away from the car towards the hotel entrance.

"What is necking?" he whispered. We walked behind my annoying uncle and his bitchy wife.

"Kissing," I whispered back.

"Oh."

The topic of kissing silenced us.

CHAPTER FORTY-NINE

"I swear she's like an angel from heaven." -Brian Cobb

Candlelight flickered in the darkness, a beautiful accompaniment to the white lilies and roses. A hundred white chairs with pink ribbons were full of guests to see the beautiful bride and Dan Margo do what he said he would never do. It's funny what ultimatums can do for a woman.

We climbed over wedding guests to get to the middle of the aisle. I sat next to Gina's mom, where my dad had saved us seats. He continued reading a pamphlet he picked up in the lobby.

It was awkward sitting next to my date. A guy like Iain wouldn't be at a middle-aged couple's wedding in Oakville. A small part of me felt insecure. People assumed he was my boyfriend. Iain did a poor job dispelling this notion as his hand rested on my thigh.

My dad noticed the hand and grinned.

The harpist plucked the strings of her instrument in the corner. The beautiful melody summoned the bridesmaids with white roses and groomsmen. The whole event was very cheesy. I couldn't get past the fabrication of love and happiness. It wasn't only my aunt, magazines and television shows loved the pageantry of weddings. It was all sickening until Gina Cobb appeared arm and arm with her father.

Wow.

The designer dress glided down the aisle with Mr. Cobb stumbling to match Gina's steps. When the guests stood, I noticed my Aunt Penny eying my date. I groaned when I thought about another cheesy wedding tradition—the bouquet toss. Whenever I knew the flowers were flying, I made sure I was in the restroom or outside. How embarrassing would it be to catch a bouquet?

I needed to stop stressing.

As much as I wanted to blame my inner turmoil on my family, I knew the actual cause sat beside me. I hated the playing with fire feeling.

There was a familiarity between us that was undeniable. Our conversation was so easy and enjoyable. How many dates had I wanted to leave after five minutes? I continued to stew over Iain, missing most of the ceremony, not that it mattered. Uncle Dan had already violated every vow he was taking, most I had witnessed in person.

"I now pronounce you Mr. and Mrs. Dan Margo," the reverend said.

Dan had Gina in a dramatic lean back kiss before he was told to kiss the bride. The guest cheered at the not-so-new couple making their way down the aisle to start the proverbial happily ever after.

The professional portraits were endless. Gina told the photographer how she wanted the shots posed. Everyone played it smart and did as told.

My dad and I posed next to a rose-covered archway waiting for the photographer to test the lighting. The signal to smile came when the photographer raised his hand in the air like we were dogs begging for treats. Before we could get up, the high energy professional had Iain by the arm posing him behind us.

"Let's get a shot with your husband too."

"Um…we…no…"

The photographer's hand went up, and our threesome smiled for the camera. He shooed us away for members of the Cobb family to get portraits.

"I tried to correct him." We trailed behind my dad to the reception area.

"I want a copy," he said.

Iain cried in my stairwell a week earlier over the thought of having his picture taken for a tabloid, but tonight he posed for a professional portrait. I wondered if he was testing my trust.

"Only if you hang it in your office."

"A challenge, huh?" Iain studied my face. "Consider it done. I may have to disguise you. Perhaps a fake mustache and hat? Frank looked rather smashing in that pink tie."

We laughed.

"He rocked the pink tie." My smile hurt. I couldn't remember the last time I'd enjoyed hanging out with someone. Iain pulled out my chair.

"I can hear everything you're saying," my dad said. He scanned the room until he found the bar. "You guys want a drink?"

"Nothing for me. Water is fine." I sipped from the glass on the table.

"I'll have what you're having, Frank."

Having whatever Frank was having was not the best idea. He was not the high-end wine drinking kind of guy.

Wedding guests mingled in the reception area for the wedding party to finish their private cocktail hour downstairs. Iain and I sat in silence. Soft music played near the dance floor where the little kids danced or dragged each other around the slick floor. Haley ignored me when I waved, too caught up in her seven-year-old dance partner.

I didn't know if I should laugh or cry when I spotted my father with the drinks—Pabst Blue Ribbon in a shiny,

Americana can. Nothing said class like PBR.

Iain raised the can to his lips. My father sat next to Iain, drinking his own can of beer.

"This is quite good," he said.

"My beer of choice since the 70s." Guests settled into their assigned tables awaiting dinner. "I am starving. We should have grabbed a bite beforehand. I didn't know about hours of pictures and private cocktail parties."

"Something wrong?" Iain put his arm around my chair and leaned close to my ear. He smelled amazing. The tips of his fingers brushed my shoulder.

"I'm nervous. Gina asked me to say a few words before the dancing starts."

For weeks, I tried to write a speech, but couldn't. I hoped standing in front of Gina would inspire meaningful sentences.

The room stood, clapped, and cheered for the wedding party's arrival. Fuzzy pink handcuffs bound Dan and Gina. Who wanted that mental image before dinner?

Like clockwork, servers brought plates of food to the tables. The place cards for members of the Cobb family sat at our table untouched. I guessed they were no-shows.

"Yep. This is us," a man said. His date had larger-than-life blond hair. I didn't know the woman's age—she could have been thirty or fifty. The purse on her shoulder rivaled her big hair. There was no doubt these people belonged to Gina. "Hi folks, Brian Cobb." The overweight, balding man extended a hand. My father stood.

"Frank Margo, I'm Dan's brother."

Brian smiled. He was the ignorant bliss, always smiling kind of guy. Brian reached for Iain.

"I'm Iain. It's a pleasure to make your acquaintance." Iain had the seamless ability to go from casual to business. Brian cocked his head to the side. He wasn't expecting a foreign accent.

"Sarah, Frank's daughter." I gestured towards my father shaking hands with Big Hair, Big Purse Lady. Brian walked around the table and hugged me. I didn't hug him back.

Brian pulled away and observed me like the chosen one. "I have heard much about you. It's nice to put a name with a face."

Gina may have spoken about me, but she never spoke about Brian until yesterday. "You are a teacher, right?"

"It warms my heart Gina talks about me." Brian hugged me again. "Gina says you live in New York City and work as an engineer."

My date narrowed his eyes, displeased by Brian's over-friendliness. Iain made this face often at work when his expectations weren't met.

"I love living in the city. Frank is also a mechanical engineer. I guess it runs in the family."

Brian put his hand in his pocket. The servers reached around us to fill up drinks.

"Brian honey, sit down," Big Hair, Big Purse Lady said. She fluffed her hair with her hand.

When I returned to my seat, Iain stared with intensity. We didn't blink until Brian spoke again.

"Ivan, can you pass me the salt shaker?" Brian pointed at the glass bottle with the metallic top.

Iain didn't like people calling him Iain, let alone the wrong name altogether. My lips spread into a smile.

"You are trouble," Iain whispered. He put his cloth napkin on his lap. The Southerners and my dad were busy eating a salad.

"If I'm trouble, what are you?" I stabbed a tomato with my fork.

"You tell me."

CHAPTER FIFTY

"Y'all remember when y'all did jello shots." -Tara Tarleton

The toasts at weddings were the same. The best man attended undergrad with Dan—they got drunk, chased girls, and Gina was the one. Tara, who said *y'all* fourteen times during her speech, gave the typical we have known each other since second grade.

When the emcee introduced me, I thanked him and accepted the microphone. I was tall in my fancy heels.

Please don't trip.

Gina had tears in her eyes, which made me more nervous. Did the words appear as planned? No. Was I winging it? Yes.

"I met Gina for the first time at Lake Minnow. Our family used to go boating there every summer when I was a kid. One summer, in particular, about twenty years ago, my uncle brought a beautiful girl on a date to the lake. This girl wore the craziest, largest hoop earrings."

The crowd laughed.

"Still does," someone shouted from the crowd.

"She was the coolest." I smiled at Uncle Dan. His eyes watered. Since when did he become sentimental?

I took a few steps towards the bridal table until I stood in front of the bride. "You have always been there for me. Anytime I needed help or someone to listen, I could always count on you. We have been through ups and downs, sorrow and joy." Taking a deep breath, I tried not to tear up but did. "I should be up here speaking of the love you share with my uncle, but today is much bigger. You have always been our family. We are so lucky to have you. I'm excited it's official." Everyone clapped, which almost made me forget my purpose for being on stage. "It is my privilege to bring Mr. and Mrs. Margo to the floor for their first dance as husband and wife."

Handing the microphone back to the emcee, I hugged my aunt and uncle before moving off to the side of the dance floor. The band Bread blasted from the large speakers. Was it corny? Yes, but I could not help the tears staining my cheeks. The emcee announced the wedding guests could join the couple on the dance floor. As I turned to find my way back to our table, Iain waited with his hand out to dance.

It never occurred to me that I would have to dance with my date. I didn't plan on sleeping in the same bed with him either.

With perfect posture and steps, he led me around the dance floor. I wasn't a good dancer. Was this a Waltz? As the music tempo picked up, he spun me around.

"Give up my life, my heart, my home…"

"You know this song?" I asked.

Iain pulled me closer, and fancy danced me around the floor once more.

When the music stopped, we broke apart for a moment until the emcee announced the bride and groom had a second song. Leave it to Gina to have two first dance songs. The middle-aged crowd cheered when the first beats of Ginuwine played.

We swayed to the beat for a moment before his hands reached for my hips and pulled me against him. I ran my hands up the front of his chest until my arms wrapped around his neck. It turned into slow dancing meets club dancing. *What the hell were we doing?* I buried my head on his shoulder in embarrassment, and he hugged me tighter.

"Your speech was brilliant," he said into my ear.

We stood closer in height with my stilettos. Iain moved his face near mine and closed his eyes.

"Can I cut in?" My slow jam high was ruined by Brian Cobb.

The hands on my hips tightened. He didn't want to give me to the balding man.

Iain flashed Brian a fake smile. "I will find Frank."

The R&B song stopped, and a soda shop oldie played. Brian's eager face said he had his heart set on slow dancing. I avoided his grabby hands by starting to imitate the older crowd doing their version of the jive.

"Do you have fun with your friend?" Brian asked.

Was he doing the twist or trying to adjust his pants? I hated fifties music. I could see the family resemblance to Gina, but she inherited the better genes.

"Yes. We always have fun together."

Brian Cobb was a nice person, but I didn't want to hang out with him. If this weren't his sister's wedding, I would have told him no. I couldn't stop thinking about Iain's hands on my hips, or the way he grinned while twirling me.

"There is more to life than good looks and fun." Brian moved closer, beady green eyes following my every move.

I thought back to my fight with Gina. She threatened to tell her brother I liked him. Did she? Had my troublemaker uncle rubbed off on her?

His arm reached for my waist. I shot Iain a desperate plea. He twirled Haley in a circle, her laughter louder than the music.

"Where is your date? I shouldn't be monopolizing you." I gave Brian the same irritated vibe Debbie received whenever she asked me to do a meaningless task.

"Who Tisha? Her daddy is cousins with my mama. She didn't want to come alone." My question distracted Brian for a moment. I kept my eye on his stubby fingers, ready to pounce on me.

"I'm dancing with your boyfriend." Haley giggled.

Happiness filled every crack in my closed off heart. She cuddled closer to Iain. It appeared happiness was filling his cracks too.

"Can I have him back?" I touched Iain's dress shirt. Haley threw her arms around him and shook her head no.

"There is plenty for both of you." He ignored Brian who continued to dance. "Would you like to get a drink?"

I nodded, relieved to be leaving the dance floor. It was only a matter of time before another slow song started.

"Thanks for the dance, Brian. If I don't see you, safe travels back to Georgia." I walked away, but he grabbed my arm.

"We will see each other again."

I couldn't hide the look of horror. Brian Cobb thought he had a chance with me. Was he delusional? Why did he assume Iain was only a friend? I wondered if everyone thought there was no way Iain could be my boyfriend.

This was exactly why I didn't want a relationship.

Haley and Iain tried to figure out which juice box they wanted—grape or apple. She recommended the apple and explained it doesn't stain your shirt if you spill it. I stood behind them. Iain ordered me a glass of red wine and tipped the bartender. They sipped their little, orange straws.

"Excellent choice, Haley." Iain sucked his child-sized drink. Haley's crush grew even further. Her admiration did not last long when she noticed her seven-year-old dance partner on the floor. Haley wiggled out of Iain's arms; her focus on the boy. Without a word, she hurried to the dance floor with her juice box. Iain smiled at Haley before turning my way. "Would you care to go outside?"

Grabbing his suit jacket off a chair, Iain wrapped it around me before we exited to the terrace. Several people were outside huddled around the propane heaters, enjoying the quieter space. The city lights illuminated the ripples in the rushing water below. The river did not have a choice where it ended, and I found myself envious of the luxury.

Why was I discontent? The past five years had been great in New York City, although I felt myself wanting more. What more meant, I wasn't sure.

The cold, iron bench on my bare legs sent a noticeable chill up my body. Iain wrapped his arm around my shoulder. I leaned into him. We sat in companionable silence, watching the river and enjoying the distant beat of party music. Brian appeared on the terrace but didn't see us in the corner.

A devilish grin flickered across Iain's face. "Brian wanted some of your dirty dancing." He smiled. I stuttered. "Don't deny it."

I warmed from embarrassment. For a minute, on the dance floor, I forgot myself. He had the ability to lower my guard.

"I will blame it on the alcohol. Doesn't that work?" I fluttered my eyelashes.

He twisted his lips and narrowed his eyes. I pressed my lips together to keep from laughing. This tension, the back and forth, was addictive.

"It is a valid excuse on occasion. In this circumstance, no. You had water for dinner," he said like a trial lawyer.

How could I top his checkmate?

"You're hot. I couldn't keep my hands off you."

He cocked his head to the side.

"How's that for honesty? I am a victim of your cougar ways." He loved our dangerous game.

"What? You're older than me."

"How do you know?" he asked.

"I read it on the Internet. You are four months older."

"What else did you read?"

"You like men, work too much, and you're a snob," I said.

Our banter came to a halt. My comeback reeked like a pile of shit.

"It could be worse, I suppose." He gazed at the river. "Shall we go back inside?"

I brought something to the surface inside him. Whatever it was, whether true or not, he didn't like my response.

After an hour of mingling, I was ready to go home and get out of my ensemble. My feet ached, my hair itched, and the tape Gina insisted I use to keep *my girls* in place chaffed my skin. It's wonderful to have arrived at an age where others feel the need to tape your breasts to make them *not saggy* as Gina put it.

"Dad, we are leaving," I said to my father who sat at our table laughing with Tisha. I told him many times to find a woman, but I hoped Big Hair, Big Purse would not be the one. He ignored me, enthralled in Tisha's story.

"Can you believe him? I got snubbed for Big Hair Lady," I said to Iain. We headed to say our goodbyes to the bride and groom.

He stayed quiet.

"Where were you?" Gina asked. She sipped a glass of wine. "You missed the bouquet toss. Tara wrestled Connie to the floor." Gina found this amusing.

"Darn. I'll be a spinster forever."

"My brother is interested." Gina grinned.

"What did you tell him?" I asked. She laughed. "If you told him I was interested, you are starting off your first official day as a Margo very poorly."

"I am kidding. Are you coming to Lake Minnow tomorrow?"

The bridal party rented cabins at the state park to party all weekend. Camping was not my scene. My dad said he wasn't going.

"No. I promised my dad I would help him grade papers. We have spent little time together the past few months." I wanted to curl up on the couch and eat dinner at home.

"What about you, Iain?" Gina handed her empty wine glass to a waiter.

"Thanks for the invitation. I have remote meetings tomorrow," he said.

"Constant work must make it hard for a personal life," she said.

My aunt's intentions were to shut down any notion I had about a relationship with Iain Mackgale. I didn't blame her, but I could live without her meddling.

"Yes, it does," Iain said.

He knew what Gina was doing. I fidgeted with my bracelet. Could this be more uncomfortable? Uncle Dan returned at the perfect moment and shook Iain's hand.

"Nice meeting you. I hope you had a good time tonight," Dan said. His face was flushed from alcohol and dancing. The last time I saw him this drunk, he hit on me at a family reunion.

"Congratulations." I hugged my aunt and uncle. A weird emotion came over me, and my stomach ached.

Iain waved goodbye to someone across the dance floor.

Everyone knew they wouldn't see Iain Mackgale again.

CHAPTER FIFTY-ONE

"Warren telephoned me about the girl. How disappointing. Iain won't take my calls. I left him a message and urged his immediate return." -John William Mackgale, Lord Crossleigh

The night air rustled through the maple trees in the front yard, the ones I used to climb in junior high. I dug through my purse for the house keys. Yellow light glowed from the porch light, making me feel at home. My father was convinced the yellow light bulbs kept away the bugs, but they still swarmed around looking for any warmth. Who could blame them? People needed warmth just as bad, but we were less obvious.

Iain and I didn't speak on the car ride home. I said true, yet hurtful, words. My curiosity wanted to know if any truth lived in the rumors. I wasn't thinking. This was Iain's life.

Once inside the house, he carried my bags to my room. I sat on the couch and removed my fantastic heels. My feet ached. I massaged the ball of my foot. There was no way I would wear these shoes again unless I had an amazing date. I wanted to laugh at the thought.

"What's going on?" I asked.

I stood, much shorter without my shoes.

The odd stare continued. He remained still, face darkened by shadows. The only light came from the kitchen.

"Thinking." Each breath was slow. He loosened his tie and unbuttoned his cuffs.

"Can you unzip me please?" I turned my back towards him. His warm fingers touched my skin. The zipper glided in slow, calculated tugs. He stopped near my panties. Even though the dress was loose, I couldn't breathe.

I climbed into the daybed next to Iain. He rolled onto his side to face me.

"I'm sorry. I didn't mean to offend you."

"No need to apologize," he said. We stayed quiet for a moment. "Is Haley sleeping here?"

"No. Jim carried her into the den. She danced herself out."

Haley made me reflect on childhood innocence. I wondered when she would discover how screwed up and complicated the world can be.

"Tell me about the psychiatrist." He nestled into the bed ready to hear the entire tale.

"What? That is personal." Not to mention, I didn't want to discuss sex with Iain Mackgale.

"I'm curious. The situation is out of your character." He analyzed the details he pieced together. "I would snoop in your HR file, but those details are not on employment contracts." I laughed. He looked serious.

"You have snooped at my file?"

"Yes. I viewed your employment file before we met. I review anyone invited to our senior-level projects. You made the cut with your excellent grades, recommendations, and employment reviews." He let out a breath, still waiting for me to begin my story. "Okay, you win. You can have equal privilege with my personal life, and you are welcome to see my transcripts."

"Deal."

His transparency bargain made me tell him what I had never told my closest friends—the sorry tale of Lee Abrams. I left out some of the details.

"He actually told you he would be more discreet next time?"

The fact he knew about Lee made me uncomfortable. He would have found out somehow.

"I should have said no. I never liked him." Iain's stare in the darkness was intimidating as if he was reassessing his original opinion of me. "I've never told my friends in New York I moved there because of—"

"Wait." Iain rubbed his chin. The daybed shifted. "You relocated because of him?"

"Yeah. My dad—"

"Frank knew? Did Frank want to murder him?"

Iain waited for an explanation.

"Frank Margo is the most reasonable person I have ever met. He wouldn't waste his energy on a lost cause. I was a consenting adult. When I told my dad, he said the real sign of maturity is knowing what to do when you know you have made a mistake. I wanted the job in New York. I was sick of the drama in Oakville."

"Did he agree with your decision to move?" The intensity never left his face.

"Yes. The job opportunity was amazing for someone just out of college. I wanted a new beginning. Everything was overwhelming."

"We all get lost sometimes. We wish for new beginnings too. Why are you so nervous?" The fan hummed in the corner.

"Wouldn't you be nervous? You said yourself you come from a world where people are not open with their personal lives." I shifted my weight to get comfortable.

"I never said I preferred my upbringing. For years, I saw my parents only on holidays. Their only concerns were that I was alive, not disgracing the family, and my grades were satisfactory." He collected his thoughts. "I love my parents, but they did me a disservice by sending me to California for five years."

"Why?" I didn't understand his meaning.

"I prefer when people are more upfront and forthcoming rather than implied. This is obvious in my business practices, which sometimes makes me unpopular. I would have been different if I remained in Berrell."

"What you are saying is you have been hanging out with wild, free-spirited Americans and now people don't like you?"

"Yes and no. I am a melting pot thanks to my travels. I hope you use your time traveling to your advantage." The professional edge in his voice faded away. "This is getting work-like."

"Let's move on then. Tell me about the supermodels and the private planes." He cocked his head to the side. "Hired guns. Lap dances. VIP." Iain stopped my rambling with his index finger to my lips, letting it linger for a moment. I wondered what he would do if I sucked his finger into my mouth.

"You have been reading too many of those smut rags under your bed," he said with narrowed eyes. I wanted to defend my guilty-self, which was obvious from the mouth open expression on my face. Iain smiled satisfied, and I had no defense.

"What were you doing under my bed?" I narrowed my eyes back at him.

"First, it's not a bed. Neither is this contraption." He rocked back and forth, and the metal squeaked. "Are you averse to sleeping in a proper bed?"

"You are avoiding my question." I rolled onto my stomach, causing my side to touch him. He was right. The bed was small and crappy—what was I thinking?

"No supermodels." He fluffed his pillow. "I own two planes. The only females on board are staff or family. No woman has ever given me a lap dance, a drunken rugby mate once." Iain regretted bargaining our secrets.

"I was kidding." Not true. I wanted the scoop on private jets full of supermodels like my smutty, romance novels. Would I be jealous? Yes! I did not want to share him with anyone. "I indulged you in my relationships; now it is your turn."

"Like you, one serious relationship." He said, face inches from mine on the pillow we shared. "We were together a year when I was twenty." I gave him a puzzled look. Was this everything?

"She broke your heart?"

"It was brutal at the time." He ran his fingers through his damp hair.

"Maybe she didn't…" I couldn't find the right words.

"Please don't tell me I was a bad lover." I laughed. He must have considered this before. "I will need the number to your psychiatrist." Iain propped his body up on his elbows, staring down at me.

"He isn't into guys." The corners of his mouth lifted at my smart remark. "Maybe your ex felt too young for a serious relationship?"

He blew out a breath. "She married the next summer to a man with more money." The ex irritated him. "More money at the time. She is now divorced. After our breakup, I drowned myself in school and started the company. I made my first million within a year. My second cousin died, and I inherited a title. She regrets dumping me, but for the wrong reasons. I am told people would trade places with me. How much is your privacy worth?" Iain fell back onto the pillow. "I am very fortunate. Please do not think me ungrateful."

"I would never think you're ungrateful," I whispered.

"This stays between us, right?" We gazed at the dark ceiling together. Iain yawned.

"Of course. You know my secrets too. The last thing I want is my drama published in the company newsletter."

"We don't distribute a company newsletter," he said.

I smiled in the darkness.

"Goodnight," I said.

"Sleep well."

CHAPTER FIFTY-TWO
"I prayed for the gray yoga pants." -Iain Mackgale

My eyes fluttered opened. Iain's face hovered inches above mine. He wore a gray jacket and running pants. Why did he feel the need to wake me up? I glanced at the alarm clock and groaned at the time—5:30 am.

"Get dressed. Let's go running," he said.

Running before daylight? Nope. Not happening.

"I don't need to run because I already have a hot body." I flipped the purple and white comforter over my head. Iain tugged my arm from its warm hiding spot. "Okay. Fine."

Five minutes later, I stood in the living room in yoga pants and a sweatshirt, messy bed head in a ponytail. I yawned. Nothing about me was pretty.

I shivered in the cold morning air. My gym stayed seventy-two degrees, with flat-screen televisions and a juice bar if you didn't want to run.

Iain started slow but accelerated when we approach the end of the lane. We turned right and stayed on the sidewalk next to the main road. Only a few cars were out. No one else was crazy enough to run before daylight.

Iain slowed his pace, glanced at the fancy contraption on his arm, and looked back at me. I smiled like I wasn't dying.

"Two miles. Not bad." He seemed pleased with my athletic abilities. "Are you ready to go back?"

I nodded. Who runs after three hours of sleep? My only consolation was his tight pants and jacket. It would've looked terrible on most men, but his body looked amazing. I didn't mind running behind him at all. He slowed to run next to me. I blushed, convinced he read my mind again.

Early riser, Frank Margo, sipped his second cup of coffee, leisurely sprawled out in his recliner. The morning light spilled through the large picture window and ruined my thoughts of going back to bed.

"I am impressed," my dad said to Iain at the sight of me dressed and awake.

"I told you I would have her ready to work by eight." Iain looked at his watch and then looked at my father. "She even has time to shower."

"I need a shower," I said on my way to the bathroom. Their conversation echoed down the hall. I needed sleep too.

When I stepped out of the shower, I realized I didn't have clothes to change into. I peeked my head in the hall and tip-toed to my room in a towel. I almost jumped out of my skin when I saw Iain crouched on the floor digging through his laptop bag. He had his phone balanced between his face and shoulder. Quickly grabbing my clothes, I headed to the bathroom to put on my jeans and t-shirt.

Two hours later, I walked past the den with my dad's laundry. Iain sat at the cheap desk typing away on his laptop. He wore a call center headset. The carefree, relaxed expression from last night was replaced with an intense scowl.

"Get Alfonso on the line, inform him of the terms. I am not making concessions." He gave a shy smile. I continued to the laundry room, unable to escape eavesdropping. "Two hours...I'll let her know...Ten million...Absolutely."

The washer made its signature swooshing sounds. I turned around and bumped into Iain. I didn't realize he was no longer on the phone.

"Do you require laundry services?" I smiled.

"No. Martin picked up my laundry this morning. Are you going out?"

I narrowed my eyes in thought. "Martin is here, in Oakville?"

"I told you. I never travel alone." Before I could ask another question, he changed the subject. "Frank said you're running errands."

"He wants cottage cheese and lunch meat," I said. Iain winced. "He isn't eating them together."

"Do you care if I join you? I need to breathe before my next call."

"Sure. We won't be gone long." Iain nodded and stepped out of my way. My dad sat at the kitchen table grading a stack of papers. "We will be back soon." Frank looked up briefly giving a shadow of a smile before returning to his work. He looked tired.

"He is never behind on his grading," I said when we got in the rental car.

"The wedding perhaps?" Iain shrugged. "It's not hard to fall behind at work."

"Don't remind me."

The traffic light on the corner of Cannon and Regency Road always had a long wait. Iain sighed. I watched him type on his phone in the passenger seat. The corners of his eyes wrinkled from either the sunlight or stress. He tapped the phone's case.

"I don't know how you do it."

"I am not sure myself." His eyes stayed on his phone. After typing a reply, he shut off his device and placed it in the console. When I glanced over, his dark blue eyes were studying me, making me self-conscious.

"Are we on the same flight tomorrow?"

"No. I am flying private. I have urgent matters which require my presence." His ambiguity created distance between us. No matter how close I felt to him, he could shut down our connection in a second. "Thanks for allowing me to accompany you. I really enjoyed your family. This experience was new and different. You were right. I needed to get away."

Gina's harsh words from her bathroom scolding surged through me—new and different.

The best case is you have a broken heart. Do you want to lose your job?

We carried the Walmart bags into the kitchen. Iain helped me put the cold items in the refrigerator. He checked his watch, then his phone, and opened a bottle of water. Something had changed. He was no longer relaxed. Our fun banter, gone. I didn't know if it was me or work or something unrelated.

"You're back," my dad said. He wiped his feet on the back door mat. "What's with all the bags?"

Iain's phone rang, he answered the call and walked into the living room. My dad watched him leave and looked at me with the same thought.

"Iain's first visit to Walmart." I shrugged.

My dad peeked into the gray plastic bags. I inherited my curiosity from him. Iain purchased three iPads, several t-shirts, an electric razor, and random snack foods. I wondered if the snacks were reminiscent of his childhood years in California. I didn't ask. Iain returned to the kitchen, phone back in his pocket.

"Did you see your middle school friends at the deli?" my father asked.

"What are you talking about?"

"The blond and the redhead?" Iain laughed. My dad nodded. "Sarah hid behind a rack of pastries. They must not be great friends."

"I have never been friends with Adrianna or Mindy. Why didn't you warn me they worked at Walmart?"

284

My hands moved to my hips. Imagine ordering lunch meat and seeing two of your archenemies bringing out tubs of macaroni salad and fried chicken from the back. I didn't want them to see me. Would they have recognized me? I imagined Mindy calling me Chunk even though she now weighed three of me.

"They are nice girls. When I told them my daughter went to Green Street, they said to tell you hello. Mindy's little boy—"

"Mean girls never grow up, Dad."

Had my father never had a bully? If I felt like a debate, I would bring up my mother. Had she changed?

My dad smirked. "Let the past go."

It seemed like a nice sentiment. Everyone always said to let the past go, but did they? Was it possible to take an experience so rooted and rid ourselves of the memory? Letting go of the past often involved forgetting. It was hard to forget how awful those girls were and impossible to forget the triangle tag on the back pocket of my mother's Guess jeans when she walked out the door.

"How about we drink tonight?" Iain asked. His clairvoyance was on point today. I needed a drink.

"Sounds like a plan."

My heels were in the grass. I sat beside the fire pit, on a blanket, with a glass of bourbon. Iain lounged in the lawn chair, bottle between his legs.

"Frank has excellent taste in spirits," Iain said.

An empty bottle laid near a log where he discarded his jacket. He pushed up his sleeves, face red from the fire and alcohol.

"I don't think I've…" I laughed, collapsed onto the blanket, and hit my head. "Ouch." I rubbed my hair. Iain joined me on the ground.

"You okay?" He smiled. I nodded. "Alcohol doesn't affect me until I lay down." He laid next to me. We gazed at the stars, clear in the chilly night.

"Thanks for coming, Iain Mackgale," I said. My eyes were too heavy to stay open.

"I have to piss," he said. I opened one eye, unable to move my head. Iain's breathing slowed.

"Get up." I nudged him with my hand. His fingers threaded into mine. The base of his palm warm. The band of his watch cold.

"Don't worry, Sarah Margo," he mumbled. The wind rustled through the trees, in the darkness. "It hangs to the right. You're on the left."

Before I could respond, the alcohol dragged me into a numb sleep.

Bright light, like a beam, shone into my eyes. By reflex, I shielded my face with my forearm. *Oh no, not the police.* I shook Iain's hand, still locked with mine.

"It's the police, Iain," I whispered. He groaned.

"Worse. It's your father," a voice said. The beam left my face. I sat up. The fire had burned out, porch light on. "What the hell were you two thinking? It's forty-eight degrees."

Iain sat up and pressed a button on his watch.

"It's ten after five," my dad said. He picked up a bottle and looked at the label. "Go inside. I would never expect behavior like this from either of you."

"We have no excuse, sir," Iain said.

My dad blew out a breath and chuckled.

"You two will restock my liquor," he said, tone back to bad guy.

"Okay," I whispered.

"Not the cheap stuff, either."

My head throbbed from drinking too much and sleeping on the cold ground. I glanced at my phone. Gina said she'd meet me at the airport for lunch at one. The newlyweds didn't leave for Hawaii until Monday.

I checked my phone again, not for the time. My heart hoped for a text. Nothing. Iain left early, in a car, with his driver. Everything about Iain Mackgale was strange. We would get closer, feel like good friends, but he would pull away. When we had amazing moments, I forgot his importance. Other times, I couldn't understand why he had anything to do with me. Somehow in my crazy mind, I concluded I had a chance with him.

She hugged me, smelling of perfume and a charcoal grill.

"Hey," I said, caught off guard.

Gina had on over-sized sunglasses and her hair in a ponytail. No one would guess this woman was older than me.

"Does this airport have salads? I have spent the last forty-eight hours with men grilling slabs of meat," she said with a smile. Gina pushed her sunglasses on top of her head. She looked tired but content and relaxed.

"Yeah…" I recognized him from a distance. The same mischievous face and long hair. He tried to wave, attention on me, but his hands were cuffed. Two police officers escorted him.

"Sarah!"

I wanted to climb under the table. Gina whirled around to see who was calling my name. She strained her eyes.

Should I tell her I don't know the guy?

"Sarah Margo!"

Scratch that.

"Do you know him?" Gina hissed.

"You are hot. Call me," Brent said. The officers moved their prisoner past us.

"Please tell me you didn't date him," Gina said. I gave her an offended look. She waited for an answer.

"No. We went to middle school together. He was always a troublemaker." We watched Brent and the cops disappear around the corner. "Why do I see people from my past? Doesn't anyone move away?"

Gina smiled. "It's the same for me when I visit Georgia. Nothing has changed. You would think high school ended a week ago."

"You were right," I said.

"Are you ill? Since when do you admit—"

"About Iain."

We paused for a moment. Tears started to form, but I told myself I wasn't crying over a guy.

"I'm sorry. I want you to be happy."

"I know."

I wished she realized how much I appreciated her caring for me. She always had, no matter how much we argued back and forth.

"Dan has a young friend he golfs with at the club, Robert."

"No thanks. Let's get lunch." A church group wheeled their luggage past us. They wore matching yellow t-shirts with a crucifix on the back.

"Let's get you back to New York before you're tempted to get the felon's number."

"He was kind of cute."

CHAPTER FIFTY-THREE

"Deana had to be number one. She couldn't stand the thought of Sarah dating Iain Mackgale." -Cassie Long

My luggage rested under the window, behind my bed, six days after returning from Oakville. I glanced over at my bags. Alex sat on my bed laughing with Cassie about a meme on his phone. Deana knocked and let herself in.

"Hey Mama," Alex said to Deana. Her damp hair looked brown. "How was work?"

"Long. I have a new client who complains about everything. She won't work for the results. I tried to get Nathan to take her. She says she doesn't want a male trainer." Deana smiled. "Did you order the food?"

"Yeah. About ten minutes ago," Cassie said. She handed Alex his phone.

I stood in the room, watching my friends. Their conversation blurred. I tried not to think about not hearing from Iain. No texts. No calls. Nothing. On the plane, I told myself to forget about him. At night, I woke wanting his warmth, the smell of him, the sound of his light breathing next to me. I glanced at my suitcases. They needed unpacked. Tonight.

No more thoughts of Iain.

"How was the wedding?" Deana asked. I looked up from my daze to find my friends staring at me.

"Beautiful. They are in Hawaii. I will show you pictures when they return."

Deana picked up the silver stilettos next to my bag. "Are these the shoes from the wedding?" I nodded. She looked at the designer tag then to Alex. "Too bad I'm not a size eight. These are killer. Too bad you didn't have a date."

"She had a date," Alex said. I shot him a warning glare. I didn't tell Deana. "Her work friend."

"Oh. Ethan went?" Her brows raised.

"Iain Mackgale," Cassie said in a confessional tone. I never told Alex and Cassie Iain's last name. Deana cocked her head to the side.

"What?" She released an uncomfortable laugh. "Is that a code name for Ethan?"

"What's going on?" Alex asked.

"Iain Mackgale. *Cross Hill Manor*," Cassie said to Alex.

"He's an actor? No way. That guy can't act. He works with Sarah." Alex looked at Cassie confused. Deana stood with her hands on her hips.

"*Cross Hill Manor* is a period drama based on Iain Mackgale's family. Drew McGrew plays him in the show," Cassie said.

"Oh. I know what you're talking about now. He's much better looking than Drew McGrew. Nicer too."

"Are you serious? You invited Iain Mackgale to Oakville? How do you even know him?"

Alex bit his bottom lip in a dramatic way. Cassie looked at the ceiling.

"He's—"

"The CEO of your company and a titled aristocrat. How did you meet? Why would he want to be your wedding date?"

"I—"

"He's a terrible person. Have you ever watched the show?"

"No."

"You should," she said.

"I'm not talking to him again. It doesn't matter."

Why was I on the defense? I didn't need Deana's permission. She had dated most of Manhattan and half of Brooklyn, maybe a quarter of New Jersey. Was she mad I didn't tell her? She never got jealous of me, but when did I date anyone?

"Did you order a side of marinara?" Alex asked Cassie. For the first time, Alex assumed the role of peacekeeper.

Tim clicked the remote to the projector. Ethan stood at the front of the room presenting the new 3D CAD software. Debbie sat in the back, in a maroon pantsuit, clueless to the world of engineering. She had the same expression as the time I tried to explain to her what cybernetics meant. I returned my attention to the slides but lost focus when my phone vibrated.

Dad: I am flying home tomorrow. Can't wait to tell you about my trip.

Me: Okay. Be safe.

Raj and Luke argued over the screen resolution recommendations for the software. I looked around the room, missing female interaction. Some days it felt like I lived in a dorky male fraternity. Tim tapped his iPhone to make a call. Two minutes later, they had an answer about the monitors. They were both wrong.

My phone vibrated. This time it had to be Gina with details of their honeymoon. I slid my device out. Debbie would go crazy if she caught me texting.

Iain: My grandfather is in the hospital. I look forward to seeing you.

Was his grandfather a good enough reason? He didn't have an obligation to me. I went a week or two without talking to my friends. Why was I holding him to a higher standard than Alex and Deana? I hated this. He would not see me again. I decided I wasn't thinking about him. We were wrong for each other. I turned off my phone.

"Earth to Sarah," Tim said with his hand waving in front of me. Debbie made a note on her planner. I would get lectured about daydreaming later. "Are you done with the Randall project?"

"Yes."

"Good," Tim said. He picked up a folder. "Raj, Luke, Ethan, and Sarah." Tim coughed and sipped water. "Friday, you are traveling to Berrell for ten days. I received the email from leadership this morning. Katie will send you the details via email."

"I can't," Raj said. He grumbled under this breath.

"The request came from senior leadership. Unless you have a good excuse, you're going." Tim didn't like Raj. He never said as much, but Raj never followed the chain of command and complained to everyone's manager.

"Why the abundance of travel? My wife is angry she has to take care of the children alone. I don't like the food in Berrell. The hotel is terrible."

"I agree with Raj," Luke said. He closed the folder on the table in front of him. "I don't want another trip to Berrell. It's like I work there."

"It's boring. No ESPN at the hotel," Ethan said. The guys turned to me.

"Um. The airport is too small." The guys looked at me with the same dumbfounded expression.

Real smooth.

They continued to chatter with each other. I didn't need to ask the reason. At that moment, I knew why.

Me.

CHAPTER FIFTY-FOUR

"He forgot his position and duty to Berrell. If he thinks our people will be happy for him, he is mistaken." - Warren Wallace

Raj stood next to me on the concrete curb, pissed at the world, ready to leave the moment we arrived in Berrell. I tried to make conversation with him but everything reverted to how much he didn't want to travel to hell in the English Channel. Luke exited the airport sliding doors. Mist fell from the sky and I buttoned my coat.

"The hotel shuttle is on its way," Luke said. He threw his duffel bag over his shoulder.

Everything about Luke, from his middle-parted bowl cut to his outdated dress shirts, screamed 90s cliché. Luke didn't like me. He once called me high maintenance because I liked Earl Grey tea better than the generic tea bags our company provided. I had a strong suspicion him and Raj whispered about me on the plane.

"I don't understand why it's taking so long," Raj said. He studied his watch.

"Dunno man," Luke said.

Droplets hit the pavement and splashed my boots. We waited under a bus shelter. I examined my surroundings—the gray sky, mossy rocks, trees with few leaves, and open fields with tall, brown grass. You couldn't gaze off into the distance in New York. A breath of fresh air in the city was impossible without the smell of exhaust fumes and dumpsters.

"You happy to be back here?" Luke asked from behind me. Raj whirled around to see my response.

"Tim said we don't have a choice. No sense crying." I wiped my daydreaming face away. Raj was suspicious. Luke wanted trouble.

"Hey," Ethan said, out of breath. He exited the sliding doors with his suitcase rolling behind him. "I thought I missed the shuttle. So hard to find bathrooms here."

"Nope. We are still waiting," Luke said. He shifted his weight to the side, placing a hand in his faded jean pocket. "What's that?" Luke pointed to the case strapped to Ethan's luggage.

"My new tablet. I am not missing baseball this time. The hotel said none of the rooms have TV, only the lounge, and no ESPN," Ethan said.

Luke looked indifferent. He didn't care about sports. I pictured him loving *Saved by the Bell* reruns and *The Naked Gun* movies. I bit my lip to stop my smile.

The shuttle pulled alongside the curb. Nomen, the driver we had the last visit, said hello and loaded our bags. The four of us climbed into the shuttle, Luke up front, and the rest of us in the back.

"The rain caused a rock slide outside the city," Nomen said, pulling the shuttle out of the airport. "We have to go through Rowan."

Raj sighed in frustration.

Nomen made a right, a way I had been before towards Iain's house. Within minutes, Rowan's wooden sign appeared.

Ethan strained to read the sign. "Dona Nobis Pacem?"

"Grant us peace," I whispered.

"Few live beyond this sign. Most of the lands belong to his lordship. Up ahead is Castle Rowan." Nomen pointed. When I looked up, I gasped.

"Beautiful architecture," Ethan said with his head against the window.

"It's very Châteauesque," Luke said.

"It used to be a defense against the British. In the nineteenth century the earl removed the ramparts," Nomen said with pride.

"Can we stay there? Maybe they have ESPN," Ethan said.

"No one lives there. An earl must marry to occupy Rowan; a rule set hundreds of years ago to guarantee the succession. The Sixth Earl waited five years to occupy. He died in an accident two days before his wedding. His fiancée received nothing, and the title went to a distant cousin."

"Are we close to the hotel?" Raj asked, tired of hearing a history lesson from the shuttle driver. Castle Rowan disappeared in the distance.

These projects were a waste of time. Our jobs were a small part of what Mackgale-Berrell did as a whole. Even Tim agreed. He told us traveling to corporate looked good on our employment reviews, but he didn't see the purpose. Was I crazy for thinking Iain wanted me here? Yes. A successful, titled CEO spent thousands of dollars on worthless projects to see me? I could hear laughter in my head. I needed to find answers before returning to New York.

After six days, I didn't have an answer.

On the first day, I checked into the hotel to find I had a large bed, television with satellite, and a mini-fridge full of American snacks. I binged on Oreo cookies while watching a rerun of *Sex and the City*.

On day two, Warren Wallace gave a presentation to us about the importance of heterogeneity in the corporate office. He told us our presence was more important than the projects.

Before day three, I went to the fitness center with the hope I would run into the CEO. The janitor emptied the trash can and changed the paper towels.

After day four, I walked to William's Folly and stayed on the sidewalk. I realized my level of crazy. The answer appeared on day two. We were the cultural liaisons for curious employees who never left the island. Iain Mackgale had nothing to do with our presence. It didn't explain the big bed, television, and snacks, but I wasn't going to question my upgrades.

In the middle of day five, I had lunch at the Bistro with Ethan. I scanned the crowd of tourists while Ethan talked about his new roommate.

On the sixth day, I gave up. I wanted to go home. My emotions were as tired as my jet lag. Iain Mackgale was nowhere to be found. How I came to the conclusion Iain was interested, I wasn't sure. Relationships and Sarah didn't mix. No wonder my dad never dated. We were biologically doomed not to find a partner.

"Hello," Joan said. She sat in the fold-out seat next to me.

The Adrianna and Mindy of Berrell took the seats across from us. I couldn't remember their names. What did it matter? Joan said hi to them. I ignored them like we were middle schoolers.

Nigel stood at the front telling everyone to take a seat. I had no idea what he did for Mackgale-Berrell. He was important, worked on the fourth floor with the other leaders, and had a British accent.

The doors opened, and Iain entered with three guys in suits. He didn't see me. I looked towards the wall and watched him with my peripheral vision. Iain took a seat near the front. My eyes shifted to Nigel, at the microphone, but my attention stayed with Iain. Everyone laughed. The world unfocused like Rowan in the distance from a hotel shuttle. He was here for a meeting. Not by coincidence or for me. He owned the building and the company.

I was embarrassed for thinking he liked me. Not just liked me, but really liked me. I inhaled a slow breath. He glanced at me, and the corner of his mouth lifted.

I checked my return flight home.

After two hours, half the employees surfed on their devices. The locals wanted to start their weekend, and the travelers wanted to go home.

My phone vibrated in my bag, but unlike the others, I ignored it. Iain turned around and gave me a strange expression. When I shrugged my shoulders, he waved his device. I pulled my phone out of my bag.

Iain: I am leaving at seven. Meet me in my office at six? It's Friday. Chinese and a movie?

My heart thumped against my chest. I concealed my phone from Joan. She busied herself with outlining the unicorns in her adult coloring book.

Me: My flight to London is tonight. I have checked out of the hotel.

Problem solved. Insanity with Iain over.

Iain: I can move your flight. You can stay in my guest room. I might need a shoulder to cry on.

Me: Please remember our balls conversation the last time you cried on my shoulder.

Enough of his profile was visible to see a smile.

Iain: My balls are safe in your hands?

Air blew out of my lips. *In your dreams.*

Me: Whatever. I'll be there at six.

CHAPTER FIFTY-FIVE

"Sarah wasn't on the flight back to New York. I emailed Debbie, not because I cared what happened to her. I hoped she did something to get fired because I wanted her sweet office." -Luke Stern

The fourth floor housed the offices of senior leadership. I had been there before, by accident, the day I ran into Iain while searching for a vending machine. Later, I found out no one was allowed on the sacred fourth floor without permission. When I stepped off the elevator, I froze. What would I say if someone stopped me? My brain had been in overdrive since Iain texted me.

I walked around the corner towards his office. The same woman worked at a computer. She glanced up, expression unchanged, and waited for me to speak.

I mustered all my courage. "I am here to see Mr. Mackgale."

"Your name?" She flipped an appointment book page.

"Um... Sarah Margo."

"Please go through. He's expecting you." She returned to her computer screen.

I opened the door to find Iain at his desk on the phone. He motioned for me to have a seat. The conference table brought back anxiety. I wondered what happened to Alan and Jessa. No one saw them again.

"I will be there Monday," Iain said to the caller. His suit

jacket hung on the chair, cuff links and tie on the desk. The sleeves of his white dress shirt were pushed to his elbows. I'd never found someone so sexy. "We can move dates, but I am booked this calendar year. I can send Nigel." I shifted my attention to the window where the remaining sun peaked out from the clouds. "Coordinate with Jane... Bye."

Iain returned the phone to the cradle. He leaned in his chair for a moment grinning. We started another staring contest. I didn't know if I should laugh or die of a heart attack.

"I need a favor," he said. Iain glanced at this watch. "Shit. I have a call in ten minutes with Renee." He said it as if I knew Renee. "I need a database adjustment."

My heart sank to the floor and slithered out the door. He brought me here to work on SQL. Why did I keep doing this to myself? I was a pathetic person. "You want me to work on databases all weekend?"

Iain laughed. "No. Only until seven. Then we are leaving to have dinner and watch a movie." I couldn't alter the confused expression on my face. "Everyone is leaving at six. This call will last until seven. I liked the way you set up the filters last time. It would keep you from boredom."

"Oh," I said because I lacked intelligent words.

Warren walked into Iain's office with a stack of papers. He eyed me with curiosity. Iain said nothing.

"Is there something we can assist you with?" Warren asked. He assumed I wandered to the fourth floor to bother the CEO.

"Sarah fixed the SQL mess last time we had an issue," Iain said and closed his laptop. "Barry's office is vacant. Why don't you work in there?" He gestured for me to follow.

"Let me fetch my briefcase. I was using Barry's office earlier," Warren said, irritated.

I waited in the doorway. Warren shuffled a mess of documents on the mahogany desk. The only item in the office was a fake plant. I wondered what happened to Barry. My wondering stopped when Iain's hand grazed my back. Maybe he didn't realize he touched me. Warren looked up. My expression remained impassive, but I was about to combust.

"There's no computer in Barry's office," Warren said. Iain tapped his laptop in his hands. "You are allowing a level three employee to use your computer?"

"I have another in my bag and a desktop at my desk. I'll manage." Iain pretended Warren had a problem with the computer and not me.

Iain placed his laptop on the desk and leaned over to enter his password. I kept my distance because I was an employee, not a woman who had slept against his fantastic body in my daybed.

"Did you need something?"

"No. I am leaving," Warren replied.

"Okay." He stood up straight when the home screen loaded. "Bring the documents we discussed to the London meeting on Wednesday."

Warren left, but the tension remained.

At seven, he stood in the doorway, coat and glasses on with a messenger bag over his shoulder.

"I'm finished." I closed the laptop.

"Good. Thank you. Let's go before it pours. We have severe weather moving in," he said.

"I need to get my luggage from E3," I said in a panic. I hoped it somehow didn't end up at the airport.

"It's at my place."

"Oh. Okay."

Iain moved with a sense of urgency to the elevator. When we exited the side door, the wind took my breath away—fast, chilly, and mixed with light rain. White clouds moved to allow the darker clouds. I hurried to the Lexus, parked in the ally, next to the hotel shuttle. We closed the car doors and looked at each other. Rain pelted the windshield.

"Hi," he said.

"Hi."

"I'm sorry we haven't talked."

"Oh, I didn't notice. I've been busy with…stuff," I said. The wind howled through the alley and rocked the Lexus.

"I'm glad you said yes to dinner and a movie." A loud crash of thunder echoed in the distance. "We better go."

Iain put the car in reverse. We turned towards William's Folly.

"Isn't the road closed?"

"It reopened today," he said.

I wanted to drive through Rowan, past the castle. My curiosity needed to know more. Did he plan on living there? What was the place like? I couldn't bring it up without him doing so first. He would think I had an ulterior motive like the people who used him for their advantage.

"I have a surprise for you." He moved his hand from the gear shift on to mine. At that moment, I knew he liked me.

Rain poured over the edge of the roof, outside the garage, creating the illusion of a waterfall. Iain pressed his remote to close the door. I loved being inside while it rained. Thunder rumbled in the distance, a sign we made it before the heavy part of the storm hit.

Iain held the entry door open. I stepped up into the corridor between the garage and living room. Iain's dry cleaning hung on a peg with the name Ogden on the tag. Was Ogden his assistant, a girlfriend, or a relative?

The aroma of Chinese food overpowered the living room. How much did he order? Iain looked over his shoulder with a smirk. I followed him to the kitchen.

I halted, like a dog at the end of its chain, at the sight of chefs cleaning the edges of plates. One man bowed and said something in Chinese to Iain. He handed the chef an envelope, smiled, and replied in Chinese. The men departed through the front door.

"I didn't know you spoke Chinese." I felt stupid as soon as the words left my mouth. How much did I know about Iain?

"I don't." I quirked my head to the side. "I looked up how to say thank you between meetings." We shared a smile before checking out the food.

Ten gorgeous plates of food lined the kitchen island. A part of me was afraid to look at Iain. The extravagance of private chefs made me feel out of place and somewhat embarrassed. I didn't want him to read my mind, know this wasn't normal for me. Although, he had met my family and friends. I needed to stop obsessing.

"Is this local?" I ran my fingers along the granite surface.

"No Chinese food in Berrell. The chefs are from a fantastic place near my grandfather's city residence in Saint-Germain-des-Prés."

The dishes were suited for a food magazine. When our eyes met, everything stopped in my mind. His face said he wanted me to see he recreated Friday night Chinese and a movie. I was happy he made an effort, but why hadn't he talked to me?

"I am sorry about your grandfather. Is he better?" Maybe asking about his family would give me an answer, or I could learn more about them.

"Thank you. No, he's not. Most of last week I was in France. I'm the heir to his company. I'm sure you are aware because the media discusses it daily."

"I watch little television."

"It adds more complication to my life." He frowned.

I wasn't sure what message I was sending, but I felt

conflicted. Let's say he liked me, wanted more from me, how would we work? Images of Castle Rowan and lofty townhouses in London and Paris drifted into my mind.

My hand knocked the chopsticks on the floor. They scattered in a mess with fresh flower petals and bamboo. I panicked. Iain smirked, opened a drawer, and place two forks on the counter.

"I've never been good with chopsticks. Let's eat. I am starving," he said. I picked up the fork from the counter. Perhaps we weren't so different. Iain picked up a spring roll and took a bite. I grinned. "What? It's not like we are at the restaurant. I can pick what I want."

"I am the last person you have to defend yourself to."

"That's why I enjoy hanging out with you."

"Because I am a no-rules, uncouth person?"

He let out a deep laugh and coughed. I patted his back by instinct. He stopped laughing when I touched him. We stood close, hovering over our food.

"You're funny," he said. The lights flicked, rain poured, and lightening flashed. The thunder was much louder than home. "Frank is just as hilarious. He has a dry, sarcastic sense of humor—very witty. Have you talked to him since he returned?"

"No," I said, disappointed. "We keep playing phone tag."

Iain retrieved a bottle of wine from under the counter and a corkscrew from a drawer.

"He went to my BBC interview. I dread them, but Frank had my team laughing the entire time. I'll let him tell you." The corner of Iain's lips curled upwards. He tugged on the cork until it popped. "Do you want wine?"

"Can I have water?"

"Sure," he said. His tall, fit frame reached into the refrigerator for a bottle of water. I needed to keep a clear head.

After an incredible meal, we went to the living room. I sat on the couch while Iain looked for the remote. He ran his hand through his hair and twisted his lips. Then he realized the remote was in a drawer below the television. He joined me on the furniture, sinking into the cushions next to me. I turned my head towards him. He loosened his tie and removed it.

"Much better. Do you like foreign films?"

Why was this man so gorgeous?

"I don't know."

Iain scrolled through a list of movies on the television until he found the one he wanted. "It's French."

I didn't know the title of the movie. I couldn't think of any French words I knew other than ménage à trois. That's the last fact I wanted to drop.

Iain turned off the light switch and returned to his spot next to me. Our legs touched like we were high schoolers hoping to go to second base. I didn't dare look at him, although he turned his head towards me a few times.

My focus needed to be on the French movie I wouldn't be able to understand. Subtitles flashed on the bottom of the screen.

Angeline: You get out of here!

Max: No. No. No. You!

The male character blew cigarette smoke in the woman's face. She smacked him. The couple kissed with passion on a chaise lounge.

Did he want to watch this movie? I would have rather watched *Antique's Roadshow* and see who could have guessed the value of nineteenth-century porcelain from Dresden.

Out of the corner of my eye, I could tell he wasn't watching the movie. Our faces were illuminated only by the soft light coming from the television. He licked his lips. Did he choose this movie so we wouldn't watch it?

Thunder crashed. I jumped and let out a yelp. Wind knocked debris onto the roof, and the lights went out. I wrapped my arms around Iain before I realized what I was doing. He pulled me close without hesitation.

"It's okay," he whispered. The wind and rain pounded harder against the house. We didn't move.

"Do you have any candles?" My head rested on his dress shirt, against his pounding heart.

"No. I'm a man. I don't burn candles."

"What if the electricity goes out?"

"I am never here."

"Oh."

We remained in the dark for an hour, listening to the storm in silence. Our bodies stayed connected as if we found the perfect excuse to be together. Iain yawned. I was tired too.

"What time is it?" I asked.

He pressed his watch, causing a glow to light up the room.

"Eleven. Maybe we can lie down until the lights return," he said.

I kicked off my dress shoes, still in a pencil skirt and dress shirt, and laid down in front of him. He wrapped his arm around me. This beat the movie for sure. I shifted my weight to find a position where my skirt wasn't so tight. My hand tugged at the hem. Iain pushed my back forward and unzipped my skirt.

"Take it off," he whispered into my hair. Did I hear him correctly? "It's only us."

I wiggled out of my skirt until it fell to the floor next to my shoes. Iain pulled me close, nose in hair, our entire bodies touching. His hand drifted on my side to the edge of my hip bone where my panties started. I pressed my butt into his groin. Did he want me?

I waited for his next move, rain pounding the roof, heart

racing until I heard Iain snoring.

The electric didn't return until the next morning. We showered, in our own rooms, and met in the kitchen. Iain busied himself with a serving tray.

"The sun is out. We can eat on the terrace before your flight."

We didn't talk about sleeping together on the couch or the fact he saw me in my panties this morning. It wasn't the first time we shared a bed, but last night felt different.

Iain handed me a bottle of wine. He picked up a tray, and I followed him through the formal dining room to a set of french doors. We stayed near the house under a pergola. Iain placed the mini sandwiches and pastries on the end of a lounge chair. He opened the wine, poured me a glass, and took a sip of his own.

"What is your best attribute?" he asked.

I found the question strange, but it had to be better than why were you wearing old lady panties?

"When I was growing up, being weird was not cool. As an adult, I find weirdness to be my greatest attribute. Nerdiness pays my bills."

Iain leaned back, wine glass and sandwich in his hands. I took a small bite of a flaky roll with white filling.

"You are not weird. Brilliant yes, but not weird," he said. I flushed. What could I say to that? "Fancy another glass of wine?" I gestured no thanks when he offered me the bottle after he refilled his own.

"I am still recovering from passing out in my dad's backyard with you." I smiled. My head needed to stay free of alcohol. I recalled what he told me before he passed out.

"Memories of that evening are muddled."

"You don't want to know," I said, somewhat embarrassed.

"Now I want to know more."

"You told me your *friend* hangs to the right." The skin on his forehead scrunched. "But you didn't use the word *friend*. I don't remember what you called it."

"It? My… oh, that *friend*," he said. His blushing cheeks confirmed he was serious when he shared this tidbit. "Why did I enlighten you with this information?" The corners of his eyes crinkled as he prepared himself for the explanation.

"You were reassuring me you wouldn't pee on me." I released an uncomfortable laugh. My face burned warmer than the sun.

"What the…" A raindrop hit his face. We were so engrossed in conversation we didn't notice the dark clouds. We picked up our stuff to move inside. "I did not show you my *friend*, did I?" I almost dropped the platter of food. Was it small?

Iain opened the door.

"Oh my God. I can't believe we are having this conversation."

"The fact you aren't answering my question tells me I did something foolish," he said.

Large splattering raindrops fell after we crossed the threshold.

"No. But you confirmed today it hangs to the right."

We laughed.

"I have done no such thing. Why are we always talking about my cock?"

"You are the one always bringing it up. I'm the victim," I replied in mock disgust.

Iain sat the bottle of wine on the kitchen bar next to the platter. We stood in the kitchen embarrassed, laughing, and relaxed. Our conversations were always great, and even the meaningless ones were entertaining.

The expression on Iain's face changed as if he was thinking

the same as me and then changed his mind. Maybe he realized he shouldn't be hanging out with an American girl from Oakville.

"Mackgale," he said. I didn't hear his phone ring. "Please have Robbie take the accounts." He flashed a shy smile. I retrieved a bottle of water from his refrigerator. "I have plans, and it can wait."

CHAPTER FIFTY-SIX

"Sometimes the truth isn't politically correct." - Dan Margo

As soon as I set my luggage inside my apartment, my cell phone rang. The cat jumped into my arms and snuggled around my neck. I put the phone to my ear.

"Hello, Father. I'm glad you called," I said.

He laughed. "Are you home?"

"Yes. I arrived two minutes ago. How was your trip?" The cat jumped off my shoulder when I opened his cat food.

"Great. I toured the National Portrait Gallery and Napoleon's Tomb. Iain and I ate at a swanky seafood place. I'm glad he paid for it." He laughed. "I went to Iain's BBC interview. Talk about neat."

My body sank into the pillows on my bed. "Sounds fun."

"I hadn't planned on visiting Berrell, but Iain insisted. He set me up with a tour of Crossleigh Manor and Castle Rowan. Talk about incredible. Next time you're home, I'll show you pictures. How have you been?"

My father usually spent an hour talking about travel. Like when we returned from Canada, he talked about Jasper for weeks. He was being short, but I couldn't focus after he mentioned Rowan. The castle didn't allow visitors.

"Good. How was Rowan?"

"Breathtaking. Iain is something."

"You like him?" I asked.

"Who wouldn't? He's a great guy."

"I need advice about relationships."

"Gina may be better—"

"She will tell me to find a bank manager and sleep with him on the third date."

He groaned. "Okay. I'm listening."

"Why haven't you dated anyone? Is there something biologically wrong with us?"

"I thought this was about you."

"Iain makes me crazy. Maybe you and I aren't cut out for relationships."

He chuckled. "Honey, no one is made for relationships. There is nothing wrong with us. Before your mother, I had other girlfriends. I was lucky enough to become a father. People don't believe me, but I am happy single. I love my job, have a wonderful family and many friends. Iain makes you feel crazy because you like him. He likes you."

"How do you know?"

"Iain Mackgale is a successful man. The last thing he—"

"You think I am not good enough for him?" If my reasonable father said yes—the answer was yes.

My father sighed. "Let me finish. The last thing he needed to do was entertain me. Not to mention, you're all he talked about."

"Really?"

My dad laughed.

"If you want to stop driving yourself crazy, tell him your feelings. If he's not interested, you move on."

"Thanks, Dad."

"I need to go. One last piece of wisdom," he said.

"Okay."

"Don't sleep with him on the third date or ever."

Over the next two weeks, Iain called and texted me daily. I thought about my dad's advice and decided to show Iain I wanted more than friendship.

Next weekend was the annual Margo Fourth of July picnic and fireworks. My family drew names. Dan won hosting July Fourth, and Ted won Thanksgiving. Why grown adults needed to do a drawing was beyond me.

I would invite Iain to Oakville.

"Mackgale," he answered.

"Hi."

"Hold on," he said. He talked to a man. The phone brushed against an object and made a loud noise. "Hello."

"Hi."

"You're day going okay?" he asked. People chattered in the background.

"Yes. It's almost over. You're working late."

"I'm in London having dinner with clients. These events are always later than expected. I planned to travel to Berrell tonight, but I will stay at the townhouse."

"Okay." My voice was small and mousy. When had I ever invited a guy?

"Something wrong?" Iain said something to a passerby.

"No." I took a deep breath and wanted to hang up the phone. "Would you like to go to my family's Fourth of July picnic?"

The phone was silent. Did he hear me? My heart pounded. Stomach acid rose in my throat. Even the cat hid under the table. He peeked out from behind the chair as if he had the stupidest owner alive.

"Sarah…I…This—"

"Forget I asked. I thought maybe if you didn't have July Fourth plans…" I stopped talking. July Fourth plans? He wouldn't have July Fourth plans. He wasn't American!

"It's a bad time," he said in a dreadful tone.

"I get it. Don't worry."

"It's not that—"

"I need to go."

I hung up the phone before he could say another word. My back fell into the comforter, and I stared at the smooth, white ceiling. There was a water stain from the leaky bathtub upstairs. I tried to focus on the spot, not my rejected soul. I vowed after Daniel; I would never put myself in a vulnerable position.

I had escaped rejection until today.

The warm water glided over my skin, and the pool noodle kept me afloat. The rest of the party remained on the patio chatting about work and the food. I closed my eyes to enjoy the sun. I heard my name, but if it were important, they would leave their patio furniture and tell me.

"The lone swimmer," Uncle Dan said—a few people laughed.

They could make fun of me all they wanted. I needed my swim time.

Dress shoes appeared at the edge of the pool. My sunglasses had smudges from sunscreen. I cringed. Maybe he would go away. I told Uncle Dan twice I was not interested in his thirty-five-year-old golf buddy, Robert. Besides the beautiful weather, too-tight polo Bobby was one reason I stayed in the pool. He kept going on and on about investment real estate.

"Are you ignoring me?"

I flipped off my noddle, splashed into the deep end, and emerged spitting water.

"Oh my God. No." An injured sea turtle could have swum to the pool wall with more grace.

"I'm happy to see you too." He grinned.

"I thought you were someone else," I stuttered. I attempted to get out of the pool in the deep end and realized I wasn't strong enough to climb out without the ladder. Getting older sucked. "I wasn't expecting you."

"Stay in. I will join you." His hair blew in the wind, expensive sunglasses on his face. "I need to change."

"Okay."

Iain disappeared into the house behind Uncle Dan. My heart raced now that I had a moment to process Iain Mackgale being in Oakville. Why was he here? Wait. You invited him. But that means… what does it mean?

Iain appeared on the pool deck. I walked up the shallow end steps, drops of water falling behind me. When he turned around, his eyes went to my bikini.

He removed his t-shirt and stood in front of me in European swim trunks.

"Do you need sunscreen?" The words croaked out of my mouth.

"Yes," he said.

Iain removed his sunglasses then turned his back to place them on a lounge chair. I reached for the can of sunscreen and sprayed his back.

Iain whirled around like a ninja. "That's cold! I thought you were using your hands." I misted him again. He jumped. "Hey!"

"I charge extra for rubs."

He grabbed the can. With a swift motion, he picked me up and tossed me into the pool.

313

When I emerged, he was next to me in the water with a pool noodle. We floated in the deep end, enjoying the warm sun. We were so close that our skin touched, neither of us attempted to separate.

"Dan said you were here," Gina said to Iain from the ledge of the pool. "Did you eat Sarah?" I shook my head. "We are putting away the food. Everyone is heading to the fireworks. Do you want a plate?"

"Yes. I am starving."

"Then why didn't you..." I looked towards Robert talking to my cousin, Andy. "I see. He told Dan he likes you."

Why were we having this conversation in front of Iain?

"He knows nothing about me." I paused. "I wish people would stop setting me up without my knowledge."

"You say no every time anyone asks," Gina said. "Would you like a plate Iain?"

"That would be nice, thank you," Iain replied. He faced me once Gina left. Our thighs bumped against one another as we moved to stay afloat. "Did I ruin a potential date?"

I shook my head no. My insides tingled when my stomach touched his muscular abs.

"I am glad you are here," I whispered.

Gina yelled from the back door. Our moment disappeared.

We floated to the stairs, and he offered his hand to help me out. He wrapped a towel around my shoulders before wrapping a towel around his waist.

Our plates of food were waiting on the patio near the house —only Andy and Robert remained outside. I didn't bother with introductions since Andy met Iain at the wedding and Robert said hello to Iain when we approached the table.

"Dan said you are single," Robert said. He nodded towards Iain as if I owed him an explanation.

Shirtless Iain chewed a large bite of his hamburger.

"Are you interested?" Iain asked.

Andy made an excuse to go inside—he didn't want to join the awkward conversation.

"Are you saying you're not together?" Robert waited for me, but I kept chewing.

"No," Iain said.

He was playing along like Alex had many times, except this time my heart ached. I sat in front of an interested guy in my league, but my eyes were on the one who would never work.

"How did you meet?" Robert asked. He wasn't buying our relationship.

"We work for the same company." Iain took a bite of potato salad. He made a weird face, not expecting the tangy flavor.

"Are you an engineer?" Robert leaned forward. Iain crossed his leg and leaned back into the patio chair.

"No, management."

"I got my MBA two years ago if you need any pointers," Robert said to Iain.

I laughed hard, and a fry popped out of my mouth. Iain patted my back like I was choking.

"You okay?" Iain asked me.

"Perfect," I said.

"Thanks, Robert," Iain said. He dabbed his lips with a napkin. "I'll keep your offer in mind."

We changed out of our swimming suits and joined the last of the picnic crowd in the living room. Haley stood by the front door, hand on hip, screaming for her grandpa to hurry. Uncle Ted picked up his keys on the bar before taking his granddaughter outside. Iain and I sat on the couch, people watching.

"Do you need a ride to the Riverfront?" Uncle Dan asked.

He moved his Ray-Ban sunglasses from his head to his face. My uncle didn't act like he was on the verge of senior citizenship.

"I have Dad's truck," I said.

"Okay." Uncle Dan disappeared through the front door. He yelled at Teddy. My family laughed outside.

"Frank isn't going?" Iain asked. He shifted his weight to face me. The tips of his cheeks were pink from the sun.

"He has a cold. I hope I don't get it. Debbie has me scheduled for twelve hours Monday and Tuesday."

"Why?" The base of his thumb pressed his lips.

"She's kissing up to Marco by expediting projects. Never get a boss," I said with a slight smile.

"I don't intend to."

"Tim is great." Iain shrugged. "Tim Sanders." He looked clueless. "He runs my division. Middle-aged. Very cheerful. Used to work in Oakville. He spent a month in Berrell."

"He doesn't sound familiar." I narrowed my eyes. How could he not remember him? Tim presented at many meetings. "Many people work for Mackgale-Berrell. I don't fraternize with employees."

"Yeah?" I shifted my body towards him. We were in an unnerving staring contest. Was he experiencing this tension? I was the queen of cool, yet freaking out inside.

"You were an accident, a destroyed fish sandwich accident."

I shot him a look of mock disgust. "My mother once called me an accident. I don't know how I feel about your words."

"Are you going to hang up the phone before I can speak?"

The corner of his mouth twisted upward. My mouth formed a shocked circle. I had forgotten how our conversation ended.

"Well..." I had nothing.

"I know why you hung up." He could see through me. I held

my breath. "I declined your invitation because I am booked solid until January. Don't think I didn't want to see you."

"Okay." I swallowed hard.

"I have to leave soon," he said with sadness in his voice. Iain pulled out his phone and messaged someone.

"No fireworks?"

"Sorry. I have an important meeting tomorrow morning." Iain rotated his wrist to show the time.

"It's okay. I do laundry and grocery shopping for my dad before I fly home."

"I had a great time." He stood to leave.

"Me too. I'm glad you rescued me from Robert."

"He's not your type."

"I have a type?"

"Someone like Brian Cobb."

I gave him a playful shove. He released a deep laugh. The insides of me bubbled with joy. We stepped on the front porch. The evening sky boasted shades of pink and orange.

"I can't top your Brian Cobb comment."

"I know." He reached for my cheek. The side of his thumb moved across my face with affection.

Was he going to kiss me?

"Message me when you return to the city," he said. Iain texted on his phone as he walked down Uncle Dan's driveway. A man opened the door of a gray car. Iain climbed inside, and my joy vanished.

CHAPTER FIFTY-SEVEN

"No more fake boyfriend." -Alex Winchester

I didn't like calling the place the gay bar, but that's what Alex called it. Our dive bar Wednesday hangout was my preference, but Deana couldn't handle seeing Mark. Why did Mark have to bring his sleazy new girlfriend everywhere? She had large breasts, which appeared they could explode at any moment. Perhaps Deana wasn't jealous, only avoiding injury.

"Sarah Nicole! Look at you, London." Alex strutted across the dance floor with a pink boa and lip gloss. I loved seeing him in his element. Alex gestured to my color block sheath dress in approval. I didn't bother changing after work.

"My company is in Berrell."

The club featured a celebrity drag show on Wednesdays. Lights flashed, and the crowd cheered. Wynonna Judd appeared on stage. Alex ran off with a guy wearing skinny jeans twelve sizes too small.

"The show starts in ten minutes," Wynonna said in a deep voice.

"Hey girl," Deana said over the music. "I'm glad you're home."

"Me too."

I spent days in Berrell and didn't see Iain once. My doubts about him returned. We talked on the phone a few nights. He apologized, insisted he had unexpected travel to Kuala

Lumpur. I had no idea if it was a city, country, or hotel in Paris.

"I'm getting a beer. Want anything?" Deana asked.

I shook my head. My plan consisted of leave after the show and read a book in the bathtub.

Deana walked towards to the bar. When I turned around to find Alex, Ben Wilcox appeared at the club entrance. Ben scanned the room, and my pulse moved quicker. Ben wasn't gay. Why was he here?

"Alex." I tugged his boa. He stopped flirting with skinny jeans. "Do you want to play fake boyfriend?" Alex threw his boa over his shoulder, strands of glitter falling to the floor.

"Honey, I am wearing lip gloss and have danced with half the men in here. You need to get a boyfriend or ask Deana or Cassie to be your girlfriend."

I didn't want a boyfriend. This was the lie I told myself.

Deana was nowhere to be found. Cassie chatted with Angelica, the big mouth from Queens, who used to work in my building. I needed to get Cassie away from her. Angelica wouldn't go along with my fake girlfriend charade. She was my only hope, the perfect girlfriend—almost believable.

"Cassie" My friend pushed up her over-sized glasses. "I need a big favor." My eyes were wide with panic, and she nodded.

"Talk later Mamacita," Angelica said to Cassie.

As I leaned towards her, she thought I had a secret to whisper. Instead, I wrapped my arms around her waist and planted a kiss on her lips.

Her arms circled my neck, and she deepened the kiss. When I broke the embrace, she flashed a wicked smile. She either assumed this was the favor or she had too much to drink.

"I didn't expect to find you here," Ben said.

Ever since his threatening encounter, we had not spoken, but he watched me. I brushed him off as a rejected suitor. Should I have told someone?

"I made her come tonight," Cassie said. She put her hand on my back.

"This is my girlfriend." I leaned my head against Cassie. "This is Ben. He works at Mackgale-Berrell."

Ben Wilcox narrowed his eyes. He wasn't buying our relationship. Did any of my suitors believe my fake relationships?

"Nice to meet you." Cassie turned. "Let's meet Alex near the stage," she said.

We didn't look back.

"Something isn't right," Cassie whispered into my ear.

"He followed me here."

Brittany Spears bumped into us on his way off the dance floor. Cher followed behind, pleading for a second chance.

"Maybe we should go." Cassie scrunched her face. She regretted signing up for the role of fake girlfriend. "Sarah—"

"What the hell in hotness?" Alex appeared with his new guy of the moment at his side. "Could this be the reason you're single?"

"I like guys, Alex." I touched his boa again. "Cassie and I are leaving. I will fill you in later."

"Have fun," Alex's boy toy said like I picked up a random lesbian at the bar.

"Oh, we will," Cassie said. She smacked my butt hard. I jumped.

The lights dimmed, and the crowd screamed. I scanned the club for Ben, but couldn't find him in the chaos. Cassie grabbed my hand, pulled me towards the exit. Blue and red lights flashed from the stage.

The bouncer was skeptical of us. We were leaving before the main show. He watched us, and I was glad. Cassie hailed a cab. I scanned the street, nothing but a few latecomers and a limo with cans tied to the rear.

Cassie told the driver where to go. I didn't hear, nor did I care if we went to my place or hers. My back rested against the seat; night lights brought color to the streets. We stopped at a red light where the car next to us blasted an old Usher track.

"I am sorry," I said. She had seen me use Alex far too many times.

"Did Alex refuse to play fake boyfriend?"

For whatever reason, I thought about moving to New York City and my first time in a cab. I remembered being scared and alone, but I didn't experience those feelings anymore. Until tonight.

"It's definitely not believable with a boa and lip gloss, but I asked. He told me to get a boyfriend." I held the sticky arm rest. "Why do I attract creeps?"

"Are you expecting an answer?" Cassie's voice was quiet.

"You have one?" I snapped. Cassie's eyes widened at my moodiness.

"Um. You are beautiful, smart, and will attract people in general—the good and the bad." Our faces glowed in the city lights. "Alex is right. You should get a boyfriend. It doesn't have to be serious, Sarah."

Did she not realize I had tried and failed?

"They always want to get serious. First, it is sex, then meeting the family. The next thing you know they are stalking you at work and picking out baby names." I covered my face with my hands. Cassie snorted. I uncovered my face. She laughed. "I am so not kidding."

"Do you think you are the only one unlucky in love?" Cassie crossed her arms. I shrugged. It never occurred to me my friends were single too. "Tonight was the hottest encounter I have had in months."

"It was hot." My eyebrows moved in a scandalous way.

Forget months, my hottest encounter in years.

"If all else fails, lesbianism is on the table." Cassie pressed her lips together, amusement in her eyes. The cab driver eyed us through the rear-view mirror. He pulled near my building and let the meter run. Were we considering becoming lesbians? Was this how bad my love life had become?

"You are a great friend, Cassie."

I hugged her. No sparks. No revelations—still best friends. She waved goodbye. I climbed out of the cab and back to my safe-haven studio apartment.

Don't pick Tony! Come on. He wears wife beaters and a gold chain.

I picked up the remote, ready to change the channel when my phone rang. When I saw Iain's name on the screen, I turned down the television volume, not wanting him to discover my love for trashy dating shows.

"Hey," I said in a sleepy voice.

"Hey."

"Where are you? It's three your time," I said.

"In bed. Can't sleep. I wish you were here," he said.

"In your bed?" Who hijacked Iain Mackgale's phone? He chuckled. I felt dumb for mentioning his bed.

"In Berrell. I would not object to you under the covers next to me."

"I would not object to you being in my bed, although the cat might mind." My voice stayed low like a teenager sneaking a late night call.

"I'll take his place. Where is he? On the sofa back?" He let out a relaxed laugh. "I lack the skill and dexterity to be there."

"He is between my legs." I could have told him the floor. Why didn't I lie? "He likes to be warm." This conversation moved out of my league. I giggled.

"What is funny? You think I lack the skill and dexterity to

take his place?" Thousands of miles separated us, but I knew he grinned.

"You're good at everything you do. I wouldn't want you to be somewhere you didn't want to be," I said, serious but seductive. Well... as seductive as a nerdy girl could be.

"I wouldn't object. Would I be required to do the same tasks as the cat?"

Did he admit he wants to be between my legs? This had to be a dream. Damn me for enjoying smutty dating shows before bed.

"Like licking my thigh and rubbing up against me?" I swallowed hard.

"We should end this conversation before I say something stupid," he said.

"Why? Do you regret saying it?" I asked, and he had the nerve to laugh.

"No. If we keep sexting, I may never go to sleep."

"This isn't sexting because we're not texting," I said. Wow. Did I read those words from a cheesy bumper sticker?

"How do you know about sexting?" he asked, amused.

"I watch *Dateline* now and then."

Iain burst out laughing, and my cheeks burned with embarrassment. Did I bring up a news program during a sexy conversation? This was exhibit A why I was pushing thirty and single. Why did I bring up *Dateline*? What's next—*Reader's Digest*.

"I miss you," he said after he stopped laughing. "I will be in New York next week for one day. My best friend is opening a new restaurant. He is having a dinner for the investors. Would you go with me?"

"Yes," I said with the biggest smile.

"I will try to sleep after our conversation. Unless you have advice on techniques to help one fall asleep faster. Maybe a segment you saw on *Dateline?*"

"I find touching myself helps. I would show you, but you are not here—too bad."

He groaned. "Yes, too bad. Goodnight trouble."

"Iain," I whispered and took a breath. "I miss you too. Goodnight."

CHAPTER FIFTY-EIGHT

"Her shoes didn't match her dress. He didn't care." -Tyler Blackburn

Iain and I hadn't talked in days. The pathetic part of me wanted to visit the break room and stare at the financial channel. I knew I was crazy. As I was having my irrational thoughts, I spotted Iain in the common area outside my office door, deep in conversation with Marco.

Iain and I were having dinner at his friend's restaurant tonight. He didn't mention his visit to our office. I cocked my head to the side to get a better view of his fitted suit. I forgot how nice of a frame Iain had, especially compared to Marco.

"Sarah," Debbie said in a pissed off tone. "What is wrong with you?" She hovered over my desk like a witch on a broomstick. "Mr. Mackgale is on our floor right now. Get it together." She didn't like surprises.

"Conference room in ten minutes," Ethan said. He slapped his hand against the door frame, and I jumped. "You okay, Margo?"

"Yes, fine. I didn't get a meeting invite." I scrolled through my computer's calendar.

"Impromptu with Marco and Mr. Mackgale." Ethan glanced over his shoulder and bent closer to my desk. "Marco looks like he is about to shit himself." Ethan and I shared a moment of amusement before he left my office to inform the other engineers.

Iain noticed me enter the conference room and continued typing on his phone. I was nervous, but looking around, everyone was on edge.

"I believe everyone is here." Tim closed the door. He joined Iain and Marco at the front of the room. "We are very fortunate Mr. Mackgale has taken time out of his busy schedule to spend a few minutes with us."

"No need for grim faces. I wanted to congratulate this department on an outstanding year. Revenue is up twenty-five percent over last year. We serviced ten percent more clients with a ninety-six perfect satisfaction rate." The mood lightened when the group realized our CEO wasn't here to deliver bad news. "I have an engagement in the city this evening. My purpose today is to thank you and check in with Marco. I have ten minutes. Questions or feedback before I go?"

Please do not look at me. My silent prayer went unanswered. Ethan raised his hand to ask a question.

"I'm curious if our department will expand to other sites?" Ethan asked just to ask a question. He wouldn't leave New York.

"No plans to expand out of New York, but business needs change daily. Your manager will keep you updated if you're interested in other opportunities," Iain said.

"Is our current system eligible for an upgrade?" Sreekanth asked, without raising his hand.

Even at twenty-nine, it scared me to ask a question without raising my hand as if Mrs. Crow would appear out of thin air and beat me with a ruler. My mind drifted back to the day Mrs. Crow huddled by the fire escape door. I had never thought about her until today. Did it take me seventeen years to care? Maybe Bethany was right about me. Did I only care about myself? I took a deep breath, resolving not to allow sixth grade to ruin my mood. It was in the past—ancient history. Why was it on my mind today?

"You okay?" Tim asked.

Batting my eyes a few times, I noticed the empty conference room. I hoped nothing important happened.

"Yes. Trying to remember the end date for the Evan's account." I stood up and grabbed my notebook from the table. Since Marco and Iain walked the floor, everyone returned to their offices.

"Why don't you head out early today? You have put in a lot of hours," Tim said.

"Thanks, Tim. I am glad you moved to New York."

A corner of his mouth lifted at the compliment.

"I'm not so sure sometimes," Tim said and left.

Did he miss Oakville? Every time I returned home, I looked for a reason to stay. Someone in my family always drove me to the airport.

I gazed out my office window at the bustling city. A bird flew close to my office window in search of a place to land. There wasn't many trees or backyard barbecues. Kids didn't run through sprinklers or wade barefoot in a creek. This city had strengthened me, but wouldn't be my forever.

I picked up my bag to leave. My phone buzzed with a text message. I leaned against my desk to punch in the password.

Iain: The car will pick you up at seven.

Me: Was this meeting part of your get to know the employees program?

Iain: No. I wanted to see you.

Me: You held a meeting only to see me?

Iain: Yes. I do nothing without a purpose.

The driver stopped, between streets, next to a dumpster. The door creaked open, and he waited next to the car. A cab driver would have told me to hurry my ass up. When I step out onto the pavement, I smelled trash. Did I overdress for the friend's restaurant? I assumed the friend didn't run a hot dog stand.

"Is this right?" I asked. The driver tipped his black sunglasses down.

"We're around back. Boss' orders."

I smoothed my dress down and fluffed my hair. My stomach filled with imaginary butterflies. Did I look good enough in one of Gina's hand-me-downs? The off-white cocktail dress hugged my body, a size too small. The strapless top squeezed my breasts to the point one spilled over the fabric under my armpit. I had a third boob. It wasn't bad unless I lifted my arm. Who needs to use their right arm? I didn't have the extra money to buy a new dress. If I didn't save, I could never go back to school and teach.

I followed the driver inside a back door through a dark hallway with boxes stacked against the wall. My heart thumped against my chest, either from the odd surroundings or the thought of dinner with Iain. We ended up in the kitchen. The back of the house busied themselves with preparing the dinner service. The staff didn't move from their stations.

A tall, black man in a charcoal suit with a salmon dress shirt and tie appeared through another door. He smiled when he saw me, teeth whiter than pristine sand. The driver acknowledged the man and left.

"Welcome, Sarah." The man reached for my hand and kissed it. He was around my age and fit. "Welcome to my restaurant."

This guy was Iain's best friend?

"Thank you. I'm excited to be here." The man didn't tell me his name. I didn't want to be weird and ask.

"E-mack is upstairs." He led me through a door to the dining area.

The ambiance comforted me—metallic decor and lighting in clear glass. Iain's friend had a knack for attention to detail. People in fine clothes chatted to one another in the dining area. Waiters in tuxedos poured wine. Waitresses with trays served hors-d'oeuvres.

A stairwell lined the side of the room, near a hostess stand, with a reserved sign hanging from a red rope. He undid the gold clasp and gestured for me to go upstairs. I held the handrail to steady myself in my hand-me-down pumps. Iain waited at the top of the stairs, dressed in a gray suit, hair styled to perfection. I couldn't help my smile. He walked to greet me, took my hands in his and kissed my cheek. The skin of his cheek grazed mine. When he released my hands, I pressed my palms against my dress to keep from shaking.

"She is gorgeous," the friend said in a flirty way. He scanned my outfit and looked at Iain, who didn't seem to mind the flirting.

My doubts crept into my insecure brain. The men were talking, but I wasn't listening. I knew why I kept having these feelings. The last thing I wanted was heartache. I had a good career. People respected me. After I gave up Oreos, my figure thinned out. I knew I was a strong person. No one realized I had feelings of self-doubt. I didn't want to let anyone close enough to damage me. My mother destroyed me the day she walked out. Whether Iain liked me or not, the damage was done. If he decided to never speak to me again, I would be hurt.

Iain pulled out my chair. The private room overlooked the main dining area. Candles burned on the empty tables. A waiter brought up a bottle of wine. He poured and left without a word.

"I have investors' asses to kiss downstairs. Let Christopher know if you need anything." The friend touched Iain's shoulder. "Are you in town this weekend?" Iain looked up at the tall man. They shared a history together. Anyone could see they meant something to one another.

"I am leaving after dinner. Grandfather needs me in Athens for an acquisition." Iain removed his suit jacket. I fidgeted with my clutch before placing it on the table.

"Next time," he said. Before he descended the stairs, he

stopped with his hand on the rail. "A pleasure meeting you, Sarah. Please enjoy my food." The friend disappeared downstairs.

Iain stood up and reached for my hand to bring me to my feet. His arms enveloped my body. I pressed my cheek against his chest, lost in his warmth, only he could make me feel as if I could float. "It's great to see you. This dress is breathtaking," he said.

"Thank you. You look okay," I said. The vibration of his laughter rumbled against my cheek.

Christopher appeared with a platter of appetizers. We returned to our chairs. A Rob Thomas song played downstairs; the ironic lyrics drifted up the stairs and stuck in my head. *Maybe someday will figure all this out. Try to put an end to all our doubt.*

I looked around for a menu. Iain raised a brow.

"What kind of restaurant is this?" I asked.

Iain put one of the hors-d'oeuvres in his mouth.

"Tyler says sophisticated Southern. He grew up in North Carolina," Iain said with a grin. "That's his way of saying he's doing whatever he wants."

"How do you know Tyler?" I asked.

"Boarding school. We were roommates for three years. Most of the students were white Americans. We were the two odd ones—the foreign and black kid. The headmistress paired us in a dorm room. I can't cook. Tyler was twelve and preparing gourmet dishes on a hot plate. His parents wanted him to join their telecommunications company. A corporate job was never for Tyler. He's been successful being him." Iain took a sip of his wine.

"Are you one of his investors?"

The corner of Iain's lip curled.

"Yes. It's expensive to open a restaurant. Tyler was short with the initial investors. He didn't want to take my money, but I insisted. He talked about opening his own place in New York when we were kids. This restaurant is his dream. Tyler has always been there for me. I take care of the people I love. It's who I am, contrary to what the media reports."

Christopher appeared with two plates of pasta. Iain looked pleased and declined the extra cheese.

"Cajun chicken pasta is one of Tyler's specialties." Iain wasted no time picking up his fork.

I took a bite of the casual, yet elegant dish. "This is great."

Iain nodded with a mouthful.

We continued our conversation, easy as always until we finished our meal. My dress couldn't handle one more ounce of food.

Iain pulled his sleeve up to see his watch. He gave me a strange stare. "I want to memorize this moment."

"Yeah?" My cheeks warmed. He wasn't being professional or reserved. Iain nodded with a serious expression; eyes fixed on mine. His words made me crazier than before.

"Are you ready for dessert?" Christopher brought us out of our moment. I took a deep breath and exhaled.

"Can you package dessert to take with us?" Iain asked. I admired his profile. The lines of his face were beautiful. My heart was in trouble.

"Yes, sir."

"Meet us at the back door. I have a plane to catch," Iain said.

Christopher left, and Iain stood. I placed my napkin on the table. My fingers squeezed my clutch with the purpose of calming my nerves.

"I wish you could stay." I kept my right arm against my dress to keep my third boob under control.

Iain reached for my left hand. "Me too, darling. Will you do me a favor?"

"Sure." Did he want his databases fixed?

"I have a table for Tyler's official opening. It will be posh. I can't make it. I want you to take your friends," he said.

Tyler came up the stairs.

"Dinner was excellent. Thanks for making us an item not on the menu," Iain said. Tyler beamed at his friend's words. He let go of my hand. "Sarah will take my table for the opening. I won't be able to attend."

"Your ass always bails on me," he said. Iain's smile disappeared. "I am joking. It's fine." Tyler pulled a card from his pocket and handed it to me. "I will add her to the list."

"Thank you," Iain said.

"I will walk Sarah out. There are photographers downstairs," Tyler said.

I flashed Iain a shy smile.

"I'll call you," Iain said.

I hated leaving him. Iain pulled his phone out of his jacket. I took one last glance before I disappeared down the stairs with Tyler.

Photographers were everywhere in the restaurant. I didn't like being hidden from association with Iain, but I didn't want to be in a tabloid. I glanced at the business card—*Tyler Blackburn, Restaurateur and Chef.* The slip of paper slid into my clutch without opening the clasp. We pushed through the kitchen door towards the rear exit.

The Rob Thomas lyrics circled in my head. *Maybe someday we'll live our lives out loud. We'll be better off somehow. Someday.*

Alex and Deana eyed me getting out of the car in a cocktail dress. I thanked the driver. Was I supposed to tip him? I didn't, and he seemed okay with it. Alex whispered to Deana. She laughed. Were they making fun of me? I met my friends under the entrance light.

"Explain," Alex said. From the smell of Alex's cologne and

Deana's heavy eye makeup, they had been out tonight.

"What are you two doing outside?" I asked. Since when did we hang out on the sidewalk after dark?

"Don't avoid my question." Alex looked at Deana. She had her hand on one hip. We had talked little. Neither of us asked why.

"Dinner with Iain at Tyler Blackburn's new restaurant."

Alex put his hand over his mouth to stifle his gasp.

"Tyler's new restaurant isn't open yet. It's very exclusive. Are you sure you had dinner there?" Alex cocked his head to the side. I pretended to think.

"You're right. I was mistaken. We went to McDonald's, and I had a six-piece." I walked past Alex towards the door. Alex opened his mouth, but no words came out. Deana laughed.

"I am kidding, Alexander." I smiled and pulled out my keys. "Iain and Tyler are good friends. The restaurant opens in two weeks. Tonight was an investors thing."

Deana blew out a breath.

"You met Tyler Blackburn?"

"Yeah, so?"

"You live in a bubble! He is the hottest chef in America right now and gay." I recognized the look and waited for the begging. Alex's words hit me. Iain wasn't bothered by Tyler's flirting because he knew his friend wasn't interested.

"Do you want to attend the opening?" I asked.

I turned towards Deana to extend the offer, but she ignored me, arms crossed and nose in the air. She didn't like me talking to Iain.

"Oh my God. Oh my God." Alex jumped.

"Calm down. It's only dinner. He invited all of us. I wish I could get this excited about men."

CHAPTER FIFTY-NINE

"I don't know how these girls got invited to Tyler Blackburn's opening." -Driver

"We are the new *Sex and the City*," Alex said.

The four of us admired ourselves in my full-length mirror. Deana was in a red strapless. The plum A-line fitted snug on Cassie's bust. Alex had on a charcoal suit with a white dress shirt. I wore a conservative black cocktail dress and silver wrap.

"They didn't have a gay guy in their friend group. Anthony and Stanford don't count," Deana said. Even though she disapproved of Iain, she agreed to go.

"The producers had no one as good-looking as me to cast," he said. The three of us laughed. Alex remained serious. "I am not joking."

"We know. That's why we are laughing," Cassie said. She picked up her handbag from my kitchen table. Deana applied pale pink gloss to her upper lip. She smacked her lips together.

"Let's go. The car should be downstairs," I said. My friends followed me.

A black Cadillac SUV waited near the curb. The same driver waited near the door. I wondered if he worked for Iain or Tyler. My curiosity wasn't strong enough to ask.

Ten minutes later, we pulled up to the front of the restaurant. A line of people waited.

Tyler Blackburn appeared outside, and the press wouldn't

stop. He wore a three-piece suit with a purple dress shirt and handkerchief. *Should I approach him?*

"Miss Margo," a woman's voice said. I whirled around, not prepared for press questions. What if they asked about Iain? "I am Rebecca. I will take care of you and your friends tonight. Shall we go to your table?"

Alex hooked his arm into mine. His head leaned close. "I am loving your boyfriend."

"He's not my boyfriend." We followed Rebecca past the line into the restaurant. Celebrities and athletes were everywhere.

"Why are we the only scrubs here?" Alex nodded towards the bar. His questions were valid. I had been pondering my relationship with Iain for months.

"I'll be back," Deana said. She hurried through the crowd and greeted a man holding a cocktail.

Alex leaned close to me. "Are you two okay?"

"Everything is fine with me. She has a problem with Iain. We aren't talking about it," I said. Deana dated losers. Her disapproval of Iain annoyed me.

"She's jealous," Alex said. "No boyfriend for years." I narrowed my eyes. "All of a sudden you snag the richest, hottest man on the planet. It's enough to shock anyone."

I shoved his arm. "Thanks a lot. You make me sound pathetic."

He grinned. Cassie texted on her phone since her friends were excluding her from their conversation.

"Cass—"

"This is from E-Mack." Tyler Blackburn stood at our table with a bottle of wine. "A little pricey, but he can afford it."

"Thanks." I introduced Alex and Cassie.

"You look familiar," Tyler said to Alex. I hated when men used that line. It was a stupid way to start a conversation. I wanted to roll my eyes.

"I do portfolio management. Maybe you're a client at my firm." Alex switched into serious catch mode.

"A friend manages mine. Let's enjoy a drink before I'm needed in the kitchen." Tyler nodded towards the bar. "We can figure out where I've seen you." Alex left with Tyler. Cassie looked up from her phone. She was one friend away from eating alone.

"Don't worry. I know no one here," I said.

Cassie tucked her phone into her handbag.

"Do you think Tyler Blackburn was hitting on him?" People were still being seated around us.

"No clue."

"You and Alex are dating celebrities. I can't get the guy in the next cubicle to go to Panera Bread for lunch," she said.

Since when was Cassie sad?

"Are you okay?" I asked.

"I never thought I'd be this old and single." She sighed. We looked pathetic. Deana returned to the table. "Who were you talking to?"

"Ryan. We went out a few times." She was being mysterious. She told us every detail, down to the moles on their butt cheeks. Ryan was never mentioned.

Tyler and Alex returned to our table, drinks in hand, laughing as if they were on a date. "Nice meeting you, Alexander. I have a restaurant to open." Tyler flashed a large smile. "Enjoy yourself."

Alex sat in his chair like a king on a throne. Before we could ask questions, Rebecca was at our table explaining the dinner options. I checked my phone to see if I had any missed calls or texts. None.

Two hours later, we had eaten chicken, lobster, and a fancy version of peanut butter pie. Our usual friend group vibe wasn't there.

Tyler greeted several tables in a black culinary coat. Another chef stood next to him with his arms behind his back. Tyler approached our table and placed his hand on Alex's chair.

"Dinner was perfect. We had an amazing time," I said, although we didn't.

"Glad to hear," Tyler said, distracted. We picked up our belongings to leave. Before I walked away, Tyler reached for my arm. His touch startled me.

"I have never seen E-Mack into anyone, not even his ex." Tyler paused. "I think you're a nice girl, but E-Mack will never be with you."

I narrowed my eyes. What I did wasn't his business.

"Who says I want him?" I shifted my weight. Tyler's hand rested on my shoulder.

"I have met his parents. They're not welcoming to outsiders. Iain is traditional. He won't go against their wishes. You aren't on his level."

The color drained from my face.

"I have your wrap." Alex appeared out of nowhere. He placed the silver pashmina over my shoulders.

"Thanks, Alex." I strained to smile.

"We should have dinner sometime," Tyler said to Alex, changing from delivering bad news to flirty. Alex took my arm. Deana and Cassie waited by the door.

"You seem nice, but you're not on my level," Alex said before spinning us around towards the door.

"Alex. He is totally interested in you." Alex pulled me close to him, leaning his head against mine.

"Pretty boy should have kept his opinion to himself." Alex squeezed me tightly. "No one hurts my girl's feelings."

"You're so sweet." My friend snubbed a gorgeous celebrity for me. "Why can't you like women?"

"Why can't you be a sexy man with a penthouse apartment?"

We laughed.

Once a project ended, a massive amount of paperwork followed. My latest client insisted on being anonymous. All the paperwork had Italian Client X as the company name. The box of parts they sent for testing had stickers with the company's actual name—geniuses. My desk phone beeped, and the screen showed reception.

"Sarah Margo," I said.

"Miss Margo. Tyler Blackburn is here to see you," the receptionist said with excitement. She sat at her desk with a book and Diet Coke, never speaking to anyone unless necessary. I needed to watch more television; even she knew the chef.

"Send him back, please."

What did he want? Did he have to visit my place of employment? I inhaled so deep my head spun.

Seconds later, his tall frame appeared in my doorway dressed to perfection. I bet he looked great in his underwear. Not that it mattered, he was a snob who liked men.

"Hi. Can I come in?" I gave him my corporate smile and gestured to one of the open chairs. He placed a brown paper bag on my desk—the smell of food was heavenly. The man could cook. "Eggplant parmesan, E's favorite." An upset shadow crossed his face, followed by a forced smile. "A few desserts because I didn't know what you liked."

"Thanks." We assessed each other.

"Have you talked to E-Mack?" He sat up straight with hands folded on his lap.

"Briefly. He has been traveling."

Tyler rubbed his head. He kept his hair very short and neat.

"He always travels." Tyler paused as if recalling a

conversation. "I told him what I said to you, and he was… pissed." He avoided eye contact. "Iain is the first person I told I was gay. I was thirteen, and I told myself if my best friend hated me because of it, I would kill myself. You get to a point when you can't keep things inside anymore." The tortured expression on his face made my heart sink.

"You're still here," I said without thinking. Tyler suppressed a grin. I leaned into my office chair. Did he have a point?

"He was supportive. I have had many dark hours in my life. Iain has always been there." Tyler grinned. "When I told him I was gay, I hoped he would say the same."

I could not hide my uncomfortable expression. At least when Alex talked about men, he was being obnoxious and funny. I didn't understand straight relationships.

"He is good-looking. I am sure he was then too." I attempted to lighten the mood. Tyler smiled and nodded.

"I'm not one to get emotional." Tyler let out a breath. "I care for him, more than anyone."

"I get it, Tyler. There is nothing wrong with wanting what's best for your friends."

"Even if it's not you?" The words escaped his mouth quicker than a flaming arrow.

I wouldn't back down. If he thought he could dictate my life, he was mistaken. "Why are you here? To remind me I'm not good enough for your friend. Are you in love with him?"

"No." The matter-of-fact tone was clear. "I had hopes years ago, but we were kids. Haven't you ever had a crush on a friend?"

My thoughts went to Daniel, sitting on the grass in my backyard in Hidden Meadows. When I closed my eyes, I could feel the warm sun, gentle breeze, and hear the neighborhood kids playing. Honking horns and construction outside jolted me out of my daydream.

"E's thirtieth birthday is in two weeks. I included my recipe for eggplant parmesan in the bag." I looked at him surprised. "E says you possess some mad culinary skills." I doubted Iain said mad culinary skills. "Go to Berrell. Surprise him. I included the codes to his gates."

"One minute you think I am not good enough, the next you are giving me top-secret recipes and telling me to fly to Berrell. You are one confusing man."

"Oh girl, you have no idea." Tyler leaned into his chair, more relaxed.

"Won't his family be there?" I muted my ringing phone.

Tyler shook his head. "I asked. He has no plans. Work as usual," he said. I studied Tyler for a moment. He grinned. Tyler had an agenda for visiting me.

"This peace offering comes with a price, doesn't it?" His mouth spread into a large smile. I wanted to laugh.

"Alexander." He licked his lips. I couldn't blame him. Everyone I knew crushed over Alex. "I enjoyed having a drink with him. When he snubbed me for you, what a turn on. I need a fine, loyal man." Tyler did an exaggerated head nod.

"We go out on Wednesdays. I'll text you the address." Should I get Alex involved? I pictured Alex running around screaming hallelujah at the mention of Tyler Blackburn. "You better be good to him. If I show up at your work, I won't be bringing gifts." He smiled and stood to leave. "Good luck with Alex."

"Good luck with the Mackgales."

"They can't be that bad," I said.

"The mother will have your ass for breakfast."

He opened the door to leave. My coworkers were hovering outside my office pretending to use the copy machine and get office supplies. I took a breath and waited for the questioning about Tyler to begin.

CHAPTER SIXTY

"A surprise from a woman means she wants something or you're in trouble." -Dan Margo

Alex went out with Tyler. Deana refused to go to wing night because of Mark's girlfriend. Cassie said no to eating out. Without Alex, I said no to the gay bar.

The three of us ate Deana's tofu scramble at my apartment. I had leftover pizza in the fridge I planned to eat as soon as they left.

"Is this a bad idea?" I asked. Deana glanced up from her bowl of bean curd. I fidgeted with a pen on the kitchen table.

"What? Flying thousands of miles to break into your high-profile manager's house?" Deana said. Cassie nudged Deana hard, which resulted in a dirty look.

"He is not her boss. She is surprising him for his birthday, not breaking and entering," Cassie said. They talked as if I wasn't there. "They talk every day. This has been going—"

"He has had plenty of chances and hasn't made a move." Deana looked at me. "I'm not being a downer."

"You're not?"

I sat the pen down and walked towards the kitchen. My stomach growled for real food. After I opened the fridge door, I removed a slice of cold pizza from the box.

"He has two titles. He's a CEO. The man is always on television. Have you ever asked yourself why you?"

Was her question rhetorical? If she had an answer, I hoped she would share.

"He took her out to dinner a few weeks ago. They have spent days and nights together." Cassie fought my case.

"Has he even kissed you?" Deana turned her head from Cassie to me. My face grew warm with humiliation. He had kissed me, just not on the mouth. My silence was the answer she expected. "A thirty-year-old guy who doesn't kiss a single, attractive girl he's been talking to for months? Something isn't right." Cassie looked helpless. Deana made a point even the hopeless romantic could not argue. "Have you watched *Cross Hill Manor*?"

"No." I didn't want to watch the show. "I've been busy."

"You and Alex were shopping for food bowls for a dog he hasn't adopted yet. You're not busy," Deana said. Cassie sunk into her chair, afraid to get in the crossfire. My pulse echoed in my ears. The cat scurried to the bathroom to hide. Before I could respond, Deana pointed her finger at me. "I will tell you what you're avoiding. Iain Mackgale has a gambling problem. He likes pretty women and has slept with most of his staff. One of them has an illegitimate child who looks like him. This girl's father was found dead when he threatened to expose Iain. Last summer—"

"He has never confirmed these rumors," Cassie said in my defense. The pizza floated upward in my esophagus.

"Go to Berrell. Put him to the test. If he declares his love, great. Maybe you'll find out he is a loser. His life makes great television, not so great for a boyfriend." Deana picked up her plastic container of tofu and left.

"Enjoy your trip," Cassie said and waved. She closed the door behind her.

A week later, I was on a plane over the Atlantic Ocean. I arranged with Tim to work the weekend for three weekdays off. Part of me felt bad for telling Tim I had a family issue in

Oakville. Debbie was upset I went over her head, but she would have told me no. That crazy woman monitored my personal and vacation time like the family jewels.

"Ladies and gentleman, we are making our final approach to Heathrow International. It's currently fifteen degrees in London. We thank you for using our airline and hope you enjoyed your flight." The captain made his announcement. I was staying the night in London and taking a short flight to Berrell in the morning.

What if he freaks out? What if he had plans but didn't tell Tyler? Maybe Deana's suspicions were true. I pictured a casino table with two women hanging off his arm.

Too late to turn back.

I showered, fell asleep, and found myself back at Heathrow. Two hours later, I stepped out of the small plane on the airstrip in Berell. What a change from London.

When I flashed my New York driver's license, the woman at the counter smiled and slid paperwork towards me. It was the typical name, address, and insurance information sheet. I signed the form.

"You work for Mackgale-Berrell, do you?" The sixty-year-old woman zipped up her company jacket. I was too nervous to notice the chilly air.

"Yes." She handed the keys to another employee.

"Did you want the expense charged to the company account?" Her eyes crinkled. People in Berrell were skeptical of Americans. They didn't live in a melting pot like we did. Outsiders were much easier to spot.

"The American office will expense the rental." This made no sense at all, but the rental car clerk didn't question the inner-workings of the corporate world. "Thank you for your help today."

She moved my paperwork to a back counter.

A guy in his early twenties waited in the parking lot. His

accent was so thick; I didn't have a clue what he said when he gestured to the black car parked next to a van. He seemed excited, so I laughed.

Rule one of not understanding foreigners—mimic their tone. Rule two —agree and thank them.

"Cool. Thanks." I placed my bag on the passenger seat.

"In the boot, ma'am?" The ruddy complected guy motioned his hand towards the trunk. I didn't want to admit I opened the passenger side door mistaking it for the driver's side.

"My bags are fine in the front." We said our goodbyes and I climbed into the seat with the steering wheel.

This was my first time driving on the wrong side of the road—thank God I was in Berrell and not London. I shouldn't have made fun of Iain's driving. This would require a level of concentration I didn't possess today.

"Shit." The gearshift laughed at me. I knew how to drive a manual, but it had been awhile. When I moved to New York, I sold my car. I didn't need it and couldn't afford to park it. Putting the car in reverse for the second time, I spun the tires and stalled. The rental car employees watched me from the glass window. Once I got the car to move, I squealed out of the parking lot in the wrong lane.

Way to be incognito, Margo.

Grocery shopping in Berrell was like going to a fancy wine shop to find food. It was better merchandised, much smaller, and junk food was not on every end cap. Double-checking my list, I made certain I would not have to come back. Being here uninvited to see Iain Mackgale was nerve-racking.

I was starting to get familiar with Berrell, knowing most of the small city and route to Iain's neighborhood. As I pulled up to the gate, the security guard was on the phone. I punched in the code, and the gate opened. At Iain's gate, I punched in another code, which thankfully also worked.

I parked near the front door. Deana's words stung. *Why you?* I needed to find out why me and the truth about *Cross Hill Manor.* Uncle Dan always said every rumor possessed some element of truth. My gut said to forget Iain so many times over the past nine months. Why didn't I listen to myself?

The electric garage door opener creaked when I punched in the code from Tyler's list. I smiled when I spotted Iain's discarded t-shirt and a bag of pretzels on the sectional. I was comfortable in his home, but I felt weird being uninvited. I hoped he would be pleased. If all else failed, I had a rental car to leave.

I sat the brown paper bags on the island. The kitchen had everything I needed to cook Tyler's eggplant parmesan. Unzipping my carry-on, I removed the pre-mixed flour and yeast zipper bag with instruction. Tyler did not trust me with the recipe for his famous bread.

At 3:30 pm, my phone vibrated.

Iain: I received the cannolis from New York. I've been craving another since we left the bakery. Thank you! They are hidden in my office to avoid sharing.

We had not talked since Tuesday. I was already in Berrell. The surprise couldn't be ruined by calling him.

"Hello," he said in hushed tones. People talked in the background.

"Happy birthday. Are you busy?" I hopped onto the counter to sit. The timer on the oven counted down another minute.

"In a meeting. I only answered because it is unusual for you to phone during the day." Someone asked Iain a question. "Your ringtone is *Blame it,* as in blame it on the alcohol, so naturally they are curious."

"Cute." Even his ring tone mocked me. "I'll let you work. I have a surprise being delivered to your house at six. Can you go home to sign for it?" I could actually hear him cringe.

"Is now a good time to mention I hate surprises?" He let out a breath.

"So exotic dancers for your birthday was a bad idea?" He choked, followed by a loud cough. "Kidding. Be home at six, okay?"

"You are quite bossy today." The amusement was back in his voice.

"I learned from the best. Chat later."

At 5:30, the bread was ready, and the house smelled wonderful. At 5:45, my phone rang. I smiled at the sight of his name.

"Hello," I said in a calm, yet freaking out voice. I wasn't sure what would happen tonight.

"I am driving home, per your instructions." As usual, he got straight to the point. "I am nervous. You promise nothing outlandish? No dancing women or petting zoo?"

I laughed. "No, sorry. You pay my salary. I don't have the means to rent animals for your birthday."

"I attended a village birthday party when I was nine. The parents had a petting zoo. Nasty little farm animals sniffing the corn cakes. I can't tell you a time I'd been more disgusted."

"What a hard life you've lived. I picture you searching for a cloth napkin while goats run around the foldout tables." I chuckled at my joke.

"Laugh all you want. It was traumatizing. No farm animals?"

"No. Relax. Nothing crazy, something American."

"Please tell me I didn't leave work early for pizza." He groaned.

"You hate surprises?" He made an agreeing noise in his throat. I couldn't get my hand to stop shaking.

"My drive is ahead. I see a parked car. Let's hope it's not the surprise. The wheels are muddy."

I drove into the mud trying to get into first gear—details he didn't need.

"The car is not the surprise."

The garage door creaked open. His car door shut, and the garage door closed. How would he feel about me inside his house, uninvited?

When he walked into the living room, he stopped mid-step when he saw me. My nervousness progressed to a ten at the site of the black tailored suit, navy tie, and glasses only he could make sexy. What if he wanted sex? I panicked and hoped he couldn't read my mind. Why did my mind go there?

With bags and keys in hand, he looked stunned.

"Happy Birthday. Is this a bad surprise?" He said nothing. "Would you rather have pizza, strippers, and goats?"

He let out an uncomfortable laugh, sat his bags on the floor, and rushed towards me.

"Heavens no," he whispered and folded me into his arms. I inhaled the smell of him, enjoyed the scale of him against me. "A great surprise." He broke our embrace. "Are you cooking?"

I nodded. "Tyler—"

"Is Ty here?" Iain's eyes lit up.

"No, only us." He pulled me close, rocking us back and forth. From this moment, I couldn't imagine being without him. I didn't want to consider the unknown. "Tyler gave me his recipe for eggplant parmesan." Iain squeezed me again.

"I can't wait." He stroked my cheek with his thumb. "How long are you here?"

"Tonight. My flight leaves early," I said in an unintentional seductive tone.

"We will make our time worthwhile." He took my hands and placed them on his chest. The warmth of his fingers covered mine. "You being here means so much."

I explored the fabric of his suit. Iain's fingers caressed my

347

arms. I didn't ask his permission to remove his coat, but his eyes said go ahead.

"You won't need this for dinner," I whispered, not taking my eyes from his. His hands left me when I slid his suit jacket off. I tossed it towards the sectional and missed. He glanced at the garment crumpled on the floor. "I hope it wasn't expensive."

He smiled. "Rags."

The warmth of his fingers loosened my scarf. His touch was so intense. I closed my eyes. This wasn't our usual touching. I opened my eyes to find him closer, breath warm against my cheek. I was about to jump out of my skin when he kissed my neck, moist lips lingering a moment. Iain pulled back to see me.

I traced along the curves in his tie. "This pattern is beautiful." My attention stayed on the navy silk with subtle embroidery.

"You are beautiful," he said.

I removed his tie and unbuttoned the top two buttons of his shirt. Iain ran his warm fingers along my skin above the waist of my jeans. A wicked smile spread across his face.

"The food is getting cold."

"I like cold food. Come," he whispered and took my hand. He led me towards his bedroom.

We were almost to the double doors when the doorbell rang. We stopped and looked at each other. The doorbell rang again. He ran his hand through his hair, causing it to stand up.

"Looks like they aren't leaving," I said.

He groaned. "My senile neighbor has lost her bloody dog twice this week." He looked so helpless when the doorbell rang a third time. Letting out a breath, he kissed my hand before letting go. "I'll get rid of her." He unlocked the front door. A quick glance at me said it wasn't the neighbor.

"Took you long enough," she said. The door opened to reveal a tall, pale women who looked like a Chanel rack.

"Happy birthday. You are a mess." She smoothed his hair when she walked past him.

"What are you doing here?" he asked.

My stomach grumbled and not from hunger.

"I planned to stay the night," she said. Her small suitcase sat inside the door. "When were we last together?"

"I'm not sure." He blew a breath out of his mouth.

I scanned the room for the keys to the rental. It was time to leave. The reason he hadn't moved our relationship forward was standing in front of me. I didn't even need to ask myself how I could be so dumb.

"The charity dinner at Michael's. You are always traveling." Her chin pointed towards him.

Could he have at least chosen someone prettier than me?

"Oh," she said stunned when she noticed my presence. "I didn't realize you were entertaining."

Welcome to being the other woman.

"Sarah, this is my sister, Iris." He had a blank face. "Iris, this is Sarah."

"Lady Iris Mackgale. How do you do?" She had the same eyes as her brother but didn't share his demeanor.

"Fine, thanks."

Iain put his hand in his pocket.

"You are American." She glared at her big brother. He smiled. "I thought Sarah worked for your company?"

"In New York," he replied.

Iain had told his sister about me.

In the last ten minutes, I had experienced every emotion known to human existence. Our threesome became more awkward when Iris studied Iain's appearance, the discarded coat, and my guilty face. I wasn't sure if Iain and I had a clue what we were doing, but Iris did.

"Oh, I hate New York. The weather is dreadful." Iris removed her gloves. I was unaware women still wore dressy gloves.

"I made eggplant parmesan. You are welcome to eat with us," I said. Her eyes widened. "Did I say something wrong?"

"Of course not. Please stay for dinner, Iris," he said.

"I need to speak with you regarding an important matter. You didn't mention plans."

She wanted me gone.

"Sarah surprised me as you have."

The flight, the feelings, and Lady Iris Mackgale were too much.

"Are you staying in town?" Iris asked me.

I grew uncomfortable. What was the right answer?

"She is staying here," Iain said.

"You can't stay alone together. What if the press were alerted? You don't need speculation," she said.

Before he could respond, Iris wheeled her suitcase towards the double doors, his room, where we would have been if she had stayed wherever she lived.

"I don't need a chaperone, Iris," he said. She disappeared. "Do you remember in Oakville when I said you don't have the monopoly on crazy relations?"

I reached up and planted a kiss on his cheek. "At least she didn't show me her butt." He laughed. "Happy birthday."

Iain squeezed me to his chest. Iris cleared her throat. Iain released our embraced, and we went to the kitchen.

"You made toasty bread," Iain said. He moved to the counter where Tyler's famous bread cooled. I nodded and thanked Tyler Blackburn. Iris pursed her lips together. "It's unbelievable he gave you the recipe."

"He didn't. The dry ingredients were pre-measured."

"Classic Tyler." Iain smiled.

"You know Tyler?" Iris questioned. I forgot she was in the kitchen.

"She met Ty at his restaurant opening."

"Tyler gave me the recipes for a date with Alex." I smiled.

Iain dipped a chunk of bread into the eggplant parmesan pan. Iris grimaced.

"Alex is his type. I knew he would be interested." Iain grinned. He looked so carefree and happy, making the expense of the trip worth it.

"You seem to know one another well," she said. Iris underestimated her brother's closeness to me. Iain took another bite of bread. "Iain, please, let's serve the food. Let's not eat from a pan."

"I am starving. It's my birthday." Iain smiled. "I am glad to spend my thirtieth with my favorite women."

Iris was a stickler about everything. She insisted on the formal dining room with knives we would never use and cloth napkins with tags still attached. As I watched Iris dissect the food, I came to a realization. I couldn't be Lady Iris Mackgale, and I didn't want to be. Throughout my life, I had struggled being comfortable with myself, but tonight I was perfect in my own skin.

No one talked until Iain started a safe conversation about Tyler helping remodel the kitchen after he bought the house. We both knew this was a lame, scripted conversation. The high society of Berrell couldn't talk about whatever they wanted like the citizens of Oakville.

"It's late," Iris said. She placed her napkin on her plate. When she stood, Iain stood too. "It's time for us to retire." Iris stared at me. She wasn't leaving me alone with her brother.

Iain smiled. "Thanks for dinner, ladies. I have an early meeting. Martin will escort you to the airport." He opened his mouth to say something else but didn't.

"Goodnight," I said. Iain disappeared into the kitchen. I didn't get the answers I needed, and Iris didn't help my cause.

CHAPTER SIXTY-ONE

"Iain Mackgale doesn't play by the rules. He takes what he wants with no regard for the consequences." - Ryan Bolton

A week had passed since my trip to Berrell. I left the next move up to him, and he did nothing. We were stuck in the same flirty friend zone purgatory he didn't want to leave. I wanted out.

I couldn't focus at work or sleep at night. Something about the relationship between Mr. CEO and myself didn't make sense. The logical step would be to ask Iain, but I feared humiliation.

"Hey girl," I said when Deana answered her phone.

"What's up?"

"I'm sorry things have been awkward between us." The line stayed silent. "Hello?" I brushed bronzer across my cheeks in the bathroom mirror.

"It's okay. Want to hang out this weekend?"

"Are you going out tonight?" She was going out. I was fishing for an invitation because my makeup said night out.

"Yeah. Ryan is having a party." Deana told a coworker goodbye. She clicked her tongue. Was she debated whether to invite me? "Do you want to come?"

She expected me to say no.

"Yes. I want to pick up dudes." My tone was serious.

"What?" Deana laughed. "No one says pick up dudes. I guess last week didn't go well with the boss."

Iain was more like Marco's boss's boss's boss.

"He's interested, but something is holding him back. Too much drama. Let's go pick up dudes, good ole American ones."

"Have you been drinking?" she asked. We laughed together for the first time in weeks. I put on my lip gloss and puckered my lips.

"No."

"I'll see you in twenty minutes."

The cab stopped on the curb of one of the most exclusive buildings in Manhattan. When she said a party at Ryan's place, I pictured a food truck employee who lived with four other guys in a two-bedroom dump. I picked a good night to tag along.

"What does Ryan do again?" I asked.

"Ryan is a real estate investor. He owns the building where I work."

Her expression bothered me. Before I could ask, she whirled through the revolving doors. The doorman smiled politely, not stopping us.

Deana strutted in heels across the marble floors to the elevator. I stepped inside. The doors closed and the beat of music grew louder as we ascended to the penthouse apartment. The elevator doors opened to a large space packed with people. As I scanned the room, I was glad that Deana insisted I wear my black cocktail dress and heels.

"Hello foxy," he said. He was in his early thirties and well-dressed. Deana hugged him. His hands went to her behind. They were better acquainted than I thought. "You look great, baby. The Manolo Blahnik pumps make your legs look killer. "

354

Deana kissed him on the cheek. He flashed a slimy grin. I recognized this face—the player. One of my blind dates was a guy like him. Over dinner, he spent thirty minutes talking about his abused rescue dogs and how he made Christmas dinner for homeless veterans.

This guy's talking point was his money. I glanced at Deana's shoes. She couldn't afford Manolo Blahnik.

"You are too sweet." Deana smiled and turned to me. "Sarah Margo, this is Ryan Bolton." We shook hands in a professional way. "Sarah is my friend who works at Mackgale-Berrell."

"How impressive. Dee has mentioned you." Ryan kept eye contact with me. I couldn't shake the strange vibe. If I were a teen, I would call my dad for a ride. "Have you ever met your CEO? I hear he is an interesting guy."

Deana disappeared into the crowd. Did she intentionally leave me alone with him?

"Yes," I said, my tone professional. "I have visited Berrell for a few conferences." Ryan's stare was unnerving. He wanted more information. "He is hands-on with his company."

I wished my CEO were a little more hands-on with me.

"Let's grab a drink, Sarah," Ryan said and put his arm around me. "What else do you know about Iain Mackgale?"

The modern apartment had a beautiful bar near the window. A blond in a skimpy dress shook a martini. I cringed. Only an amateur shook gin.

"Why do you ask?"

Ryan handed me a blue glass with a lemon wedge. I took a sip but didn't allow the liquid into my mouth.

"I'm a businessman," Ryan said. He left his drink sitting on the bar. "Iain Mackgale runs one of the most successful companies in the world. Everything he touches turns to gold. I am curious because he is private. Anytime he does interviews; he is vague." Ryan scratched his chin in thought. "Mackgale-Berrell is privately held. He doesn't have a board or shareholders to please."

"Do you want to learn how to mimic his success?" Why would Ryan find information about Iain valuable? Ryan laughed at me before summoning a waiter.

"I am successful on my own." Ryan grinned like I'd asked the stupidest question in history. "Your CEO purchased valuable real estate I was interested in last year. Somehow, he negotiated a steal of a price. If I could screw him over, I would."

I pretended to be unaffected by his declaration.

"I'm a low-level engineer who tests automotive parts. Before moving here, I lived in a small town. Mr. Mackgale writes my paycheck. That's all."

Ryan studied my face and nodded. Reaching into his pocket, he pulled out a business card, placing it in my hand. His fingers closed my palm and didn't let go.

"We both know you're lying. If you ever run across information." Ryan's green eyes blazed with a threat. "My contact information is on my card."

My insides ached at the thought of selling out Iain. Is this what he experienced daily?

"I doubt I will be helpful." I scanned the room for Deana with no luck. "It was nice meeting you." As I turned to go, Ryan hadn't released my hand.

"I pay well for information." Ryan saw the panic in my eyes. He released his grasp. "Please, enjoy yourself tonight."

I didn't have time to process what had happened. My phone rang in my handbag. Without looking, I answered it, saying hello over the music.

"Are you out?" Iain asked in disbelief. My heart pounded. Should I tell him about Ryan Bolton?

"Picking up dudes."

Real smooth Sarah.

"Why would you be looking for men?" He sounded upset. Why should he be hurt? Iain had every chance to claim me but did nothing.

"I'm close to thirty and single. Why shouldn't I be out picking up dudes? It's not like I have a boyfriend, right? Maybe I should get one." It spewed out like nasty word vomit.

"Do whatever. Goodnight," he said. Iain disconnected the call.

I didn't want to stay at this party. Who was I kidding? I didn't want to pick up dudes or continue saying dudes. Standing up to Iain should have made me proud, but instead, I felt terrible. I never wanted to hurt him. If I were truthful with myself, I was to blame too. I didn't come out and say, I'm sick of being your buddy. Standing in the foyer of Ryan Bolton's penthouse apartment, the obvious hit me.

I am in love with Iain Mackgale.

This was not a crush or a fling—I had real, very scary feelings for him.

CHAPTER SIXTY-TWO

"I couldn't continue my employment with Mr. Mackgale. People tried saying he was different from his father." -Mrs. Ogden

Two days after I upset Iain, Debbie called a morning meeting to inform us we were traveling to Berrell the next day. Raj went crazy and threatened to quit. Debbie called Tim. He showed Raj the email from Iain Mackgale. Senior leadership needed engineers for an emergency project due to the acquisition of an automotive plant in France. The reason appeared legit, but Raj didn't buy it. I didn't either. The CEO used his power to keep me from picking up dudes. I wasn't sure if I should be flattered or pissed.

Thursday morning I woke up with a fever, chills, and a runny nose. I dragged myself across the street with a box of hotel tissues. Most of the morning I huddled near the toilet, and every time I said restroom, my coworkers didn't have a clue where I was going. The people in Berrell viewed relieving yourself as a sacred, not talked about event. Americans talked about their potty habits like the weather forecast.

I rested my head against the wall, in the empty hall on the third floor, trying to regain composure before returning to the conference room. My only hope was a short meeting. I wanted to hide in my temporary cubicle and be miserable alone.

"You are leaving," he said.

I turned my head, eyes red and nose running.

According to the others in the office, he had been in France. I hadn't spoken to him since the night of Ryan's party.

"Fetch your belongings. Martin is downstairs." He studied me with the same scrutiny he would give a spreadsheet.

"I am fine." I hadn't moved from the wall.

"You are not fine. Jane says we have an illness going around. I'm instructing leadership to allow ill employees to leave." Iain turned towards the elevator. No goodbye. He was all business.

The elevator opened in the lobby. Martin waited near the front and opened the rear door of the Mercedes. It was a waste of Martin's time to drive me a block, but I had trouble standing. When we passed the hotel, I leaned towards the driver's seat.

"I am staying at Hotel Rowan."

"His Lordship instructed me to take you to his residence." The fifty-something-year-old man in a suit provided no further explanation.

"Are you sure? This isn't a good idea." My voice croaked, and I touched my aching throat.

"It isn't my position to question His Lordship's judgment." Martin's eyes returned to the road with a blank expression.

I received a text. My heavy eyes blinked to see.

Iain: Make yourself at home.

Me: I would have been fine at the hotel.

Iain didn't text back.

I closed my eyes. A whoosh of cold air filled the car. I opened my eyes. Martin held the door frame and waited for me to exit. When I stepped out, I noticed the sea to the right of the house. I took a moment to inhale the salt water into my nostrils.

"Thank you," I said to Martin. My eyes stayed fixated on the water. Martin cleared his throat and held open the front door. I stepped into the foyer.

A gray-haired woman in a simple dress greeted me. She cocked her head, alarm on her face. Martin placed my bag on the hall table and left us alone.

"You're the girl in the picture," she whispered. Her hand moved to cover her mouth. The older woman stood frozen.

How had she seen a picture of me?

"I'm Sarah."

"Why are you here?" Her eyes widened. She flexed her fingers into a fist. I wondered if Iain forgot to tell her I was coming. Martin let me in the door. Why was she frightened?

I am American. Don't worry. I won't rob you blind or eat your children.

"I am sick."

She shook her head and raised her voice. "You shouldn't be here. You should return to where you came from and not set foot on Berrell again."

I didn't move.

Without another word, she moved past me and out the front door. I couldn't tell if my illness or her warning gave me the chills. Did she know something about Iain? I could kick Alex for making me watch scary movies. I should be happy being in Iain's home—this is what I wanted—but I wanted to leave.

In the guest room, I stripped to my bra and panties and slipped on a company t-shirt from my laptop bag. The shirt smelled like work, but I didn't want to search for clothes. Exhaustion washed over me. I was glad to climb under the pintuck duvet. My last thought was the incredible feeling of the linens.

My eyes blinked open when a hand touched my shoulder. I flipped over on my back, scared and disoriented. He sat on the edge of the bed. The light from the hall lit up his figure, still in work clothes. Cool fingers touched my forehead and cheek.

"You're warm. How are you feeling?"

"Terrible." I winced from the pain of speaking.

"I'll let you rest." Iain stroked my cheek.

"Can I leave this room?" I sat up. "I can't sleep anymore."

"Of course," he said. "Why don't you watch a movie, and I will make you soup."

Without thinking, I got out of bed, went into the attached guest bathroom, and plopped on the toilet. Iain eyed me doing my business. He didn't say a word—no wonder the housekeeper didn't like me.

"Your maid left."

When I returned to the room, Iain noticed my lack of clothes but acted oblivious.

"I know. She quit." The sorrow in his voice went through me like a knife into skin.

"Why? I don't understand."

"Mrs. Ogden shouldn't worry you. Let's go find a movie" Iain took my hand. I followed him to the living room. His demeanor made it clear the conversation about the housekeeper was over.

I felt worse as the hours ticked away. Iain stretched out behind me on the couch. I rested my back against his chest, and he pulled me closer. The television played a British movie about a preacher building a town, which neither of us watched. We were busy processing. He kept his thoughts to himself. Mine stewed inside.

"Did she quit because I'm American?" I reached for my throat in pain. Iain shifted his weight, followed by a sigh. My curiosity wanted to know. I didn't care if I pissed him off. "She said I'm the girl in the picture, and I should return to where I came from."

"You are the girl in the picture," he whispered into my hair. The warmth of him melted me. I loved him, but couldn't say the words. "I don't want you to return to where you came from." I could feel his breath warm on my neck, and the feeling was enough to make me forget what I asked, but I didn't.

"You didn't answer my question." My voice was barely audible.

"I'm not answering your question," he said.

I was too sick to find a tactful way to get my answer. The room went black.

When I woke, Iain typed on his laptop near my feet. Did he ever sleep? The contemplative look on his face softened when he noticed my open eyes.

"Feeling any better?" Iain cleared his throat, wincing in pain. "It appears I have caught the plague too."

"Oh no," I whispered. My head wouldn't move. "I didn't want to make you sick."

Discarding his laptop on the table, Iain moved closer. "Most of the office is ill. It's not your fault." He sneezed.

My head ached, feet hurt, and my spine felt like a bus hit me. Thank goodness I was not at Hotel Rowan. His hand touched my foot when he repositioned the quilt. It occurred to me it was Friday. Daylight poured in through the windows.

"Aren't you going to work?" I asked.

"No."

"You aren't needed at the office?" A part of me felt bad. He was missing work because of me.

"In the words of Frank Margo, what's up with the twenty questions?" Iain stood to retrieve his phone from an end table.

I laughed, and my body ached.

"Bad habit." I tried not to speak too loud or move.

"Mrs. Willis," Iain said to the person he called. "I need

Charlotte…Tomorrow is fine." Iain scoffed. "Mother will not mind. I am certain." The call ended. Iain sat on the corner of the cushion, phone in hand, deep in thought. "Charlotte will fill in until I can replace Mrs. Ogden."

"Will she tell anyone I'm here?" The thought of people finding out about my unconventional relationship with Iain Mackgale was never a big worry, but after Mrs. Ogden's sudden departure, I felt uneasy.

Iain rolled his eyes in disgust. "She has a television show based on her indiscretions. It's safe to say she wants no more trouble." Iain left the room towards his office. Was he referring to *Cross Hill Manor*? As much as I wanted to know more, even I knew not to push further.

My stomach grumbled because I hadn't eaten in two days. I went to the kitchen in search of food. The refrigerator was well-stocked, and there was everything I needed to make scrambled eggs. As I worked, I felt better. Maybe it was moving around or distracting myself from the fact I was staying at a man's house who could never be with me. *Sound familiar, Sarah?* I groaned to myself. Lee never bothered me. Iain Mackgale made me crazy.

"Are you cooking something?" He stood barefoot in sweats and a t-shirt.

"Is that okay?" I asked, but he didn't answer. Instead, he looked into the pan. "You are pissy today." I decided on a statement rather than a question.

"Pissy?" He stared at the eggs.

"Irritated, upset, grumpy…"

"Yes. I am familiar with the term," he said.

"Iain, if I have upset you, I am sorry. I can leave. You're housekeeper—"

"Mrs. Ogden is staff, Sarah. She's an employee." His tone was harsh. "I have no personal connection to her." After he ran his hand through his hair, he looked like a madman with tufts of reddish brown hair shooting in all directions. "I'm sorry. I am being an ass."

"Talk to me, please." It was a plea to put us out of our misery and bring us out of this fucked up purgatory we couldn't escape.

He closed his eyes.

CHAPTER SIXTY-THREE

"I wasn't surprised to find them in flagrante delicto." -Nolan Martin

The room remained dark. In minutes, the progression to light would begin. We were awake, staring into nighttime, without words. The silence passed each minute until the room shifted from black to shades of gray. The lines of Iain's face appeared in front of me. He rested against the sectional, propped up on his elbow. Something weighed on his mind, but he wouldn't talk.

My eyes shut. I couldn't take the silence. The sensation of his fingers moved along my cheek to my jaw. I opened my eyes. He inhaled a sharp breath.

The palm of his hand pushed my back until my body pushed against his chest and stomach. The skin-to-skin contact of my skimpy, loose tank top and his shirtless chest made me forget why I ever had reservations. He pushed his thigh between my legs, and I knew I couldn't say no to whatever happened next. Light filled the room and my distracted mind.

This was a bad idea.

When I tried to pull away, he tightened his embrace. I moaned from the pressure. Iain trailed soft kisses down my neck and shoulder. I told my inner voice, who warned me a few moments ago, to step outside for a break.

My hand moved up his back and over his chest. Somehow in my fog of pleasure, he worked his way on top of me. His mouth rested against my collarbone. He ran his hand down my arm and along my side, stopping where my panties met my thigh. The tips of his fingers toyed with the fabric before deciding to explore my bare behind.

Iain released a ragged breath then stopped. His heartbeat pulsed against me. He removed his hand as if he had an epiphany.

Yes, I want you.

Pushing my tank top strap down my arm, he pulled the fabric to reveal my breasts. My hand traced the outline of his back and found my fingers at the waistband of his boxer shorts. His mouth hovered above mine, warm breath against my mouth. I arched my back. He grinned and touched my lip with his finger.

At the moment when I worked his boxer shorts over his hips and my nipple was between his teeth, Martin appeared in the living room. The older man stared at us in horrified embarrassment. Iain laid on top of me to hide our bodies.

The party was over.

"This isn't what it looks like," I said to Martin. My heart thumped to the point of explosion. Iain chuckled whether in amusement or humiliation.

"I'll be outside, sir." Martin wasted no time exiting. His workaholic boss in the throes of passion was too much. Iain sighed and rested his head on my bare chest.

"This is absolutely what it appears," he murmured into my skin. He kissed my chest before pulling up his shorts. I saw a peek of him nude, which only made me more upset Martin walked in.

Iain went to his office to work. I remained on the couch—sick, confused, and hopeless. Daylight had arrived, but I couldn't see.

The housekeeper had a tri-tip roast wrapped in the

refrigerator. She wasn't coming back to cook it, and I was hungry. When the oven pre-heated, I set the timer for an hour and chopped carrots. Exhaustion and sickness made it hard to stand on my feet, but the cooking was a welcome distraction.

"Don't apologize for phoning." Iain's voice moved closer to the kitchen. "She is here. We have been ill. She slept most of the day." He appeared in jeans and a button-up with dark-framed glasses. "Would you like to speak with her? It appears she is cooking dinner." Iain laughed. "I will tell her. Bye Frank." He placed his phone on the counter and peeked into the oven.

"I found a roast in your refrigerator."

Iain stood close. I tilted my chin upward to look him in the eyes. My lip quivered in response.

"Frank was worried about you. He wants you to call him when you return to New York." Iain remained expressionless.

"I will. Thank you." My voice seemed so small. "Dinner should be ready in an hour."

I didn't know what to say about the housekeeper, her replacement, Martin, or this morning's events. I went with my old standby do nothing approach.

Iain leaned against the bar. He observed me slicing the roast on a cutting board. I plated the meat with the roasted carrots and potatoes. When I moved to the sink to wash my hands, Iain continued to watch my every move—it was unnerving. What was his problem? I knew one piece. We moved out of the friend zone and into the half-naked on the couch zone.

"This morning shouldn't have happened." The directness and certainty in his voice irritated me to the point I shook. I ignored him. "Did you hear what I said?"

His question sounded like stupid stuff my mom would say when I was growing up.

I understood you. You are being ignored.

"Can you please speak?" A few minutes of silence passed.

Sitting the bread knife on the counter, I looked up at him with my eyes blazing. He should have thanked his lucky stars I could not shoot fire or laser beams. A smart person like Iain couldn't think of a more tactful way to bring up this morning?

"What do you want me to say?" I inhaled an exhausted breath. His face showed he assumed we shared the same opinion.

"Are you mad at me?" Disbelief was all over his face. Why were men so stupid? "I am trying to be honest."

Enough with the martyr's face, Mackgale. Why wasn't I gay? I would consider lesbianism when I returned to New York.

"Message received," I said, detached. I stepped away from the counter and towards the guest room. I did not get far. He reached for my arm. We stood connected for a moment, another staring match.

"Why are you being cold towards me?" He pressed his lips together and exhaled a deep breath through his nose. Did he want an answer? "I received my travel schedule on Wednesday, and it's brutal, with little time in Berrell and no time in New York until March. I didn't want to sleep with you and then disappear for six months." He let go of my arm.

"It didn't appear that way this morning. Without Martin's interruption, we would have."

He paced in the kitchen. When he looked up at me, he looked conflicted, and I felt terrible. Why should I feel bad?

"I am human too." He choked out the words in a sob. "Does anyone not realize I am a person? I am not perfect." For whatever reason, I was unmoved by his performance. "I'm trying to do what's right."

"I'm going back to New York in the morning. Enjoy your dinner," I said.

"Sarah."

I turned around. "What do you want me to say, Iain? I don't

have feelings for you. What happened this morning means nothing? I am unaffected? I'm human too. Are you happy now?"

"No, I am not happy!"

I stormed past him to the guest room and shut the door. My body slumped against the wall, tired and sick. If he invited me back to Berrell for a worthless conference, I was quitting Mackgale-Berrell.

CHAPTER SIXTY-FOUR

"I had no issue with her, but my employer paid me to get rid of the problem. She happened to be the problem, and I needed cash." -Ben Wilcox

After two weeks in New York, life fell back into place. Deana wasn't as pissed at me. Raj had calmed down to a level of sanity. Iain hadn't called or texted me. I hadn't cried over it in six days.

I buttoned my trench coat near the elevator. Warm days were over, and when the sun went down, you needed a jacket. Summer never lasted long enough, but neither did most good things. I picked up my handbag, looked at my watch, and pressed ground floor on the keypad. My stomach growled.

"Miss Margo." The receptionist hurried to catch me. "Your father called twice today. He said he lost his cell phone and only had your work number. I couldn't find you earlier." She handed me a yellow slip with his information.

I felt like a piece of garbage because I didn't call him back two weeks ago. My mind was so warped with Iain; I didn't notice he missed our Saturday call. He would forgive me, but I couldn't believe I had been so distracted.

"Thanks. It's fine. I will call him when I get home. If he calls tomorrow, transfer him to the lab." The elevator doors opened. "Judy, you can call me Sarah."

I decided on pizza from the dive between work and my apartment. The project we were working on needed a finalized write-up. I could work on my report while watching a movie with my cat.

Shoes hit the pavement behind me. I'd lived in New York City long enough to know the sound of a typical passerby. I ignored my inner voice on occasion but not now. My pace quickened, and the steps behind me matched my acceleration. I looked over my shoulder. Anyone could walk down this street in a hat, but I knew him. Why in the hell was he following me?

Calm down.

Without looking, I fumbled in my bag for my phone. I couldn't risk taking my eyes away from the pavement for a second. I needed to call someone, but couldn't think of who and didn't have time. My phone opened to a list of recent numbers. I pressed the last person I called. The phone rang.

Someone, please pick up.

"Sarah?" Iain's sleepy voice sounded worried.

Shit. Had I called no one since Iain? It was past midnight in Berrell.

"Yeah. I am on my way. You think I should get a cab? Good idea." My voice shook with each word. I put my hand up and moved at a pace my heels didn't like.

"Are you okay?" My heart ached when I pictured sleepy Iain with messy bed head. I still loved him.

"No, but I'll see you in a few minutes. Everyone will be there, right?" I fake laughed.

"What's going on?" The sound of his breath was audible through the phone. My chest squeezed until I couldn't take a breath on my own.

"I wish I knew." A cab pulled to the curb. "Hang on baby. I am getting into the cab." I gave the driver my address but told him to turn right and circle the block. Cab drivers were used to weird requests. "I am being followed. I am in a cab." My teeth chattered. "I didn't mean to wake you. I pushed the last person I called."

"Do you know who is following you?" Iain's voice was harsh. I didn't know if he was worried or mad.

"Ben Wilcox. He manages the temp employees." I tried to calm down. "I think he has followed me before."

"When and where?"

I told him about the gay bar and pretending to be Cassie's girlfriend—I left out the kiss. He was strictly business tonight, and I didn't want to test him with my adventures in lesbianism.

"Go to your flat and lock the door. I am staying on the line." His laptop chimed a second before he started typing. "Do not answer the door for anyone. Do you understand?"

"Yes."

The neon sign for the twenty-four-hour market flickered. I hoped I could make it to the door. I tossed the cab driver a twenty before bolting towards my building.

"Hello, James. I'm sorry to phone at this hour. I need you to run Benjamin David Wilcox, employee ID 390872." Iain made another call, but I was too busy running to make sense of the words.

The hall was empty. My hands shook violently when I tried to unlock the door. The deadbolt clicked. I slammed the door, locked it, and slid to the floor. I had never felt so comforted by a plug-in air freshener in my life.

"Are you serious?" Iain said to someone else. "Heads are going to roll over this one. I want you on the next plane to New York... Not good enough!" I had never heard him so angry. "Call Henderson, take the company jet. I landed in China four hours ago, James. I cannot leave. My meetings start in an hour. Ring when you land."

He's in China?

"Sarah?" Iain was calmer but still angry.

"Yes." I hated getting him involved. A creep following me was not Iain Mackgale's problem.

"Are you in your flat?" My heart rate started to descend. The door was locked. I was in my apartment.

"Yes. I'm sorry," I whispered. Often I apologized to people and truly didn't feel sorry. Tonight, I felt sorry. "I shouldn't have bothered you. I didn't know you were in China." He didn't say anything. "I am sorry, Iain. This isn't your problem."

"My problem? Your well-being is absolutely my concern!"

"You made it clear two weeks ago it isn't." My voice had a bitter edge.

I stood up to remove my coat. My stomach realized the danger had lessened and growled. Since I didn't get pizza, I would have cereal for dinner.

"I didn't want to sleep with you and then disappear for six months. I never said I didn't care about you." He silenced me with his feelings. "Ben Wilcox is using a fake social security number. HR missed a different name on his background check. James is looking into it and will be in New York tomorrow. Whether you intended to call me, it was the right thing to do. I need you to call in tomorrow and not leave your flat."

"My personal time is used."

"I added sixteen hours to your time bank," he said as if no big deal.

"Can you do that?" I asked.

"I can do whatever the hell I want."

Really? Why aren't we together?

When I got out of the shower, I had three missed calls.

"Where were you?" Iain demanded when he answered the phone.

"In the shower—"

"Has anyone been to your flat or tried to contact you?" His demands made me uneasy.

"No." I pulled my towel tighter. "Your accent isn't as diluted when you're mad."

"That's offensive," he said. I made a mental note to walk on eggshells.

"Sorry." He appreciated humor and sarcasm, but not tonight —he ignored me. A knock on my door increased my heart rate times ten. "Someone is at the door," I whispered. "I think it's Deana." Her voice echoed through the hall with Mrs. Martinez.

"Don't answer it," he said with fear in his voice.

"It's probably only my neighbor and Deana—"

"I beg you, Sarah. Please don't answer the door for anyone until my security team gives the okay." I pictured him pacing in a hotel room, running his hand through his hair.

"I can't see my friends? You think my friends are involved? That's crazy."

"Have you noticed anything different about your friends or coworkers? Strange behavior towards you? Lavish purchases?"

"No."

The sparkle of the Manolo Blahnik pumps on Deana's feet dulled my mood.

"People betray for money." Iain let out a jagged breath. "Trust me. I know from personal experience."

"Okay." A burning sensation covered my face. I pinched my nose to keep from crying.

"My intention wasn't to upset you." Iain paused. "I have never experienced such helplessness in my life. My chaos is now at your doorstep."

"You don't know this is because of you."

"Yes, I do. Try to sleep. I'll phone in a few hours," he said.

"Okay."

Sleep wouldn't happen.

"Promise me you'll stay in your flat and not answer the door."

"I promise."

CHAPTER SIXTY-FIVE

"The Indian kid had one hell of a conspiracy theory." -Marco Romano

My calendar popped up a fifteen-minute meeting reminder on my computer. I prepared for the time-off interrogation. The benefit of personal time was to use it for something personal, but Debbie made everyone's life her business. When I had a doctor's appointment, I would get a return-to-work excuse as proof for these pointless conversations. Today, I had nothing. It's not like she could fire me for using my benefits. I hated listening to her complain.

To my surprise, when I walked into Debbie's office, Marco and Raj were sitting in chairs. Raj looked his usual pissed. Marco looked intrigued.

"Sorry, I didn't mean to interrupt." Were we doing employee reviews? I turned to exit.

"Raj and Marco are here for your meeting."

I surveyed the motley crew. What issue could Raj and Marco have with me? I was surprised Marco knew I existed since he once called me Brittany. Sitting in the chair between them, I smiled business-like at Debbie.

"Tell us what's going on," Debbie said. She showed up to play hard-ass boss.

"I was sick, a stomach bug. None of my projects are delayed." Leave it to Debbie to get an audience to rehash why I used personal time. Debbie shook her head like *nice try* and folded her hands on her desk. "I threw up a few times and had a fever."

"What about the sixteen hours of personal time?" Debbie eyed me like a homicide detective.

"HR?" Since sixteen hours of personal time appeared at random, her questioning was valid. I would go with ignorance and hope she believed me.

"We would ask the HR manager, but as of yesterday, she is no longer with the company," Marco said. He implied I was responsible. "An employee from home office took her place. Don't you find the situation strange?"

"I'm an engineer. The inner-workings of human resources isn't my expertise." They didn't buy my innocence.

"Different approach," Marco said. He looked at Debbie and then my direction. "Raj is convinced he is invited to Berrell because of a connection you have to someone."

"Connection?" I tried to act appalled. "I am from Oakville. I have no connection to anyone overseas. This is insane. Why would Raj be involved? We aren't friends."

"Ben flirts with you, and then he's gone," Raj said. The office shifted to a courtroom. "Why weren't you in your hotel room? How do you get first class upgrades on full flights?"

"How is my life your concern?" I fired back at Raj.

"You don't deny your actions?" Raj's dark brown eyes blazed. "I don't want to travel every month. You're the reason. We are your cover-up."

Debbie enjoyed the show.

"I wasn't aware Ben flirted. I only spoke to him a few times. If he left his job, how am I involved? We aren't in the same department. As far as being in my hotel room, I confess, I visited sights on my time." Raj doubted himself for a moment. A part of me felt bad making him appear crazy. "I have no control over the airline. Check the expense reports. I didn't pay for it. The ticket guy offered to buy me a coffee on his break.

Maybe he hoped to impress me."

"Your last return flight was not on the company account." Debbie produced a spreadsheet with a blank space below the date.

"I was sick and moved my flight. I put it on my credit card by accident." *Please don't ask to see it.*

First, I did not have a credit card and second, Iain booked my flight. The thought of Iain made me empty. I wanted nothing more than to climb into his lap and feel his warmth.

"Are you saying this is a misunderstanding?" Marco asked. His hair gel made his hair look like plastic.

"She knows this isn't a misunderstanding!" Raj smacked his hand on Debbie's desk. I flinched. Raj's volatility compared to a drunken public house brawler. "The hotel said you checked-out." Raj stood in front of me, surprising Debbie and Marco. Was I getting an ass whooping? "Tell us what you're doing." He looked at Marco. "Check her company email."

"We have. There is nothing," Marco said.

I tried to hide my fear. They investigated me. Marco concluded I had a powerful connection. Why else would he be here?

"Check her phone," Raj said.

I did not like him. Five years of working together and he undid our work relationship in minutes.

"You can't check my personal phone." Sometimes Iain sent me a selfie at night before bed. I never deleted them. What would Marco think of the shirtless CEO on my phone? "Do you want to go to my apartment and see what I hide in my panty drawer?"

"Sarah!" Debbie scolded. I forgot she was in the room. "That is not appropriate."

"None of this is appropriate," I said. I looked at Marco. "I am being accused of having someone fired and—"

"Explain the celebrity chef," Raj said. Marco looked at Raj. I shrugged, not able to think of an answer. "See, I told you she is hiding something."

Marco's eyes narrowed. Debbie leaned forward. Raj hovered over me.

"Ty is dating my best friend. They like to keep it private. You remember Alex, Raj. He used to work in our building. I used to eat lunch with him downstairs," I said without emotion. I looked at Debbie. "Do I need to account for how I met Alexander Winchester? We can call him or show up at his employer and search his emails."

Debbie looked at Raj with sympathy. His behavior said raving lunatic.

"Why did you tell Ben you have a girlfriend?" Raj asked. Marco grew uncomfortable with the inappropriate question but said nothing.

"I didn't tell Ben anything." My voice was sharp enough to cut whatever came near it. "I was at a club with my girlfriend, and he ran into us. We said hello, nothing more." My back dripped with sweat. Luckily, I wore a suit jacket.

"You're not gay." His brown face said checkmate.

"Have you ever seen me with a man or heard me talk about a boyfriend?" I gave Raj my best you-outed-me expression. Being a spinster had an advantage.

"No," he said. Raj returned to his chair.

Marco sighed.

"I am done with this meeting," I said to Marco. "Next time, HR will be present. If you want to search my panty drawer or discuss my sexuality, I recommend a lawyer."

I returned to my office. Even though I put on a decent performance, I wasn't in the clear. As I pretended to work on my computer, they watched. I could do nothing out of the ordinary.

My instinct said tell Iain, but he needed no more stress. I

couldn't let my connection with him get out—no matter what.

CHAPTER SIXTY-SIX

"Each time I picked up the phone, I burst into tears." -Gina Cobb-Margo

I didn't speak to Iain. We texted a few times—him checking on me. He never revealed what happened with Ben, and I didn't care to ask. Someone from his security team stayed in New York. I didn't know who they were or if they watched me.

I told myself the time zones kept us apart, but we had managed distance before. We were both hurting, mourning the loss of what would never be. *Oh, Iain*, I whispered into my pillow. Tears streamed down my cheeks and onto the cotton fabric.

The top of my dresser vibrated with another missed call. I shut my eyes and returned to my darkness.

Why had she called four times today? It was unlike her not to leave a message. Why didn't she text me? I tossed the comforter aside. My feet didn't like the cold floor. I retrieved my phone.

She answered in a low whisper.

"Hey." I tried to pretend I was fine. She didn't speak, only breathed. "Aunt Gina?"

She took a deep, ragged breath. Fear pulsated through ever vessel—something had happened. Did Uncle Dan want a divorce?

I will disown the bastard.

"You have to come home." The words cracked, almost unrecognizable. "Tonight if you can."

"Tonight? Why?" Uncle Dan's stupidity could wait until the weekend.

"I don't want to discuss this on the phone." Gina sniffed and sobbed.

My heartbeat raced at marathon speed. I sat up. The cat jumped off the bed and sneezed.

"You are scaring me, Gina. Please."

My heart couldn't take anymore. I lost the only man I ever loved. There would be no one like him. Silence. I glanced at my phone to make sure I didn't lose the call.

"Frank…isn't well."

"What do you mean he isn't well?" He said nothing about being ill. I remembered I hadn't called him.

"He has cancer." Gina sobbed. "Please come home."

My hand went to my chest to stop my heart from coming out.

"I'll talk to HR on Monday. I am out of personal time."

"No. Frank won't make it past Christmas." Gina couldn't stop crying.

"But there are treatments. People beat cancer all the time. They do."

"His body isn't responding to the treatments. It has spread. He's doing palliative care for the pain," Gina said and sobbed. "Please don't be mad at Frank for not telling you. You've been happy in New York and—"

"Are you saying everyone knew but me?"

"Don't yell."

"I can yell if I fucking want. No one seems to care—"

"Stop! Your dad thought he'd tell you once he was on the

mend. He didn't want you moving back here."

Gina and I sat in silence for a moment like two raging female bulls contemplating whether to tear the other one to pieces.

"I'm taking the next flight." I flipped on my light, opened my drawer, and tossed clothes into my gym bag.

"Good. Text me. I will pick you up at the airport. Please don't be mad at Frank. He's so worried you'll be mad."

"I'm not mad. I am terrified."

CHAPTER SIXTY-SEVEN

"Several times in our lives I told Sarah everything would be okay." -Frank Margo

The man sleeping in the recliner was not my father—impossible. Frozen in the middle of the living room, I couldn't accept reality. He was fine last summer. What would I say to him? He didn't tell me because I would worry. I would drop everything because let's face it—Frank Margo was my world. We had been each other's strength through every storm. He should have allowed me to be there for him.

What the hell was I going to do?

When his eyes opened, dark brown against his pale, sunken skin, I felt the sting of oncoming tears. I walked towards him for a hug, not wanting him to see how shocked I was by his frail appearance and patchy hair. Nothing could have prepared me for this moment.

"Hey, Dad." He put his arms around me while still in the chair. He squeezed me, and I could feel how much weight he had lost. I bit my shaking lip to keep from letting out a sob.

"Sarah." His voice shook. "I'm sorry."

I told myself on the plane I wouldn't cry. *Don't let him see you cry.* My mantra had no effect, and I lost it.

"It's okay, Dad."

The fact remained everything was not okay. Looking at my father, I was so helpless and lost, feelings I hadn't felt since the fall of Hidden Meadows. I was a child then, clueless to the world around me, but everything I had learned since seemed to dissipate. I lacked reason, thought, sense, and time. The only person who could carry me through this was Frank Margo. "Many people beat cancer."

"Basic probability, honey," my father whispered. He wiped my face with his hand. "You of all people should understand someone is always on the losing end of odds." He closed his eyes, perhaps not wanting to admit the truth aloud. "This time it's us."

The words shredded through me, ripping my soul to pieces. I sat on the couch afraid I would fall to the floor. We sat in silence with only the buzz of the corner lamp. I hated that damn lamp.

"How's Iain?" He asked like we weren't discussing his demise two minutes ago.

Did I tell him Iain and I weren't speaking? I was losing both men I loved more than life. No words could describe my despair.

"He is working a lot," I said, and it was true. Thinking about Iain hurt.

"I have only ever tried doing the best for you. Do you forgive me?" My father's eyes watered. I had never seen the light out in his eyes until this moment. His typical joy, sarcastic, life-loving-self wasn't there.

"Of course, Dad. I love you more than anything."

The blue Silverado rattled up to the gate at Pine Ridge. I needed to talk to my aunt. I didn't text her my flight. A cab took me to my dad's house. I needed time to process and talking about cancer with my father would end in sobbing tears. I couldn't let him see me desperate, hopeless…lost.

When I pressed the black button, no one answered. I had watched Gina enough to memorize the gate code—her birthday. The truck's brakes squeaked when I parked behind Uncle Dan's boat, covered in a tan tarp for winter. I would wait for my family to arrive home.

An hour passed, I sat on the single stair leading to the covered front porch. Uncle Dan had river pebbles in his flower bed rather than mulch. Two large aloe plants were near the sidewalk—Grandma's favorite. My elbows rested on my knees, palms of my hands cradled my cheeks. The sun sat low in the sky; darkness would soon shadow Oakville as much as my heart.

Shoes swooshed in grass blades, but I didn't bother to move my head. If it were my uncle and aunt, I would have heard the garage opening. Gina would have yelled hello from the car. A person sat next to me. Tall, in a suit, the smell of expensive cologne—a little too much. The view of argyle socks from the corner of my eye confirmed the person. He never wore solid socks.

"You okay?"

I looked up at Roddy King. Seventeen years ago, I saw him for the first time on these steps. He now had a few lines on his face and dark circles from late nights at the hospital, but his eyes were the same chocolate shade lined with dark lashes.

"Define okay," I whispered. A blond in a red dress waited in the Kings' driveway. She watched us.

"I am sorry," he said. The clarity of his voice resonated deep within my broken spirit. He knew too.

"Tell me," I said.

Roddy pressed his lips together to stop the quivering. He glanced at his date pacing near the beige SUV on the blacktop. Our eyes locked, mine watering, his full of fear.

He sighed. "It's not good. The cancer has spread. I am so sorry."

I knew the stages of grief from a college psychology class— denial, anger, bargaining, depression, and acceptance. I was in denial. No chance in hell could I accept my father would be dead by Christmas.

My mind went to Iain. Would I return to New York to work for Mackgale-Berrell? I sent Debbie and Tim an email requesting a leave of absence and boarded a plan. I didn't wait for an approval. Maybe they would fire me. I would never see Iain again, other than on television or a tabloid. I moved straight to depression.

"Go home, Sarah. Your uncle and aunt are at a charity event downtown with my parents. That's where we're heading." Roddy's date tapped her watch with an exaggerated eye roll. He adjusted his suit when he stood. "Don't be angry with your family for concealing Frank's cancer. It does no one good to harbor bad feelings. I would know."

CHAPTER SIXTY-EIGHT

"When I saw her on the steps, my feelings turned upside down. I had an engagement ring in my pocket for the woman waiting in my parents' driveway. If Sarah wanted to leave together in the beat-up Silverado, I'd go."
-Roddy King

"Do you want me to cook dinner tonight?" I asked my dad. He hadn't moved from his recliner since I had arrived in Oakville.

"No. Gina dropped off pasta salad a few days ago. I didn't eat it." His eyes shut.

I hadn't slept in three days. Roddy wouldn't leave my thoughts; memories played of us when we were younger. The days before we had lines on our faces and had lived in the real world. I wondered if I had made a mistake ending our relationship. Maybe I should have stayed in Oakville, been with my dad the entire time. Roddy and I would have gotten married, moved into a house close to Oakville State. I would have accepted a faculty position under Frank Margo. Students would wonder which Margo was teaching the statics class. Our kids laughed in my mind, dark lashes and tan skin like their father.

Life seemed utopia in our heads. The reality was Roddy meant something, but I didn't want to be with him. The kids waved goodbye in my thoughts and climbed into a car with Roddy. I loved someone else.

I sunk into the couch. My father dosed in and out while watching television.

The landline rang.

I pressed the talk button on the cordless. I couldn't believe people still used home phones. "Hello."

"Dan made reservations for the Riverfront," Gina said. I figured she would yell at me for not calling her at the airport. We ignored our problems for the first time in our lives.

"Okay."

"We will pick you up around five." A speaker made an announcement. "I need to go. I am helping Shantel with the holiday displays." She didn't say goodbye.

A car rumbled across the broken asphalt where the maple tree roots had grown under the driveway. I peeked out the picture window at the blue SUV. I asked my dad if he recognized this type of vehicle. He shook his head. A man in sweats and a baseball cap got out and opened the back door. He wore dark-framed glasses. Iain? It couldn't be. I ignored his call yesterday.

The stranger outside had the wrong house. Maybe it was the neighbor's estranged nephew who mixed up the three and five in the address. Wrapping my robe around myself, I walked to the driveway to greet the man. He turned around with a laptop bag on one shoulder and a messenger bag on the other.

"Iain?" Underneath his eyes were dark from travel and time zones. I threw my arms around him. He squeezed me.

"For someone who is ignoring me, you seem glad I'm here." His head rested against me. I stayed quiet for a moment, not moving my face from his sweatshirt, afraid I would burst into tears.

"How did you know I was here?" My voice soft and muffled.

"Human Resources." He didn't let go of me.

"I thought HR was confidential?"

"Human Resources doesn't question the CEO. You aren't mad, are you?" Iain pulled away to study me. He brushed my hair out of my face. I looked terrible—tired, no make-up, and I did not bother getting dressed.

"I am glad you are here. It's…" Tears hurried down my cheeks.

"I know." His large hands cupped my face. If the situation were different, he might have kissed me. "I am here."

My dad didn't leave his room all afternoon. I decided not to push him to come out. The medications made him tired. No matter how I reasoned with myself, the entire situation seemed unreal. I had many memories in this little brick house—all included a larger-than-life Frank Margo, not a dying cancer patient.

I cringed. Did I admit the truth to myself? Dying cancer patient. I swallowed hard, and tears fill my eyes. Maybe the diagnosis was a mistake? A medical error or a switched chart. Any minute the cordless would ring, and the doctor would apologize. I let out a ragged breath.

The shower turned off.

I pulled myself together, wiped the tears, and pulled a fishing magazine from the newspaper rack. I flipped through it as if I needed a new bass boat. Iain would return to the living room any minute. I couldn't let him see me a mess. Things were awkward between us. Neither one of us seemed to know how to remove the tension. I didn't understand why he couldn't see me for six months, but somehow he could drop everything and be in Oakville.

Iain sat on the opposite end of the couch. My gray sweats and ponytail paled in comparison to his black pants and rolled up dress shirt. I watched him out of the corner of my eye pushing up his glasses and checking his phone.

"Are you becoming an angler?"

I placed the magazine on top of the Sunday paper. "I'm considering it," I said with perfect posture. He wanted to laugh. I did too, but we didn't.

Was it okay to laugh?

Laughter echoed outside as if God answered my question. A fountain of blond hair moved outside the picture window with my tall uncle in tow. She came through the front door, without knocking, her hands full of shopping bags. Uncle Dan carried more.

"Hey baby," Gina said to Iain. She hugged him. Since when did she like my work friend?

Uncle Dan placed his bags near the ones Gina left in the middle of the floor. He touched my shoulder. I didn't leave my spot on the couch.

"Where do you want the bags?" Uncle Dan gestured towards the mound of shopping totes. I looked at him confused. Why would I want this stuff?

"What is this?" I asked, not hiding my contempt. The last thing I wanted was gifts to lessen the your-dad-has-cancer blow. Clothes, shoes, pillows, and towels spilled out of the tops. "I can't accept these gifts. It's too much."

"It's not from us, honey," Gina whispered next to Iain.

"Neither of us has much here. I asked Gina to purchase clothing and household items. I flew here from China with only work attire. There weren't many options at the airport."

"These items are expensive." No one bought me extravagant gifts. Uncle Dan touched his head and looked at Iain.

"If a man gets out his credit card, the polite thing to do is thank him." Gina gave me a mother hen glare.

"Thank you," I said to Iain. His eyes on me made my stomach flutter with more feelings than I could process.

"Y'all ready to get something to eat?" Gina asked.

"Let's see if Frank is up to a night out." Dan gestured for

Iain to accompany him to the bedroom where Frank slept.

I opened a box of women's shoes. "Running shoes?" Iain smiled, and I missed us before our fight.

"Sticks and stones, baby," he said with a grin. I laughed even though I had no idea what he meant. He disappeared down the hall with my uncle.

"These boots are four hundred. I could never afford these items," I whispered to Gina.

"He said he wanted the best we carried," she whispered. Gina eyed her reflection in a wall mirror. "He was specific on what to buy." She reached to touch a nearby frame. "When I fall, you will catch me," she whispered.

"You talked to him on the phone?"

I ignored her words. Now was not the time to be spiritual. I couldn't handle talk of God's will or whatever direction Gina was going with the catchy poem.

"He was worried about you. Don't give me that look. He is trying. I know I wasn't his biggest fan in the beginning, but he seems to care about you. He and Dan talked for a while on the phone. Dan says Iain dropped big things at work for you." Gina glanced at the hall to make sure the men didn't hear our gossip. "Show a little appreciation."

"How much did he spend?"

"Around seven thousand," she said. My hand went to my mouth. "It's not all yours." She leaned closer as if telling me a secret. "He can afford it, baby. Why do you think your uncle never questions the money I spend?" I shrugged. She smirked. "Thank him in the bedroom later."

My mouth dropped open. Gina laughed at her dirty joke. Studying my face, she read my mind.

"You haven't?"

"It's complicated."

"It's not complicated. If you don't want to thank him, I

will."

I opened my mouth to speak, but nothing came out. Gina laughed again. It's not like I didn't want to sleep with him. I wasn't telling her I had tried and failed.

"Why am I always discussing my sex life or lack thereof with my family?" I forgot to keep my voice down. The men returned to the living room. "I will crawl into a dark hole now."

How many embarrassing moments can one handle in a lifetime?

Uncle Dan laughed. "How about the Riverfront instead of a dark hole?" Dan wrapped his arm around my shoulder. I nodded. "Good girl. Please take a bag and change out of your sweatpants."

"I wouldn't want to ruin your reputation."

CHAPTER SIXTY-NINE

"He slammed me against the wall. I should have called the police." -Jeff Layton

Gina handed me a garment bag. My heart sank when my fingers touched the black suit and matching hosiery intended for my dad's funeral.

Turning around to face the wall, I sucked in a deep breath to keep my composure. Gina hooked another bag to my door and returned to the living room. I wasn't sure if she left for my benefit or hers. When I turned around, a blue chiffon dress hung on my door above matching pumps on the floor. I changed and didn't bother seeing how the dress fit. I didn't care.

"Your new suit looks great," Gina said to my father. I entered the living room. He flushed with embarrassment and eyed the sleeve of his gray pinstripe coat. "Where do you keep your ties?"

"I don't have ties nice enough for this expensive suit." My dad squinted his eyes. "I don't know why you had to buy it. I'm getting buried in it. My suits would work fine for the dirt."

Dan watched his brother fight with his wife. Iain threaded a red tie through his dress shirt.

"Oh, Frank," Gina grabbed his suit jacket. "The restaurant requires men to wear a tie."

"I have plenty of ties, Gina," Iain said. He put his arms through his suit jacket sleeves. "They are hanging in the utility room; take whatever you need."

My father gave him an irritated look as if Iain had joined Team Gina. She smiled and hurried towards the laundry room. Everyone waited for the blond boss to return.

"Here we go, Frank." Gina held a blue silk tie with embroidery.

"I love that tie," I said.

I watched her thread the material around my unwilling father's neck. Iain wore it on his thirtieth birthday. He smiled when I looked at him. For once, I read his mind. I wondered all the time what would have happened in his bedroom if Iris never showed up. Would we be different now?

"It's beautiful," she said. My dad allowed his sister-in-law to tie a Windsor knot.

Grabbing his blue Oakville State baseball cap to cover his balding head, my dad looked at his brother. "Let's go before these women put lipstick and a wig on me."

My dad smiled for the first time since I'd been home. Half my heart filled with joy, the other piece cracked.

Iain placed his hand on my lower back. My eyes watered, either from wanting or not wanting his touch. He ushered me to Dan's X5 where I climbed into the back seat. Seeing the blue tie made me so empty; although I missed something which didn't exist. Iain's rejection and the cancer news left me sad and helpless. I wondered how long I would feel broken. Iain and Gina climbed in the back. I had the privilege of the middle seat, made for baby seats and ten-year-olds.

Everyone gazed out the windows in silence. This group was never quiet. I couldn't tell if we were hungry or depressed.

His finger brushed against mine. I assumed his touch was an accident since the back seat was like riding in a sardine can. When it happened again, I glanced out of the corner of my eye, dark blue eyes not disguising their direction. I wanted to stay mad at him.

He said our intimacy should have never happened—rejection in its purest form. It's like telling someone their breath stinks and then asking to kiss them. I was mad at him, afraid to get close again. I moved my hand back to my lap and turned my face towards Gina. Her artificial nails tapped the glass on her phone, a text to her mom in Georgia.

We arrived at the restaurant and waited for the valet attendant to give Dan a ticket.

The restaurant's main attraction was the glass wall overlooking the river. Soft music played, and a couple slow danced on a small dance floor.

"Right this way." The hostess led us to our table, stopping for a moment to do a double-take at Iain. The length of her blond ponytail ran across his arm when she turned to hand him a menu. Jealousy bubbled inside me, an emotion I hated. Iain didn't notice and pulled out a chair for me to sit.

"Your dress is lovely," he whispered and opened his menu.

Why are you in Oakville, Iain?

"Ditto." I opened my menu. Gina kicked me under the table, followed by one of her harsh looks. Iain smiled at my asinine response.

"Any wines on this list you recommend?" Iain asked Dan.

The manager stopped by our table and put the conversation on hold. Dan Margo was the Iain Mackgale of Oakville. Maybe the manager wanted to thank him for dining at the restaurant or wanted to offer us a complimentary bottle of wine.

"I'm sorry, sir," the manager said to my father in hushed tones. "We don't allow hats in this restaurant."

Gina and I shared a panicked look. We were aware of how self-conscious hair loss made my father. Even at home, he wore a baseball cap.

"I'm not going to remove it." My father returned to the menu.

All of us ignored the manager. Were we hoping Jeff, according to his name tag, would go away?

"I have to ask you to leave," Jeff said. He stepped back to allow my dad room to exit. Was the manager kicking out a cancer patient who refused to take off his hat? The situation was more unreal than actual cancer.

"Do you know who I am?" Dan asked, hands clenched into fists on the table. The tension at our table was enough to attract attention.

"Yes, Mr. Margo, I am familiar with you," Jeff said in a snide manner. "We don't allow hats in our restaurant, and we don't make exceptions, even for you."

Dan started to remark, but his brother interrupted.

"Fine. I'll wait in the car." My dad stood to leave.

I scanned the faces at the table—shock. Iain's chair screeched against the floor. He stood taller than my dad and Jeff.

"Have a seat, Frank." Iain helped my frail father back into his chair. "Outside," Iain said to Jeff. He placed his hand on the manager's arm. Jeff didn't argue with the pissed-off, former rugby player.

Our table sat in silence. No one bothered to pick up a menu. We were either bailing Iain out of jail or eating at Benny's BBQ. My family avoided eye contact. I couldn't take the humiliation on my father's face. Several minutes later, Iain returned to the table and took his seat.

"All is well," Iain said. He picked up the menu. Everyone stared at Iain.

"Did the manager know who you are?" I asked.

"No." The corners of Iain's lips turned upward to a satisfied grin. "I told him if he spoke to my family again, I would give him a proper ass whopping. Jeff is a wee man. Size matters."

Dan laughed. My cheeks warmed.

"Iain, you didn't have to…" My dad's eyes grew misty.

"Is this the place with the king crab legs you were telling me about in London?" Iain asked.

My dad perked up at the mention of his travels. Relief spread around the table. My dad would take tonight to the grave. No one at the table would forget, but for everyone's sake, I felt thankful Iain somehow saved the night.

"The Riverfront can't top London," Frank said. A flicker of memory crossed his face. "What beer were we drinking?" A small smile touched my dad's lips.

Iain laughed. "Name a beer we didn't drink that night."

"I guess you told me a watered-down version of your trip?" I said to my grinning father. "He couldn't remember the name of the restaurant and kept calling it swanky seafood. The details were patchy."

"There may have been some heavy drinking." My father returned to his menu, an attempt to avoid my interrogation.

"After you lectured us the week before for having a little too much to drink?"

Busted, Frank Margo.

He considered his rebuttal for a moment. "I didn't end up passed out near lawn furniture." He sat his menu down.

"When did this happen?" Dan asked. He hated to miss a great story.

"These two idiots broke into the liquor cabinet." Iain laughed at the fake insult. "They got shit-faced and passed out in the backyard the weekend of your wedding."

Dan laughed, and Gina disapproved. She turned her head to hide the amused smile.

"You can't judge. Frank was so drunk; he woke thinking he had relations with the big-bosomed housekeeper."

Our table roared with laughter, cancer forgotten for a moment. I closed my eyes for a second to keep the memory close, to retrieve it when the light turned to dark.

"Big-bosomed?" I questioned.

"The word *tits* is frowned upon at the dinner table," Iain said. I shoved his thigh. His hand moved on top of mine, and he didn't let go. The room spun with laughter and emotions. Even the waiter laughed and waited to take our drink order.

"I am not used to a woman walking around my bedroom. When I woke, she was looking for my pants. I assumed the worst…or best," he said, red-faced and laughing. "I told her I hoped she enjoyed herself because I couldn't remember a damn thing."

Everyone laughed but me.

"Oh my God, Dad." My attention shifted to my father's partner in crime. "What happened to you that night?"

"Martin made sure I made it to my own bed. I slept alone as I do every night."

The mood at the table changed. Iain studied my face, hand still wrapped around mine. Dan talked to the waiter, but I couldn't hear their conversation.

"Good."

He twisted his lips in thought. Iain wanted to say more but didn't with an audience.

"Would you like champagne tonight?" Iain asked, and I nodded. He turned to the waiter. "Two bottles of the best Cristal you offer."

"Excellent choice, sir," the waiter said.

"Ina has two extra tickets for the silent auction and *The Nutcracker*," my dad said to his brother. "It's a fundraiser for the university. It's in three weeks. There may be a third ticket if I'm not around."

"Frank," Gina scolded.

"The Cobbs are coming to town the second week of December. We already have *Nutcracker* tickets. Why not take

Iain and Sarah?" Dan turned to us. My dad knew the tension between us. He didn't want to suggest a date.

"We would love to attend," Iain said. I stayed quiet and emotionless. "I love the theater." He smiled at me.

The waiter returned with drinks. Iain ordered the red snapper livornese. I wanted a cheeseburger, but I ordered the same as him. When our eyes met, I glanced away. I wanted him to know I could be on his level. There was a chance I would throw up later. I picked up my glass and took a sip of champagne. It tasted familiar.

Iain smiled at my expression, clicking his glass against mine. "To Sarah Margo not getting swallowed by the sea," he whispered, face inches from mine. I wanted to kiss him, but I took another sip of my bubbly drink. I wasn't ready to consider forgiving him.

CHAPTER SEVENTY

"My good memories were replaced with him walking down the hallway of the oncology ward in a gown stamped with the hospital logo. The IV line was taped to his hand. A bag of liquid dripped from a pole on wheels. Machines beeped. People cried in the waiting room. I never forgot the sounds." -Sarah Margo

This wasn't my first university fundraiser. They were always the same—a catered buffet, a silent auction, and a performance afterward. I had never seen *The Nutcracker*.

Iain pulled the rental up to the curb and made a joke about how I would break my neck walking several blocks in heels. He was making excuses. My dad knew it too but gave up fighting with everyone on what he could or couldn't do. The dark circles under his eyes were proof of his exhaustion.

My dad held my arm tightly as we entered the double doors of the student center. We were meeting Ina in the main lobby in ten minutes. I hadn't seen Ina since my graduation. There was no sign of her, only nicely dressed people picking up the silent auction brochure.

The double doors opened with a rush of cool air. Iain shivered and removed his gloves. The last three weeks he spent every day catering to our every need while running his company from the den. I wished I could express my gratitude or tell him the truth of my feelings. Whenever I tried, our harsh words in Berrell rang louder than my courage. He stopped at the event table to pick up a brochure.

As soon as Iain joined us, Ina appeared through a different door, smiling warmly. I was happy to see her until I noticed her son. Maybe he had grown-up. After all, I had not seen him since dating Roddy. They attended the same snobby high school. Jacob Rosenberger thought he was a gift from God.

Ina hugged my dad, tears streaming down her face. She was always professional, and I found her emotions alarming. As my dad and Ina exchanged words, Jacob ignored me and turned his attention to Iain.

"Hello. I'm Jacob Rosenberger." Jacob held out his hand to Iain. Jacob looked like a little weasel in a black suit.

"Iain Mackgale," Iain said, all business. Something in Iain's demeanor gave me the feeling he thought Jacob was a weasel too.

"I thought that was you," Jacob said. He crossed his arms as if he solved a mystery. "Are you speaking tonight? The university paid a small fortune to get you here."

"No. I'm a guest." He opened the brochure to view the auction items.

"My father owns Rosenberger Investments downtown." Jacob had a snobby smirk on his face. "I would love to pick your brain sometime."

Iain removed his eyes from his reading material, irritated. "No business tonight. As I said, I'm a guest."

"Our meeting doesn't have to be tonight." Jacob was the fly you wanted to squash.

"I don't do consulting work." Iain flipped through the brochure and ignored the pest.

Instead, Jacob turned to me. When people weren't impressed, he got rude. Jacob inherited this trait from his father, which is why Ina was no longer married to Henry Rosenberger.

"Roddy got engaged over the weekend. His parents are ecstatic the Kirk's are joining their family. Do you know

Lindsay Kirk?" I opened my mouth to respond. "No, you wouldn't know her. Lindsay's parents own Kirk Pharmaceuticals, and she graduated pharmacy school last summer."

"I'm happy for him." I had no ill feelings towards my ex-boyfriend. If he wanted to marry a stuck-up rich girl to please his parents, that was his business.

"Are you waiting for someone? Did you need directions?" Jacob asked Iain.

Iain chuckled. "No. I'm fine. Thank you." Iain's expression softened when he leaned closer with the brochure. "What should we bid on?" I shrugged, not sure how practical a gas grill or a riding lawn mower would be for people like us. "How about the trip to the Cayman Islands in April? Three days of pristine beaches and world-class, all-inclusive dining." Iain read the description. "You said I should holiday there. It's only right you come and assess the hype."

I laughed. It felt good to be happy.

"You don't forget a thing."

He placed his hand on my back and pulled me against him. He kissed the top of my head. I wanted to stop being mad.

"No, darling girl. I do not."

"You are here with Sarah Margo?" Iain and I looked up at the pest. We forgot he was next to us. Jacob stepped back, over-dramatically making a coughing sound. "Wow. Can't you get any woman with your money?"

"Sarah is the only woman I want," Iain said. The room stood still for a moment, lights sparkled, and the chatter disappeared. "Gold-digging half-wits get old fast." Iain squeezed me as if steadying himself not to beat the shit out of Jacob in the student center.

"But…"

"We aren't your concern." Iain threaded his fingers between mine. "Frank is inside. Let's go."

People crowded near the door. I leaned close to Iain. "What about the press? I forget you are you sometimes."

His head leaned against mine. "I'm glad you do. It's handled."

I narrowed my eyes. "Jacob recognized you."

"Jacob watches too much television."

"Your name?" a woman with a list asked.

"Sarah Margo."

"Table fifteen. Auction starts at seven. The winners are posted after the performance. Please pay within twenty-four hours. All checks should be made payable to Oakville State University." The woman sounded like a recording. She handed us drink tickets.

"No worrying tonight," Iain whispered.

Easier said than done.

Our table had a centerpiece which read *Dr. Rosenberger, College of Engineering*. Six chairs with outdated maroon covers lined the table.

"You have grown up." Ina hugged me. She was never affectionate. Was it because of my dad's fate? "You should be so proud, Frank."

My father's lips lifted into a small smile. The paleness of his skin and the dark smudges below his eyes worried me.

"It's good to see you, Dr. Rosenberger." She brought back memories of graduate school, and I found myself missing academia.

"Hello. You must be Iain," she said. Iain took my former professor's hand, pleased to meet my mentor. "Frank shared his London photographs at our department meeting. I never forget *I* names."

"I have a sister called Iris and a brother, Issac. It's a pleasure

404

to meet you." Iain held her hand for a moment. The older woman formed tears in her eyes.

"Enough of the dramatics, Mother." Jacob appeared at our table. "It's our turn to get food."

Ina followed her son to join the others in the food line. My dad observed his friends and colleagues chatting at tables and near the buffet. Their world would go on without him.

"Twenty minutes left to bid on auction items," a voice yelled from the front of the room.

"Go bid on our vacation," Iain whispered. His lips touched my ear by accident. It tickled, and I giggled. "I'll stay with Frank."

My dad turned in his chair, to soak in as much as he could one last time. I struggled tonight—one minute I couldn't contain the flutters of happiness with Iain and the next my heart ripped to pieces over my frail father. He possessed the parental skill of intuition. I knew he wanted to comfort me, but didn't—what could he say to make my pain go away?

"How much should I bid?" I asked Iain. Our faces were close. Why was he so good looking? I flushed.

"Let's do ten. I doubt anyone will bid higher."

"Ten dollars?"

Iain snickered and kissed my cheek. "Thousand. Your bid. My check."

"Good. Ten dollars was my budget." My dad watched us with a shadow of a smile.

"Sarah is bidding on the Cayman Islands vacation," Iain said to Frank.

The doctors had told my dad to continue living his life, but everything was a constant reminder he would not be around to keep sharing ours. Frank would never meet my husband, his grandchildren, or the simple details of a vacation in the spring. I felt guilty bidding on a beach vacation. Was this a symptom of survivor's guilt?

"Good," he said.

I scanned the auction table until I found the sheet for the beach vacation. Three bidders. Arthur Klein had the highest bid at four thousand dollars. I scribbled my name and ten thousand dollars. Iain's money never interested me, but I was Hollywood outbidding an ophthalmologist by six thousand dollars. I strutted back to my seat.

Iain and my father were not at our table. Panic surged through me until I saw them at the bar, my father holding on to Iain. The doctor had told him not to drink alcohol with his medication, but my dad looked the happiest he had been all night next to Iain with a beer. An older man and his wife stopped to say hello and shook Iain's hand. I wondered how many people recognized him. Not to mention, how he handled the press. I scanned the banquet room. No cameras. No press. I joined the men at the bar.

"The bidding is closed." A gavel banged against a table.

The three of us moved towards the buffet line, Frank clutching his beer. He said he was not hungry, but I told him he needed to eat something. The eye roll he gave rivaled my own. I was happy to see where I learned my bad habit.

"I am tired," my dad whispered. He grasped Iain's jacket to steady himself. "This will be the last time I'm out. Flanker, can you take me to the table?" He shared a slight smile with Iain.

I wanted to reassure him he would be better tomorrow, but couldn't.

"Sure. Anything." Iain handed me his plate of food and took my dad's plate of scalloped potatoes and cookies.

I wanted to bring a wheelchair, but my father said no. The last thing he wanted was for the people who respected him to see him at his worst. Most everyone in the room knew about the cancer—Frank was the chair of the Department of Engineering. He stepped down and was no longer teaching after seventeen years.

When I returned to the table with food, our group had returned to their seats. Ina and Frank were talking. Iain texted on his phone to avoid Jacob. A sixth person sat at our table but turned around to socialize with the group behind us.

Iain didn't acknowledge the food or my presence. I ate the catered food and avoided Jacob.

"Sarah." A hand touched my shoulder. When I turned, Aaron Wells towered over me, sophisticated as ever. I stood, and we hugged.

"What a surprise," I said.

Another man with his arms around me caused whatever was so crucial on Iain's phone to take a backseat.

"The city has been good for you." Aaron held my hands to survey my dress. "I am sorry we keep missing each other. You've been out of town the last two times I've been in New York."

If Iain weren't sitting next to me, I would have felt sorry too.

"I've traveled a lot this year." I smiled at Iain. Aaron's familiarity irritated him.

"Hello." Aaron reached around me to extend a hand to Iain. "I'm Aaron. Sarah and I grew up in the same neighborhood, a lifetime ago."

"Iain." They shook hands.

"This is my father, Jared," Aaron said when Mr. Wells appeared.

"Mackgale-Berrell?" Jared asked. He eyed the young CEO.

Iain nodded. "The very one."

"Your company is impressive. It's a pleasure to meet you. Are you speaking this evening?"

"No. I'm visiting my girlfriend," Iain said.

I hoped the shock of his words wasn't evident on my face. Aaron looked surprised. If my childhood friend only knew we found out about my relationship at the same time.

"You're a lucky man," Jared said and turned to his son. "We need to find your mother. We'll be in trouble if we're late." Jared waved at Frank and Ina. "It was good seeing you and nice meeting you, Mr. Mackgale."

Aaron leaned closer with a solemn expression. "Call me at the office when you're ready to meet. We can do lunch." Aaron hugged me. Iain scowled.

"I will. Thanks, Aaron." My emotions bubbled to the surface. I had managed not to cry all evening. The moisture in my eyes filled my tear ducts.

When Aaron and Jared left, I grabbed my clutch from the table. "I'm going to the restroom."

I gasped when Iain stalked into the restroom behind me. The two stalls were empty.

"You can't be in here." I raised my voice, outraged he was in the woman's restroom.

"Why are you meeting Aaron?"

"Are you jealous?" The thought of two successful, gorgeous men fighting over me was fun. It wouldn't happen, but a girl could fantasize.

"I don't get jealous." He ran his hand through his hair. "But I am jealous. You make me absolutely crazy."

"You make me crazy. One minute you want me, the next you don't. Tonight, I became your girlfriend because you want no one else interested." Emotions surfaced, burning and tightening my throat. I bit my shaking lip to keep from getting more emotional. "Are you ashamed of me?"

"Are you serious?" Iain moved closer. I stepped backward until my lower back touched the sink. "How could you think such nonsense?"

"What is the truth?" We needed to put this insane relationship to rest and move on.

"I can't tell you," he said. I started to leave the restroom, but he stepped in front of me.

"All this time and you can't tell me? You either don't trust me or what you're hiding is bad. Or both."

"No. You are the only person I trust. I have signed legal documents and cannot disclose. The last thing I want is to involve you. Look at the trouble I have already caused."

"If you're here for guilt, please go." I gestured towards the door.

"I am here for you."

"Why are you in Oakville? What happened to six months with no time off?" Asking the question which loomed in my mind felt great.

"Do you know how much money the company is losing with me gone? Senior leadership is upset I have left and won't say why." He fidgeted with his watch.

I was close to losing my crap on him. "I didn't ask you to drop everything."

"It was my decision." The edge in his voice softened. A toilet trickled in the stall next to us. "I can't lose you. After seeing your pal Aaron all over you, I have no doubt I should be here."

"The Wells own a law firm, Iain." Weeks of lack of sleep caused me to tire easier. I sighed. "I am meeting Aaron to go over my dad's last will and testament."

"You can't be in here, sir," a woman said to Iain. We didn't realize three women entered the bathroom.

"Call security, Anita," the heavy-set senior told her friend.

Iain muttered apologies, and we returned to the lobby. The Rosenbergers and my dad waited near the double doors. Most people had left for the theater across the street.

"Iain." I stopped to face him with a glance towards our party. He looked at me, exhaustion all over his face. "You are the only man I want."

There was no time for further discussion. Jacob stormed towards us. "Where the hell have you been?" Jacob tapped his watch. "We have been waiting for ten minutes!"

"We'll meet you there," Ina said to her son.

"Do you mean it?" Iain whispered.

"It's always been you."

I was so caught up in *The Nutcracker* I didn't speak to anyone. When it was over, Iain smiled. His mood improved since our restroom showdown. We admitted we wanted each other. It didn't solve the hundred other problems.

People were leaving. Ina had her hand on my dad's back for support. They moved to the end of the row and waited for us. Jacob jumped a row below to speak with someone he knew.

"I will bring Frank home," Ina said. I didn't feel comfortable leaving my father. Iain squeezed my arm. Ina wanted her final memories of her friend before letting him go. The thought was too much to stomach. "Will you offer Jacob a ride if he needs one?"

"Sure."

My dad didn't say goodbye. They moved through the crowd.

Iain led me up the aisle to the exit. Outside the auditorium was a table with the auction results. Two men wrote checks, and their dates held spa gift baskets. Iain scanned the list. He blew out a breath of irritation.

"J. Rosenberger outbid us by one dollar." He chewed his lip.

"We are not offering that prick a ride," I said and took Iain's hand. "Let's get out of here before he sees us."

The SUV shut off and woke me from my sleep. At least twenty years had gone by since the last time I fell asleep in a car. Wiping the drool from my mouth, I unbuckled my seat belt. My body ached from lack of sleep.

Iain opened the car door and helped me in the darkness. We had forgotten to leave the front porch light on. My hand slid under Iain's suit jacket, fingers enjoying his linen shirt. He illuminated the driveway with his phone. The tips of his fingers dug into my backside. The warmth and feel of him made my body forget the fatigue. This connection between us was frustrating. The tension between us needed to find release. Why we couldn't get past this state of miserable purgatory—I had no idea.

I was in love with a man who wanted me, but couldn't have me. Tyler's nagging voice played in my head. *Iain's a traditional guy; he won't go against his parent's wishes.* There had to be more.

"Does your secret pertain to Charlotte?" I asked with one foot in the living room. Iain turned on the lamp, expression bewildered.

"It is not a secret. It's a non-disclosure agreement." He sat on the chair. "What does Charlotte have to do with us?"

"Everyone says you had an affair with her and your father disapproved. She had your baby. Her father was killed when he tried to make it right for her. Deana says you're a bad person. You sleep around, gamble too much—"

"You know I despise that bloody show." He placed his hands over his face in frustration. My heart sank when I had a strong inkling the rumors were true.

"Oh my God." I didn't mean to utter the words aloud. "It's true."

I added crushed and devastated to the long list of emotions. He uncovered his face with an expression I was not expecting —embarrassment.

"You never asked. I didn't want to tell you." His voice was low. The light from the lamp made his skin appear golden. "I never told you because I am ashamed."

"What else are you keeping from me?" I kicked my shoes off my feet.

Iain's lip trembled. "I didn't want you to judge me because of my family. Your family is lovely and…" He inhaled a deep breath.

"What does your family have to do with your stupidity?" My evil glare caused the wrinkle on my forehead to become affixed.

"Charlotte's relationship wasn't with me." His dark eyes did not move from mine. "It was my father. The child is my brother. Most everything you said is true, even the murder." I gasped. Iain covered his face again.

We sat in silence for a moment.

"Does your mother know?"

"Yes. Divorce is frowned upon. She wouldn't give up her position. My grandfather would never allow her to cause further scandal." Iain moved his hands on his lap.

"What about you? Everyone thinks this show is based on you."

"You shouldn't be surprised what people will do for money," he said.

The familiar line rang in my head.

CHAPTER SEVENTY-ONE

"Who wakes up at four to run?" -Penny Margo-Burns

Sleep deprivation had no effect on my ability to close my eyes. Rest didn't happen. Most nights I stared at the popped ceiling from my daybed. I tried not to remember why I was home. One night, I tried fooling myself into believing it was Christmas break. We made fettuccine for dinner. I hummed "Silent Night" in the shower. My plan didn't work.

My feet kicked off the purple and white comforter, and I climbed out of bed. I peeked into my dad's cracked door. He snoozed in the middle of his bed. Ina had brought him home as promised. The clock chimed four in the morning, and I tip-toed towards the kitchen for a glass of water.

When I glanced into the den, Iain typed on his laptop in the middle of the foldout in only pajama bottoms and glasses. I turned the cold handle and filled my cup with tap water. The liquid soothed my dry throat.

"Come here," he whispered. His laptop clicked shut.

I turned around, yellow light from the oven hood illuminated us. When I set my glass on the counter, it echoed in the silence. I stood frozen. Iain had a particular look about him, one which said he wanted purgatory over. I wanted nothing more than to move our relationship forward, but my heart was skeptical. He placed his laptop on his suitcase, reaching a hand towards me.

My bare feet moved across the cold floor to the carpet in the den. He moved the fingers of his outstretched hand. I reached for him like I was reaching for hot coals. He leaned forward, grabbed my hand, and pulled me into this lap. I collapsed on him in a clumsy way.

When we sat up, I straddled him. It wasn't intentional, but he planted his hands on my hips to keep me in place.

"Do you like this?" I whispered.

He nodded and caressed my cheek. We were inches from each other's face in a quiet house. I inhaled a breath.

"You look so beautiful in this light," he said.

Iain leaned forward to kiss my lips. His mouth was delicious and soft. He pulled away to study my reaction. We stared at each other like we had many times.

"I'm sorry. Hurting you was never my intention. Please forgive me. I want to fix us after..." Iain stopped. He wanted to say after Frank dies, but he caught himself. "When we return to our normal lives."

I appreciated his apology. At no point did I think he was a malicious person trying to cause me pain. I had every intention to give in to whatever he had planned on this fold out, but I wasn't ready to unlock the gates to my heart. Our back and forth of emotions the past few months had taken a toll on my already low tolerance for the opposite sex.

Iain pulled me against him. After a few gentle kisses, he parted my lips with his tongue then broke our kiss.

"Are you going to tell me we shouldn't be kissing?" I kept my voice low and impassive.

"No," he replied. His face was serious. "We should be more than kissing, but not with your father here."

"No door either." I kissed him.

Why did we wait so long to kiss?

"Squeaky, rickety bed."

I gave him my fake concerned face. He tried hard to suppress a smile. "You couldn't handle me, anyway."

"Don't you worry about me." He continued to kiss me. I wrapped my arms around him tighter. His hands moved under my nightshirt and over my bare skin. "I don't have a condom."

"I take the pill for cramps," I whispered.

Without warning, he flipped me to my back, pinning my arms over my head. I laughed when the foldout creaked. Iain kissed me to muffle my laughter.

"I want you," he murmured against my neck.

The tips of his fingers slid under my panties, pulling them across my thighs and over my feet. I breathed heavy with anticipation. Iain climbed off the foldout to remove his pajama bottoms. My mouth went dry at the site of him. Alex would be so jealous. *Should I be thinking about Alex?*

He climbed on the bed and lifted my nightgown. I hadn't had sex in six years. My pulse ticked with every kiss he placed on my thighs. His palm moved across my stomach. With his other hand, he parted my legs and kissed my hipbone.

I moaned.

"Quiet."

He moved his finger in and out of me, wetness hitting the sheets. I had never experienced want on this level. My back arched in response to the delicious high. He had the most satisfied grin on his face.

A noise came from the living room. We were close to nude, uncovered, with the lights on. My dad was upset about drinking last summer. He would be mad about screwing in his office.

"Wait," I whispered.

"Wait?" His offended expression was cute.

"I heard something," I said.

We sat on the fold out and listened—a few coughs followed

by an object falling. He reached for his pajama bottoms. Pulling my nightgown down, I hurried through the kitchen and into the living room. I saw him on the floor. Panic surged through me. My feet became twisted in the rug.

Darkness followed.

Warm blankets pressed against my arms, heavy and soft. My eyelids wouldn't open. Sleep deprivation must have won. I couldn't remember getting into bed or setting an alarm. The constant beeping was too much for my aching head. I opened one eye. The ceiling had tiles. Metal rails were cool to the touch. Strange curtains hung from a rod. I touched a bandage on my head.

Where am I?

"Lay down. You're okay," Iain said.

I could not put together the words, but I did not feel okay.

"Frank?" I murmured, recalling how I used to call him Frank to be funny when I was little.

"Your father is being admitted to the ICU." Iain squeezed my hand.

"I need to go." I tried to sit up.

"No," he scolded. "Dan and Ted are with him. Once he's settled and you're discharged, we can see him." I touched my aching head. "You tripped and fell on the hall rug. Your head hit the door frame." Iain kissed my hand.

I couldn't recall anything.

"There y'all are," a panicked Southern accent said and pulled back the curtain.

It occurred to me I wasn't in a room, but a patient bay in the emergency department. Gina hovered over me, without makeup. I blinked a few times. It was strange to see her bare, tired face. She wore a wrinkled cardigan. Iain had on pajama pants and an Oakville State sweatshirt. I had on a hospital gown with a bandage on my head—we all had seen better days.

"Oh, baby," Gina gushed with tears in her eyes. She touched my head. "Are you okay? I told Frank to get rid of that rug."

"The doctor left a few minutes ago. She is being released," Iain said to Gina. She touched Iain's arm in thanks.

"You called 9-1-1? You knew how?" I asked.

Iain grinned. "I attended school here. Stop, drop, and roll. Dial 9-1-1 for a fire." Iain recalled a memory. "I never thought it would prove useful."

"Did you fill out the paperwork?"

"Yes." He pulled his phone out of his pocket and waved it. "You work for my company."

"Didn't the hospital staff think—"

He laughed.

"Enough with the twenty questions. They seemed more concerned with your bleeding head than who filled out the paperwork. Besides, I told them you're my wife." He was not joking. "The nurse said family only."

"What if someone alerts the press?"

"Look at me right now. No one would believe me if I said I was the king of the dumpster." He gestured to his pajamas.

"What were the two of you doing awake so early?" Gina asked. She looked at me and then to Iain. "I see."

"I have no defense," Iain said.

"Penny has been asking. Come up with another explanation," Gina whispered. Her lip quivered. "If you wouldn't have been awake..." She broke off, tears streaming down her face.

I wasn't following and shrugged.

"Frank would have drowned in his own vomit," he said.

I sucked in a shaky breath and closed my eyes. The mental

image of my dad unconscious on the carpet outside the bathroom flashed in my memory. I wanted to wake up, take two ibuprofen for this pounding headache. I should have been in New York, waiting for my dad to call to tell me he planted marigolds over the weekend—the only flowers he could get to live.

A doctor entered the room and spoke to Iain. "She is ready for discharge. Plenty of fluids and rest, over-the-counter pain medication for the headache, and follow-up with her primary doctor if there is any concern."

"Thank you," Iain said.

I winced in pain when the nurse removed the IV, placing another bandage on my hand.

"Do I have any clothes here?"

"Your nightgown has blood on it. Martin is on his way with clothes for us." I needed to relax. Iain was a professional at taking care of any situation.

"Sometimes I forget about your drivers, security team, assistants, and intel resources." The corner of my mouth lifted. I was so tired.

Gina stepped into the hall.

"They can be helpful on occasion. Wear the hospital gown until Martin returns. I would give you my sweatshirt, but I am not wearing a shirt underneath."

My mind drifted back to shirtless Iain. Life was unfair for so many reasons.

We arrived in the ICU waiting area. Gina paced, talking to someone on her cell phone. People cried in the hall. Machines beeped to a hollow rhythm. Hospital staff in scrubs hustled behind the nurse's station.

"Can I see my dad?" I asked Gina after she put away her phone.

"Hospital policy doesn't allow more than two people at a time."

"I am his daughter!"

Iain held my arm to either stabilize me or keep me from charging through the doors. Dizziness came over me, and I sat down.

"Your uncles will argue Frank is their brother." More relatives were on their way to the hospital. "I spoke with Dan a few minutes ago. The critical care team is trying to stabilize him. Why don't you rest for an hour?" She worded it like a suggestion, but it was a command.

"Okay."

"Praise Jesus, Sarah Nicole listened to someone." Gina smiled with tears in her eyes. "Not the miracle I wanted."

"Rest your head against me," he said.

I snuggled next to Iain on the waiting room sofa. A woman and her teenage son slept with hospital pillows and blankets on two of the couches. Gina stepped into the restroom when her phone vibrated.

Ten minutes later, Martin brought our clothes. He didn't like me before. I doubt he loved hanging out in Oakville for weeks. Iain didn't like me asking questions about the people who worked for him.

I changed into the yoga outfit. It was one of Iain and Gina's purchases. The pale gray color worked well with my complexion, and the form-fitted zip-up made my breasts appear bigger. Martin had my make-up in the bag. I applied powder, eyeliner, and lip gloss. If it were not for the bandage on my head, I wouldn't be half-bad considering the circumstances.

Iain stood outside the restroom. He changed into dark denim, a white button-up, and a navy sweater. Why did he always look so good? My mind drifted back to the site of him standing nude in the den.

Sarah!

"We can go see your father now," Iain said.

He put my bag over his shoulder and took my hand. I followed him to the locked door. A nurse slid open a window and allowed us access.

A woman sobbed, which elevated my anxiety to a ten. The sterile smell created a sickness in my stomach. I inhaled shallow breaths to calm myself. The hospital did not try to make this unit pretty—no potted plants, wall décor, or educational posters.

Squeezing Iain's hand tighter, he looked over at me with fear. My family stood at the end of the hall looking through a glass window. At first glance, one would think they were gathered around a newborn nursery, but the expressions on their faces were less joyous.

CHAPTER SEVENTY-TWO

"Jesus answered him, "Truly I tell you, today you will be with me in paradise." - Penny Margo-Burns

Gina had quoted the Bible three times in the last ten minutes. It was her way of coping, and I found talk of God's will annoying at the moment. Aunt Penny egged on her religious talk.

I stood in the hall, on the other side of the glass, numb to my surroundings, with my aunts and Iain. Uncle Ted and Dan were in chairs at my dad's bedside. Ted wouldn't stop crying. The nurse pointed towards us. My uncles stood. Dan touched my dad's arm before joining us on the other side of the glass.

"You girls can see Frank." Dan walked out of the room. He didn't stop. Ted followed.

Gina grabbed my hand and squeezed. I was in a full panic attack by the time we stood at the bedside. My father had a breathing tube and an IV. His eyes were closed. My ducts became heavy with tears. They spilled over my cheeks and splashed onto the floor.

This was the end.

Penny joined us. The nurse wasn't enforcing the two people rule.

We held hands. My head ached from the fall and crying. Nothing mattered standing in this room. My aunts whispered in unison. I put my head down, not able to escape their prayer.

Our Father who art in Heaven,

Hallowed be thy name;

Thy kingdom come

Thy will be done

On earth as it is in heaven.

Give us this day our daily bread;

And forgive us our trespasses

As we forgive those who trespass against us;

And lead us not into temptation,

But deliver us from evil.

When I looked up, my dad's eyes were open, sunken and melancholy.

The hot water cascaded over my skin, hospital smell spiraling down the drain. I hadn't showered in three days. My dad insisted we leave until morning. He was tired, sick of our crying and hovering. We agreed to go back to Uncle Dan's until morning. He lived the closest to the medical center.

I only agreed because three doctors were meeting Uncle Dan to discuss my dad's status. Two of the physicians lived in Pine Ridge, one being Dr. King, Roddy's father.

Clean clothes and washed hair improved my mood. I walked up the stairs to the living room. The physicians greeted Uncle Dan and Iain. Gina motioned for me to join her on the couch. The tall man in his thirties was Dr. Harper. I used to see him at my gym. We never talked. He hit on the leggy blonds. The older man with a potbelly and gray hair shooting from his ears I didn't know.

"I'm Chase Harper." He shook Iain's hand. "I don't believe

422

we've met."

Dr. King entered without knocking. I leaned against the couch to hide behind Gina. She turned to see my face. I shrugged. My aunt knew I was hiding from my ex's father. She tried not to smile.

"Iain Mackgale. It is a pleasure making your acquaintance." A spark of recognition crossed Dr. Harper's face.

"Dr. David King. Are you in business with Dan?" David looked at Dan in question. He recognized the young CEO too.

"No. Sarah is my girlfriend."

Whether I was Iain's girlfriend didn't matter, I enjoyed David King's shocked face. I told no one the mean remarks he had made. Whenever the memories played in my head, I shut them down. No one wants to be told they aren't good enough or will end up like their crazy mother.

One night Dr. King followed me to my car and offered me money to break up with Roddy. I told him he could shove the thousand dollars up his ass.

I zoned out, not hearing most of the conversation between the men. My uncle wanted a last-minute miracle for his favorite brother. *A dying man saved by an experimental treatment wasn't supposed to live past Christmas* would be the story headline. I pictured the news station interviewing us around a table. There would be a ham and mashed potatoes, pillar candles burning in the centerpiece. My father would ask for another piece of cake. We would laugh. Even I wasn't this delusional. This was Dan's final attempt to do what he could. Gina coped with the Bible. Dan searched for the last minute miracle.

"Are you suggesting you have been holding out because of money?" Iain raised his voice. Dan put his hand on Iain's shoulder.

"Of course it's about money," the older doctor replied. Gina dug her manicured nails into my thigh. "Someone has to pay —"

"You're worried you won't get paid?" Dan exchanged a look with Iain. "This is my brother!"

Gina stood, and I tugged her down next to me. We didn't need the South to come alive.

"Do you have a money tree, Mr. Margo? It's costly, and insurance doesn't cover experimental treatments." The older man crossed his arms. "I doubt your department stores are profitable enough—"

"Are you fucking telling us Frank could get better with these drugs?" Iain mimicked a raging bull. "How much do you want? Ten million? Fifty million?" The doctor laughed. "I am not finding humor in the situation, sir."

"Is that all you have?"

"A scratch on the surface. You clearly don't know me."

"You seem like a young kid who doesn't know how the real world works."

Before a fight broke out, Dr. Harper said, "There is a drug, but it won't cure Frank. It's in trial. The only benefit is it may allow Frank to live a few weeks longer. It will not change his outcome and will add more agony for your family. I looked at Frank's latest PET scan this morning."

"We wanted to be sure we had done what we could for Frank…" Dan choked up.

"Thank you for taking time to speak with us," Iain said.

Dan had his hand on Iain's shoulder to steady himself. The physicians walked to the door and reminded each other of a colleague's birthday party on Saturday.

"It's over," I whispered. Gina squeezed me, sobbing into my wet hair. I was helpless—my life would be less without my father.

Iain stood in the kitchen, eyes watering, watching us. My feelings were dead on the inside and dying on the outside.

"Let's get cleaned up and sleep. We can head back to the

hospital around six." Uncle Dan pressed a button on his watch.

"We can't stay here!" I stood, ready to return to the hospital. My uncle's tired face disagreed. "No. No. No. We can't stay here!" I sank to my knees in the living room.

"Sarah, baby." Gina wiped her bloodshot eyes with her sweatshirt. "Your uncle is right. Everyone is exhausted. Teddy and Penny are with Frank. We can leave early tomorrow."

Iain took my hand and led me downstairs to the guest bedroom. The calming earth tone décor was an improvement over the tacky trophies and daybed in the hobby room. He pulled down the duvet and helped me in bed.

"I am in need of a shower." He kissed my forehead. "Try to sleep."

I reached for his arm. He turned around. "Thank you for being here."

"There is no place I'd rather be," he said.

"Not even the Cayman Islands?"

His grin revealed more tired lines.

"Only if you're there too."

Iain disappeared into the guest bath. My body gave in to sleep.

CHAPTER SEVENTY-THREE

"Iain spent weeks sleeping on my couch and running his company from a hospital waiting room. You may be just friends, but he isn't." -Frank Margo

The elevator opened and the four of us entered. Uncle Dan hit the seven button to take us to my dad's new unit. No one talked. We were in an elevator staring at the walls the way strangers do. My eyes gravitated towards a poster hanging above the keypad. I squinted my eyes to make sure I wasn't playing games with myself. It was him, Lee Abrams, advertising the hospital's psychiatry department.

I thought I'd care. In the past, I would have freaked out about running into him or get stressed if someone knew about our relationship. Today, I didn't care. Whether from my dad's cancer, or Iain, or growing up, I forgave myself for being stupid. If the elevator doors opened to Lee on the other side, I'd give him an eye roll and keep moving.

My stomach growled. "What are we having for lunch?"

"It's not even seven."

The elevator dinged. I followed my family into the hall. Uncle Dan looked at the directory on the wall. Two older people bought a soda from a vending machine.

I shrugged.

"You are no different now than you were at ten-years-old," Gina said.

"I still get hungry." I zipped up my jacket.

She laughed. "Let's check in on Frank. Once he's sick of us, we can go eat."

Our banter amused Iain. He placed his arm on my back and pulled me against him. We walked behind my aunt and uncle. I slept in his arms last night. The smell of him lingered on my skin. I hadn't considered what would happen after Oakville. He never said we would be together, only fix us. Would we return to texting buddies, using work to cover-up our visits? The memory of Raj going crazy over travel caused me to grimace. I needed a new job. Maybe move. Even the fun of living next to Deana vanished.

Nothing stayed the same forever.

The new unit had no people restrictions. My dad's room looked like a high school kid's party while the parents were out of town. Paper cups everywhere. People were standing, sitting, and loitering near the door. I wanted to tell them to leave, but how could I justify I was more important?

Iain said hello to my cousin, Andy. I waved at Mr. Burns when he looked my way. He was Aunt Penny's third husband; no one could remember his name. My back rested against the wall near a dispenser of barf bags.

"I have a conference call scheduled and emails to answer," he whispered, then kissed the side of my head. "I'll be in the waiting room."

"Your dad wants to talk to you alone," Uncle Dan said on his way out. The family followed.

A minute later, I was alone with my father.

I sat on the corner of his bed. His face was pale, eyes tired, and he didn't move.

"Finally. A moment of peace," he whispered. The heart monitor moved but made no sounds.

I didn't know what to say. My instinct was always humor, but

I could find nothing funny about cancer. I wished I would have prayed harder with my aunts or searched for a miracle drug with my uncle.

"I love you, Dad."

"Sarah." He struggled to swallow. "You are the most important person in my life. I could never tell you how much you mean to me. One day you'll become a parent and know for yourself."

The burning in my chest produced tears in my eyes. I wanted to say I couldn't survive without him, but I took a breath instead. He lifted his hand. I squeezed his fingers.

"I'm proud of you. What you have accomplished thus far is only the beginning. An amazing life is ahead of you."

"Thanks, Dad," I said.

"I'm tired," he whispered. His eyes closed for a moment. "Don't visit me at the cemetery. I need you to move on with your life. Wherever you go, I will always be with you."

His dark brown eyes burned fiercely as if he had used every ounce of energy to relay a message. I froze. I needed to say something meaningful, but my words were lost. My body hovered over this moment watching. This was our last conversation.

"I love you so much. I couldn't have had a better dad." I placed a tissue over my mouth and nose to conceal my sobs.

Gina opened the door. Iain followed her into the room.

"Everyone is going to eat," she said.

My stomach growled.

"Flanker can stay with me," my dad whispered.

"Why do you keep calling him Flanker?" Maybe the cancer medication made him confused. I felt bad for asking.

"It's a rugby position," Iain said.

"I thought you were a hooker?"

Gina glared at my vulgarity.

"Another rugby position," Iain said to my aunt.

My dad smiled.

I recalled the day we received the keys to the little brick house. He promised me everything would be okay. I believed him.

CHAPTER SEVENTY-FOUR

"I said my final words to him, in my mind, at the casket as a crowd of people watched. Today they pitied me, and I didn't like it." -Sarah Margo

No part of me wanted to move. I remained on my daybed with the hope reality would change. My eyes were half-swollen and itchy. The hair on my legs prickled against the sheets. I had only showered once this week. I didn't care.

God, take me too.

"We have to leave soon." Iain stood over me. I couldn't see him, too tired to move my head, but I could feel his presence. "You must get a shower. Come."

No.

If I removed myself from this bed, I would have to deal with the truth. Who wants to go to their father's funeral? My dad would be disappointed I grieved in such a way, but I had no control over my emotions. The sorrow ran deep into my bones.

Life couldn't go forward.

"Sarah, are you listening?" He touched my shoulder. "You leave me no choice."

Strong arms slid under my stomach. My limp body molded to his chest when he picked me up. The blurry popped ceiling came into view when my eyes opened. The light hurt.

Iain dropped me on the bathroom floor. My back crashed

into the vanity, too numb to feel the impact. Iain hovered over me—waiting—his lips moving inaudibly. Was he saying my name?

I had given up.

Iain grabbed my arms hard and pulled me to my feet. I wobbled. The tips of his fingers dug into my flesh; drowsy thoughts whirled around until Iain lifted my t-shirt over my head. He wasn't gentle.

"Do you think this is how I wanted to undress you for the first time?" Iain's emotion jolted me out of my trance. I lifted my head to meet his eyes, angry and sad. "You are not the only one who lost Frank. People are expecting you." He paused. "They need you."

"I can't." The back of my throat ached when I spoke.

Iain reached behind the curtain to turn on the shower. The sound of water beating against the metal tub was soothing, but I didn't want a shower. What was the point of bathing?

"Fine." He wrapped his arms around my body and lifted me into the tub with him. Warm water soaked my bra and underwear.

"Hey!" I screamed. He didn't say a word, only held me while the water beat against us. His dress pants and shirt plastered against him from the moisture. "I'm not okay," I whispered into his chest.

Iain lifted my chin, the shower cascading down over us. His lips touched mine. To feel something besides grief made me feel alive.

"No one is okay," he said. A moment passed before he stepped out of the tub, his leather shoes leaving a trail of water on the bathroom floor.

The staff at the funeral home discussed their Thanksgiving plans in the corridor while my family waited to be told we could go to my dad's visitation. We had an hour of private time before we had to face the hundreds of people Frank Margo knew over his lifetime.

Uncle Dan paced the room even though Gina told him to stop twice. Uncle Teddy and my two aunts talked about the changes at the airport where they spent their morning picking up family.

I waited in the middle of the room, on an oriental rug, next to the wooden podium where people would sign the guestbook. What was the point of a guestbook? The funeral director told Iain it would be mine to take after the service. Why? I would not sit around reminiscing like a high school yearbook.

My family stood and followed the funeral director into the next room. Iain took my hand, guiding me to the moment I feared most. With each step, my heartbeat quickened, the numbness wore off, and I was left with every feeling I wanted to avoid.

In a moment life flashed in my memory—his laugh, that smile, the way he looked in the rear view mirror when I sat in the back seat, our vacations, and the early Saturday morning phone calls. We were on a boat, a train, in New York City, and now here.

Vibrancy turned to dullness, joy to sorrow, liveliness to fatality in a second. I stepped towards the casket—bouquets of flowers on stands and on the floor. I released Iain's hand as my aunts and uncles moved for me to have a spot in the middle. I closed my eyes, sucked in my bottom lip, and felt the uncontrollable shaking begin.

"Sarah." Gina pulled me closer. The scent of her perfume provided a small amount of comfort.

"I can't do this," I whispered.

Gina didn't respond. I heard Penny whisper to someone that Frank looked good. I opened my eyes and shot an irritated look at my aunt. She eyed the floral arrangements.

Frank looked good? Really?

The sight of him took my breath away. He was very thin, pale, covered in makeup with his lips glued together. Someone had cut his hair and not in a way he would have liked. A satin blanket covered his new suit. Tears welled in my eyes at the sight of the blue tie.

The weight became too much, and I dropped to my knees—hands covering my face—tears staining my black dress. Gina wrapped her arms around me, whispering words with no meaning.

"Why?" I whispered. "I want to know why."

The meteorologist said on the morning news Oakville had never had eight inches of snow before Thanksgiving. I wore snow boots—the ones I kept at my dad's house in the hall closet—with a dark gray dress and matching overcoat. A crowd of people huddled under the tent, near the blue spruce, fighting off the cold, to say goodbye to my father.

The priest handed me a wand. I mimicked his actions, dousing the casket with holy water. Everyone chanted a prayer. When I looked up, I spotted her from a distance. She opened a car door to leave. My mind wandered back to the visitation.

My mother leaned against the wall, not coming to the front to see her ex-husband. She looked older—more gray and wrinkled. The last time I saw her was my graduation party six years ago. Today, she didn't show up to start trouble. She didn't come for me. Lori Margo came to pay respects to a man she shared a past with. For once in my life, I respected her.

"Come," Iain said. He placed his hand on my back. The fresh, white powder moved under my feet. I left the grave and climbed into the limo.

I didn't look back.

CHAPTER SEVENTY-FIVE

**"I was relieved to be on a plane heading home." -
Iain Mackgale**

A faint glow appeared through the mini blinds, brighter than usual from the snow. Iain was next to me with his hand resting on my stomach. The house was quiet. No morning news played in the living room. The smell of brewing coffee absent. Snow collected on the sidewalk with no one to shovel.

"My flight leaves this afternoon." He wasn't asleep either. "I have an important matter to handle." He repositioned himself.

"I should go back to New York. Maybe tomorrow or Saturday. I need to return to my life."

"Good idea. Me too." Iain removed his hand from my stomach. "I need to pack."

He closed the bathroom door behind him.

When he returned from his shower, he wore jeans and an Oakville State sweatshirt he acquired during his stay. Iain hadn't shaved, and his reddish-brown stubble matched his shaggy hair.

"Something wrong?" he asked.

"Are you keeping the beard? No one will recognize you."

A wicked grin appeared on his face. "Exactly. It's growing on me." He scratched his facial hair. "You not like it? I think I look American."

His faux accent made me happy.

I got out of bed and stood in front of him. Reaching up, I touched his face with my fingers. He placed a hand on my cheek. "I like you better without a beard," Iain said. My lips curled upwards. "It's good to see you smile."

I stood on my tippy toes to kiss him. His warm mouth met mine, and he squeezed my waist. We were a slow-burning fuse.

"I need to go. We'll talk soon," he whispered. He planted a chaste kiss on my lips and then reached for his bags. "Safe travels home."

I was alone in the little brick house.

Sitting around an empty house made me upset. I packed five minutes after Iain left and booked an evening flight to New York. I texted Gina for a ride to the airport, then went through the house to make sure it was okay to leave. Iain cleaned out the refrigerator and parked my dad's truck in the garage.

The front door opened. Snow from her boots landed on the rug.

"You are early. That's cute." I motioned to her bag.

"New at the store." She smiled. "Let's eat before you go."

"I'm not hungry." My carry on sat next to the door with my dad's overstuffed suitcase. I didn't have to worry about returning it, and my eyes watered.

"I didn't ask if you were hungry." She gave me the stance. I had seen Uncle Dan try to fight Gina with this look—he never won.

"Okay." I handed Gina the manila envelope from the table. She noticed the law firm seal.

"Aaron Wells dropped this paperwork off last night. It's everything I need to sell the house. Aaron recommended I use Amber, one of our mutual friends to be the real estate agent. The for sale sign should be in the yard tomorrow. Uncle Dan

435

said he would move the contents of the house into storage until I decided where it should go." I gestured towards the envelope. "The power of attorney allows Uncle Dan to close on the house."

"Aren't you rushing into selling?" Gina sat on the couch.

"My dad's medical bills are expensive. He gave more to charity than we knew. I can't afford to pay for this house and my apartment. I don't want to move back to Oakville."

"Dan and I will help however we can. We can help you financially if you need us," she said with a slight smile.

"I'm fine. Thank you. I feel like I rely on you too much."

"Nonsense. We're family. Besides, one day you'll be the one picking my nursing home. I'm staying on your good side."

We shared a chuckle. I missed us.

"Iain is gone I assume?" Gina looked around the living room. All that remained belonged to my dad—his television, couch, recliner, and blue afghan.

"Yes." I missed him before he pulled out of the driveway.

Snow swirled in the wind outside the window.

"You will be okay. Promise me you won't jump off a building?" Gina's face was serious as if she wanted reassurance I didn't have my demise planned.

"You know that's a tad dramatic for even me. I will be fine. I need to return to my life."

We loaded my bags into her car. I kicked snow from my boots before turning on the porch light. My hand pulled the knob to close the front door. I turned the key for the last time. A brisk wind bit at my cheeks. By selling the little brick house, I was losing part of my soul. I figured out why my dad never moved. This was our place.

Once in the car, I checked my phone—no calls or texts. I had to tell myself he was in the air somewhere without service. Leaning my head against the back rest, I closed my eyes. When

I opened them, my past was gone.

CHAPTER SEVENTY-SIX

"She knows." -Deana Dash

The familiar old building smell of my apartment washed over me when I opened the door. I dragged my bags inside. A black ball of fur scurried under the table.

"Hey old friend," I said to the cat. He peered out from his hiding spot skeptically. If he could talk, he would have said, *where the hell have you been?* My friends fed him while I was away. "I am going to unpack. You can come out and see me." The cat went further under the table.

It was late. New York City was quiet other than an occasional car. I stood at my window, flakes of snow falling. The city I had grown to love didn't feel like home anymore. I kept telling myself I had only been back an hour—I needed time to adjust. My discontentment wouldn't go away. My stomach ached, my head throbbed—I wanted my overall feeling of hurt to go away.

Someone knocked on my door.

"You are up late," I said to Deana. I hoped she didn't want to talk about my dad.

"I had a drink after work. We had primal class tonight."

I cringed at the thought of Deana's primal class. They hung upside down from an elastic band in some attempt to rip their core apart while draining the blood to their head.

"Thanks for taking care of my cat. I'm glad to be home," I

said. The cat ran to Deana and rubbed against her leg.

"Alex picked up a few groceries for you," Deana said, gesturing towards my refrigerator.

"He's the best." I was too tired to go anywhere. If he bought cereal and milk, I would be okay.

"Stupid contacts." Deana set her phone on my table. She hurried to the bathroom with her finger in her eye.

The phone vibrated. When I glanced down, I saw my name on her screen.

Ryan: Did you talk to Sarah about Iain Mackgale?

I pressed my lips together to hide my reaction. My feet hurried to the refrigerator. "Good. Alex bought milk. He knows how much I like cereal."

Deana exited the bathroom. "Yeah. I think he bought you the chocolate puffs you like."

"Goody," I said.

Her eyes widened before picking up her phone. Deana tucked her device into her back pocket. "Whatever happened with you and Iain Mackgale?"

My heart sank. There was no turning back. Our friendship was over. Was she selling me out for money?

I shrugged. "I haven't talked to him. You were right. It wasn't going to work out. He wanted a no-strings hookup."

"You don't know where he is?"

I gave her a dirty look. "Is he missing? I've been in Oakville."

"Um. No. Okay." Deana fidgeted.

I wanted her out of my apartment. If she could lie and betray me, what else was she capable of doing?

"I'm going to bed. Tomorrow I pack. I decided to move back to Oakville." I had to lie.

"Oh," she said. Deana gave me the fake disappointed face she used on men when she turned them down. "That sucks."

"It definitely sucks."

My dad always called on Saturday mornings before he started his day of lawn work. Eight o'clock in the morning like an alarm clock. I never slept past eight on a Saturday. It was eleven. Half the day wasted, and my dad gone.

The cat snoozed between my feet. He narrowed his eyes when I reached for my phone. I hated my track record of unavailable men. If my dad was right and Iain had feelings for me—he couldn't entertain them. I sighed, resulting in another annoyed look from the cat. When I saw the screen, Iain had called—eight times. I turned my ringer on.

A part of me jumped up and down; the other dreaded calling him to say Deana joined the dark side. I questioned my other friends. Who could I trust? I needed to think before I called Iain. My phone rang and scared me.

"Hello," I said to Gina.

"You received an offer on the house."

"What? It's only been two days."

Ice formed on my window from the cold. I climbed out of my bed and dug a pair of sweats out of the drawer.

"The neighbor waited for the house to be listed. He's buying it for his daughter," she said.

The house selling fast wasn't part of my plan. I had hoped it would sit for months, and I could go home another time. Now a spoiled brat would live in my house for free.

"What did they offer?" I hoped it was a low-ball, one I had to turn down.

"Asking price. It's a cash offer. They want to close in two weeks. The daughter wants to be home by Christmas."

"Okay. Fine. Accept it. Whatever." I pulled a sweatshirt over my head. "Aunt Gina, I have to go."

"We'll accept the offer. I will call you next week," she said. We said goodbye and ended the call.

My boots pounded the stairs, down to the first floor, where a vendor parked on Saturdays. I needed caffeine and time alone to think. A line of people waited at Ralphie's cart. He sold magazines, coffee, hot dogs, souvenirs, and whatever he could wheel along the sidewalk.

"Go ahead," a man said. He studied the handwritten coffee menu.

"Thanks."

Ralphie's wife restocked newspapers and magazines. Iain's face caught my eye. He was on the cover, but I couldn't see the text until she moved.

Billionaire to marry Lady Clarisa Lusterville.

Their two-million dollar wedding plans.

Exclusive pictures of the engagement in the French Riviera.

"I don't have a lifetime," Ralphie said. He did an exaggerated hand motion. The line behind me grew restless. "You want a hot dog or not?"

"No thanks. I changed my mind." I turned around to go inside.

People from the line stared at me. I was in shock. Iain had a matter to handle. I assumed he meant work-related, such as buying a company or firing one of his sycophant leaders.

As I scaled the stairs with my angry boots, my phone rang. It was Iain. He was calling to tell me about his unexpected engagement. I imagined he would tell me he felt bad about the trouble he caused, which is why he stayed to help with my dad. Maybe he would say he couldn't marry me because I'm not a titled twit with a large ass nose.

"I don't want to speak to you again," I said when I answered.

"Sarah—"

"Every five years, my life becomes a shit show. That's where I am right now. I'm in the shit show. Guess what? I will get through this mess, move on, and be—"

"Your dad didn't want me to tell you—"

"Don't you dare bring my dad into your… your dumbness. Lose my number."

I hung up.

I stomped through my front door and to my window. My hand turned the dust and grime covered latch. I pushed open the pane of glass to a whoosh of December air.

"I loved you," I said to the phone before tossing it out the window.

CHAPTER SEVENTY-SEVEN

"Lady Clarisa Lusterville wore a silk tie blouse by Versace while on holiday in France with Lord Rowan, known in business as Iain Mackgale. Sources say he proposed on a thirty-one-meter yacht owned by shipping mogul, Aldric Aleron." -Magazine

A destroyed phone was peaceful—no buzzing, ringing, or voicemails. Two weeks of absolute bliss. I had shut myself out from talk of death, a backstabbing friend, and a man who lied about marrying someone else. Stop thinking about your problems was the fifth step in the self-help book I purchased over the weekend. I became so great at this tactic; I stopped reading the book.

"Are you sure you don't want to help clean?" He opened his eyes just enough to acknowledge my voice but went back to sleep. A small sliver of December sun hit the back of the sofa bed. He stretched his paw to enjoy the warmth.

I continued to scrub the stove, careful to avoid getting cleaner on my favorite yoga pants. My television played an ad for an online relationship site. I scoffed. Dating was pointless. It took away from the important things in life like cleaning one's stove.

Someone knocked. I walked to the door with rubber gloves in the air to avoid dripping water on the floor. Alex said he'd drop off boxes after work. The door wasn't locked.

"It's open," I yelled.

I returned to the stove. Why did I think it was a good idea to attempt to make caramel sauce?

"You shouldn't leave your door unlocked."

When I whirled around, I dropped my sponge.

"Can I help you, Mr. Mackgale?" A slice of bread had more emotion than me.

"Everyone is worried. You shut off your phone and took an extended leave of absence." Iain unzipped his casual winter coat. He eyed the moving boxes near the window.

"More like threw my phone out a six-story window."

I removed my cleaning gloves to wash my hands. When I reached for a towel, he handed me one. He looked great. The awful heartbroken fog reentered the room.

"You can see I am fine. Did you need anything else?"

"Sarah." Iain gave me the sad face. What reason did he have to be upset? He decided to get engaged to someone else. "I am sorry I didn't tell you. Frank—"

"Look. I am sick of hearing about you and Lady Lust. It's bad enough I have to see your engagement photos on the newsstand every morning. Congratulations. Don't be offended when I don't RSVP."

Iain laughed. I let out a frustrated sigh.

"Are you plotting with my mother?" I leaned against the kitchen counter. "Since she can't kill me physically, are you trying to kill me emotionally?"

"You are being dramatic." He smiled.

I needed him to leave. No part of me wanted to talk to a man promised to another woman. I couldn't stop loving him. His presence hurt more than the magazine.

"I am not engaged, Sarah. Did you not read the article?"

I shook my head no. He confirmed my dad told him not to tell me about his arrangement.

"This engagement wasn't your secret? Or what you discussed with my dad?" I crossed my arms.

"No. I was with you for weeks. A source told the papers I was in France with the Lustervilles. I haven't spoken to them in years. Clarisa is my ex-girlfriend." Iain closed the distance between us. "I told you my history with her."

I walked around him. After racing down six flights, I was on the sidewalk without shoes, keys, or a place to go.

"Where are you going?" His hand reached for my arm. I jerked away.

"Somewhere far away from everyone's drama."

"Shoes might help your journey," he said.

I whirled around in the opposite direction. I needed to get away from him. He stalked behind me.

"I can't do secrets. This is enough to drive someone insane."

His eyebrows rose as if I was already there.

"Let's go upstairs. I will tell you," he said. I walked away, but he tossed me over his shoulder in a quick motion.

"Hey! Put me down! You're making a scene."

"No, darling. You're the one yelling."

I didn't fight him up the stairs. Iain closed the apartment door and returned me to my feet. I sat on the bed, dizzy from being upside down. I had no choice but to hear his side.

"The confidentiality agreement is due to the sale of Mackgale-Berrell." It took a moment for the words to process. "The company purchasing mine is publicly held. They insisted we keep the sale private and requested I do nothing to cause bad press for Mackgale-Berrell."

"Such as dating an American who works for your company?" Iain nodded. "How long has this been going on?"

"Since after I met you." He moved closer. "It takes time to find buyers with enough funds."

"Why sell?" I couldn't help being skeptical. Why would he sell an empire he created?

"I want more out of my life. For the past few years, I've had a strong feeling that I'm missing a part of me. I cannot keep working at this pace and expect to have a serious relationship or family." He reached for my hand. "I met you. What I want from life has changed. I am keeping the real estate, but will no longer be CEO."

"You are not engaged and selling the company?" Whatever he promised my dad had to be bad news. "What did you promise my dad you wouldn't tell me?"

"I am in love with you." The words rolled off his tongue. "He didn't want you overwhelmed. He assured me you wouldn't run off with Aaron Wells. Frank wanted me to let you decide how fast to move our relationship." He paused "He told me you're in love with me too."

"What does Frank Margo know?"

Iain smiled. I wrapped my arms around his waist, pressing my cheek against his chest. He pulled me tight.

"You told my dad you love me?"

"Yes. We had a long conversation one evening regarding my intentions. He loved you very much. You were his entire world."

"He was mine too."

"I don't want to spend another night without you," Iain said. His lips touched mine softly at first until we were making out like teenagers. He pulled away. I moved closer to him because I wasn't done. He smiled. "Pack up your belongings and come to Berrell."

"Now?"

He nodded.

"For the week?"

He shook his head no.

446

He kissed my lips again. "We will work out the details later. Right now, I want you to come home with me, to our home."

"This isn't a rash decision you will regret later?" I had to ask because that's what I do—ask questions.

"No. I have wanted you to move to Berrell since the night I fished you out of the sea." He made me smile. "My plane leaves in two hours. The closing of the company is tomorrow. I came to New York as soon as I could manage. There is a gala hosted by my mother next week. I would love to introduce you to my family." He squeezed my palm. "Our relationship will be public, which means tabloids and opinions. If you don't want the stress, I understand. I want to prepare—"

"I'm coming with you." My lips kissed him with more force than I had intended. "I don't want to spend another night apart either."

CHAPTER SEVENTY-EIGHT

"He never cared about women until her." -Nolan Martin

Two large suitcases sat near my apartment door for Martin to carry. He called me ma'am, and no longer gave me disapproving looks. It hit me I was in a relationship with Iain. He referred to me as his girlfriend in Oakville, but it was different. I didn't believe him, and we weren't in his world. Everyone would know. My heart pounded. Would I be as famous as him? I never considered how I would feel about being in the public eye. I loved him for him, not his position.

Iain leaned against the wall, on his phone. Martin and another man picked up my luggage. The cat meowed from the pet carrier, worried he was going to the veterinarian. In an hour, the cat would take his first flight over the Atlantic to his new home. So much had happened, and I found myself adrift. At least I could be with Iain. I hadn't lost them both.

"Are you okay, darling?" Iain tucked his phone into his pocket and pulled me into his arms. I savored his smell and warmth.

"What about my apartment?" Before he arrived, I had packed to leave with no plans.

"We will return after Christmas or hire a mover. I don't want you worrying." He knew my next question before I did. "I told Gina we would visit Oakville for Christmas, and you would phone her when we landed." He reached into his pocket. "This is yours."

Before I could object to the iPhone, Martin told Iain we were ready to go.

I climbed into the backseat of the town car and into the front seat of Iain Mackgale's life—my new life. Martin hurried to the passenger seat next to the driver who he referred to as Douglas.

Six years ago, I moved to New York City to start a new life. I took every memory with me. The time had come to move on. New York had been good, but I wasn't sad to leave.

"Where are we going?" The sign for the Lincoln Tunnel was ahead. Traffic backed up. Cars honked their horns as if that helped.

"Teterboro," Iain said.

I wondered why we weren't going to JFK.

"I received confirmation the plane is on standby, and our flight plan is acceptable," Martin said.

"Warren will be on our flight with his team. He had a financial meeting with Marco and asked to join my return flight." He leaned closer and lowered his voice. "Remember to keep what we discussed earlier to yourself."

Were we flying on a private plane?

"He doesn't know?" My attention went to his lips, so pouty and moist. If we didn't have two drivers in the front seat, the possibilities were endless. Iain smiled. He read my mind.

"He does, but you shouldn't. There are legal ramifications," he said.

I leaned my head against his shoulder, not caring who witnessed the affection. Iain said nothing further. The buildings became smaller with each mile.

Girls like me didn't fly on private planes.

Iain guided me across the runway to the aircraft with a Mackgale-Berrell logo. The wind had picked up, swirling old snow into the air. Warren waited near the folding stairs in one of his tweed suits. He wouldn't stop staring at me.

"Good evening, Warren," Iain said. His arm still around my back. "I believe you have met Miss Margo."

"Yes," he replied. "Can I have a word with you?"

I recognized Iain's polite smile, the one reserved for when he did something he didn't want to do.

"Trina." Iain motioned for a woman at the top of the stairs. "Will you settle Miss Margo? We shall be along in a moment."

After Trina helped me on the plane, I lingered close to the door.

"Can I fetch you a drink, Miss Margo?"

She smoothed her flight attendant uniform with her hands. A few strands of her Nubian twists were a deep purple. She smiled when she caught me eying her hair. I wanted to tell her I loved the style, but I wasn't sure if I should be chatty with the staff.

"Water would be great. Thank you."

Trina disappeared through a sliding door. The sound of a nearby jet made it difficult to eavesdrop.

"I questioned you about her months ago. How do you explain she is moving to Berrell? What about your parents?" Warren asked.

"My personal life isn't your concern. My parents will meet Sarah on Friday. They know about her, and she has met Lady Iris."

"She can't go to the gala. I have asked for an invitation for years."

Trina brought me a bottle of cold water. She shot me a wicked smirk. We listened together. I wondered if Trina

450

thought I was like Iain—wealthy and titled.

"I apologize I have never asked you to be my date. It's Lady Crossleigh's event. She makes the guest list."

"The people of Berrell will not—"

"This conversation is closed. Be polite or find your way to Kennedy Airport."

Footsteps hit the stairs, and I hurried to the built-in sofa. Trina stood like we were talking the entire time. I liked this girl.

"Through the sliding door sits six seats for guests. We are in Lord Rowan's private quarters which boasts a sitting space, kitchen, lavatory, and a sleeping compartment." Trina opened the restroom door and moved a curtain to reveal bunk beds. She reminded me of the time I went RV shopping with Uncle Ted.

Trina continued talking, but my mind drifted to Rowan. I'd never been around Iain outside work, our places, or Oakville. When he spoke about his sister to my family, he called her Iris. We used his first name. He never corrected us. Around others, he called his mother and sister by their titles and didn't flinch when called lord. I decided to be cautious until I the learned the rules.

I kicked off my shoes and curled up on the built-in sofa along the wall. His life was intimidating, but I could get used to flying private.

"We are preparing for take-off, Miss Margo. Please ring if you require assistance." Doors shutting and confirmation checks made my stomach flutter with excitement.

Iain entered the sitting area. Warren sat in one of the two dark brown chairs. He placed his bag on the table. Shouldn't staff be up front? I know I had been here two minutes, but I wanted Iain to myself. We had much to discuss, and I couldn't have a conversation in front of disapproving Warren.

Iain took a seat next to me. An irritated glare was exchanged between Warren and Iain, but nothing verbalized.

Iain pulled his laptop from a bag. "I have work to complete. My tablet and headphones are in the drawer below if you want to watch a movie." He touched my face. "It's a long flight, but worth it."

"Anyone in the lav?" Warren asked Iain. He gestured towards the closed restroom door. Iain looked up from his laptop.

"Only Dr. Margo," Iain replied. He scooted closer and glanced at his iPad in my lap. He was running a billion dollar corporation. I was playing Angry Birds. Iain smirked. "Can you fix my spreadsheets? If you're not too busy. I cannot figure out what's wrong."

"I'm at a good stopping point." We laughed. He handed me his computer and watched me work.

"I think your formulas are off somewhere because C:11 is blank," I said. Iain pressed his fingers against his forehead. "Don't worry. I can fix it." Iain grabbed my head and kissed my cheek.

"You're the best, which is why I have a surprise." Texting on his phone, Iain walked towards the mini kitchen. He opened the refrigerator.

"Is that what I think it is?" I gushed over the pasta tins from Tyler's restaurant. We left in a hurry. I hadn't thought of food.

"Cajun chicken pasta and Tyler's bread." He held up his hand in a stopping position. "Fix my spreadsheet, and it's all yours." Iain returned to the sofa.

"Should someone check on your friend?" Warren paced outside the restroom door. For a moment, I forgot he existed.

"Who?" Iain asked. He leaned his chin on my shoulder, not looking at Warren, who huffed closer to the restroom.

"Sir." He knocked on the door. "Are you okay?"

No answer.

Iain and I looked at each other. I covered my face to avoid

bursting into laughter. Iain buried his face against my shoulder.

"Dr. Margo?" Warren gave me an irritated look since Margo had to be one of my relations.

"Dr. Margo is a cat." Iain's smile was as large as his face. Warren opened the door to find a pet carrier. Doc meowed. "Sarah's father wouldn't let her have a pet growing up. She adopted a cat her second year and—"

"You brought a bloody cat on a plane?" Warren raised his voice.

"We had an awful time applying for a passport." Iain tried to lighten the mood.

Warren slammed the door. Trina peeked in to check on the commotion.

"Done." I handed Iain his laptop. "Trina, would you like to try Tyler Blackburn's pasta?"

Her eyes grew large. Why was I the only one who didn't know Tyler? Trina's eyes moved towards Iain. He nodded. She followed me to the refrigerator. I slid one of the large tins off the shelf and placed it in her hands.

"I love Tyler Blackburn," she whispered.

"Can you share with the others up front?"

"Yes, ma'am," she replied with a smile.

Warren exited the restroom to see Trina carrying food from Tyler's restaurant. "You'll fit in well with the Mackgales," he mumbled.

"I am ready to eat," Iain said and joined me next to the fridge.

I wanted to say something to the CFO, put him in his place, but I remembered the time I let the Guess overalls and orange lipstick go to my head. Time to adult, and let it go.

I leaned close to Iain. "Was it okay to share the food?"

"Yes," Iain said in hushed tones. His lips brushed against

453

mine. "Never stop being generous." We opened another tray. "Besides, Tyler made enough food for a reception."

With a blissful smile, he kissed me and moved his hands to my hips. My body gravitated against him. When he tried to pull away, I grabbed his tie for another kiss. He moaned with regret.

He leaned close to my ear and whispered, "If you keep playing, I'm fucking you in the bathroom."

I stepped back, mouth in a perfect circle. He grinned like a man who wasn't joking. I contemplated if I was willing.

"Considering?" Iain asked.

"Possibly."

He kissed my cheek. "Not the first time. Let's eat."

It was unspoken between us, but we knew once in Berrell we were making us official. I turned away to keep the embarrassment to a minimum.

Warren witnessed the exchange with no attempt at disguising his displeasure. Iain offered Warren pasta, but he declined because of the time.

Iain scooped pasta on a plate. "When we land, I must go to the office. Martin will take you home. I will return as soon as I can."

Warren's unzipped bag on the table caught my attention. At the top of a folder inside, I noticed a familiar logo. Why did I feel weird? Warren's eyes met mine. Panic raced through my veins. I remembered the embossed logo, smooth to the touch, music thumping to the rhythm of my pounding heart.

Ryan Bolton's business card.

CHAPTER SEVENTY-NINE

"She changed him. For the first time in his life, a weight had been lifted." -Mallory Wallace

Warren rode in the front seat of the Mercedes next to Martin. I needed to tell Iain about Ryan Bolton. When I glanced at him, his eyes stayed fixed on his phone screen. I should have told him before I noticed the logo.

"Renee is at the office," Iain said to Warren.

"I will be in late." Warren turned to see Iain. "Do you mind if Martin takes me home?"

"That's fine. Martin is taking Sarah home. I am leaving after the paperwork," Iain said. He clicked his phone off. "We aren't telling the employees until after the new year."

My head tilted to the side. Did Martin have his gun? I couldn't believe Iain was leaving me alone with Warren, but I was the one who didn't tell him about Ryan and Deana. My leg spasmed. I bounced my foot up and down to release my pent-up energy. My chest squeezed with each passing minute. What if Martin couldn't be trusted?

We parked in front of Mackgale-Berrell's corporate headquarters. For the first time, I wouldn't be here to work on meaningless projects. Martin opened Iain's door and handed him a messenger bag. He didn't say goodbye. Martin climbed into the driver's seat. Iain disappeared into the main entrance.

We rode in silence, heading the opposite way to Iain's house. Maybe they were taking me somewhere. After ten minutes, the landscape changed from city to rolling farm hills. Sheep grazed in the spacious fields. Wooden fences stood on both sides of the unmarked lane. We passed a Crossleigh Village sign nailed to a roadside tree.

Martin turned down a narrow dirt path. When we pulled into the driveway of a two-story stone house, an older woman hurried inside. She had been loading boxes into a car. Warren got out of the vehicle, without a word, and went inside. One would think my anxiety would have lessened, but it didn't.

Martin placed my luggage in Iain's master bedroom. A strange feeling came over me when I realized I lived here. Martin left the double doors open, revealing the only room in the house I had never set eyes upon. I stepped inside the large space and stopped. One picture frame sat on the nightstand. I picked it up and smiled—our tour ponchos were too stylish.

When I opened the door to the master bathroom, I admired the jetted tub. I turned on the water and squirted the lavender bubble bath. Hot water filled to the top, unlike the Hotel Rowan.

Hanging behind the door was his bathrobe. I smelled the sleeve. On the counter, a toothbrush dangled from a holder next to his shaving supplies. Toiletries were organized the way one would expect.

I sank into the tub, suds up to my chin. The bubbles calmed my stress, but our troubles weren't over. When Iain came home, I would have to tell him. I didn't want to think anymore.

After ten minutes, I dried myself with a towel fluffier than my comforter. Exhaustion came over me, and I needed sleep. I wrapped Iain's robe around my bare skin, too tired to unpack, and climbed into his bed.

Hours later, I woke to keys hitting the table and the door shutting. Iain stood at the bottom of the bed. I sat up, embarrassed to be in his bathrobe. He didn't say I could take over his room.

"Sorry, I'm in your bed." I brushed my damp hair from my face and pulled the bathrobe tighter after I caught him eying my exposed skin. Why did I feel shy?

"You in my bed is a gorgeous sight." His hand ran across the footboard.

"Did everything go okay this morning?" I tried to change the subject. I had wanted this man for months. Why was I so nervous? The jet lag didn't help. I needed to focus and tell him about Warren.

"No work discussions," he said with a seductive edge. "I want a shower, sleep, food, and you."

My mouth went dry, and when I opened my mouth to speak nothing came out. He tossed his phone and wallet on the dresser.

"In that order?" I croaked. He nodded. It was a relief he hadn't planned on pouncing right now.

"I'd like to sleep a few hours. Will you prepare or order food?" Iain removed his cuff links and loosened his tie. He had bags under his eyes. "Martin will help, or you can take one of the cars." Iain retrieved a shirt and pajama bottoms from his closet. "The keys are hanging in my study."

"You trust me to drive your expensive Lexus?" I removed myself from his bed and straightened the pillows. He grinned at either my comment or the fact one of my breasts peeked out of his robe.

"I have excellent insurance." He removed his shirt and kissed my forehead. I eyed his chest. The cocky bastard knew I wanted him.

He disappeared behind the bathroom door.

The refrigerator had nothing useful. I wasn't eating fish from a tin can. My once-a-year-food-from-the-water quota was met with the red snapper at the Riverfront.

The keys to Iain's cars hung beside the bookshelf. The clear choice was the zero to sixty in four seconds Lexus.

I opened the door to the coupe like a teenager stealing their dad's car. I pressed the button to open the garage door and started the sports car. The aftermarket racing petals were intimidating—was it necessary for a daily driver? When I put the car in reverse, the Lexus squealed out of the garage. I hoped Iain was asleep. Perhaps the petals had a purpose. I buckled my seatbelt and sped along the country roads like a police chase.

I could never afford this car. An odd thought crossed my mind—I now could drive his flashy vehicles whenever I wanted.

"Shit." I ramped the Lexus onto the curb in front of Wallace's. When I got out, I surveyed the wheel, which had survived my driving.

The door jingled. It had been a few months since I had shopped at what the locals referred to as Mal's.

"Are you searching for a trolley?" Mallory Wallace, the owner, asked. I turned around. The older woman stocked can goods in an apron. "Hello. They have you working over Christmastime?" Mallory pulled a cart from behind the partition wall and pushed it towards me.

"Thank you." I accepted the cart. "No. I'm returning to the States for Christmas. Do you have any of your biscuits or cream cakes?"

I lost ten pounds from the stress of losing my dad. Splurging on baked goods wouldn't hurt. Mallory smiled and removed her apron. She walked behind a new display case.

"We prepared the cream cakes this morning. Would you fancy a fresh mince pie?" Mallory handed me a small pie with pride. "Happy Christmas."

I took a bite, without a clue what mince meant. Moaning in satisfaction, I gave her a thumbs up. She waved at another customer entering and smiled.

"So delicious. Make me a large box of biscuits, cream cake, and mince pies. I am not watching my figure this holiday season," I said. I went in search of real food.

When I pushed my small cart to the counter, Mallory eyed the Lexus parked outside the store. How many people in Berrell could afford his car? Maybe I should have had Martin run the errands. Our relationship would be public knowledge in a few days, but seeing Mallory make conclusions made me uneasy. Did she think I wasn't acceptable for Iain Mackgale? Should I care about Mallory Wallace's opinion?

As I was having unpleasant thoughts about Mallory, she surprised me with kindness. "I am very sorry to hear about your father. His lordship told me on the phone." I gave her a strange look. "I'm his tenant."

Tears pooled in my eyes. Our tree and stockings would remain packed away in a storage unit off Regency Road. The cozy fireplace would burn this holiday season, but not for us. I hated the girl moving into our little brick house even though I did not know her.

"Shall I charge this to his lordship's account?"

I remembered my checking account balance and nodded. "Thank you."

"Please enjoy the pies," she said.

"We will. Merry Christmas, Mrs. Wallace."

I didn't contact my friends or family after I tossed my phone out a six-story window. When I think back, I was nutty. I had no sane explanation for my actions and was thankful Iain didn't want to discuss my loony decision.

When I tapped Gina's name on my iPhone, the call played through the speakers in the Lexus. I had no clue how it happened.

"What the hell were you thinking?" A Southern woman scolded me in surround sound. "No, Darlene. I'm not talking to you." People chattered in the background. "No. I said I am not talking to you. I know you were…"

"Hello?"

"Hold on, Sarah." A few moments later, an elevator dinged. "What the hell were you thinking?"

"I'm sorry. I was a mess and then Iain…"

"How could you believe a tabloid? He was with us the entire time this supposed engagement took place." She waited for me to provide a sane explanation.

Keep waiting.

"I didn't read the article." How could I be upset over a story I didn't bother to read? "He said my dad told him not to tell me. I assumed he meant the engagement."

"What did Frank not want him to say?" Gina asked, irritated at me. I waited for the you-need-to-pay-more-attention speech.

"He's in love with me," I whispered.

Gina sighed. "Anyone with eyes in their head knows he loves you and you love him." Gina paused. "You had us worried. Don't ever do anything stupid again. No one could reach you and thank the Lord Iain called us. I packed for New York." Her voice shook with each word. I bit my lip to keep my emotions under control. "Iain said you're coming home for Christmas."

"Yes." I was a terrible person for adding more stress to my family.

"I'm thankful you're safe. We can talk when you're here," she said. "Iain asked if y'all could stay with us. The hobby room is yours. My parents will be here."

"Okay. Sorry, Aunt Gina."

"Don't be sorry," she said.

Tears streamed down my face as we said our goodbyes. The guard opened the gate when he saw the Lexus. Before I hit the garage door opener, I stayed in the parked car for a moment to regain my composure.

CHAPTER EIGHTY

"She washed away my grief." -Iain Mackgale

Iain typed on his laptop on the sectional. When he noticed my full hands, he placed his computer to the side and took the box of sweets I balanced. He followed me to the kitchen.

"You didn't sleep long?" He looked tired, still in pajama bottoms and a t-shirt.

Iain studied my face. "You've been crying. Are you okay?"

Iain leaned against the breakfast bar. I felt terrible for upsetting Gina. Iain looked just as upset.

"Yeah." I didn't convince him or myself. "I talked to Gina on the way home from Mal's. My stupidity caused everyone to worry."

"I should have told you about the company and how I felt about you, but I'm thankful you're here now."

I kissed his lips then pulled away. "There's something about Warren."

He shook his head no. "I can't talk about work. My nerves are frayed. I need a night of peace."

One more night couldn't hurt. The company was no longer his, and Warren wasn't his problem.

"Would you like a mince pie?" I opened the box of sweets. He raised his eyebrows, not expecting baked goods to be my response. "I am tired of being upset. Let's eat desserts and watch holiday movies."

"I love when you cook dinner."

Only one cream cake and two biscuits remained in the pastry box. The credits rolled on the holiday movie. It was a made-for-television with humor I didn't understand. Iain laughed a few times, which was funnier than the lines. He peeked into the Wallace's box.

"Are you still hungry?" I couldn't eat one more ounce. He sank into the couch with his hand on his stomach and grimaced. "I feel bad we didn't eat real food."

"We had protein, carbohydrates, and fruit. I count this as a proper meal," he said and smiled.

"We didn't have protein." He covered his face with his hands. "Are you laughing at me?"

He removed his hands to reveal a broad, joyous smile. "I am laughing with you. What did you think the chewy bits were in the mince pie?" He threaded his fingers with mine.

"Chewy fruit?" I shrugged. He laughed again. "It tasted like raisins." He kissed me hard on the lips.

"You had meat tonight, darling. We keep our mincemeat authentic," he said with pride.

"Please don't tell me what I ate. Let's stick with chewy fruit." My face hurt from smiling.

"Sarah Margo, what am I going to do with you?"

"That is the question of the hour." We both knew what was happening tonight. The tips of his fingers brushed against my jaw, and he kissed me. "Are you nervous?" I asked when our lips parted.

"You shouldn't ask a man if he is nervous. I have done this before."

I kissed him slow and deep. "Confident, are we?"

"No. I am terrified." I looked for a sign of humor, but he was serious. "Let's say I was bad in bed and you moved back to New York. I would be devastated, wouldn't go to work, people would lose their jobs. The shops would close. Buildings would crumble. All because one woman didn't like my cock." Our laughter disappeared when our lips touched.

"We over-think everything we do," I said against his lips.

Iain jumped to his feet almost taking out the table.

"No more over-thinking. Meet me in the bedroom in five minutes. We are getting this over with." Iain walked towards the bedroom door.

"Way to be romantic! What are you doing?" I had trouble believing him.

"Brushing my teeth." He grinned. "Four minutes."

Iain disappeared.

The lights were off in the bedroom. Iain waited for me next to the side of the bed. My heart thumped in my ears to the point I couldn't hear. I ran my finger down his bare chest, not taking my eyes off his face. Iain pulled my shirt over my head. His warm palms ran up my sides and over my breasts. I pulled his face to mine, kissing him with all the pent-up feelings from the last year.

"I need you," he whispered in-between kisses. With a quick motion, he tugged my shorts down. I enjoyed his hands—worshiping and warm.

"Then have me…finally."

He tossed me on the bed. I squealed when he jumped on top.

I knew I would relive tonight in my mind for the rest of my life. This was love and how it should have always been.

CHAPTER EIGHTY-ONE

"John told me I couldn't start trouble with Iain because of our money issues. What he doesn't know won't kill him." -Eloise Aleron Mackgale, Lady Crossleigh

Light filtered through the curtains. The alarm clock on Iain's nightstand displayed eight minutes after ten. I sat up and touched my head. My hair felt like a bird's nest. I smoothed it down with my hand and hoped Iain would stay asleep until I made myself presentable. I leaned closer to listen to his breathing.

"What are you doing?" His eyes were closed, arms wrapped around his pillow. Sleepy Iain was a beautiful sight—why couldn't sleepy Sarah be the same?

"Checking to see if you're alive."

Amusement spread across his face as his eyes opened.

"You weren't that rough on me. If you want to try killing me again tonight, I'm available." I shoved him, and he pulled me on top. Our bare skin melted against one another. I kissed him.

"You never sleep past daylight. It's after ten."

He hugged me to his chest. My cheek on his shoulder.

"I have a reason to stay in bed." He sucked in a breath.

"What?" I lifted my head to look at him.

He flushed. "Has it always been good for you?"

I tried hard not to smile.

"No. I wouldn't have gone without sex for so long." His arms squeezed me close once more. When I lifted to look at his face, he looked concerned. "What's going through your head?"

"Clarisa," he said.

I quirked a brow—one of the mean, jealous looking ones. "You're thinking about your ex?"

"She phoned yesterday to give her sympathies for the fraudulent engagement story. I hadn't found the right time to tell you."

He selected the moment I was nude in his bed. I didn't know if I should laugh or be pissed off. It occurred to me I could write a book about the dumb comments men make.

"Who offers sympathy for a story they likely helped fabricate?" I rolled off him.

Iain smirked. "Some women love games. I don't care either way. No reason to be jealous, Sarah Margo."

I opened my mouth in a way suggesting his accusation was outlandish. "I'm cool. Totally fine with Lady Lustypants."

"She is going to my mother's gala—"

"What? Why?" Perhaps I wasn't a mature grown-up okay with hanging out with my boyfriend's lie spreading ex.

"I don't make the guest list." I rolled my eyes and recalled his I-can-do-whatever-the-hell-I-want line. "She asked if I would accompany her."

"Don't you think the tabloid and her recent interest in you screams guilt?" He said nothing because he knew. "Let me be clear. If you said yes, I will throw more than my phone out the window."

He kissed me. "I told her I've been hopelessly obsessed with you since the day we met, and we're making our relationship public at the gala." He smiled. "I didn't want you taken by surprise. That's all."

Large hands cupped my behind under the comforter. He planted kisses on my neck. I didn't want to talk about Clarisa.

The doorbell rang.

"I thought you locked the gate." I pictured Iris at the door with her petite suitcase ready to ruin my day.

Iain had one mission on his mind.

"They'll go away," he mumbled.

"Mr. Mackgale," a voice shouted from outside.

He rolled off me. I admired his figure when he left the bed to slide on pajama bottoms. Iain muttered inaudible words in the hall. I wrapped his black bathrobe around me. The front door creaked when it opened.

"Sorry to bother you, sir. Your phone was off."

I stepped into the hall. Robbie handed Iain a stack of magazines. He waited with patience in front of his boss. Iain's attention stayed on the print.

"Fuck."

"Hello," I said to Robbie. We worked together on two projects this year. He didn't look surprised to see me at the boss's house. Robbie acknowledged me with a nod.

When I saw the magazines, my eyes did a double-take. Me at work. My senior picture. Iain and I on his plane. The kiss between Cassie and I at the bar. What the hell?

"Warren cleaned out his office and left a notice of resignation," Robbie scratched his head. From the look of the situation, neither Iain nor Robbie expected the CFO to resign. I should have told Iain about the woman loading boxes into a car. "He asked me to wire eight million to his personal account rather than a check."

Iain laughed.

Robbie and I shared a look of confusion.

"I need Nigel here."

"He's returning from France at half past two."

"Effective immediately, you report to Nigel." The color drained from Robbie's face. Iain liked playing God.

Robbie nodded. "What about the press? Lena's inbox is full."

"Do nothing. My relationship with Miss Margo will soon be public."

Beads of sweat collected on Robbie's head. He was the messenger, a number cruncher on Warren's team.

"Lena asked if legal should get involved."

"I'll discuss with Nigel this afternoon."

Iain's business demeanor worried me. I withheld information from him. Last night made me forget his CEO role, always in charge, because he willingly surrendered to me.

I went to the kitchen.

My palms pressed against the countertop. Stomach acid moved into my throat. The front door closed and echoed through the house.

His bare feet made a distinctive sound on the wooden floors. Iain went to a cabinet between the fridge and formal dining room. He placed a bottle of whiskey and a glass on the counter before pouring a healthy amount.

"You are drinking liquor in the morning?" I asked. He put the glass to his mouth. "At least allow me to make you something to eat if you're going to be stupid." He sat at the bar, golden liquid in one hand and tabloids in the other. I cracked eggs into a skillet. "Are you mad at me?"

He turned around on his barstool. "There are no words to describe how mad I am, but not at you. An explanation why you were getting off with Cassie would be nice."

"The night Ben Wilcox followed me to the club, Cassie and I pretended to be a couple. I was scared." I flipped the eggs. "He didn't believe I was gay."

"That bastard!" Iain slammed the glass against the bar. I flinched. "Warren hired Ben Wilcox to follow you." He held up the magazine. In the picture, my head rested against Iain. The other was me holding his tie kissing him. "Warren took the pictures, and he hired Ben."

"Iain," I whispered. He lifted his eyes to meet mine. "Do you know Ryan Bolton?"

He nodded. "You know?"

"Yes. Deana…"

"I'm sorry. I knew she was familiar with Mr. Bolton. When you went to his flat, I had you followed." My lower jaw dropped. "Don't be upset. He's dangerous."

"You arranged for me to return to Berrell to protect me?"

"No. Separation from dudes." We shared a small smile. "I didn't know Deana's involvement until last week. She accepted money for information regarding our relationship and my whereabouts."

"Are my other friends involved?"

"No. I advised Tyler to have Alex keep his distance from Deana," he said.

My chest lightened a little. I didn't want to lose Alex or Cassie. My luck wasn't good with blond friends.

"On the plane, Warren had a folder with Ryan's business logo." The mood shifted back to dark.

"Are you sure?" Iain scratched his head.

"Yes." I plated the eggs and walked to the bar. "You don't seem surprised."

"This is my life, Sarah. Why do you think I tried to keep my distance?"

"I thought I wasn't good enough for you."

He reached for my hand. "You are perfect. Beautiful in every way. You're not interested in my title or money. I worried you

469

would decide I wasn't worth the trouble."

"You're my best friend," I said. He pulled me close. "Why did Warren do this?"

"I discussed the possibility of selling the company in the spring with him. He disagreed, but I insisted on looking for potential buyers—"

"Warren thinks too highly of himself." I placed my fork in the middle of my plate. Iain took a drink of my water, abandoning his alcohol.

"Warren often forgets his place."

"Why did you keep him around?"

Iain returned the bottle of whiskey to the cabinet.

"He is brilliant. His father worked on the estate for my grandfather. Warren attended university in London and worked for years at an automobile company. When he returned to Berrell, I hired him. I didn't know the hostility he harbored towards my family. Warren wanted to think of him and I as equals."

"But, you're not?"

"A degree and hard work will not move you into certain circles. This isn't America where one can shift from one group to the next. Most people in America consider themselves middle class, a classic example of an egalitarian society. No ambitious individual here wants labeled average."

I had immense pride in where I was from. "I'm a middle class, average American. What about me? How can I be with you if I can't ever be on your level?"

"Birth or marriage, darling. I'm not marrying Warren."

I hadn't thought about marriage since the day I stormed out of the courtroom and slumped against my dad's rental car. I am never getting married echoed in my mind. The words were an absolute truth. Did Iain want to marry me? I thought none of this through when I said I'd return to Berrell with him.

"I don't understand why he hates me enough to have me followed and sell pictures to a tabloid. Did he really get eight million dollars?"

I wondered how much Deana profited. Her eyes lit up when we were somewhere expensive. I tried to ignore my heartbroken feelings when I saw the text of betrayal.

"It's me. He can't stand who I am. You would think I would have known, but often the ones we think we can trust are the ones we shouldn't." He reached for my water glass and took a sip. "Warren didn't go to the closing yesterday. He assumed we'd close before the papers came out. New owners often let senior leadership go. I offered him eight million as a severance package. The money would be his as soon as I signed."

"Did you offer a severance to others?"

"No. Mackgale-Berrell isn't closing, only changing owners. I would have offered to Nigel, but he will assist with my real estate," he said. I shrugged. "He's our chief operating officer. We have known each other since school. He is to inherit Wester Park when his father dies. It's a beautiful place on five thousand acres. Nigel lives in London, next to our townhouse."

Warren was getting eight million. Nigel a fancy house on a lot of land. I inherited a 1994 Chevy Silverado with crank windows.

"Our?"

He nodded with satisfaction. "Renee and his son came to finalize the sale. He's a former business partner of my grandfather." He adjusted his body to face me. "Renee asked for a ninety-day extension. He plans to make his son CEO of whatever Mackgale-Berrell becomes and asked me to help with the transition."

"You still own the company?"

Iain spread his God-like smile. "Warren receives nothing because the sale didn't go through."

I scratched my head. "Wow. Karma at its finest."

"Are you pursuing legal action against Warren?"

"No. He did enough damage to himself. We need to find out why he's in contact with Ryan Bolton. Please stay close to my security team and me until we figure it out. I can't stress enough this man's ruthlessness."

I wanted to ask more about Ryan, but I feared I would make myself afraid. My emotions were exhausted. I needed time to heal, process my life without my father. Dealing with drama on this level wasn't my strength. I needed Iain to carry the burden for now.

"What do we do now?" I asked.

"We go to the gala. Sunday we fly to Oakville to celebrate the holidays with your family. After the new year, I will work between Berrell, London, and Paris for three months. You can work with me or relax. Do you want to start a Ph.D. program in the fall?"

I grimaced. "I can't afford school. My checking account balance is seventy-four dollars."

"I added you to my accounts. Finances won't be a concern. Research programs." I opened my mouth to object. "Your life has changed. Get used to it and allow me to share my success with you."

"My application will be late. What about you?"

"You have stellar reports. You'll get in where you want. I told you I am going whenever you go." He kissed my forward. "After the company sells, I'd like to holiday before I lose you to academia."

I wrapped my arms around him.

CHAPTER EIGHTY-TWO

"American girls lack sophistication, among other qualities." -Lady Clarisa Lusterville

The living room filled with garment bags and boxes. Women in black aprons and dress pants hustled to set up. I did a head count—seven women from twenty to fifty. I stood near the door and wondered what I should be doing. Should I help them unload or offer refreshments? I wasn't sure what the protocol was for having a designer come to your home to style you.

"Do you need a hand?" I asked. The women scurried past me, not making eye contact.

Iain reappeared from his study and ignored the women taking over his living room. He kissed the top of my head.

"This seems like a little much," I whispered.

"You'll want to be dressed by a professional for this event. Please trust my judgment. After you see what these parties entail, I will let you decide."

A tall, glamorous woman entered the living room and greeted Iain with a kiss on the cheek. I didn't like seeing another woman touching him, a feeling I had never experienced, but he was distant and professional.

Elle Ella was an elite designer from London. She styled the wealthy and famous. Gina earmarked pages in magazines of Elle Ella's couture line and often tried to find pieces similar for the department stores. No one in Oakville could afford Elle and her entourage.

Iain introduced me, and she kissed my cheek uttering words I didn't understand. I gave her my fake polite smile and shrugged at Iain. Ms. Ella turned her attention to a young woman wheeling in a set of trunks.

"She knows you don't speak French," Iain said. His fingers caressed my neck. A phone rang. "Mackgale…What is on my schedule?"

My mouth opened to speak, but he was in route to his study. Two of the women pressed tape measures against my legs and then my arms. I trusted Iain's judgment and allowed these women to have their way with me.

Over the next several hours, I was prodded, plucked, cut, and highlighted. Elle Ella stood me up next to the full-length mirror. She gestured to one of her assistants about the dress. I did a double take when I saw myself. The long, silk dress reminded me of the night sky—a dark blue with black lace wrapping from my chest to my hip. The soft curls in my hair reflected the new golden hues. Elle showed the hair stylist a diamond barrette. She pushed up my hair and snapped it above my ear.

Iain appeared.

"You look beautiful." He planted a chaste kiss on my lips.

My reflection disappeared when the assistant picked up the mirror to leave. Butterflies filled my stomach. It was time to jump into a foreign world.

Iain spoke in French to Elle. She placed a green velvet box in his hands. I gasped when he revealed the necklace.

"Turn." His warm fingers touched my neck. "Perfect."

My palm grazed the cluster of diamonds on my chest. Iain eyed me with warmth.

"The jewelry is on loan. If you love the pieces, we can purchase."

"You would let me keep the necklace?"

He nodded.

I turned to an assistant. "How much is this?"

I knew she spoke English, but she hesitated. Iain lowered his chin as if giving her permission to speak. For whatever reason, she wasn't supposed to be talking.

"Thirty-five thousand pounds, ma'am," she replied.

"Holy shit," I said.

One assistant coughed, another snickered. I violated some rule about women using profanity. When I risked a glance at my boyfriend, he pressed his lips together.

"I need to change into my holy shit expensive dinner jacket." He cracked a smug smile.

We drove for an hour, through Berrell City and into the countryside where the land had more grass than houses. Iain didn't say much, hand resting on my thigh, watch sparkling on his wrist. The soft glow of sunlight below the horizon disappeared with each kilometer.

"There will be a vast amount of press tonight. Smile. Don't worry about being polite or answering their questions," he said. Martin glanced in the rear view. "Remember pudding in America is not the same as pudding in Berrell. If you don't care for dinner, I will have food sent to your room later."

"We aren't staying in the same room?"

"No. We aren't married. You will have your own set of rooms."

"Set of rooms?"

He placed his hand on my chin to move my face towards him. "Besides my mother and sister, you will be one of the most important women at this gala."

"Um. Okay."

"You're strong. I've never met someone with such confidence and tenacity."

Was he talking about me? I wanted to search the backseat to be sure. He pressed my hand against his cheek.

The enormous estate was in the distance, fire-lit lanterns lined the long drive. The sight was unreal, like the television show I never watched. Crossleigh wasn't châteauesque like Rowan, more Jacobethan with tall towers and large windows. I grew nervous as the walls of the castle came closer.

Martin stopped the car near the entrance.

"You grew up here?" I whispered.

He nodded. "Yes. When not at school. Are you ready?"

Before I could reply, the door opened, and the cameras flashed.

CHAPTER EIGHTY-THREE

"Everything I was taught said I shouldn't like Sarah Margo. Then I saw her dancing with my brother, admiring him for his true self." - Lady Iris Mackgale

Two sets of doors, made of ornate wood, opened to an entry hall. Iain ushered me inside with a few guests. The shouts of the press diminished and were replaced with the cracking of the fire in the marble fireplace. Above the mantel was a coat of arms; on the floor were antique rugs. The walls had paintings of previous generations of the Mackgale family. Gold lamps created enough light to illuminate the murals on the ceiling.

"May I have a word, my lord?"

We followed an older woman to a stairwell. I assumed she worked at Crossleigh by her plain dress and pinned up hair. Guests whispered when they passed us tucked away. Tonight felt like one of those strange dreams one has after eating Mexican food after midnight.

The woman regarded me with curiosity and then shifted her attention to Iain. If she thought I'd wait in the hall during their secret meeting, she was in for a shock.

"Her ladyship doesn't have a room for your companion, but we prepared accommodations downstairs," she whispered.

I made this woman nervous.

Iain shook his head. "Please move Miss Margo's luggage to my rooms."

The woman leaned closer to Iain. "Are you quite certain?"

"Yes."

"Very well, my lord," she said and left us.

"I'm fine downstairs," I said.

"It's where the staff sleeps."

We stood close; dim light beamed shades of yellow on his face. It took me a moment to realize his mother's intentions.

"Your mother doesn't approve?"

My delusional mind convinced myself our differences wouldn't be an issue. Why was I surprised? The Kings thought I wasn't good enough for Roddy. The Mackgales were far above two doctors from Oakville.

"You will have to earn your place," he said.

"Earn it?"

He nodded.

How does one earn acceptance in a world they don't belong?

I had figured life out before. The back of his hand slid behind my neck, and he kissed me. I would become one of them somehow because I wasn't giving Iain Mackgale up.

"You don't belong here," Dr. King said. He looked over his shoulder at Roddy in conversation with a high school friend. "How can you not see my son isn't right for you?"

Soft Christmas music played at Oakville Country Club.

"Why do you hate me so much?" I asked.

Dr. King glanced at our surroundings to be sure no one overheard. "My son wants to marry you. He's determined no matter what I say. You'll embarrass him. It's unlikely you'll finish college. I wouldn't be surprised if you sold cars at your uncle's dealership. Roddy will have an important position in this city. He needs a wife to match his caliber."

Roddy joined us, a large smile on his face. It was Christmas, a time to be happy, but I was miserable.

"What's going on?" Roddy asked.

"Your father wants me to break up with you. The last time I saw him, he offered me money."

Roddy looked at his father with outrage.

"Is this true?" Roddy stepped closer to Dr. King.

"It's her or us, son," he said without an ounce of emotion.

"You want me to choose between my girlfriend or my family?"

A part of me hoped Roddy would pick me up and carry me out of the holiday party. He would say his parents didn't matter, tell me I would be successful and do great things. But he didn't. He remained still.

It became clear we didn't have a no matter what relationship. We had cracks in our love that our history couldn't repair.

"Don't worry about choosing, Roddy. I am done."

Iain touched my face. My eyes blinked a few times as the memory from a Christmas a decade ago faded. A man said hello to Iain. He gave a nod of recognition. We stood in the hallway outside grand doors with two men in livery. Orchestra music and chatter exited with each guest who entered. We were fashionably late.

"Thanks for coming tonight. I'm grateful," he said.

I smiled as the doors opened to another world.

Crossleigh was far from the banquet room at Benny's BBQ where we held our parties. I risked a peek at the ceiling, ornate wood and murals surrounded by immaculate chandeliers. The floors were shiny marble with gold detailing. I tried to keep my eyes forward, not be intimated by the grandeur.

Iain led me through the crowd. He was right about hiring a designer. I spotted Iris. She wore a pale pink gown with a fur collar. Her nose lifted in the air when she saw us. The man next to her must have been Trevor, the fiancé she cared nothing about.

In front of us stood Iain's parents. His father had a ruddy complexion and auburn hair. Next to him was his wife, tall and glamorous as one would expect from a French woman. She passed her beautiful features to her son.

"May I present Miss Sarah Margo?"

Everyone nodded. No one spoke. We walked away.

A loud noise sounded twice.

"It's the dinner gong," Iain whispered. A man pointed at me. "My father likes to use it during these events. Most of the time, it collects dust."

I was too caught up with my surroundings to care about the history of a gong. He had introduced me to his parents, which seemed like the most overrated moment of my life. Before I could analyze his parents' lack of conversation, I sensed eyes burning into me.

There she was, the ex-girlfriend who broke Iain's heart, across the room. She moved towards us, flaming red hair, pale skin, and freckles covered her nose. The sides of her green gown swished back and forth with each step. Iain didn't see her.

"Excuse me for one moment, darling," Iain said.

He walked off with the guy I assumed was Trevor. Could I run in these heels? I didn't want to talk to Lady Lustbucket.

I cocked my head to the side and flashed a fake ass smile.

"It's impressive you are here," she said.

"I feel the same way about you. I thought you'd be busy selling stories to the tabloids," I said.

"There's always some truth to the papers."

"Really? You were engaged to my boyfriend last month?"

"He would have married me. I chose better at the time. I won't deny I want him back, especially since he inherited his cousin's title and is still in line to inherit Crossleigh." She paused. "I'm here to examine the competition."

My cackle laugh drew a few glances from the surrounding people. Clarisa narrowed her eyes at my outburst.

"We are competing for nothing."

"I wouldn't be so certain. Do you honestly believe you'll last?" She gestured to the glamorous party-goers.

"We have the love that fills the cracks."

"Is that an American euphemism?"

"It means we aren't your business." I stood with my hands on my hips. This girl was the reason I destroyed my five-year-old phone.

"Iain will want to marry someone with a title." She lifted her chin so high; I was afraid her neck might snap.

"You're right, Clarisa. Thank God I have one."

She flinched at my familiarity. The woman should have been glad her name was all I called her.

A woman about twenty-five with bird feathers in her hair appeared next to Clarisa. "Does she?"

"Hidden Meadows. We are distant relations to the Earl of Grey and the Burger King. Excuse me, girls."

"Do we know anyone in Burger?" Clarisa's companion whispered.

I strutted across the room, all eyes on me, to greet Iris. No longer would I be afraid of mean girls.

After a lavish dinner in the dining hall, we returned to the main room for dancing and mingling. Most people at the gala approached Iain. I had met a prime minister, two princes, a handful of lords, and Nigel, who worked for Mackgale-Berrell but was also in line to inherit a title. He mentioned his land three times as if I cared.

I was finally the cool girl, the one everyone wanted to meet, but I didn't get the satisfaction I thought would come with the attention. They wanted to know me for all the wrong reasons. Perhaps the cool girl persona didn't exist. It was an illusion we put in our minds from our own inadequacies.

"One last dance before we go upstairs," Iain whispered.

A beautiful male voice sang with the orchestra. Iain led me to the middle of the floor. He pulled me close. The lights of the chandeliers twinkled through the crystal.

"She's the one who knows the Burger King," Bird Lady whispered. Her dance partner eyed me with suspicion.

"That's Lord Rowan," he whispered to her. The couple watched us dance.

"Do I want to know?" Iain asked against my ear. His warm breath stirred something inside me. I was glad to be sleeping in his room tonight.

"Honestly, I wouldn't ask."

"Let's go," he said.

Iain led me through the crowd and into the hall. A man lounged on an antique bench with his phone. We entered a room with two billiards tables. Against the wallpaper were leather armchairs. Above the windows hung stuffed horned animals. He grasped my hand when we went through another door into a dark hall with a small staircase.

I hesitated.

"We are avoiding the main staircase. It's called fashionably disappearing," he said.

Our dress shoes thumped against the wooden stairs. At the top, there was no door knob. Iain pressed his hand against the wall until light spilled into the stairwell. We stepped into a hallway lined with tapestries and gold. When the door closed behind us, it blended in with the surroundings. I touched the wall with curiosity.

"It's the servants' stairs, which allowed the staff to be

invisible to the family. We now call them employees and rules are more relaxed."

"Crossleigh must have a lot of history."

"Yes," he said with caution. "One day I will share with you." A dark shadow crossed his face. Our eyes stayed locked for a moment. "I had food sent up."

Did he notice I pushed my dinner around my plate? The fish had eyes and an open mouth. I couldn't muster enough courage to attempt eating the scaly thing in front of a hundred people.

Iain removed a key from his pocket to unlock his room. All the ceilings and doors were tall. I remained in the entry, shocked by the extravagance. The walls were cream, outlined with wood and gold.

"This is your childhood bedroom?"

He nodded.

A fire roared in the fireplace. I touched a photo on the mantle of him and another boy with the same colored hair.

"That's my brother, Issac." Iain only talked about Iris.

He studied me taking in the surroundings. I acted as if the gala was nothing new for me, but I was having trouble pretending his childhood bedroom was my normal.

"This furniture is beautiful."

"Chippendale," he said.

"Like the dancers?" I asked.

"Like the furniture maker."

"Are you sure you're okay I don't have a title or five thousand acres like Nigel?" I removed the barrette from my hair.

"Darling, I have loved you since the beginning. When I say you, I mean exactly who you are. This life is a part of me, but not all of me. I'm sorry I haven't been vocal about my feelings in the past. There's nothing I want as much as you. Even if you think Thomas Chippendale is an adult entertainer."

I made my fake outrage face. "You love embarrassing me."

"You give it right back to me."

Iain wrapped his arms around me and kissed me with passion. I pulled him against me tighter, warmth from the roaring fireplace radiating against my gown.

Someone cleared their throat. We broke our embrace to discover his father standing in the doorway. "I need to speak with you."

"I'll be along in a moment," Iain said. His father left us.

"People are always interrupting our fun."

Iain kissed me again. "I promise I won't be long."

I was too tired to wait up. My dress slid to the floor, and I climbed into his childhood bed.

Guests who stayed at Crossleigh attended an early luncheon in the solarium. In between large pots of plants, tables boasted fine linens and gold candelabras. The waitstaff from the night before served us roasted chicken with a variety of small sandwiches and desserts. I had no problem cleaning my plate.

Through the glass walls, I watched a tree in the distance, swaying in the gusty sea breeze. On the right side, the foliage was very much alive, full of bright green leaves. The same wasn't true for the left. Many of the leaves had fallen, and the few that remained were leaving with the wind. Even the branches didn't look as strong.

I found myself drawn to the tree.

"I'm going to step outside," I said to Iain, who was busy debating with Nigel about rugby. He nodded and returned his attention to his friend.

When I opened the door, the cool breeze traveled underneath my flowy blue dress. I shivered but was determined to get a closer look at the half-alive, half-dead tree. The frozen grass crunched beneath my heels until I stood on a hill, next to the tree, sun and sea in the distance.

I glanced over my shoulder at Crossleigh, amazed by how long this wondrous place had stood the test of time. Then I focused on the tree. I could relate. A part of me was very much alive, invigorated by love and new beginnings. The other remained dead to the world, mourning the loss of my father and the betrayal of my closest friend.

"Do you Americans have thicker skin?" Iris rubbed her palms against her upper arms.

I smiled. "Not likely. This tree is fascinating. It looks dead, but it's not."

"For as long as I can recall, this tree dies on one side. Naturally, you would assume the rest would be doomed, but it somehow grows stronger," she said.

A tear rolled down my face. I hoped I could be the tree. My eyes gravitated towards the clouds. He said he would always be with me. A gust of wind swirled our hair with the falling leaves.

"You did well last night," she said.

"Thank you." I turned to my boyfriend's sister. Was Iris softening to the idea of me?

"Can we go inside now? Iain said he'd take me to London this afternoon if I could find you."

Guess not.

We walked in silence back to the solarium where Iain waited to take me home to Oakville.

CHAPTER EIGHTY-FOUR

"Don't worry about the blond. She's no longer a problem." -Ryan Bolton

The car slowed and drifted towards the exit ramp—my dad's exit. Panic surged through my veins like electricity through a wire. I glanced at Iain, calm and oblivious, before I took another look out the window. We were almost to the traffic light. The green turning arrow on the dashboard flashed right. Why? There was nothing off this exit. We didn't need gas or to go to Walmart. My mind scanned every business on Regency Road. Iain didn't need his nails done or a cheap haircut. He didn't eat fast food either. We turned on the street towards the little brick house I called home for half of my life.

"Wait," I said. My arm crossed Iain's chest as if shielding him from a hard stop. "I don't do the Memory Lane thing." He parked near the curb. When he looked at me, his face was relaxed. The exact opposite of mine. "I have a confession. The house...I didn't want to sell." My chest burned. "I regret it so much."

"Gina said it would do you good to see the house." Iain moved the gearshift into drive.

"This is a bad idea. If you're going to subject me to Memory Lane, I need a bottle of wine at dinner." I shifted in my seat.

He smiled. "Deal. Cabernet Sauvignon okay?"

I shook my head, irritated at him for not understanding I couldn't see the house. The thought of my dad not living there crushed me. In addition to the fact I didn't want to sell my safe place to strangers. I wanted to keep a part of Frank Margo, more than his belongings still in storage.

Memories of last Christmas drifted into my mind, the fire, plates of fettuccine, my dad's booming laugh when his brother called to say dinner had been pushed back an hour. I couldn't do it, but I had no choice. Iain pulled the car into the spot where he usually parked.

"You can't pull into the driveway! Someone lives here."

Iain turned off the engine.

"The place looks nice. You were right. I feel much better. Let's go. Wine time. I might need two bottles, nice ones that cost a fortune."

"Let's have a quick peek." He opened the car door. I reached for his arm but missed.

"Iain Mackgale! I swear on everything holy."

I jumped out of the car. The blacktop was freshly paved, bumps and tree roots gone. When I looked up at the house, the roof and windows were new. My focus moved to the bench on the front porch. Gina must have forgotten to tell the movers the outside stuff went to the storage unit too. My heart sank to the growing pit in my stomach. I helped my father make the bench.

Our former neighbor stepped outside to retrieve a package from his doorstep. He gave a polite smile and a wave. My cheeks flushed. I waved back, humiliated he caught me snooping at the house his daughter bought. I imagined him telling his son-in-law who would reply, next time we will call the police if they trespass.

"I love you," Iain said. I shot him a hateful glare. He took my hand and placed cold metal between my fingers. "The house is yours."

"What?"

"I didn't think you were ready to let the house go." Water

filled his eyes. He didn't want to let it go either.

The keys hit the pavement when I covered my mouth—either in shock or joy. My knees mushed like gelatin. When I wobbled, Iain grabbed my arm.

"Hold on to me," I said.

"Always." He retrieved the keys from the asphalt and led me back to Memory Lane.

When I entered the living room, nothing had changed as if Frank Margo would come home from work, and we would eat frozen pot pies on the couch while watching the news. The tips of my fingers traced along the picture of us in Canada. The larger-than-life expression on his face brought tears to my eyes.

After a moment of examining the room, I sat in my father's recliner, eyes shutting for a moment. My lungs welcomed deep breaths, and I found peace. I could feel his presence, smell his cologne, see the lines on his face, and hear him saying—it's okay, Sarah.

I would ask Iain to stop at the cemetery before we returned to Berrell. My father asked me not to go, but I was afraid if I didn't see reality in front of me, I would continue to hold on to the notion my father wasn't dead. The worthless glimmer of hope that somehow this was a mistake, a bad dream, or whatever my mind could conjure.

"Sarah?"

My concerned boyfriend stood over me with his hands in the pocket of his pants with the hope he didn't break me by buying the house.

"Thank you," I said. His posture relaxed to a more casual stance. I took his hand when he offered and wrapped my arms around his waist. "What are we going to do with this house? You don't want to live here, do you?"

"No. We have a place to stay when we visit. Neither of us like hotels." He brushed a strand of my hair from my face. "I made changes after the closing. Dan and I discussed the construction at length. He said you'd love it. I hope he's right."

"Where?" I scanned the living room, which hadn't changed.

Iain gestured towards the kitchen. When I peeked around the corner, the dark brown 70s cabinets were still intact. The wallpaper still had a rip near the ceiling, although my dad had glued it a dozen times. I shrugged. Iain pointed towards the den, where the fold out had been. At the moment my feet crossed the threshold, the light from the new windows and fresh paint hit me.

A new door was next to a leather chair. I expected a closet, but instead, I entered a hallway. We passed a new exterior door. When I looked out the window, the old lawn chairs remained by the fire pit. I turned a doorknob to find a master suite the size of my New York City apartment. I beamed a joyful smile at Iain.

"You approve?"

"Yes!"

I repositioned the throw pillows. He remained quiet a few moments while I took in the new space.

"There is a—"

"Bathroom! Wow," I said.

"I'll let you decide what to do with the other rooms."

"This must have been expensive."

"We will never get our money back." Iain kissed my cheek. "There are more important things than money."

"Like what?" Uncle Dan said from the hallway.

Iain shook my uncle's hand.

Gina rolled her eyes at my uncle. I hugged my aunt. There was no doubt she helped with the remodel.

"We'll be outside," Dan said to Gina. Iain followed my uncle.

"What do you think of the house?" Gina asked.

"Oh my God. I am in shock. I can't believe he bought this house for me. Thank you for helping him with the remodel. I know you did. Your style is everywhere."

"Now you have a place to stay when you bring my little ones home," Gina said with a grin.

"Let's not get crazy."

We laughed.

"I never thought I'd enjoy hearing the G word, but I would love to be a Glamma."

There was always a comfort with Gina I never had with anyone else. Our humor was set aside during my dad's final weeks. I wanted nothing more than to have a sliver of the past back.

"Why didn't you have children?"

A look of sorrow engulfed Gina's face. I blamed Uncle Dan. Heaven forbid baby stuff cluttered his house and kept the bikini models away.

"I had a hysterectomy when I was eighteen. You didn't know?"

"No."

I remembered my graduation party. My mom yelled at Gina, something about she couldn't have her own children. Why was I so oblivious? I assumed Dan didn't want children, and Gina loved being a trophy girlfriend.

"I had terrible endometriosis. The doctors tried everything, but we ran out of options. My high school boyfriend broke up with me the night before my surgery. For years, I was depressed, but I met Dan. He didn't want children. No man in my small town wanted me. You are not the only one to move to escape the past, baby girl." She laughed with tears in her eyes. "When I met y'all at the lake, I wanted to be a part of this family."

"Teddy must have been on vacation."

Gina smiled as she recalled the past. "You're right. Ted wasn't there." We giggled like middle schoolers. "That day seems like another lifetime."

The past loitered in my mind like an unwanted visitor. Gina grabbed my hand and squeezed. She read my thoughts. Tears welled in my eyes.

"Let's forgive ourselves. Let's love ourselves. Let's be thankful for life and its many blessings," Gina said.

"Amen," I whispered.

CHAPTER EIGHTY-FIVE

"Three years ago, I saw Sarah's dad at the barbershop. He told me she moved away and to never contact her." -Daniel Klein

My eyelids fluttered open, laced with the remnants of forgotten dreams. The bright light through the window wouldn't allow my sleep to continue. I yawned; the way one does when sleep deprived. Memories of last night caused a salacious grin. I loved Iain more every day. His voice echoed from the kitchen.

I admired my new room, but couldn't avoid the pang of sadness. I imagined my dad joking with Iain about pitching the metal desk. The same one the university threw in the trash in 1995.

My hands covered my eyes to shield more hypothetical memories. I needed to stop feeling sad. My dad wouldn't want me upset. After all, it was Christmas. Iain bought the house to remind me of the good times. I needed to cherish those memories and let go of what I couldn't control.

The smell of coffee lingered into the room, telling my tired body to join the world. I shivered when my toes touched the hardwood floors, and I tip-toed to retrieve socks from my suitcase. Most of my clothes were dirty. I wondered if Iain had replaced the washer and dryer. I hadn't been in the laundry room or bedrooms. Perhaps I was overwhelmed being in the house I thought I'd lost.

Iain paced in the den, one hand fidgeting a folder, the other holding his phone. He nodded, took a breath, and smiled when he saw me pouring coffee. Why did he love me? My sweatpants and bed head paled in comparison to his polished appearance. With a few strides, he met me halfway and kissed my messy hair.

Iain placed his phone on the table before he removed the coffee cup from my hand. I gave him a strange look when he placed my caffeine fix near the conference call he had abandoned. Before I could speak, he wrapped his arms around me in a warm embrace. My cheek rested against his soft sweater.

I raised to the tips of my toes to kiss his lips. My eyes drifted towards the bedroom. He groaned. "The HVAC company will be here in thirty minutes to install the new unit before we leave in the morning. Do you mind handling the repairman?"

I kissed him again. He deepened the kiss. I moaned. He pulled away, hands on my shoulders to keep his distance and laughed.

"I have a special dinner planned tonight," he said.

"We were at the Riverfront last night. Where could you take us that's nicer?" I matched his smirk.

Iain pointed towards the backyard.

"Okay. I can be a cheap date. You did buy me a house."

"Checks to pay for the heating unit are in my bag." Iain picked up his phone and continued to chat as if he didn't miss a minute of the call.

The doorbell rang. When I answered the door, the repairman was at his truck, digging in a cardboard box on the driver's seat. His sagging jeans revealed the crack of his butt. I pretended to adjust the wreath on the door, embarrassed I glimpsed his hairy behind. The man tugged at his pants before pulling a work order from his shirt pocket.

The repairman eyed me with suspicion when he approached the sidewalk. Perhaps he thought my sweater dress and boots were too fancy for having my heating unit replaced. He stopped in front of me, scratched his beard, and scanned the work order.

"Do I know you?" he asked. The tip of his finger traced along the paper, stopping at Mackgale.

I shrugged. How on earth would I know him? I hoped my snobby thoughts weren't visible on my face. Hairy Butt and I were not acquainted.

"No. I am not from here."

"Are you sure?"

Was he really questioning if I knew where I was from? New York City. A place where people like belts. Was he hitting on me? Guys at the gym always tried the do-I-know-you line.

"I am sure. Please come in. I will show you to the utility room." I opened the door for the repairman.

He picked up a picture frame on the end table.

"You're Sarah Margo," he said.

I quirked a brow. What was this guy's problem? We didn't know each other. I wanted to yell for Iain. Maybe this guy had something to do with Warren Wallace and Ryan Bolton. He wasn't the repairman. This guy was here to hurt me.

"I can't believe you don't recognize me. Dan Klein," he said. The lines around his eyes crinkled when he smiled.

I stood in the middle of my father's living room confused. The only Dan I knew was my uncle.

"Daniel?"

He chuckled, and it reminded me of playing neighborhood baseball. The boyish face and athletic figure were long gone.

"Are you okay with departing before seven?" Iain entered the living room with his phone in hand. "Oh, my apologies. I didn't hear the door." Iain moved to my side where he put his hand on my back. Daniel studied us for a moment.

"Do you guys live here?" Daniel asked with a look of skepticism.

"No. This is a secondary property," Iain said.

"Where's your dad?" Daniel asked.

"He passed away last month," Iain replied for me. The sting of tears returned, but I kept it together. Any bit of joy on Daniel's face drained. "Do you two know each other?"

"Yes. We lived in the same neighborhood as kids." I forced a smile.

"Hidden Meadows," Daniel said with pride.

Iain's phone rang and saved me further awkward conversation between my boyfriend and the boy who first broke my heart. Daniel watched Iain leave the room.

"I have work to do." A big lie. "Let me know when you need a check."

I retreated to the master bedroom in a full-blown panic attack. After all these years, I run into the boy who broke my heart. He acted like he forgot how our friendship ended. What was I expecting—an apology? So much for forgetting about the past. The worst part was realizing how much I obsessed over Daniel throughout my life, often comparing this perfect vision of him to every guy who didn't make the cut. To see him now made me seem delusional. I spent my twenties rejecting good-looking, nice professionals for an overweight repairman who ditched me for an easy seventh grader. Let's not forget the hairy ass.

Iain entered the room, closing the door behind him. "Are you okay, darling?" He joined me on the bed.

"Yes. I wasn't expecting Daniel to be the repairman."

"Let's get out of here," Iain said. His hand folded into mine. "We need supplies for tonight."

CHAPTER EIGHTY-SIX

"Everyone has cracks. It's understanding their pain to know how they need loved." -Sarah Margo

Flames roared from the fire pit—large enough to make me wonder if sitting outside was safe. Iain poked the flames; I observed from the warmth inside. I unpacked plastic containers from Benny's BBQ. When he said special night, I didn't expect pulled chicken next to an outdoor fire during winter. The local meteorologist predicted six inches of snow after midnight.

"It is frigid." A burst of cold air followed him through the door. He rubbed his hands together.

"Does this special night include who survives?"

"We both know you would win. It's not so terrible near the fire." Iain glanced at the food with approval. "I am changing before we eat. Perhaps a second pair of pants."

I loved his boyish grin.

"Me too. I hope my snowsuit is still in my closet."

"I believe it is, next to the death trap bed and horse figurines."

"Those are fighting words, Mackgale. You know how I feel about my daybed." I pointed my finger in an authoritative way. Instead of being intimidated, he laughed and went to the bedroom.

"I'm taking my plate outside," I yelled. We didn't have time for lunch. My stomach rumbled at the site of the baked beans.

When I opened the back door, the whoosh of icy air traveled through the fibers of my clothes. I hoped Iain was right about the fire. Tonight was the coldest night of the year.

Iain joined me with a plate of food. We ate in silence with the occasional crack of fire or gust of wind.

When we finished our food, he placed the plates in the grass. He turned towards me and reached for my hand. I should have worn gloves. We underestimated the power winter had over a fire.

"One of my favorite memories is when we dined outside. I can't cook, worked late, and fed you cottage pie. It wasn't a date, but I worried you wouldn't speak to me again. You weren't put off by the lack of grandeur. Instead, we enjoyed an evening of great conversation under the stars. A few weeks later, I came to New York and stayed with you. I could have found a place to stay after the first night, but I enjoyed being with you." Iain blushed.

"I know," I whispered. Tiny snowflakes spat from the darkness above. "I didn't want you to go either."

"I can be my true self with you. I never have to put on a facade or watch what I say. We have the most incredible banter —no one makes me laugh and smile like you."

I leaned forward to kiss him.

"I am pretty funny."

"You get your humor from your family. I love how hilarious they are when together. That's why I couldn't let this house go. I became close to Frank this year. He wanted me to deliver a message."

I froze like an animal in front of headlights. What kind of message and why? I couldn't handle more surprises. Iain's hand shook either from the cold or nerves. He tugged something inside his jacket. When the greeting card appeared, I gave him a puzzled look. All this build-up for a bent envelope with a coffee ring stain on the back? I eyed the beat-up gift when he placed it in my hand.

"Interesting," I mumbled.

"It's not from me. Disregard its condition. It has traveled around the world in a suitcase."

I opened the envelope to find a flimsy card, one purchased at a discount party store. The cover had pink and blue balloons in the clouds. This card was selected by someone who didn't have many options. Tears streamed down my face. I knew the handwriting.

Sarah,

Words could never express, my child, the love I have for you. Even in the darkest times, you have always been my light. Cherish our memories, but don't hold on to the sorrow. Live. Experience new adventures and bring me with you in spirit.

I wish you a lifetime of happiness.

Love,

Dad

I looked up from my father's final message, blinking tears, to find Iain on one knee. He reached for my hand before removing a box from his pocket.

"Allow me to be your light. Let's start a new adventure. Will you marry me?"

"Yes."

I fell into his arms where the cold was forgotten.

EPILOGUE

Strands of her dark hair collected snowflakes in the blustery wind. With each footstep, her silhouette diminished in the fog to Frank's grave near a blue spruce. The tree shared a memory with Sarah and her father, which was evident when she selected the plot, but I didn't ask. Everyone should have moments they keep to themselves. My most cherished recollections were filled with Sarah, proof the best memories are the ones never shared.

I turned the car's heat to the highest setting, exhaust fumes creating clouds of wintry smoke. The outside temperature gauge displayed seven degrees.

She crouched next to the new headstone and ran gloved fingers along her last name. The white rose she insisted on bringing rested in the snow. She asked me to stay in the car, told me she was fine, but I knew otherwise. As the past upset Sarah, the future had me anxious.

She believed our meeting happened by chance. In a sense, she was right. I didn't plan on colliding with her on the fourth floor. My mind drifted back to the unhappy day I argued with my father over money when Warren came in the door with a stack of employee files for a pointless conference. That's when I saw her beautiful face, pinned with a paper clip to the top of a manila folder. After examining her records, I approved Warren's request. I knew I was crazy and resolved not to seek her out even though a small voice inside told me I needed

Sarah Margo.

If I cared about her, I would have let her get on with her life with someone normal. Her lawyer friend or Dan's golf partner perhaps. I couldn't entertain thoughts of Sarah with someone else.

My phone rang. I glanced in the rear view at the car behind us. Douglas held his phone to his ear. I answered.

"Sir, we received confirmation Heather Ann Murphy, alias Deana Dash, is dead. The police found her body in the Hudson this morning."

Stupid girl. It's what happened when dumb bitches mixed with the wrong men for money. Why was Sarah friends with her? Instead of sympathy, anger boiled inside me. I was acquainted with too many of these men. My father included. I asked God so many times—why Frank? Why not my own father?

"Not a word to Miss Margo. I will tell her once we're home."

"Very well, sir. We believe one of Mr. Bolton's associates is waiting at the Oakville airport. Martin advised the flight team to land at a regional airport in the next county."

Thanks, Deana. I hope the shopping spree and free rent was worth your life. You are the reason your friend is in danger.

Sarah was often oblivious, too preoccupied with family or work to notice we were always followed—a parked car, a man trying too hard to blend into his foreign surroundings. I passed off my anxiety as work when she would ask, but I feared for her life more than my own.

"Miss Margo shouldn't be much longer. We will follow you."

The day I would have to tell her secrets, dangerous secrets, played in my mind. Would she leave me? A sick sensation rose from my gut to my throat, but I smiled softly when she returned to the car. Sarah sat in silence for a moment before removing her glove to wipe her nose with a tissue. A grin spread across her face when she caught a glimpse of her engagement ring.

She loved me.

"I'm ready to go to Berrell," she said with watering eyes. Relief surged through me. We were safer locked behind gates with a security team in remote Rowan.

"I love you." The tips of her cold fingers touched my face and sent warmth through my veins.

AKNOWLEDGEMENTS

It's two in the morning, and I write this with a proud, thankful heart. Bringing a story to life can takes years. This book took me four years to complete. I learned so much and faced many challenges on the page and in my personal life. Writing a novel is often a book lovers dream. Without a reader, stories have no purpose. Thank you.

I hope you'll forgive me for leaving so many unanswered questions. There will be a second book, *The Rise of Rowan*, told from Sarah and Iain's perspective. Rowan will introduce the Mackgales and Sarah's new life. A short story parallel to *The Fall of Hidden Meadows* told from Iain's perspective will be released soon.

Many people have touched this book. There is no possible way I could thank every person by name. I would forget someone and feel terrible. To everyone who believed, helped, and offered professional magic—thank you.

Maybe I'm weird, but I always wonder about the dedication when I start a new book. Richard is my father. He had Non-Hodgkins Lymphoma. It was stage four. He fought for years, and the treatments were too much for his body. In remission, he had an aneurysm and died twelve hours later. We were blind-sided, misled by how life should have been, and frankly —destroyed. That's a line from the prologue and very true to me personally. I was eleven.

I went twenty years without talking about my father. A few years ago, I was having a conversation with a good friend from college. She asked if I knew my father. I thought it was the craziest question, but how would she know? I had never mentioned him. So I started talking, and I found the more I talked, the more people could relate.

My father was a lot like Frank. He was a family person with a great sense of humor. Like Frank, he wanted me to move on. During his treatments, we often had conversations before bed about life. Perhaps he knew his fate and wanted to leave me with final wisdom. He told me one night not to be afraid to do big things.

I didn't name the type of Frank's cancer. To me, it didn't matter for the story. I wanted the reader to focus on the loss, not the treatment or prognosis. In the end, cancer sucks no matter how you label it.

I hope you enjoyed this book. Reach out to me on social media. I would love to hear from you. For more information about me or my work, visit JennaVeirs.com.

ABOUT THE AUTHOR

Jenna Veirs told her parents in fourth grade that she couldn't survive another winter in Cincinnati, Ohio. After a few states, she now calls Florida home. She is an autism and homeschool advocate, loves cooking, hates cleaning, and attempts Pilates. This is her debut novel.